THOMASHEEN JAMES
MAN - OF - NO - WORK

Man-of-no-work but of many wiles, Thomas James O'Doran ("without the Esquire"), Thomasheen James to his intimates, is one of the most engaging and amusing vagabonds that ever came out of Wicklow. In his own language, so rich in humorous turns and racy expletives, if you meet him "wance" you are not likely to "disremimber him twice." Thomasheen James's fund of anecdote and adventure is as inexhaustible as his thirst, as quaint and irresistible as his wooing of Peg Kate, and once more Maurice Walsh proves himself a master hand both at drawing and at drawing out the incorrigible yet captivating characters of the open road.

By MAURICE WALSH

THE MAN IN BROWN
THE SPANISH LADY
THOMASHEEN JAMES, MAN-
    OF-NO-WORK
THE HILL IS MINE
THE KEY ABOVE THE DOOR
WHILE RIVERS RUN
THE SMALL DARK MAN
THE ROAD TO NOWHERE
GREEN RUSHES
AND NO QUARTER
SONS OF THE SWORDMAKER
BLACKCOCK'S FEATHER

BOOK
PRODUCTION
WAR ECONOMY
STANDARD

THOMASHEEN JAMES
Man-of-No-Work

BY

MAURICE WALSH

W. & R. CHAMBERS, LTD.
11 THISTLE STREET, EDINBURGH : 38 SOHO SQUARE, LONDON

First Published 1941
Reprinted 1941, 1943, 1946

Printed in Great Britain by T. and A. Constable Ltd.
at the University Press, Edinburgh

DEDICATED

TO

HUMPHREY KERINS

Who ought to know better

CONTENTS

CHAPTER I

THOMASHEEN JAMES AND THIRTY
PIECES OF COPPER

I

THOMASHEEN JAMES, when he first contacted me, was poor; he was as poor as a church mouse. No! "Poor" is not quite the right word; for poverty implies having something, however little, and at that time Thomasheen James had nothing. He had, indeed, as he himself said, "the daylight and the wather," but these great gifts are distributed so providentially that a man possessing only them still believes that he possesses nothing. The sun will shine and the air go drifting alike for man, mouse, or millionaire; and we are only barely on the brink of that millennium when none but the taxpayer and his chattels shall acquire their bellyfuls of piped spring water.

Thomasheen James was not ever in this complete state of destitution; occasionally he was just plain poor. In a five-mile tramp through horrid suburban streets, and by a keen use of tongue and eye, he might reap a harvest of stale bread and boiled tea, with an infrequent generous copper from someone nearly as destitute as himself; and on notable days, with angels about and the devil more than usually busy in business quarters, evening might find him with the wherewithal to pay for a cubicle and a clean bed in a red-brick institution outside the walls of Saint Patrick's Cathedral. He was, like many of his class, peculiarly nice in habit and person, and to lie between clean sheets was about as near to felicity as he could ever hope to get on top of earth.

He was a communist by conviction—"a convicted communist," as he put it—but a muddled sort of conviction; for he had, naturally enough, a complete contempt for an invertebrate proletariat, and expressed an unlogical admiration for the culture of that class he erroneously assumed to be the aristocracy. His greatest handicap was a mordant tongue employed in an uncompromising criticism of man and his institutions; and his notable virtue—if any—was a dislike of Woman, even though it was a dislike based mainly on fear. "They haven't no dam' mercy, women," he proclaimed. "They do things for their own reason, and you might as well be talkin' to them as the wind and you wantin' to change it." Behind that criticism was a thought that he could never clearly articulate.

His intelligence was of no mean order, and another turn of the screw or another scrap of grey matter might have made him a philosopher, a revolutionary—or even a poet. Instead, he was the born drifter.

His life, which I hope to picture in these misadventures, had drifted aimlessly from a back lane in a Wicklow seaport town, and drifted far; for there was a trace of tinker-gipsy blood in him, and that strain will take a man to the world's end and back again. During the middling-great war of 1914-18 he had got as far as fabled Stamboul in the stokehold of a transport-ship of the British Navy, and had garnered a store of interesting and, I hope, unreliable information. Some of that information, even duly censored, I do not hope to retail.

I first made his acquaintance through the medium

of a claw-hammer. I was amateurishly putting a new roof on my summer-house at the garden-foot, and the hammer, after the way of hammers, slid away from my fingers and disappeared over the eaves. A startled "Wow!" accompanied by a sacred epithet came up from below, and I nearly followed the hammer as I craned over the edge.

I was looking down on Thomasheen James.

A live, wary, china-blue eye was contemplating me from each side of a sharp peeled nose standing out of a lean freckled face. An old felt hat was in one hand, and the other hand was caressing the crown of a short-cropped sandy head. He grinned at me, but not amiably.

"Becripers!" he said. "'Tis lucky me dome's solid."

"What do you want?" I enquired inhospitably. No disreputable hobo had any right in my garden.

Thomasheen James still contemplated me. I was collarless, in stained overalls, and I probably needed shaving. He gestured a thumb over his shoulder.

"I hear the man-o'-the-house is amiable to a bit of a hard-luck story?"

"Not on your life," I said. "All the pickings are mine, and I have to scratch hard for them. You get out!"

But I could not deceive Thomasheen James for long. His grin became more amiable.

"My mistake, sir," he said, "and I ax your pardon. After havin' your bit of a joke, would the duck-egg you laid on the roof o' me skull be worth a tanner to you?"

"Not in these trousers."

"Sure there's no hurry," he agreed. "Let us go on with the work!"

He retrieved and reached me up the hammer, and

busied himself gathering scattered tacks off the grass. In a little while he was perched on the step-ladder, nursing the saw, holding down felt, passing me nails, propping me with a broad hand in dangerous postures; and he talked—talked me into his toils. In something less than an hour he got a whole florin out of me.

He looked at the florin in his palm, and he looked at me. If I am any judge of looks there was a gleam of possession in his eye. I was his meat. I was, and I am. The curtilages of my house became his stamping-ground between wandering fits, for he would always wander. He might be away for months on end, but he always returned, and in time I used look forward to his return. Some sort of informal tie established itself between us, a kind of frank tolerance that flattered my inner revolt against suburban respectability. Sometimes I was pleased to think that but for my anchorage Thomasheen James would have drifted into that slough of degradation that is the doom of his kind.

I never hired him to work, never hired him at all. He came and went as the spirit moved him; and when the spirit moved him he had a busy way of fussing about the garden and the tool-shed. He was really efficient with a yard sweeping-brush, and no dead leaf was safe from him in the shadiest of corners; with a hoe he was deadly dangerous to weed and vegetable alike; and with a spade—let himself speak: "Becripers! I couldn't sleep sound an' a spade under the same roof." Probably he was a rogue by all accepted definitions, but he was never pettily dishonest. For instance, we could safely leave the house unoccupied, the back door on the latch, and Thomasheen James grooming the garden path. And . . . But let his character develop itself as we go on.

On a certain Tuesday afternoon, after an absence over the long Easter week-end, I was sitting in my open-fronted summer-house when Thomasheen James came down the garden path behind the handles of a wheelbarrow that held nothing but his brush and two dead cabbage leaves. He set the barrow carefully down on the plot of grass fronting the house, and calculated me with a cold and wary eye.

"Get out!" I said, looking at him sourly over the top of my writing-glasses.

"You're back?" said Thomasheen James.

"Obviously. Get out!"

I was endeavouring to put a few profitable words on a writing-pad, and not succeeding very well.

"A bad time to talk to a man," said Thomasheen James distantly, "an' him with a sore head after his week-end in Kerry! But talk I will. I'm in trouble."

"I gave you five shillings last week——"

"The week before last—four and a tanner to be exack. The trouble concerns the both of us."

"The devil it does! How much do you want?"

"Do you recolleck them fishin'-boots o' yours?"

"The black rubbers? You can have them—they leak in ten places."

"Not them. The yellow boyos with the nails in the sole that come up below your oxters."

"My new waders? If you dare put as much as a finger——"

"They're in the pawnshop this solid minit," said Thomasheen James solidly.

I was on the point of explosion, but took a second thought.

"Who put them there?" I enquired, mildly enough.

"I did—Holy Thursday evening."

"A holy evening, and a holy thing to do!"

Somehow my urge to explode vanished, and was replaced by an unpleasant sinking feeling. Thomasheen James had broken trust. The old careless tolerance that existed between us was in real danger for the first time, and I was actually distressed.

"Am I to understand," I enquired patiently, "that you lifted my only decent waders and pawned them?"

"I knew you'd be takin' the dam'dest view you could," he said sadly. "I got nothin' for them anyway."

I found the relief of anger. The waders were first-class articles, and could be pledged in any Dublin pawnshop for at least twenty shillings.

"Don't say it," besought Thomasheen James. "Don't never say I up and stole your waders."

"I'll say more than that." And I did. Unfortunately I can be occasionally guilty of language to astonish even Thomasheen James. I invented a family tree for him and detailed the fate of it, branch by branch. No one, not even Thomasheen James's father, knew who Thomasheen James's father was, but I traced that reprobate's progress as far as the hangman —and after—and drew pointed conclusions. "For," said I, warming to the subject, "any so-and-so nurtured in my bosom who would repay me by stealing my new waders at the peak of the salmon-fishing—the only decent waders I had—the only pair of waders that never soaked a drop of water——"

"Who declaims on such marvellous waders?" said a pleasant voice at the garden gate behind my left shoulder.

year or a bit more, you've been idling and pandering in this place, but you will neither work nor idle in it for another day—and that's flat."

"Order in the court!" commanded Justice. "Go on, Thomasheen James!"

"Long or short, I been workin' in this garden off and on, and if 'tisn't a wreck and a ruin let him take the credit that wants it. An' wan day I'd get a shillin', and in three days' time another shillin', an' a gintleman 'ud be feelin' generous, and a noble Christian the same as if you martyred him. Mind you, I'm not complainin'. I'm not complainin' at all. A shillin' now and a shillin' then is all I ever wanted—and a bowl of soup when it was goin'."

"These he got," I put in, "and more besides, yet where are the waders that I want to loan to the reverend judge?"

"No special pleading, please! Cut the cackle and get to the waders, Thomasheen James!"

"I'm workin' up to the bloody waders, amn't I? Holy Thursday, after lunchin'-time, an' the week's work put past me, I was sayin' to meself that five bob would be as little as himself could be handin' out to get me over the Good Friday an' the Bank Holiday at Fairyhouse Races. An' did I get the five bob? Did I, I ask you? Did I hell! A coupla hours after meal-time, an' his snooze over him, out comes himself and a friend with him—a fellow wouldn't come in a door sideways—and the two wives chit-chatterin', and two bags strapped on the heel of the motor car; and off with them laughin' an' jokin', full of food an' fun. 'We'll stop for a drink in Ard-na-Righ,' says the stout fellow. 'No,' says his missus, 'we'll have tea in Maryborough'——"

"That's where the jail is," said the sergeant suggestively.

"I know it. I was hungry in it once—and I was hungry Easter Sunday as well. For there I was left, me mouth open, an' not one ha'penny to rub aginst another; the long week-end before me, the town empty —and no one in the house but the girl an' the two young wans."

"No need for him to go hungry," I said quickly. "The servant was in the house."

"'Tis little you know her," said Thomasheen James.

"Moreover, I looked in the garden before I left, but he was not about——"

"You looked dam' hard, I know. I was sweepin' out the hen-house at the back."

"Or asleep in a corner?"

"Like me betters—and why not I? If you lifted your voice above a whisper you'd ha' heard from me. Mind you, I didn't blame you, and I'm not blamin' you. You're your own master—outside the house— an' every man has the weight of his own conscience. 'Maybe he left something for me with that servant-girl,' says I to meself, havin' the best opinion of you in spite o' previous occasions. And in I went to consort her. 'What would he laive?' says she, the mopsy. 'Hadn't you your dinner, and there's a cup o' tay in the pot if you want it. An' look here, me boyo!' says she, 'you'll cut your hook out o' this place till the boss comes back, for I'll not be the subjeck of scandal in this end o' Dublin.' An' she with a face on her to stop a clock. 'Give me the tay,' I says, 'before I lose me timper.' And I took it, and it lukewarm, sitting outside in the tool-shed. An' even then an' after all, I didn't blame you. 'He never meant to throw me distitute this way,' I colloges with myself. 'He'll be worryin' the heart out o' himself when it crosses his mind every hour. It'll be troublin' the dacent man day and night, and him knowin' that I've run out me fourteen nights in the Vincent de Paul's shelter.'"

"Oh, dammit!" I exclaimed. Truth to tell, I had not thought of Thomasheen James for a single moment during that pleasant week-end in Kerry.

"Take it aisy," implored Thomasheen James. "There's no call to be usin' bad langwidge before a priest, and him not usin' it back at you." He drew in a long breath. "It was about that time that me eyes lodged thimselves on the yalla waders hangin' upside down on the wall. What am I sayin'? It wasn't me eyes saw thim at all, but the divil lookin' through me eyeballs, and him whisperin' in me ear : 'Mullarkey at Egan's corner!' I heard the whisper plain as I'm talkin' to you this minit. 'Mullarkey would advance you half-a-dollar on them fishin'-boots. They're worth more, but you'd ax only the half-dollar. You can manage on that be the dint of the hole in your belt till the boss comes back, an' with the five bob he'll hand to you and he no more than out o' the car you'll be able to redeem the boots an' no one a penny the wiser. Go on, you cowardly skrimshanker! 'Tis what the boss would be glad you'd do, and it to aise his conscience. . . .' So I took the boots," said Thomasheen James briefly.

"And pawned them for your half-dollar?"

"That's what you think. To Mullarkey's I took them at Egan's corner. He is not me usual man o' business, but he was convanient—an' he don't know me. But, be the powders o' war! he'll have cause to know me one o' these days—if he has eyes in the back of his poll. He looked at the waders an' he looked at me. 'These are spang new,' says he cogitately. 'These things cost a fiver not so long ago. Wher'd you get 'em, me dacent boy?' 'From a fri'nd,' says I careless-like. 'He was that,' says Mullarkey. 'Is he a fisherman be any chance?' 'So he says,' I says. 'An' has he given up the foolish game?' 'He has not,' says I, the dam' fool I was. 'He'd be fishin' a splash o' water in the track of a road after a shower o' rain, an' so he might as well for all the sprats he brings home.' 'Then he must be out of his mind to present you with these,' says Mullarkey, and he went on rubbin' 'em with wan finger. And there I was in front o' him, the hooks o' desp'ration buried in me, for I saw what was in his mind, the doubtin' divil.

"And then, without another word out of him, he stuffed the boots under the counter, an' cast a red eye at the telephone in the corner. 'How much?' says I. 'Come back on Saturday mornin' like a good boy,' says he, coaxin', 'an' I'll see what I can do for you.' 'Give me back me fishin'-boots, you so-and-so,' I starts on him. But he looked at me out o' that red eye an' reached a hand at the telephone, an' whether he got a hould of it or not I don't know, for I was skedaddlin' up the street as if the divil was after me—an' so he was. An' there I was, broke to the world, an' worse off than ever!"

"I gather that you did not accept the invitation for Saturday?" enquired Justice.

"An invitation to me own wake! What sort of a omadhaun do you take me for? Wasn't Mullarkey's intintion as plain as the nose on his face, an' he goes to bed be the red light o' that. Seein' the holy evenin' that was in it, an' Good Friday followin', he had no mind to put the hooks in me till the Saturday. Why the hell didn't I go to a Jewman instead of an oul' sanctimonous craw - thumper? Saturday, how are you! an' Detective Dowd waitin' for me, the handcuffs up his sleeve. I wasn't in this end o' Dublin be Saturday. I wasn't in Dublin at all. Down be Navan an' round by Trim I was, slinkin' from door to door an' sleepin' under a hedge five nights—an' every time I seen a Guard in the distance me hair ruzz."

He lifted and shook a finger at the priest.

"An' let me tell you, me reverent gintleman, that this very minute I'd be in a safe place I know where Joe Dowd couldn't lay a hand on me, only I knew the boss 'ud be needin' his waders—and so are you. Ye know where they are now, an' me duty is done." His hand implored peace. "Don't let no wan be raisin' Cain. I won't. I'll go quiet, an' in thirty days I'll have lashin's o' time to forgive an' forget. That's me complaint, now—an' may the divil look sideways at me!"

Sergeant Joe O'Dowd thumped his massive thigh.

"Truth or lie—and I have my own opinion—that's as thorough a bit of special pleading as ever I heard in or out of court."

The priest and judge looked at me, and I noted that all the humour had gone out of his eyes.

"Joe might accept your opinion in equity," I hinted placatingly.

"I am glad you have some grace in you," said the priest.

He had stopped smoking long ago. Now he laid his pipe down and rubbed his hands through his black

23

hair as if his thoughts pained him. There certainly was trouble in his voice.

"The Lord forgive us," he said. "I wonder are we Christians at all? Thirty brown coppers were all that this unfortunate rogue wanted; consider how many you spent over the same week-end."

"I am not the defendant," I tried to ward him off.

"You are, and I am. Thirty pieces of silver were a certain price, and thirty pieces of copper would have kept Thomasheen James from hunger and from cold in the days we celebrate as the ultimate proof of our Faith. But he hadn't got them, had nowhere to get them, and had to go slinking along byways, fear in his heart. You and I ate our fill and slept softly, but this man slept hard and was hungry. Look! If we were true Christians we dare not sleep a sound wink, and food should be dust in our mouths, if we knew that there was a hungry man or a hungry woman or a child whimpering with the hunger within the four seas of Ireland. It is a beneficent small island and not crowded, generous in its soil and in its race, and in it no one need go hungry—no one at all—with a little considerate thought and less planning. Men work and eat, men are idle and look to a charity that is often cold and sometimes kind, and not infrequently thoughtless —like yours and mine. Men are idle, indeed, and many of them, including a certain one, need not be so —wastrels, drifters, incompetents. But let us not judge them. God knows why they will not work, why they are not fitted for work, what wicked curse is on them, what terrible dreaming drives them. All that we need know is that no one should go hungry in this Christian land. . . . But what is the use of talking? You know all that I would say, Mr Pagan. I will not give an opinion in equity. I will be the judge that you wanted. You have your writing-pad on your knee. Take your pen and write this:

"'Dear Mr Mullarkey—law-abiding in mere honesty —don't put that in. Dear Mr Mullarkey, the bearer of this note has my authority to pawn the pair of fishing-waders, my property, left with you on Holy Thursday evening. If necessary, Detective-Sergeant Joseph O'Dowd will confirm.' Sign it. Put the address on top."

"At last I am sure," I said, "that you will never be more than the poorest curate of the poorest parish in the diocese. There's your outrageous note!"

He took it, folded it without looking, and reached it to Thomasheen James.

"Take that, you astonishing scoundrel! Bring back the ticket to our brother here. He will do the redeeming."

Without another word the priest rose to his feet and strode to the garden gate. He left his pipe behind him.

"The waders will be here to-morrow," I called after him. "I'll send them down to you, and if they don't fill with you in a deepish place I'll lose faith in cursing."

He looked back over his shoulder and smiled a little sadly.

"While you're at it, send along that thick pair of socks too."

"Miracles 'll never cease," said Thomasheen James. "That man 'ud make a Christian out of you if you lived to be a hunderd."

Joe O'Dowd rose to his feet too and paced solidly to the gate.

"I am going. I'm going now. I do not want to be a witness to the assault and battery that is about to take place close to here in about ten seconds flat. Wait!" He beckoned me. "Come round the corner a minute and I'll instruct you how to root a man in two places without leaving incriminating evidence. I believe in strict justice, myself."

When I got back there was no Thomasheen James, and Joe O'Dowd had known there would not be.

He took full advantage of the judgment in his favour. He pawned my waders for fifteen shillings, and I had to pay an additional ten per cent. to redeem them.

That misadventure befell him and me some time ago, and Thomasheen James has his tentacles in me still. As I sit writing these last words he is coming up the garden path trundling his barrow that contains only his sweeping-brush and two half-dead leaves.

"We'll be real busy in a day or two," he says cheerfully. "The leaves is beginnin' to fall."

"I am busy now. Get to——!"

"Did you see what Pinkyvitch said in the *Moscow News* last week?"

"Who the devil——?"

"Pinkyvitch! A big professor in Moscow beyont— up above Stamboul where I belted a Turk during the Big War. He says the culture o' the West is only for pink-eyed rabbits. He says if any prooletarian gint wants to get the straight tip on culture let him come an' study it where 'tis bound to the wheel of advancement.

I wonder, now, what a ticket to Moscow would run a man in for?"

"Make it a single one," I tell him, "and you can pawn my new waders."

"May the divil dam' the mimory some people is cursed be," says Thomasheen James warmly.

CHAPTER II

THOMASHEEN JAMES AND THE
CANARY BIRD

I

WRITING-PAD under arm, I strolled down to the open-fronted summer-house at the garden-foot, seated myself in a comfortable old wicker chair, laid writing-pad on knee, carefully sharpened a pencil, and slowly filled a pipe. Like all victims of my trade, I was loth to start work, especially on this fine sunny afternoon, and, so, was not ill-pleased to see Thomasheen James, my-man-of-no-work, trundling his barrow down the garden path. A thin, wiry, long-necked, freckle-faced, sandy-haired, ageless scoundrel, he was loosely attached to me for my sins, and there was between us a tolerance based not at all on mutual respect.

The wheelbarrow contained only his sweeping-brush and a few dead cabbage leaves; and he wheeled it on to the grass plot fronting the summer-house, balanced himself on the tail-piece, drew one of my old briars from his pocket, and set his china-blue eyes fixedly on the tobacco-pouch in my hand. Grumbling a little, as usual, I threw the pouch at him, leant comfortably back in my chair, watched blue smoke drift and swirl below the eaves of the summer-house, and waited for Thomasheen James to enunciate one of his unveracious principles.

"Manalive!" he protested, wreathed in smoke. "Why don't you try a strong dacent plug tabaccy? You can well afford it."

28

And then I blinked, sat up, blew at a drift of smoke and looked again.

"What the devil is this?"

"Don't be disclosin' your ignorance," said Thomasheen James. "That's a canary bird."

A gilt cage hung from the angle of the high-pitched roof over my head, and a richly-plumaged, long-bodied canary sidled along its perch and turned its head aside to look down at me. I had never seen bird or cage before.

"Whose bird is that?" I demanded smartly.

"I'm keepin' it for a lady friend o' mine——" began Thomasheen James.

"Not here," I told him warmly. "My wife will not allow caged birds on the premises, and neither will I. You'll take——"

"Only for wan bare week," he temporised.

"Not one single hour. How long do you think that bird will last with our black cat?"

"Sure enough, he wouldn't last long," he agreed. "That little yalla boy is a Scotch fancy an' delicate kind; he wouldn't last long with your black cat—an' you couldn't blame the cat an' him hungry." He pointed and twitched a finger. "But you'll not be noticin' that I have the cage in a strateegic attitude beyond the lep of a polar bear itself. Would you mind listenin' to me for half a minute?"

"If you care to waste your breath. That cage goes out of here this evening."

"All right! All right! Out it goes even if it costs me the makin's of a good job. But sure we have the evenin' before us, and we may as well be collogin' a few words to pass the time." He pulled deeply at his pipe for a while, and I wondered how far my resolution would go in support of my wife's ukase about caged birds.

"When I was younger and had me health," he began leisurely, "I was a reg'lar hard worker late an' airly. I was so, and am yet at stated periods, only I find that a change of air does me good now an' then for relaxitive purposes. When me presence is absent from this vicinity I amn't no wanderer on the roads o' the world, an' don't you think it."

"I don't. I know."

"You are not the only string to me bow and arrow, an' me sweat spills down on many's the garden path."

"Don't tell me that you have discovered other victims?"

"Call her what you like, an' your capacity is well known. A Miss Falconer she is, a spinster-woman over in the South Circular Road, a round, comfortable woman comin' on in years, and a good enough, kind-hearted woman as women go, but, as I told you before and often, no man can't rightly put his shirt on the best o' them—an' well you know it. A small house she keeps, a bit of a garden and a servant-girl, a bitch dog an' a cock-canary. That little yalla fellow cheepin' at us up there is the cock-canary, a seven-year-old male bird fit to show, and a singer besides. I tidies up the garden for the ould dame, an' plants out a bit of salad an' such, and she pays me well for it—and better'n some I know, an' aisy for her. It was be the instrument of her bit of a bitch dog that I got me first inside grip on her.

"Divil such a dog you never saw! A bad cross betune a Irish water-spaniel an' a half-bred pug-dog —as sure as I'm tellin' you—the colour of a warty spud an' fed like a Christian. She goes waddlin' up and down the garden path, her paunch to the ground, her tongue at the side of her mouth, an' a harmless look in her eye; and the first you know, she'll have her teeth in your calf an' a screech out o' her an' you. Many's the time I'm inclined to acquaint her with the toe o' me boot, only I know better with the ould lady lookin' on, breakin' her heart laughin', an' a shillin' in the heel of her fist to restore the pain. Wait till I tell you!

"One Saturday—I mind it well—this Miss Falconer comes out to me where I am groomin' the tool-shed, with the bit of a bitch trailin' behind, hardly able to waddle a hoof, an' not enough stigma in her to nose at a rat-hole.

"'Do you know nothin' about dogs, Tommy?' she puts up to me, anxious-like. Tommy she called me always, an' nothin' worse like some I know.

"'Why not I, ma'am?' says I. 'I ownded a Kerry Blue tarrier wan time—a fightin' dog—kep' his hould on a Airedale for twenty-three minits be the clock.'

"'There is something far wrong with me little Juno,' she says. Juno, becripers! That's the name she had on her. 'She won't look at her dinner,' she says. 'The wing of a chicken,' says she.

"I knew dam' well—anyone would—the ailment that was on Juno—overfeedin' an' want o' exercise. Them pug-spaniels, if they don't get a gallop wance in a while, puts on flesh shockin'. But I had sense enough to keep me trap shut on that.

"'Do you know a good vethrinary surgeon, Tommy?' she says.

"'Them fellows, ma'am!' says I, me mind wakin' up. 'They might know this an' that about a horse or a cow, but divil dam' the thing they'd know about a delicate pedigree of a pup like Juno.'

"An' there was a pound note waiting for any judicial man to prescribe a dose of areca nut or tuppence worth o' castor-oil.

"'I have a fri'nd, ma'am,' I tells her, 'an' 'tis given up to him to be the most knowledgeable man about dogs in all Dublin. The vets themselves consults him on the sly in difficult cases—the same as this.'

"'Get him at once, Tommy,' says she, swallowin' the bait down her windpipe.

"'He's a bit of a cripple, ma'am,' I comes back, 'and don't go out in consultations. But I could take little Juno—never you fear, ma'am! I'll lift her in me arms at every crossin', an' it'll cost you ne'er a penny—barrin' a small donation of a present if you are satisfied with the cure.'

"She was so aisy, the poor ould lady, that I was ashamed for her as a sample of the boorjoo classes. In no time at all I puts the leash on Juno, an' she puts her teeth in the ball o' me thumb; an' I off with her soft and tinder down the road. But wance round the second corner I livened her up, and when she held back I gave her the end o' the strap in a safe place. I'm not a cruel man be nature, not like me fri'nd Davy Hand that every time he meets a dog gives it a root of a kick on principle, him bein' a bit of a fancier. The touch I gave Juno wouldn't bother a flay, but the noise out of her had people jumpin' for the pavement thinkin' it was the fire-engine comin' through.

"Anyways, I hauled her out to the Phoenix Park, two miles, an' ran her across the People's Garden to the edge of the dog-pond. 'Don't blame me now,' says I to her. "'Tis for your own good I'm doin' it, an' if there's anything o' the water-spaniel in you, you won't mind a drop o' moisture.' An' in I puts her, head first.

"Down she went an' up she came, an' batthered her way out yellin' blue murdher, an' when I caught her she bit me in the same place—the ball o' me thumb —an' in with her again behind-foremost. Manalive! the blood was in her right enough, for in a small while she got used to it, an' splattered round an' round, her nose up an' her eyes starin'; an' when she came out— an' me tired whistlin' at her—she shook herself in me face, an' made advances to a Airedale terrier, a big quiet fella that turned her over with a paw and walked off slow an' dignified.

"Becripers! she was gettin' livelier every minute, so I gave her freedom acrost the Fifteen Acres, and she was as proud as sin makin' a fallow deer gallop. After that I borrowed a lift on the heel of a coal-cart comin' in from Chapelizod—for meself. The bit of a pup trotted behind—she had to trot or strangle herself on the leash—an' be this time her paunch was no trouble to her, I'll guarantee. The ould lady was anxious waitin' for us be the time we got home.

"'Dear me, Tommy! I was feart you'd lost me little pet,' says she, the pup in her arms an' she kissin' the nose of it.

"'Me fri'nd, ma'am,' says I, 'spent above two hours on her'—so I did—'an' here's a special bottle has to be given with her food'—I paid thruppence o' me own money for that bottle, plain castor-oil it was. 'If you don't mind, ma'am,' I says, 'I'll take the pup down to the tool-shed an' minister the food and drink to her; the operation is not for a lady to be lookin' at.'

"'I couldn't bear to see it, Tommy,' says she, the poor woman.

"'An' it wasn't the wing but the whole half of a fine spring chicken. I shut the tool-shed door careful, an' Juno took her drop o' castor-oil be the aid of a box wrench in her gullet. It was a good chicken. There was nothin' wrong with it.

"'An' now, ma'am,' says I when all was over, an' Juno tryin' to climb the side of the ash-bin after the bones, 'don't give her as much as another wan bite of anything till to-morrow mornin', an' you'll find her a new dog be that time.'

"She was so, a new dog—what was left of her. Ten bob, there and then, I got for the fri'nd of me imagination. I expected a pound, but don't never put all your faith in female spinsters—they're closed be nature.

"Many's the time I cured me little Juno after that; an' do you know? I got to like the bit of a bitch—a source o' me regular income—an' she took to me an' no hard feelin's; an' often as not I used give her a share o' the chicken, or whatever it was, fair an' dacent.

"Wait! Wait now! For a lit'ry man you have a dam' poor choice o' words. Amn't I comin' to the canary? Hadn't I to lay me foundation an' show you that oul' Miss Falconer is as good as in me trouser pocket? She thinks me the most judgmatic man in her end o' Dublin, an' if she is wrong far be it from me to say it. That's why she left me in charge o' her canary.

"Yesterday, herself an' Juno an' the servant-girl— a poor Dublin gom—went off for ten days or a fortnight to take the waters at Lisdoonvarna. She'd ha' taken the canary as well, cage an' all, only for the faith she has in me. Too dam' clever I was, maybe. Maybe I

soft-soldered her too much. Maybe I was too bloody
perfect altogether, an' that's good for no man. Things
come right back at you when you're laist expectin'
'em, an' when you wake up you're back at the far
side of where you started from, with divil a place to
start from. I'm too honest, the Lord knows—I suppose
'tis just the twist in me, an' a great handicap often.

"I don't like the job at all. She has that canary
bird goin' on four years, an' becripers! they talks to
each other like Christians, she cheepin' at him an' he
cheep-cheepin' back, till he gets tired of her an' starts
peckin' at his lump o' sugar. I know fine be all the
instructions I got—this an' that about millet-seed an'
chickweed an' lumps o' sugar, and sponge-cake with
ca'ne pepper in it for the betterment of his colouring—
I know dam' well be the look in her eye that if anything happens to that blasted bit of yalla feathers
I'll be on the lookout for another job. Yes, job I said!
No woman was never my victim. Oh, all right! have
it your own way. Me confession is complete."

"But why choose these premises as your bird
sanctuary?" I protested.

"There's Davy Hand, o' course, but Davy's a bit
of a fancier himself, an' no more conscience to him
than a magpie. I wouldn't put it past him to sell that
bird be swoppin' it for an infayrior article if I gave him
the chance."

"How long will this trusting old lady be away?"

"A fortnight at the outside—say three weeks."

"Or a month. I'll have nothing to do with that
canary. Go and speak to my wife if you like."

"Me dacent man!" said Thomasheen James with
enthusiasm. He knew that I had hauled down my
flag, and that he would not need a broadside to make

35

my wife surrender. As a matter of fact, I was already curious as to how disaster would overtake him, as it always did even in his best-laid plans.

II

Everything went right for a week. I found myself liking that little yellow bird. Bred to captivity for generations, it seemed quite content with its gilded cage. It was strange and fluttery at first, but at the end of a week it greeted me with a cheep and a little run of high notes, and sidled along its perch to sample daintily a spray of chickweed in my fingers. In fact, at the end of that week I was caretaker of that bird and not Thomasheen James.

And then Thomasheen James made his first false step. He brought a friend to see the canary. That friend was Davy Hand, a dishonest, friendly, likeable little scoundrel out of the slums of Dublin. One afternoon I found the two in the summer-house staring up at the cage under the roof.

"Beggin' your pardon, sir," said Thomasheen James, "this is me suspicious friend, Davy Hand. He thinks he knows hell-an'-all about canaries an' fightin' dogs, and I presumed the liberty of our garden to let him see the best bird in Dublin."

Davy Hand shook my hand warmly, expressed his happiness to see me looking so well, and hoped the missus and the kids were in the prime. He was a small tubby man, with a broad simple-looking face under a bowler hat—but he was anything but simple. It was the first time that I had met him. I have met him often since, but I have never seen the bowler hat off his head, nor can I say whether he wears a vest or shirt under the

36

shabby black overcoat that, winter and summer, is always buttoned tight over a round stomach.

In the talk that ensued he ignored Thomasheen James. He pointed a thumb towards the cage.

"A nice bird, sir."

"The nicest in Dublin," said Thomasheen James.

"'Tisn't the first lie about a bird or a dog," said Davy to me. "Could I see him closer, sir?"

"If you don't put your ugly plug too near him," said Thomasheen James. He climbed on my rough deal writing-table and carefully lifted the cage down.

Davy, in a crouch, his face close to the wires, sidled all round the cage and scrutinised the canary from every angle. I could not tell whether it was he or the bird that was twittering, and the bird never fluttered, but sidled on its perch and seemed to be showing off its points.

"A nate bird, sir," he admitted, straightening up. "As nate a bird as ever I see—but I wouldn't say the natest."

"A bloody miracle an' you to say that much," said Thomasheen James.

"In the trade, sir, he is what we call a Scotch fancy —and a cock-bird, I think."

"He never laid a egg anyway," said Thomasheen James.

"He's a cock so, sir, but 'tis hard to tell be the looks o' them fancies. See the gran' shoulders to him, an' the reachy neck and the curve like the belly of a sail. Them's his points, sir, an' a bird half the likes o' him 'ud cost you fifty bob in any fancier's in Dublin. Japus, sir! What a mate he'd be for my hen-bird."

"Go to hell out o' that, Davy Hand!" snapped Thomasheen James.

"I have a hen-bird o' the same breed, sir, a great monster of a bird up to eight inches long, as near as be dam'd perfect in shape and carry, only spoilt be a cloud o' brown across his crop. What a matin'!"

"Don't be listenin' to the mealy mouth o' the scut," urged Thomasheen James. "The ould lady might be back home any day—three days at the outside."

"Three days 'ud be enough, sir," said Davy promptly. "Two days to get acquainted and wan day in the same cage—if we hadn't a louser in our company."

"I'll give you a belt in the gob, Davy Hand," threatened Thomasheen James.

"I'll tell you what, sir!" said Davy. "I'll give the pick o' the nest an' a second pick out o' six—and that's worth forty bob an' only the pinfeathers out on 'em."

Thomasheen James climbed back on the table and hung the cage in its place. From his high perch he addressed Davy Hand forcibly.

"Go home to your wife and hungry childer, Davy Hand! Go home now, or there'll be blood spilt in this respectable garden! Go on out now, Beelzybub! an' I'll folly after, an' if your blood don't fill the gutter me name's not T. J. O'Doran Esquire."

Davy Hand shook my hand warmly, hoped we'd meet again in pleasant places, and went. Thomasheen James leapt off the table and hurried after. I, prudently but regretfully, stayed where I was, for I did not want to be legally implicated in the grievous bodily assault that was imminent. Loud voices faded into silence down the hill towards the river.

And yet! That very evening Davy Hand returned amicably with Thomasheen James. They were not intoxicated but they had drink taken, and there was not a mark on either. And a square mating-cage swung from Davy's right hand. A mating-cage is divided in two by a wire partition with a sliding door. In one of the compartments was a long-bodied slim canary. It was as like our one as one pea to another, except for a patch of brown plumage high up on the breast.

"The best-shaped hen-bird in Dublin, sir," said Davy. "I hope your honour is not disagreeable?"

"Me judgment failed on me," said Thomasheen James sadly. "I gev in. The rejooced state o' this scorpion's brats would melt a iron man to a deed o' charity. Three hours it took him, but I gev in. And wouldn't it be the pity o' the world to miss such a chance of a gran' matin'?—and sure there's no mortial sin in it after all. I admit it—I gev in like a feather bolster."

Davy Hand, with the utmost care, and twittering as the canary twittered, gentled our cock-bird, got a quiet hand on it, and placed it in its own compartment of the mating-cage. Then we stood back and watched. The two birds seemed to be friendly from the very beginning. They examined each other heads-aside, fluffed their feathers, twittered, sidled up to the wires, and crossed beaks.

"Cripers alive!" exclaimed Thomasheen James. "A pair o' love-birds! They're coortin' a'ready. Open the partition, Davy Hand—or I will."

Davy addressed me urgently, his hands expressive.

"Sir, if you don't want to be private to a murder don't let no man open that slide-door for two whole days. Mind my words, sir—two days! For it often happens that the hen-bird'll pluck a few feathers out of the cock if they are not proper acquainted, an' it has been known where the cock'll kill the hen be sudden dint of affection. An', sir! if a sartin carroty-

39

polled bastar' opens that slide-door afore two days a bunch o' feathers mightn't be here or there, but if that cock-bird kills my hen—do you see that fist, sir? I'll drive it down his gullet an' pluck his windpipe out be the roots, an' after that——"

"Aisy, Daveen! Aisy now!" said Thomasheen James coaxingly. "Another dam' word out of you, an' I'll be after throwin' yourself and your mis-becoloured hen out in the street and let a bus run over ye. Are you goin' before I change me mind?"

Davy went.

III

Next morning I sought my garden as usual, and Thomasheen met me half-way down to the summer-house.

"How are the love-birds behaving?" I enquired.

"I dunno. I'm feart to look." Thomasheen James rubbed his sandy poll desperately.

"Afraid to look?"

"I am then. Maybe I did a foolish thing, an' I'm waitin' for you to restore me confidence."

"What——? You dam' fool——!"

"Damn Davy Hand, anyway—an' his consarned hen! He left the bad thought in me head yesterday evenin'. You an' him wasn't out o' the garden afore I began to repint. Comin' evints casts their shadows before, as Tom Moore says, an' me ould lady's shadow was already on top o' me long as a telegraph pole. She might take it into her head—she's that kind—to make for home before her time, an' if be any chance she l'arned that her little pet of a cock had intruded himself into a lady's chamber 'tis me she'd blame for disgraceful intintions. I didn't like the thought, I'm tellin' you, an' I went back to the summer-house an' cogitated the two birds. An' there they was as friendly as bedam' an' rubbin' beaks through the wire. The timptation laid me out like the blow of a pick. 'What's a bunch o' feathers, anyway?' says I, 'an' to the divil with Davy's hen an' she in her gore. An' sure if it comes to that I could belt that little runt the best day ever he was.' And there an' then I up and pulled at the slidin' door—me hand did it in spite o' me—and without another look I skedaddled out o' the garden an' let love take its coorse. Begobs, sir! I'm feart to look this mornin'. Maybe me judgment wasn't the rale article on top o' two pints. Would you mind takin' a peep?"

I applied an epithet just but strong and hurried down to the summer-house. As I stepped hurriedly under the open front a little fluff of whitish-yellow feathers lifted off the floor. Then I looked up at the big cage. There on the perch sat Davy Hand's hen. There was no mistaking the cloud on her breast. She was peeping down at me, her long neck out, and one pale feather jauntily acock at the side of her beak. And as I looked she sidled along the perch and twittered down at me, proud as Lucifer, as much as to say: "Come up and see what I've done!" There was no sign or sound of our cock-bird—except that one feather in the hen's beak and the many feathers on the floor.

"Cripers alive!" exclaimed Thomasheen James behind my shoulder. "''Tis like as if you plucked a yalla chicken all over the boords. Has he plucked Davy's hen, the blackguard?"

And then he stepped to my side and saw Davy's hen in her triumph. He let one anguished yell out of him, and in one leap was on the table staring into the

41

bottom of the cage. His voice was lamentable, his words a threnody.

"Wo—wo—wo! It is a terrible thing, I tell you. A shockin' thing. Here he is in the bottom of the cage in a bed of his own feathers, me darlin' little cock-bird, his poor kippens of legs stickin' up in the air, an' his weeshy tummy heavin' up and down be the dint o' him gettin' his breath. No! He's not killed dead—he's worse. He's in a state of naked destitation. The breath of life is in him and no more, but as sure as I'm tellin' you, barrin' his wings and his tail an' an odd bit o' fluff here an' there, he's as naked as the back o' me hand. He's powerful naked. That she-vixen's plucked him like you'd pluck a goose to fill a tick, an' there she is now, preemin' herself, and his last feather in the side of her bill. Ay! his last feather, an' her last one as well, for this very minit I am goin' to twist her neck fondly thinkin' 'tis Davy Hand's windpipe is under me thumbs."

His hand was already at the door of the cage when a shadow darkened the front of the summer-house. Yes! it was that fortunate or unfortunate moment that Davy Hand chose for his entrance. He had not trusted Thomasheen James, with good reason, and was come up to see if his own bird had survived the night. It had. He stood under the eaves and wondered:

"What'n hell is wrong, sir?"

"Nothin' is wrong," yelled Thomasheen James exultingly. "Nothin' at all! She only killed him, an' now I am goin' to kill you, an' everything'll be right again."

He was off the table in a flying leap, and Davy Hand got out from under. Thomasheen James wasted two seconds to arm himself with his sweeping-brush, but these did not give Davy time to open the garden gate and escape to the outside. He went up the path, his long coat in a flying tangle, and his feet spurning the gravel with extraordinary celerity. Thomasheen James moved even faster. For the first time in his experience he had found a man to turn tail to him, and that spurred him to his best effort. The tool-shed was at that end of the garden, the door ajar, and, just in time to escape the poised brush, Davy darted inside and banged the door in Thomasheen James's face. Thomasheen James broke the head off the brush against the jamb of the door.

I hurried up the garden path.

Thomasheen James was driving his shoulder against the door. It yielded six inches, but Davy Hand, inside, won them back desperately. The next furious drive made a gape all of a foot, and the door hung there astrain; but Thomasheen James, trying to get a shoe inside, lost his leverage and the bang nearly took his nose off.

"I'll have him this time," he panted, and stepped away three paces for a final prodigious drive.

It was then I got him by the jacket collar and hauled him back. He struggled, but not forcefully.

"If I throw you out you're out for good," I said.

"Very well so!" he said, quieting down. "Let him come out an' be kilt peaceable."

I shoved him away and parleyed with Davy through the closed door. With some difficulty I established a temporary armistice, and invited Davy to appear.

There was silence inside; then the door opened suddenly, and Davy sprang out, one hand on guard and the other armed with a pick-handle.

"Let him at me now, I'm armed," he cried valiantly.

43

I stepped between, and Thomasheen James made no effort to circle me. The first fire and fury had died down, and the pick-handle looked a formidable weapon. They glowered at each other like held fighting dogs, and apparently decided that if a blow had to be struck the other had better not see it coming.

Davy's nice sense of good manners still led him to ignore Thomasheen James in the presence of Thomasheen James's boss.

"Is the cock-bird killed-dead, sir?" he enquired.

"He's dyin'," cried Thomasheen James, "and the minit he's gone you've gone with him."

"If he's not dead-out, sir, I might save him," said Davy.

"Save him!" derided Thomasheen James, "an' he as naked as—as Vanus."

"I've done it before, sir," said Davy. "Beggin' your pardon, could we take him in before the kitchen fire?"

"What's the good o' wrastlin' with that deluded bit of depravity?" Thomasheen James wanted to know.

But we did. We wrestled with him for two hours. We put him in a nest of flannel before the kitchen fire, and dosed him every quarter-hour with a crumb of bread soaked in whiskey. The whiskey was mine, and there was half a bottle of it to start with. I took none and the bird took a couple of drops, but at the end of the operation the bottle was about empty, how and where I did not see. Luckily my wife had left early on a shopping engagement, and my two youngsters were at school.

After a time the frail little legs of the half-naked bird gave a kick or two, and a wing-tip fluttered. Davy loosed a hurroo.

"I'll pull him round yet," he boasted. "I'll pull him round in spite o' hell if the pride isn't broke in him."

Thomasheen James became less gloomy.

"Do you know what I'm thinkin'?" he half mused.

"I don't want to," I told him.

"I'll tell you. 'Tis about thim made matches down in the County Kerry where you come from. You know? Thim matches where a poor young fella is married on a girl after one meetin' an' maybe not as much as half an hour's coortin' in the whole ceremonial. Listen! I'm thinkin' that 'tis maybe a good thing the poor gom hasn't a coat o' feathers on him like a canary."

Davy Hand ignored the doubtful pleasantry.

"If I do save him itself, sir," he said, "it'll be six weeks before he has a clane coat on him."

I took the poker away from Thomasheen James.

"Why wouldn't you let me crown him?" he protested. "Six weeks! an' oul' Miss Falconer home any day!"

"I'll tell you what I'll do, sir," volunteered Davy. "I'll take the bird home with me out o' harm's way, an' attend to him the same as if he was wan o' me own kids."

I began to like this tubby, adequate, dishonest little man.

"I wonder, now," he said, "is this ould lady we hear so much about short in the sight?"

"She is," said Thomasheen James sourly, "but 'tisn't a bat she is, not to be scandalised be her bird's nakedness."

"There's yourself, sir, an' you wouldn't know wan Scotch fancy from another; an' how would a poor

45

half-blind single woman know? If everyone is agreeable, I'll take a turn down to Tim Mulvey's in Bridge Street. You know the place, sir? Tim Mulvey the bird-fancier! He has a million birds if he has wan, an' a power o' Scotch fancies to pick from. A fri'nd o' mine! We'll borry the loan of a bird from him for six weeks—or a week longer—an' we'll slip it across on the ould lady be the use of our tongue—if they's a tongue between us."

"I'm listenin' to you, Davy Hand," said Thomasheen James under pressure. "The tongue is in me head, and 'tis me gets thrown on the face o' the world."

"An' then, sir, after six weeks—or a week longer—an' this little mortial restored to his jacket, we could swop the birds again an' no wan a penny the wiser. That's the best I can do, sir. Can you better it?"

I couldn't. Neither could Thomasheen James, though he protested furiously at the task before him.

"I never deceived no ould lady yet," he said with complete truth.

Davy Hand scratched below his bowler hat.

"I'm thinkin', sir," he said diffidently, "that Tim might be wantin' five bob for security." He patted a slack pocket. "I'm a bit short this week."

"Ten bob he'll be wantin', more like. I'm a bit short meself," said Thomasheen James hurriedly.

Later the two left, carrying the canary in a cotton-wool nest in the bottom of its gilt cage. Davy Hand had a ten-shilling note of mine pinned for security in a vest pocket. It was only a short loan, he assured me most convincingly—a week—six weeks at the outside—and I believed him.

They were back that evening with a fully-fledged

46

canary in the gilt cage. For men who had been short of funds they showed unmistakable signs of wassail.

"We done it, sir," said Davy. "A dacent spud, ould Tim! We illustrated our difficulty, an' after he got over the crick in his jaw laughin' he loaned us our pick of the fancies on a deposit of ten—I'll be honest, sir, five bob it was—but we had to stand him a pint before to soften him up."

"An' a pint after," added Thomasheen James, "to keep him from broadcastin' the story be wireless."

"Never you fear, sir! Your money is safe," promised Davy. "What do you think o' this little boyo?"

I saw no shade of difference between the changeling and Miss Falconer's bird, and said so.

"To me experienced eye," said Davy, "he's a shade slimmer, but he has the same set an' hunch. A cockbird, I think, but one can never be sure with this kind. It doesn't matter a hair anyway for a short time like six weeks—or a week longer."

"'Tis me has to run the gamut o' thim six weeks—an' the week longer as well, you scut," said Thomasheen James. "An' if anything happens I'll hang for you."

And that was that.

IV

The new bird stayed with us for a week. It was more aloof than the old one, and entirely silent, refused to make friends with me, and when I tried to tempt it with a lump of sugar fluttered wildly against the far bars of its cage. And then, one afternoon, I noticed that the cage was gone—and Thomasheen James. I waited with interest for the scoundrel's return—if he would return. He did.

47

I heard him before he appeared. He was whistling gaily and quite tunefully, and strolled across the green, both hands in his pockets, and one hand clinking coin.

"I done it," said he laconically.

"Done what?"

"You know dam' well. The sweat is hardly dry on me yet. Me oul' Miss Falconer came home late last night, Juno an' servant-girl an' all, and Juno glad to see me. I didn't tell you of her approach because I knew you'd be makin' me hair rise with your prognostifications. The first thing she said to me was: 'How's me little darlin', Tommy?' She didn't mean me but the canary, an' the cage half behind me back.

"'I had the job o' me life with him, ma'am,' I tells her, 'day an' dark. His heart was broke after his darlin' mistress, an' I was barely able to keep the spark goin' in him'—and that was no lie.

"'The poor little dear,' says she, flattered. 'Let me see him.'

"I was for hangin' the cage high up on its hook, but she made me put it down on a small table in her sittin'-room. I was on tinterhooks, I promise you. That bird is the marrow of her own, but, as you noticed, it is inclined to be flustered be humanity. She walked all round him like a cooper round a cask, an' he fluttered away from her, an' when she cheep-cheeped at him he only looked at her in astonishment.

"'Why—why—why! He don't even know me,' she said, an' she next door to weepin' an 'wailin'.

"'He hadn't a note out of him all the time you was away, ma'am,' I comes at her, the sweat out on me. 'An' when they loses their voice that way, be heartsickness, it don't come back to them for as much as six weeks—or a week longer,' says I, an' I cursin' Davy Hand in me own mind.

"'Poor little darlin'!' says she. 'He has got thin.' She put a finger through the wires, and he hit the roof; an' when she put another finger at the other side he pegged it down good and hearty. She let a screech out of her. 'Oh—oh! He don't know me at all at all,' an' she cryin' in airnest.

"'Jealous he is, ma'am, an' a puss on him,' I explains. 'You'll have to coax him a day or two. A cannibal of a black cat I have put a fright on him.'

"Me mind was in a turmile, I tell you, for I couldn't help noticin' that there was a sartin uncalled-for suspicion in her eye as she looked from the bird to me an' back again. 'Get me a lump o' sugar, Mary,' says she to the servant-girl cold-like, an' she contimplatin' the unreasonable bit o' yalla contrairiness. Me heart sunk. A canary that won't fall into sin for a lump o' sugar isn't no canary at all. But, do you know, me prayers was heard, an' that dacent little bird took pity on her an' me; for after a piece he sidled up and had a peg or two at the lump in her fingers, his eyes wary on her; an' me breath started to come aisier.

"'He'll be atin' out o' your hand in no time at all, ma'am, same as always,' I encouraged her.

"That sort o' restored her opinion, an' by keepin' at her an' keepin' at her, an' the bit bird gettin' to like the taste o' the sugar, she swallowed her suspicious nature like dew of a June mornin'. The poor ould crathur! I was ashamed of meself takin' what she gave—an' I expected more. All the same, I came away whistlin', and down with me to Davy Hand to tell him the news. I stood him two drinks on the heads of it. Moreover, our denuded little cock is beginnin' to perk up, an' a fluff o' down comin' out on the naked patches. In six weeks from now I won't have a care in the world. Everything is set fair, an' becripers, sir! I am already lookin' forward to the time when I'll have money in the savin' bank."

"Did you give Davy Hand ten shillings to refund to me?" I enquired.

"That's Davy's private investmint," he parried quickly. "Who caused the misfortunate accident, I'd ask you? But he's an honest gom, Davy. He'll repay you wan way if not another."

The next day Thomasheen James disappeared. I did not see him for a month; but I was not surprised. It was one of the busy periods in the garden, and these usually coincided with his disappearances.

He returned quietly, and he was not whistling. I discovered him doggedly hoeing the vegetable patch, to the death of weeds and a frequent young turnip. There was a subdued look in the light eye he turned on me.

"How's our bird-fancier?" I enquired, hitting him exactly between wind and water without knowing it.

His shoulders contracted as in pain, but he said nothing for a while.

"You liked that bit of a canary?" he said then.

"The first one. How is he making out?"

"As good as new. If you was thinkin' about a bird of your own there's wan goin' cheap: a Scotch fancy seven year old, a cock-bird for sure, and a singer besides. Ten bob to you!"

"Not ten pence. Where did you steal him?"

"He was left on me hands."

Illumination broke on me. I whistled.

"What came unstuck?"

"I lost me job," said Thomasheen James wearily.

"You never had one."

"Whatever it was, I lost it." He leant on his hoe. "I'm this minit back from Davy Hand's. I wint down to drownd him in the Liffey."

"Did you?"

"He was over in The Liberties judgin' betune two fightin' dogs. I'm going down to-morrow to consolidate the job."

"Whatever happened?"

He worked furiously for a space, and then thrust the hoe deep into the soil and a turnip.

"I may as well tell you straight," he said resignedly. "If I don't, Davy Hand will—with adornments— unless I get to his windpipe first. It was a miracle that happened. Wait! I'm tellin' you, though 'tis against meself, an' you can use it for both our profits if you want to. This very mornin' it was, beyont in Miss Falconer's—the ould mistrustin' hairpin! I was groomin' little Juno across in the tool-shed, an' she called me from the kitchen door.

"'O'Doran! Come here!' O'Doran! that's me name, and that should ha' warned me, as well as the hard set of her jaw—an' the servant-girl sniggerin' in a corner.

"'Folly me!' says she, an' she led me into the sittin'-room where the cage was hangin' in the winda, an' a kitchen chair under it. 'Climb up there,' says she, pointin' at the cage, 'an' explain the consequences.'

"The bit of a bird looked as usual to me, but I climbed up on the chair, me mouth open.

"'Well, Thomas?'

"I was as dumb as the ace o' spades.

"'What do you see?'

"'A bloody miracle, ma'am,' says I.

"'Neckrymancy!' says she, whatever she meant. 'I was suspicious from the start, but now I am sure,' says she. 'I suppose your cannibal cat ate my poor bird. Very well, Mr O'Doran! Work another miracle now, or else sling your hook an' take that indecent bird out o' me cage.' Thim's not her exack words—they was worse, an' more of them. So I slung me hook, bird an' all, an' here I am toilin' and moilin' the rest o' me days."

He was about to resume his devastation with the hoe when I stopped him.

"What was the miracle?" I enquired with restraint.

"Didn't I tell you? No! There was no blottin' it out. That unnatural cock-bird had up and laid four eggs in the bottom o' the cage."

* * *

Thomasheen James did not "drownd" Davy Hand. They still run in harness to the risk of simple or designing citizens. And I am not certain if Davy has wiped out his debt of ten shillings. He insisted on presenting my wife with a canary in an inferior cage, and so worked on her that she was induced to accept it. After that I could not mention the brief loan. A new cage cost me a couple of pounds.

Furthermore, he assured me, as he hoped for a bed in Paradise, that the canary was a hen-bird of his own breeding, and a cross between a Scotch fancy and a Belgian roller. It looked familiar to me, and seemed to know me.

As I write it is twittering down at me and suggesting

a cube of sugar. A gay and friendly bird, and a hen perhaps. But I can always irritate Thomasheen James to the explosion point by wondering aloud when, if ever, it is going to lay an egg. And sometimes I wonder to myself, not too guiltily, if my wife is the rightful owner.

CHAPTER III

THOMASHEEN JAMES AND THE ABSENT-MINDED PROFESSOR

I

"You are certainly going to miss that bus," my wife warned me.

"Blazes! If you left those confounded fishing-boots——"

"On the summer-house floor where Thomasheen James dropped them? Ah! here they are. Run and you might catch it. Shall I ask some friends in for a salmon supper?"

"Fine! I'll buy you one on the way back," I shouted from the hall.

I banged the door, swished round the end of the privet hedge, and was brought up all-standing by Thomasheen James's wheelbarrow dead in the middle of the path. Thomasheen James himself, my-man-of-no-work, sat on the tail-end smoking one of my old pipes. There was nothing in the barrow but his yard sweeping-brush.

"Cripers!" he exclaimed. "Is the house on fire?"

"You and your damned barrow!" I exploded, rubbing my shin as I hobbled down the drive. He was already trotting at my side.

"Gi'e me them waders and the creel, if 'tis the nine-forty you're after."

He ambled down the hill ahead of me towards the bus-stop at the road-junction, and mocked me over his shoulder.

"Surely-to-glory! You don't fancy yourself to catch nothin' a day like this—not even the bus maybe?"

"Perfect fishing weather."

"So it always is—in the morning. You'll have a different tune at the end o' the day—like most fishermen ever I knew."

"Fat lot you know about fishermen!"

"The fill of a book, only you couldn't print most of it. Run now! Run like hell! Here she comes."

The driver of the bus saw us coming and obligingly waited; and Thomasheen James and I bundled on the platform shoulder to shoulder.

"That's our first catch o' the day—an' our biggest be far," said Thomasheen James complacently.

"Put down that tackle and get off," I ordered, the bus beginning to move. "If that lawn is not cut——"

"Aisy—aisy! the week is long. It'll be cut."

He stowed waders and creel carefully in a corner and sat down opposite me.

"Where are you going?" I demanded.

"Fishin'. But not a sprat—and mind I told you."

The conductor, an old friend, was at my side.

"One to Tober Bridge, Michael—one!" I said.

Thomasheen James looked at me, half challenge, half appeal in his eye.

"Have a heart an' start the day dacent!—Better make it two, Mick."

I nodded to the conductor. Thomasheen James was bent on coming with me, and he knew that I would not repudiate him in public. Moreover, he was good company.

"Our bit of a joke over," he said, "we'll have a smoke to ourselves," and borrowed my pouch.

I sat contemplating the lean, wiry, red-haired indestructibility of the man. He was a freer man than I was. At the loss of all respectability, at the loss of many things much more valuable than respectability, he had achieved his own freedom. He carried freedom under his hat, which was an old hat of mine. He was not my chattel; he was never legally in my employment; he was in receipt of no fixed wage and had not yet suggested one; but we tolerated each other outside the barrier of class-consciousness, and were implicit partners in a consideration of certain aspects of his own venality.

As I sat there looking at him I realised how much talent he had misused in seeking to avoid the unavoidable, all the vain and daring exploits he had just failed to pull off because of the one final, inevitable false move that had brought the shadow of Nemesis but never the complete vengeance; and there and then I realised that I was only one of a long succession, and that some day I too would throw him out on his ear to be a menace to some other member of what we call our social organisation. And then I had a feeling of dismay. Had he at last perfected his technique to the management of a final and unescapable victim? And was I that victim? I swore.

"Damn! I wish I had never set eyes on your sub-human façade."

"Don't be blaspheemious," said Thomasheen James, startled out of a day-dream. "Me what?"

"Your face."

"You never took your eyes off it the last half-hour. The next stop is Tober Bridge."

He possessed himself of waders and creel, I took the rods, and we dismounted above the strong flow of the Owenbride River. We leant over the parapet of the high three-arched bridge and looked far down at the water running strong and sternly in its gorge over smooth shelves sloping from a long cascade higher up. A little of the early sanguine mood of the angler faded in me.

"I told you so," said Thomasheen James exasperatingly. "Look at it! You could see the head of a pin in the bottom of any dam' pool."

"But the sky is just right," I persisted, "and a nice breeze to riffle the water. A twenty-pounder at least —maybe two."

"Live horse, and you'll get grass," quoted Thomasheen James. "Where do we make a start to commence with?"

"A mile up—Cloona Reach."

"Hell's blazes!" His eyes lit. "Is it poachin' we are?"

"Certainly not. I have a day's permit from Colonel Sandys to fish his lower reaches."

"And oughtn't that be a warnin' to you. That ould divil wouldn't give his own mother a day's fishin' an' the fish takin'."

"That's a straight libel on a gentleman you don't even know," I said angrily.

"Don't I? The same ould dug-out lost me the best job ever I had—an' may the divil melt him!"

"Oh! So you know him?"

"We have cause to remimber each other," he said with restraint. He lifted the lid of the creel and looked inside. "We have lashin's o' sangwiches anyway, but they'll be dry atin'."

"Plenty of water to wash them down."

"River water! That's no safe drink for a human man without 'tis polluted be a drop o' good whiskey—

57

half an' half an' plenty o' water. You'll have that bit of a tin flask in your poacher's pocket?"

I had, but I did not tell him so.

Thereafter we went fishing. And I did fish. And Thomasheen James proved himself a true prophet. The breeze was propitiously in the south-west; the sky was perfect, sheeting and shining with a warm smurr of rain every half-hour; but the water was all wrong. The water was clear and low and just one degree chilly with the melting of the last wisps of snow in the hill chorries; and in the stiffest riffle I could catch the glint of the *Blue Palmer* fly I was using. I rose not a single fish.

But the salmon were there. They were there in every pool. They came out of the water playfully—sometimes over my very cast—in a clear silver smacking curve, but never in that porpoise-like head-and-tail rise that betokens a fish ready to take. Once I hooked a playing fish in the back fin and had a furious ten seconds before the hook tore free. And that was all.

But, notwithstanding, the day was a pleasant one and passed quickly. There is more to angling than the mere catching of fish; otherwise, who would be an angler? The weather had turned definitely towards summer, and the air was all balm; the larks were soaring and singing, and the river curved and fell and sang, and smoothed itself out into shining reaches below tall banks of fresh-foliaged trees; the pastures were bright green round patches of brown tillage; and, behind all, the moors swept upwards into the flowing curves of the great hills of Wicklow, where cloud shadows running smoothly made the sunlight seem more brilliant.

It was good to loiter along the head of a bank looking over a hopeful pool; to pause, while one filled a pipe, and consider the best way of covering all the likely spots; to put oneself in the salmon's skin and choose the exactly appealing fly; and then to work down the pool yard by yard, hope never dying until the final cast into the tail riffle. One might say a few choice words then, sit on a boulder, try a small taste from the tin flask that was really silver, relight one's pipe, and discuss with Thomasheen James the possibilities of another fly.

My henchman astonished me with his knowledge of flies and fish. He would sit on his heels at my side turning over the felts of my old-fashioned leather book and wonder why, "in the name o' hell," I had cluttered it up with as "infayriour a collection of flies as I ever put eyes on."

"There now is a *Orange Grouse* that might do the trick for us if it was only two sizes smaller; and this Scottie, the *Green Highlander*, we could be after tryin' in the next bit of a shower; but when all is said and done, gi'e me a *Spring Blue*—number one—with a touch of yalla in the hackle to timpt a suspicious fish on a day like this—an' dam' the one in your whole selection."

We did tempt the fish with every possible and some impossible lures, but no fish fell. Shortly after midday the sky began to clear, and by the time we reached the head of our water no cloud marred the fragile spring blue; the breeze died away, every pool became as flat as a mirror, and the sun was as warm as in early June.

"Go on wastin' your rasher an' eggs if you have a mind," said Thomasheen James, "but if you're after that fish your missus wants 'tisn't with no rod and line you'll get it."

"I know no other way."

59

"Do you tell me that? What about that time in the Big War when I was out fightin' for your investmints and you away up in Bonnie Scotland?"

The only fighting Thomasheen James had done in the war was with his fellow-stokers in the bowels of a transport-ship of the Mediterranean Fleet.

"You haven't a stick of dynamite about you?" I suggested.

"No then. But this minit I have a stomach an' it glued to me backbone with imptyness."

So we sat on a green bank in the gentle warmth, our feet on dry gravel, and munched sandwiches. Above us a swinging footbridge spanned the water to a fine spread of parkland clumped with lindens and grazed on by deer-like Jersey cows; and at the head of the park a white square house with a Greek portico slept in the sun. I noticed that Thomasheen James kept a wary eye lifting towards that white house.

"That is Colonel Sandys's place," I told him.

"I know it. Is he at home?" he enquired with interest.

"I think so. He lost you the best job you ever had?" I hinted. "But all your jobs were best ones."

"I can't say that on the present occasion," he riposted.

"What job did you lose?"

"A good job."

"No sweat on your brow?"

"It was the reesponsibility," said Thomasheen James.

"All right! Tell me about it."

"There might be libel in it."

"There will be. Go on!"

He finished his sandwiches, looked at me with a calculating eye, and gestured widely towards the silver flask. I uncorked it consideringly and Thomasheen James brightened.

"A reesponsible job! I was the guide, guardian, an' gineral recuperator of a professor out of the univarsity."

"He never survived all that?"

"I didn't. I won't be tellin' you his name, an' if I did you wouldn't make nothin' of it, not movin' in thim advanced circles. I mind the evenin' well. I was after footin' it all the way up from Maryborough——"

"Where the jail is?"

"Do you want to gloat over me misfortunes or don't you?"

"All right—all right! Say when, man!"

"The cup'll tell you when," said Thomasheen James.

II

I was a young, strong, hardy butt of a boy thim days (began Thomasheen James), an' the longest cir-circuitest road couldn't knock a feather out o' me. I had done me twenty mile up from Ard-na-Righ, an' was makin' for the Vincent de Paul night shelter, me bein' without as much as a ha'penny to bless meself with. I had come in be the borders o' the City, when I overhauled an ould fella progressin' vagariously in front o' me. 'Twasn't the length of the street that was troublin' him but the breadth of it, for he was tackin' by an' large from sidewalk to road an' back again like a hooker in a head-wind. A fine summer evenin' at the back o' ten, an' he navigatin' his way home after bein' thrown out of a pub somewhere. A short stub of a thick-built man in a good loose flannen suit, an' a floppy panama hat on the back of his poll.

As I came up behind him he intercepted a white

lamp-post and set back two steps, liftin' his hat most polite an' "'Scuse me, madam," says he. Then he set back two more steps with no intintion an' collided on me chest. At that he faced round, swayin' on his props, an' speculated me out of an eye like a dead herrin'. A red-jowled ould buffer with a bush o' white hair, an' I saw at wanst, be his gineral appearance, that he was no customary soak, only an ould gintleman vitiated by an intermittent occasion.

"You red-skull of a prooletarian," says he, stern but scatterin', "would you assult a illustr'ous visitor to this i'noble city? But, behould!" says he, "you will find no plunder on me carcase, for I have shared me last pasedo with thirsty brothers. Begone, vartlet!"

An' he made wan almighty swipe at me with the panama hat, an' took two full circles out into the middle o' the road. I was just in time to snake him off the raddiator of a bus, an' I propped him secure aginst the lamp-post; an' he up an' apologised for beltin' me so outrageous hard. He hadn't touched me within a foot.

"Do you live hereabouts, sir?" says I to him.

"Far an' far from here, me inquirin' fri'nd," says he, sad. "A city where the unbeliever trimbles and if he don't trimble we makes him trimble. Behould," says he, "a citizen of the great accidental city o' Dublin."

"Dammit!" says I. "This is Dublin."

"Dublin!" He straightened off the post. "So this is Dublin! I know it from the mountains to the sea, but this mean street I have not seen before."

"Might I be bould to ask, sir," says I, coaxin' an' wonderin', "whereabouts in Dublin you pound your ear?"

"Ah!" says he; "the jargon o' the west! Crumlin!"

says he. "Crumlin! where the boorjoo percreate theirselves in gimcrack simi-detachable villa residences." That was true for him.

I was proppin' him up in the heart o' Crumlin that very minit.

"Whereabouts in Crumlin, sir?" I puts to him.

"I have it!" says he. "Six—three-six-seven! Yes, three-six-seven, Dunover Avenue, Crumlin, South Dublin, in Ireland."

Dunover Avenue—one o' them new roads a mile long —it was only round two corners from us.

I anchored him be one arm. "Let us see if we can locate the place, sir," says I, haulin' at him.

He brewed that in his mind, houldin' aginst me. "Very well, aborogeen!" says he then. "Let me assist your errin' steps. The members o' me hareem awaits me long—her name is Mary."

An' he started to sing. Well, sir, we went perambulatin' round two corners an' up Dunover Avenue, me eye liftin' for number three-six-seven; an' when we came to it I steered him across a bit of a lawn into a imitation of a porch.

"Here we are, sir!" says I.

"A remarkable feet of exploration!" says he. "Alas! this place looks mean an' strange after all these years." He shook hands with me. "Thanks for the use of your carpet, Harroon-all-rascal," says he. "Further larges I cannot bestow at time o' goin' to press. Call round in your next voyage."

He aimed his finger at the bull's eye o' the bell-push an' scored only an outer.

"Show me the keyhole," says he, "an' I'll find the door meself."

So I propped him aginst the door, pressed the bell

hard, an' made off down the path; for I was feart the lady he called Mary might be that sort o' woman to blame me for the biled condition of her sultan. All the same, I watched him round the corner of a lonicera hedge.

The door opened an' he fell in on the bosom of a thin woman—I knew she'd be thin—and the both o' them went back into the passage, an' I heard the clatter o' furniture an' the wallop o' chinaware on the floor, an' a screech to wake the dead, and another screech on top of it, and the bellow of a man's voice behind all. An' before I could wink twice, me ould gint comes propellin' through the door in a flyin' jump. Boys, oh boys! He had his feet under him, I tell you, and came scatterin' down the path like a tarrier dog, his hat in a ball in his fist, an' never a halt out of him till he hit the railin's on the other side o' the road. I wint across an' recovered him.

"Lids o' hell!" says he. "The city has fallen to the infidell. I seems to reco'nise you, stranger."

"Was it three-six-seven at all?" says I, havin' me suspicions.

"Six-three-seven—what else?" says he.

I near moidered me brain calculatin' the way you could mix thim figures to a strange result. Eleven, maybe? Six, is it? Anyways it looked like I had a job before me, but whin I start a thing I finish it, an' he was a dacent-like ould buffer even if he hadn't a make in his pocket. I was actin' out o' pure tinderness o' heart, and I'm drawin' your attention to the same.

So we wint tackin' by an' large up the devous long road, an', as luck would have it, struck the right house the third time o' askin'. Six-three-seven it was all right. Well I remimber it. As soon as we got inside the gate he leant down from the anchor I had on him an' extricated a plant, root an' branch, out of a flower-bed along be the path.

"Consider that!" says he, holdin' it under me nose. "That," says he, "is a akwilleesio of the genius that runs in uncles."

"'Tis what I call a columbine," says I, and so it was.

"'Zackly!" says he. "From columbus, a dove—see the five o' them in each head. My wife, Mary, paid ten shillin's a dozen for them, an' they are the apples of her lustry eye."

It was a stout dame—not thin—that opened the door to us this time. A plumpish, good-lookin', fresh-complexioned woman, and white in the red of her hair.

"Oh, John—me poor Johnny!" says she, partly in distress, but mostly relieved-kind.

"My dear," says he, makin' a bow and near buttin' her in the lower curve, "I brought you home a small gift." And he presented her with the columbine.

"How nice! Thank you, darlin'," says she, humourin' him, an' there was not a bit o' suspicion in the inquirin' eye she threw at me.

"'Tis how we lost our way, ma'am," I tells her, "an' we sailin' home from foreign parts—Stamboul, I'm thinkin'."

"I know—I know," says she, noddin', an' a kindly grip on her rambler. "Thank you very much."

I knew then that this was not the first an' only time he had been discanted on his own doorstep after varous pre-pergrinations at the other side of a coupla shots o' malt liquor.

He shook me hand in fare-you-well, an' says he:

"You will have to dispose of me services now, me

good man. Try an' navigate under your own steam. Strong drink is ragin' in you."

And there I left them, and asked for nothin'. But when I got as far as the gate the ould lady hailed at me an' came down the path.

"For your trouble, and I hope you don't mind," says she, her hand out. "I am very grateful to you for bringing me husband home."

A whole half-dollar it was, an' I was able to sleep in clane sheets that night in the Iveagh Home.

Yes, sir! I liked them two—especially the ould lady —from me first survy. She had a pleasant eye and a ginerous line to her mouth. An' durin' the watches o' the night I consaived the polite notion of payin' me respecks next mornin' to inquire if the ould explorer had recovered from his jaunt in lands beyont the main.

I did it, bright an' airly, and there he was as spry as a trout, and him just settin' off for a day's fishin' in the Tolka River; an', when I sort o' interposed that it might be impert'nance on my side if I trailed along carryin' the bag, the good woman imbraced the offer an' meself at the same time, for she hadn't a ha'porth o' faith in her ould wool-gatherer an' him out of her line o' sight. So off I wint with him, and I dunno if he knew I was there most o' the time.

That's the way it began, an', to make a long story short, in less than no time at all I was an institution. Becripers, ay! I was instigated as full-time retriever of the professor, an' me indispinsibility was as strong as a mountain.

A professor—that's what he was. A professor o' echo-nomics in the univarsity. Mind you, for nine months o' the year, he was a rock in the ocean aginst

the timptation of a thirsty windpipe, lecturin' his bits
o' false doctrine twice a day an' takin' the bus home to
his wife reg'lar as clockwork, a bundle o' books in his
oxter an' his pipe in his gob—an' nothin' in the pipe as
often as not. It was only in the long vaycation that he
was accustomed to dive intermittenly off the deep end.
He had nothin' to do, and in the garden he was as fatal
as a sow in a patch o' spuds; but let him go out his
walk alone, a few bob in his pocket, and he'd gradually
circulate himself into a pub somewhere; an' after a
second drink he lost his dimensions lock, stock, and
barrel, an' found himself navigatin' his way home from
some outrageous foreign clime—China or Peru or
Pennsylvania, or some such consarned place.

Sober and head-sore he regretted his little pro-
clivities, and be way of avoidin' the occasion o' sin he'd
arm himself with a trout-rod and lose himself in the
wilderness o' the country. Lose himself is right. For
he would go wanderin' up the riverside, droppin' in a
baited hook here and there, dramin' a bit, readin' a
book, an' wanderin' on again; and at the heel o' the
day he might find himself ten miles from home, an' the
points o' the compass twisted contrairy. More'n wance
he came back in the tail of a turf-cart next mornin's
dawn. As absent-minded a block o' l'arnin' as ever
drew breath, an' him by-way-of-an-expert to l'arn youth
the legal way of extractin' the spondulicks out of
another man's pocket accordin' to the rules laid down
be Church and State.

I reg'lated all his trapesin's. Two or, sometimes,
three mornin's a week we used set off for the country an'
enj'y life on the loose foot betune stated hours, a dollar
in me pocket—mind you that—aginst the misfortunes
o' the day, a thermos flask o' coffee, and a pile of

sangwiches in the fishin'-bag; and before the fall o' night I had him restored safe an' sober to six-three-seven Dunover Avenue, an' a hot meal waitin' for me in the kitchen. The ould lady was as contint as a clockin' hen on a chinee egg, an' in no time at all was callin' me Tommy, an' consultin' me knowledge on this an' that about the house an' garden. Thim was the days.

Fishin'! We busted no records one way or another. He was a bait-fisher, an' I can see your nose curlin' at the mention. He said that fly-fishin' was plain cheatery; and what else is it? "If a trout," says he, "can induce a juicy worm off me hook I congratulate it an' supply another, but if it fails, then its want o' circumspection ends up in me wife's frying-pan." Many's the trout we fed in the Tolka River that summer, and I heerd anglers remark that the trout was runnin' bigger than any season yet. There was one big bull of a cannibal in the Mull Pot off the Navan road, an' he imbibed half a cannister o' worms off us reg'lar, till one day I took the rod meself an' baited a stuart tackle with a felonious brander worm, an' I set that fella danglin' in a holly bush six feet out o' the water.

We had a elegant summer, I warrant you. The professor was a respected man, an' known far an' wide for his l'arnin'; an' most o' the neighbourin' fishin' proprietors, knowin' his little fault an' his harmlessness among the trout, gave him a free permit to fish where and when he liked. We tried the Tolka an' the Dodder, the King's River an' the Liffey, and this here Owenbride, an' began all over again. I used provide ourselves with a strickly limited number o' bottles o' beer at the start o' the day an' distribute them judicially betune us so as not to cumulate any bad effects; and we used daunder along the banks, fishin' when we had a mind, havin' a snooze to ourselves in the heat o' the day, an' wakin' up to argyfy the affairs of the nation an' the ingenuity of the civilised man to contribute to himself what belonged to widows an' orphans.

I used have to watch him like a hawk, for when he was discoorsin' away an' his pipe empty he would fill it often as not out o' the worm tin; an' wanst, when he broke his line an' was for splicin' it, he found it convaniant to hould the worm in his teeth. We caught fish sometimes as well, for, when the conditions wa. suitable an' no interlopers about, I used handle the rod an' bag a coupla trout to ameliate the ould lady, tellin' her how himself caught 'em, an' if she didn't believe me, he did. That's the sort o' gluggerhead he was. Mind you, me dacent man, catchin' trout with a worm in low water is no mug's game. You have to fish agin the strame, and keep the bait on a nice line, an'— All right—all right! Amn't I workin' up to me denoomong?

Yes, sir! We was the completest combination of bull-headed brain an' plain intelleck you ever heard tell of. He was the grandest talker that ever ran his tongue round words with as many j'ints as a earwig, an' me vocab'lary hasn't never recovered from contack with him. Meself in them days had a nice balance to me tongue, an' a disputatious way of interspersin' any argyment to bring him up all standin', so that he'd have to go back to what he called his first principles an' build up his conclusion again, storey be storey, an' me ready to clout it down before he had the roof on. 'Tis he made a communist out of me agin his will.

"You donkey!" says he. "'Tisn't money great men want but power with a big P."

69

"Give me the money for a start," says I back.

"You poor dumb idiot!" he comes at me as if I was one of his students—he had a hot flare o' temper. "Are you not cognising of the fact that if all the ready wealth o' the world was shared out, your share would be exackly one pound eleven shillings and seven point nine circulatin' pence per week? Therefore aggregation of capital is not only——"

"Wait!" says I. "Wait there! Gi'e me one pound eleven every Saturday night, an' you can circulate the odd coppers into your own pocket. I wouldn't call the Queen me aunt."

From that time on I was a convicted communist. Aisy now—aisy! I am comin' to the heart of it.

It was right here on the Owenbride that misfortune inflicted on me the loss of the best job I ever had. Maybe I was growin' careless, an' did not recontre me surroundin's as I ought. A day early in September, a gran' salubrious day with the corn stooks yalla in the field back of us. I should ha' looked closer at the same bloody stooks. You know the third pool we fished comin' up, the one where, be awkwardness, you broke a barb on the back cast. The Corrig Pool—that's it! All flat slabs o' rock above an' below water. 'Twas there that disaster conterracted us.

Me bould professor was sittin' on a lump o' rock, his back agin another lump, half-dozin' or deep thinkin'—I couldn't tell which—his eyes shut an' his mouth makin' small puffs as if his pipe was still in his teeth, which it wasn't, havin' fallen betune his knees. He had just polished off four sangwiches an' enclosed himself round a quart o' beer, and the food an' drink was curlin' happy inside of him.

Meself was reclinin' on me stomach, me jaw over the

edge of a rock, and the deep water a foot below me nose. The Corrig is a tarnation deep hole at that place, an' I couldn't make out the bottom; but, look you! a matter o' four foot down there was a convaniant flat shelf stickin' out, an' restin' on that was as nice a cock-salmon as ever waved a fluke, all of fifteen pounds I would say, with blue showlders on him like a Berkshire pig. His nose was agin the rock, an' his flukes gave a waggle now an' then, an' when that happened I could see the beak on his bottom jaw an' the white o' his belly. A clane-run cock-fish takin' a rest after the batter up the rapids before goin' on up to the spawnin' redds. Whisper! I saw a fish in the identic same place to-day —a bigger fish, all of eighteen. Four foot deep only, an' there's that telescope gaff o' yours in the creel—— Very fine! Very fine! I wish your wife heard you denyin' the sartinty of a fish supper!

I lay flat watchin' that salmon, an' after a time I turned me head an' cogitated the professor. He was real sleepin' at last, his mouth open—and did I wake him? No, sir! I was too busy resistin' timptation, but it was too strong for me. It always is unless it is as wake as skim-milk, an' then 'tis only a timptation you wouldn't give a dam' for. I fell—half a minute I lasted good.

I twisted the long-handled gaff we had sideways an' slipped the hook under water well behind the fish. If all tales be true you are fam'lar wi' the artifice o' gettin' a gaff under a salmon's navle. Slow an' a little at a time like the minit-hand of a clock, an' then sudden an' fast like a flash o' sheet-lightnin'—or you'll find yourself head-over-heels in deep water an' your belly full of it if you can't swim.

I didn't go into that deep hole, not be a jugful.

When I was good an' ready I let that purty fella have it, an' brought him leppin' out o' the water an' over me head an' wallopin' aginst the professor's shins six foot back. I didn't mean to do that, for I didn't want to wake him up till I was ready to explain the way he caught that fish from the butt of a rod. I'd often noticed that after a snooze on a quart o' ale his mimory went all lop-sided, an' he was liable to accept the conclusion with no laist notion o' the predispositions. Anyways, I waked him up, and he bumped his head on the rock, an' while he was rubbin' the place, his eyes shut, I reduced the salmon with a kick in the poll.

"Why, Tommy!" says he, his eyes open agin. "That's a nice salmo sailer we caught."

An' there, at that misfortunate minit, a voice spoke pleasantly from the rocks above us.

"Thanks, me good fellow. My fish!"

Yes, it was! Who else? Colonel Sandys himself. I knew him fine though the professor didn't, we havin' got the trout permit from his agent, Dan O'Shane. The ould fire-eater came down off the rocks bitin' his moustache, an' his eyes like a lump o' ice. An' the bottom o' me heart fell out.

"I needed a fish too," says he aisily, but it was the aisyness of a hangin' judge, the black cap already on his head.

The bould professor was on his props, blinkin' hard an' tryin' to remimber.

"Did you catch this fish, my man?" says he, his voice sternin', for when he was lit up be a quart he'd back down from no son-of-a-gun.

"This scoundrel o' yours saved me the trouble," says the colonel.

The professor was tryin' his dam'dest to recall the past.

"Tommy," says he, "was it me or you caught this fish?"

A man has to be bould at the right occasion, an' two agin wan is no handicap in or out o' court.

"Betune us we did it, sir," says I, bould as brass. "Twenty-two minutes you had him on when I gaffed him nate as ninepence."

And he faced the colonel.

"Fella! I have a permit to fish this stream from Mr O'Shane," says he. "How dare you claim my catch?"

"Not only do I claim it," says the other, houldin' himself in, "but I possess it as well." And he bent down to take a purchase on the tail o' the fish.

"I shall report this disgraceful insult," bawled the professor. "But manetime I insist on me rights."

He was always discoorsin' me on what he called the rights o' property, an' becripers! he could act on it as well. Do you know what he did? You don't! He up and gave the bendin' soger-man a knee in the short ribs that made him grunt an' yelp an' drop the fish to hould on to his liver. An' there an' then me gallant professor took a strangle-hold o' the salmon, both hands round the tail, an' says he:

"Your fish, you ruffian!"

At that the soger-boy saw red murdher.

"Outrag'ous!" he yelled. "Put that fish down, you blind ould addlepate!" And in with him at the professor.

That was a error in ticktacks. I was tellin' you the way the ould boy clouted me with his panama our first renconter. But it wasn't no wisp of a hat he had in his hand this time. No, sir! He was a strong-built butt of a man, an' he swung fifteen pounds o' dead salmon like a champeen throwin' a hammer. Chroosht! right under the ear with a clap o' ten wet towels rolled into wan.

The colonel had no control of himself. He went sideways like a paper flappin' the wind, tangled himself in his own legs, tee-totthered on the edge of the rock, an' yellin' blue hell went behind-foremost into deep water. It was the same as if you exploded a stick o' dynamite.

"Oh, murdher!" says I. "This puts the lid on it."

The colonel, poor fella, came up once an' spluttered, an' down with him agin; an' when he came up a second time I retrieved him with the gaff in the belly-band of his trousers. But to make sure of his discretion I be way of accident let his head under a third time before extrackin' him out on the bank.

There was no more fight left in him than a drownded rat. Dammit! he hadn't wind enough in his carcase to thank me for savin' his life. But what's the use o' boastin'? Our victory was only temp'ry, an' before we could plan a retreat we was impounded be a irruption o' three water-bailiffs lyin' in ambush among the corn stooks. We was reduced be numbers.

What more is there to tell? I am never the one to draw out me agony. That was the end o' the best job I ever had. Oh well! if you want to know. The professor had powerful fri'nds, an' influence was employed above an' below ground to keep the case out o' court. But I might as well be in jail, for I was thrown out on me ear for that wan small single lapse o' discreetness. That's it all for you now!

I looked out across the river and thought aloud.

"If this professor of yours fished only for trout and with bait, why the presence of a long-handled gaff?"

"Dam' well I know the suspicion you have in your mind," said Thomasheen James regretfully. "But if you saw the ould fool tangle his cast on top of a tree or twist it round a stone in slack water you'd know the binifit of a long-handled gaff to extricate him. Maybe you don't believe me——?"

"Not a word. How many salmon did you lift out of the river that season?"

"Go to——" He lifted to his feet quickly. "Look! Who's that comin' across the field towards us?"

A man in white flannels was strolling down towards the swing-bridge from the white house across the park.

"That is Colonel Sandys," I told him.

"I thought as much. Do you think he'd be re-mimberin' my countenance?"

"If he does," I hinted, "I get no more free fishing."

"I wouldn't want to discommode you. I'll cut me hook an' wait for you at the bridge. Hould you him in confabulation."

He moved off down the bank at an easy slouch that did not look in the least like a strategic retiral.

Colonel Sandys crossed the bridge and came down to greet me. A tall lean man with a moustache start-lingly white against a face burned brick under tropical suns, and a particularly decent man too, notwithstanding Thomasheen James's animadversion. He preserved his salmon reaches as conservatively as possible in a land of poachers, but was most generous in distributing permits amongst honest anglers.

We talked for a while, and he proposed that I take another day the following week when conditions might have improved. But as he talked his eyes kept turning speculatively downstream.

"That was your gillie?" he suggested at last, and I was ready with the reply.

"He sweeps the yard and garden path for me," I said.

"Oh, that's all right. In the distance he reminded me of a scoundrel that troubled us a good deal some seasons ago. An inveterate poacher, he used an old wool-gathering college lecturer as a cloak, and must have lifted an unconscionable number of fish out of the easy pools—with a gaff. We found salmon scales where no scales should be, set a watch on the water, and finally caught him red-handed."

He then gave me his version of that capture, and at no point did it agree with Thomasheen James's. The professor had not been implicated at all; Thomasheen James himself had wielded the poached salmon as a weapon, not on the colonel but on his bailiff; and it was Thomasheen James who had been soused to cool his violence. I will not decide who was lying. Possibly both!

After the colonel's departure I set up my trout-rod and fished the runs downwards with a cast of minute, thin-hackled wet flies. The evening rise was on, and by some fair fishing I got half a dozen takeable trout; and, as usual, I very nearly lost my bus. At the last minute I hurriedly bundled up my tackle, and it was only then that I noticed that I had lost my patent telescope gaff. There was no time to go back on my tracks, and all I could propose to do was to drop a note that night to the head water-bailiff.

As I clambered, nearly breathless, out on the road Thomasheen James hailed me reproachfully from the porch of *The Blacksmith Arms* at the bridge corner.

"I hear her comin'. Dammit! why didn't you give yourself time to stand me wan pint?"

The bus came round the corner then, and I didn't waste time to curse him as I hurried to the stopping-place. Thomasheen James was at my shoulder as I swung on. I stowed my tackle in a corner where there were two other fishing-creels, but no sign of any fish, and took a vacant seat, back to the door. After a brief time Thomasheen James took the seat opposite.

"That's another dam' day over us, glory be," he said.

"If you've been drinking beer," I said, "I have a darn good mind not to pay your fare."

"I'll be astonished if you renage me," he said confidently.

And there one of the other anglers on the bus leant forward and exclaimed warmly:

"My lord! Look at that, Tom! What a beauty!"

The man addressed as Tom looked behind my shoulder, and his mouth opened and shut. Then he stared at me.

"Sir," said he, "what marvel of a fly lured that beauty on a hellish day like this?"

I turned slowly and with discretion. Oddly enough, the first thing I noticed was the polished butt of my patent gaff projecting under the lid of the creel. But on top of the lid lay as shapely a salmon as ever came out of the famous Owenbride River. Its perfect shape denied pounds of its weight. I looked at it dumbly, and saw the gaff mark an inch above the vent. But Thomasheen James was not dumb.

"In the Corrig Pool," said he easily. "A *Black*

Doctor with a grouse hackle on a number five Limerick bend. A summer fly, I know, but wasn't this like a summer day—an' how could the fish know else? A hen-fish, eighteen pounds if an ounce, an' I gaffed him nate as ninepence after twenty-five lively minutes."

He looked at me with a calm eye.

"Have you the fare on you, sir? The conductor is waitin'."

"That's another best job lost," I said softly but grimly.

But I paid his fare.

"I can't lose what I haven't," said Thomasheen James.

CHAPTER IV

THOMASHEEN JAMES AND THE RUNNING DOG

I

THE afternoon was warm for late May, and I found writing even more irksome than usual. My characters sat on the breeching and thought of the plot that imprisoned them with cold disfavour; and my red-haired heroine said that she preferred the blond Nordic villain to the squat black Celtic hero. So did I. In slack despondency I leant back in the old wicker chair, draped a handkerchief over my eyes, and began to consider dejectedly a recasting of the whole darn thing. . . .

I was roused by the clank and squeak of an ungreased wheel across the patch of green before the summer-house, and lifted a corner of the handkerchief to see Thomasheen James, my-man-of-no-work, propelling his barrow to a strategic position facing me. He eased it down softly, and rubbed his sandy poll under a disreputable tweed hat that had been mine in its youth and age.

"God is good to some of us," he said aloofly. "Isn't it a fine sleep he's havin' to himself?"

My well-brought-up heroine had just told me to go to Hades, and I had no hesitation in consigning Thomasheen James to the Christian equivalent.

"A great pity I waked you to vi'lent expressions," said he. "There you was under your veil, an' you

79

remindin' me of them ladies I saw in the Big War over
beyant in Stamboul. I do be often thinkin' since that
'tis a shame to the world we couldn't be puttin' the
purdah on most Irishwomen ever I seen."

"The purdah?"

"That's what they call it. Coverin' em up as much
as possible in the upper storey. Cripers! isn't it a
thirsty afternoon is in it?"

Yawning lazily, I turned to the open cupboard at my
right shoulder. I sat up suddenly.

"There's a thief on these premises," I said warmly,
"and I need not go nearer than that to identify him."

"Near enough, an' you not to fall over yourself,"
said Thomasheen James.

"I could have sworn I left a bottle of lager in there
last evening."

"You might be losin' count after three or four
runnin'; an', robber or not in other walks o' life, I
never touched no bottle barrin' out o' your own hands
—an' that not often."

"Run up to the house and tell my wife to give you
one bottle of beer."

"Give *me* wan bottle, is it?"

"No! One bottle which you will bring here intact."

"Wan?"

"One."

"Very well so," said Thomasheen James resignedly,
and left me to wonder how he would account adequately for the second bottle he was certain to bring.

A lean, wiry, ageless scoundrel, with a strange
roguery strangling a stranger honesty. He had served
in the King's Navy, had cruised erratically and with
malice aforethought over the length and width of
Ireland, had lifted grapnel hurriedly out of many

doubtful situations, and was now, for a time, precariously anchored on my premises for his own purposes and my occasional profit. As a gardener he was no success, but he could sweep a path and, under close supervision, water tomatoes and cut a lawn. He was no respecter of persons or institutions, had read surprisingly but without method, used astonishing phrases wrongly but picturesquely, and yielded to an outspoken tolerance in our mutual relationship.

"That's a mighty intelligent young woman you have visitin' you," he said at my shoulder. "She was inside in the kitchen invintin' a cake in a brown bowl—God help our dygestion!—an' says she: 'Take down a second bottle, Tommy boy; me uncle will be needin' it in a small while.' Are you her uncle?—she's too good-lookin'."

"No. My wife's her uncle."

"Ah! That's where the brains come from."

"Implying that I have none?"

"Oh, you got brains of a sort all right!" he said carelessly. "But, maybe, you haven't as many as you think you have. Will I lift the cap off this second bottle for you?"

"You will, I suppose. But if you risk that beer I hope it will rend you like a bad conscience."

"Me conscience is tough—I'll risk it."

He sat on the tail of his empty barrow, poured the liquor carefully, looked through the misted amber of the glass, and took one delicate appreciative sip.

"Yes so! A intelligent young woman. Is she married that one? She don't look it."

"She is. Her husband is an Englishman."

"The poor gom! The English was always soft about women, an' 'tis no great wonder to me they are where they are with sich a disasthrous handicap on top o' them."

I eased my shoulders into the wicker chair and decided to yield to laziness for the afternoon. If Thomasheen James wanted to philosophise on woman I would listen while decency permitted; I would even encourage him.

"From certain of your remarks, now and at other times, Mr O'Doran," I said, "I am led to conclude that you are something of a misogynist."

"Cripers alive! Miss—you're not meanin' mis-cre'nt?"

"Miscreant! That also, but let misogynist suffice for this afternoon."

"Miss—miss! I mind meetin' up with it somewhere. But you're wrong. I never did the like."

"I mean that you seem to suffer from a constitutional or acquired hatred of woman."

"I got that in parts. No then, I don't. I don't be hatin' nobody no more—'tisn't worth while—barrin' a go-by of a cop, like Joe O'Dowd, askin' awkward questions, an' Mullarkey the pawn beatin' you down over the counter, an' the capitalist class as a whole, an' the heerarchy root an' branch, an' Ingland, red in coat, collar, tooth an' claw, when I've nothin' else on me mind. No! 'tisn't many people I hate these days."

"But you dislike women?"

"Don't you?"

"I married one."

"So you did—or was it she married you?"

"Perhaps your dislike is not constitutional," I began again. "Were you ever crossed in love?"

"Was I ever what?"

"Crossed in love. Loved and lost, you know?"

"An' wouldn't I be the bloody fool?" said Thoma-sheen James.

"Or had an unfortunate adventure or two?"

"You don't have no other sort—not with women—but me hands are washed clane long ago."

"Very good! Suppose, then, you finish that beer and let me get on with some work. You could cut the lawn."

Delving into Thomasheen James's past was always a matter of some difficulty unless the occasion was right. It was right now, for he knew that if I resumed work he would have to cut that lawn in the heat of the afternoon.

"Haven't we the evenin' before us?" he said hastily. "Lend me the loan o' your pouch. Manalive! This new summer daylight time makes a hell of a working day for the dumb prooletariat, an' I'll shave that lawn in the cool o' the evenin'. Speakin' on your favourite subjeck—next to urgin' me to drownd meself with pespiration—let me tell you, man to man, that most of the male sect o' me acquaintance has cause in plenty to mislike women. It would be a dam' foolish man would put his trust in the best o' them. We know that, me an' you, but we ha' done it in our time, an' look at us now. Women! they are kind enough, say with a bottle o' beer, but seldom payin' for the same, an' they are kind enough in other things as well, pay or no pay; but at the back of all they do be doin' things for a reason o' their own, an' it unreasonable to the male mind; an' then, at the heel o' the hunt, with the game in their claws, they'll up and change their mind all of a sudden, an' do somethin' so contrairy that it can be undone only wan way, and the worst way. I mind me wance down in the County Limerick meetin' a woman o' that sort—a nice woman too, as women go, and a widda woman besides."

He stopped, and an introspective look that was almost wistful came into his eyes.

"A nice woman! That young wan up in your kitchen wallopin' batter in a brown bowl reminded me of her. She has the same way of seducin' you with a bottle o' thin beer."

"Broke your heart—if any?"

"She broke many a heart, but mine is still knockin' agin me ribs in here." He considered me aside out of china-blue eyes, and I began carelessly scribbling on my writing-pad.

"You're wrong," he said, "but you're used to that. She was a moon winkin' in the sky and I was a dollop of mud under her feet. 'Tis another man I was thinkin' about, an' I'll tell you about her and him so that you won't be throwin' her in me face on a festive occasion. Take your few notes if you want to—I don't mind. There might be a dollar or two in them for the both of us."

He paused, and then went on rather slowly as if drawing on a memory that was stored down deep in him.

II

It was down in the County Kerry, as I said (began Thomasheen James), and at that time I had me health an' was a lively hard-workin' butt of a boy. I was so, and, what is more, I had a steady job an' me steady with it.

I was kennel-man to wan Captain Owen Terrie of Dromo over near the Limerick border; an' the same

captain was a gay sportin' buckeroo, a tall fair-haired
divil of a young rooster, an' another divil, but older,
lookin' out of his two eyes at any woman gintle or
simple worth lookin' at. He kep' a horse in trainin',
bred a hunter out of a half-pedigreed mare, an' had a
colt that promised to carry his colours in the Cup at
Punchestown. But strange enough, an' though horse
an' dog don't mix well, his rale fancy was dogs: runnin'
dogs, raygistered greyhounds for track or course. He
knew dogs from A to X; he knew them as well—as
well as meself, an' what don't I know? He did his own
conditionin', an' only paid me a kennel-man's wages,
but in a matter o' close judgin' he often gave me best,
him bein' a fair-minded man where dogs was consarned.

Yes, sir! I knew runnin' dogs, every turn an' twist o'
them, an' what's more, me knowledge is still in here
where I addle me brains. This very minit I know a
fawn pup be Master Ross out o' Lady Loon, an' if
you——

Right—all right! Moreover, I couldn't be after
trustin' you with a trackin' dog, an' a family man ought
to stay out o' jail. Faith! I'll admit it, I'm not to be
trusted meself aither. In me time, an' the track vet
not too particular, I could add three lengths to a dog's
paces in a three-twenty-five sprint, an' I could slow a
dog as much as a second in the full five-fifty oval. You
take a hair out of a horse's tail, black for choice, an'
the two middle nails of the near fore-paw—Dammit!
wouldn't you give me time to lay me foundations?
The widda woman won't run away, an' amn't I
overhaulin' her in proper style o' story-tellin'.

Well then! One evenin' about this time o' the year
—no, a bit earlier, for I mind the open coursin' was

85

over a month or more, an' we busy puttin' a polish on the young dogs for the track season. That was the year we got as far as the last two in the Irish Cup at Clou-nanna. We won the simi-final, but a stag of a hare foundered our dog on us, an' the captain, a considerate man with a hound, took him out of the final. Take it aisy! I'm right at the start of it.

As I was sayin'—or was I?—I had two first-season puppies out for exercise along the top o' the bank of the Moen River when along comes a young slip of a woman ridin' a young hunter: a tall slip of a young woman on a tall young colt no more than half-broke— an' she half-broke with him. She did not know me cognomen at that time, but I knew her be name an' repute. Everywan did. Any man seein' her wance was not likely to disremimber her. A tall slender branch of a young wan, black as a crow's wing in the hair, an' her face like milk with the crame left in it. Not, mind you, that I ever cared for the thin kind meself. Over in Stamboul, now, the females carry the weight in the right places, an' their faces, when you take a chance to see them, is as comely as the full moon in harvest. There was wance—— All right! if you don't want none o' me discreet experiences in the Big War! I'll get to the widda. I'm at her a'ready.

Yes! This horsy woman was the widda, young an' all as she was. Mrs Una Loftus was her name. Una Loftus of Vesey, and Vesey as sound a bit of ground in the bottom lands o' the river as you'd get in all the Golden Vein. She was a chip o' hell to ride a horse or twist the heart in a man. She didn't spit in her fists to put a twist in any man's heart, I'll say that for her, only she couldn't help herself. But how do I know? For, maybe, if she could help herself, she'd be at the twistin'

86

just as handy. Any man she looked at betune them black lashes, an' her cheek slender an' smooth with a small hollow under the bone, an' her mouth like as if butter wouldn't melt in it—any man at all, I say, would go round scratchin' his head, schamin' to keep her smile all to himself—an' more if he could. Boys, oh boys! But 'tis she was nice—nice to look at an' nice in her ways; leggin' it round the countryside like a tall slip of a lad in her ridin'-breeches, an' aisy as you like keepin' at the length o' her arms all the buckeroos, single or widow'd or married itself—it didn't matter a dam'—eager an' willin' to cherish her an' the sound acres o' Vesey.

But where was I? Ay! I encountered her on the banks o' the Moen River on a fine spring evenin', an' she drew in her dancin' young horse an' looked at the greyhounds and looked at me—an' she had a smile for me.

"Good-morrow to you!" says she. "These are Owen's—Captain Terrie's young dogs?"

That's what she said, her voice pleasant an' friendly. An' we had not been introduced to each other, mark you. Look at me! I belong to that i'noble caste that any woman, high or low, can collogue with as a perfeck stranger. Have you noticed that? Any woman that spakes to the likes o' me spakes to a animal of another order, or condiscinds to be kind, or, maybe, she's after information received. But I didn't notice none o' them things with Mrs Una Loftus. She was just passin' the time o' day with a countryman an' his dogs. "Captain Terrie's young dogs?" says she.

"They are, ma'am," says I. "A fine evenin', glory be to God!"

She laughed then. "Nice greyhounds," says she,

87

"but I have a better hound at Vesey than the best o' them."

"He's sure a topper so, ma'am," says I. "How's he bred?"

"Full brother to that fawn there," says she, "an' I got him from Owen Terrie when he was a pup—I mean the dog," says she. "Some pups never grow up," and off into her gay laugh again.

"His breed is all right anyway," says I, thinkin' in me own mind that if Owen Terrie gave her a pup o' that blood the same pup was the throw-out of the litter, or the captain had a reason of his own at the back of his mind, the playboy.

"I think Captain Terrie would like him back," says she then. "He says I am wastin' a good greyhound."

At that I cocked me ears, for once in a million years the runt of a litter grows up into a sound dog.

"I'm takin' a turn be the back o' Vesey, ma'am," says I. "Might I make bould to look at him?"

"And welcome," says she. "He'll be about the stable-yard. You can't mistake him—a black-and-white, an' he answers to the name o' Magpie." An' givin' me a whirl o' her ridin'-crop, away she canters down the bank, her black hair liftin' under the peaked cap she wore, the sun shinin' on her, and the big plain o' Desmond and the hills o' Barnagh makin' a frame to fit her. I can see her this minit.

So down I circled be Vesey at me aise, an' there was the Magpie hound gallopin' up the yard at us, and it the tidiest yard in four parishes. He had a bark to him like a mastiff, but there was no wickedness to it, and in less than no time himself an' meself an' the other dogs was acquainted an' respectful. The housekeeper, a stout woman with a tongue to scorch leather, put her head out the kitchen door.

"Go 'way out o' that, me foxy lad!" she screeches. "We don't allow no bitch dogs about the yard."

"Your bee-oligcal eddication is neglected, me good woman," says I.

"Holy Saint Joseph!" says she, consternated, an' shut the door like a belt o' thunder.

You've seen the markin's of a smooth-haired fox-terrier: black saddle an' black spectacles? Them was Magpie's markin's. 'Tisn't often you get that colourin' on a runnin' dog, an' less often on a good one, but if it is good it is tarnation good. An' Magpie looked good to me. He looked dam' good. Not a tall dog at all, but he had the longest, curvin'est, best let-down hind-legs from hip to hock I ever saw, an' you know what that means the first reach up to a hare. Have you heard the ould verse of a rhyme?

> "The Head of a Snake, the Neck of a Drake,
> A Back like a Beam, a Side like a Bream,
> The Foot of a Cat, the Tail of a Rat."

That fits a good hound to-day as well as the far-away day it was invinted by some dead-an'-gone fancier now in glory. And it fitted Magpie like a glove.

"Cripersjoe!" says I to meself, "the bould Captain Terrie was blind of both eyes the day he gev that pup away, or," say I, "the sight was scattered on him be dint o' lookin' at someone else."

An' that someone else came clatterin' into the yard on her tall colt as I was feelin' the clane bone o' her dog's fore-leg.

"Do you like my Magpie hound, young man?" says she.

"A nice pup all right, ma'am," I says, drawin' it mild. "Did you ever course him at all?"

"No! I don't like killin' things," says she, the heart-killer.

"Not even a buck-rabbit an' we ate alive by them?"

"No!" says she. "But Magpie has l'arned our hens to fly like pigeons, an' sent all our ducks wild on the Moen River," says she, laughin', an' she could laugh hearty as a boy for all the trouble put behind her—if all tales be true.

"You'll be after spoilin' the dog on us, ma'am," says I. "You'll have him chasin' cats next—or does he?"

"No! He's no killer," says she again.

"You wouldn't think o' tryin' him on the track?" I sort of coaxed at her; "an' that's no killin'. Only a bit of a block o' wood on a steel rod with the skin of a hare on it."

"Your name I don' know——"

"T. J. O'Doran without the Esquire—Tommy to you, ma'am," I tells her.

"I was only quotin' the Bible," says she, laughin'. "Your name is Tommy O'Doran, but your voice is the voice of Owen Terrie. He wants to train my Magpie for the track, but I wouldn't trust a Kerryman with a runnin' dog or a fightin' dog—an' I wouldn't trust Captain Terrie with any a dog at all." An' be the way she said that I knew it was more than a dog she wouldn't trust him with.

"I'm not a Kerryman, ma'am," says I, "an' God forbid. I'm from the County Wicklow, an' I'll train your dog for you meself. There's not a ha'porth o' harm——"

90

"We'll talk about it another time," says she. "Come into the kitchen an' have a bottle o' stout."

That's all I said that time about Magpie or Captain Owen. I thanked her for the bottle o' stout the housekeeper hoped would choke me, an' off with me back to Dromo. The captain had his watch in his hand waitin' for me.

"You dam' well walked the feet off them pups," says he, "or was it asleep under a bush you was?"

"You was asleep yourself wance upon a time," I comes back. "I been lookin' at a dog."

"You have?" says he, givin' me a slant of an eye.

"I have so," says I. "It might ha' been a good pup to give away at the time, but 'tis a dam' good pup to coax back now—if you can, an' you can't," says I.

"Oh!" says he, that way, as if I was after givin' him a prod in the wind.

"Maybe you had a good price for him—in your mind," says I careless-like.

"You go to hell, Thomasheen James!" says he.

An' I shut me trap tight, for there was a divil in his eye to help me on me way that road.

I needn't waste your time tellin' you that I had me own way with Magpie in the end. I was a persuadin' sort of a customer thim days in a thing I set me heart on, an' I had me heart set on seein' what the hound could do on the runnin' track. Yes, sir! at the end o' ten days I had Magpie in leash with his fawn brother, Brian Boy, an' him atin' out o' me hand. An', what's more, I had his owner as keen as meself. She used walk the dogs out with me, an' a dandy walker she was, straight in the foot an' wan arm swingin'. As friendly a young woman as ever was, an' she never talked down at me, pattin' herself on the back for condiscindin' to the bottom classes—like some people I know not far from here.

Before long she got to trust me judgment in this an' that about the place, an' wasn't above askin' me opinion about a horse or a cow—or a man. But she didn't mention wan word about Captain Owen Terrie, an' I noticed that. He was in her mind, but she didn't need no advice about him. She knew him an' had her guards up, maybe hopin' that he would try a belt at her in passin'. How do I know?

The bould captain said nothin' to me about trainin' Magpie. He wasn't supposed to know, but you couldn't hide much about a dog or its owner from that same boyo, an' he couldn't help noticin' that I was trottin' it down the direction of Vesey in an' out of me spare time. All he said was:

"You're puttin' a nice polish on Brian Boy for wance." That was the fawn brother to Magpie. "I would like," he goes on, "to see the dog would lead him from the back stretch."

"You'll see him if you live long enough," says I.

"I don't know any puppy that could," says he, "an' I ought to know, breedin' the best in Munster."

"You do and you did," says I, an' off I went whistlin', leavin' him cogitatin'.

That Magpie dog was the only dog, god, man or woman that ever pleased me to me heart's contint. He was kind, an' he had the heart of a line, an' he took all the polish you could put on him an' asked for more. Be this time the young widda was in a hurry to see her dog racin', but I wouldn't permit no hurry. I brought him on at me own pace to a certain pitch, an' then I tried him out agin a stop watch. A fri'nd o' mine was sec'etry to a home-made track over at Ballydowd on the Kerry coast, an' wan mornin's dawn I slipped across there with Magpie. He did the three-thirty sprint in nineteen an' a half seconds. "Only fair to middlin'," says me fri'nd. "Give him a good rub, an' we'll try him the full course." An', as sure as I'm tellin' you, Magpie did the full five-twenty-five in a fraction under thirty-one.

"Jerusalem!" says me fri'nd, listenin' to his watch to see if it was stopped on him. "There isn't a three-year-old nearer than Dublin to beat that—much. He's a distance dog, slow from the trap but like a wind out o' hell from the back stretch."

"Keep your thumb on that," I warns him, me fist under his nose. "Keep your thumb on that, an' you'll not loose by it." An' back I went to Vesey at peace with the world, an' me plans growin' like a mushroom on a harvest mornin'.

"Is he good—is he good enough, Tommy?" the young widda wanted to know when we got back.

"Good enough, ma'am," says I, "if I have the choosin' of his races."

"Why not you, Tommy?" says she. She always called me Tommy now. "But I'll have no tricks," says she, threatenin' me with her finger.

"Ne'er a trick in the world, ma'am," I promises her, "only wait till I give the word before you lay your money on him."

An' I went to puttin' the last shine on Magpie. An' then, wan day, sort o' be accident, the captain met us an' we out with the dogs. He took no laste notice o' me, but to the lady he says:

"L'arnin' to train a hound, Una?"

"I am, Owen," says she, quiet.

93

"Would you mind takin' a second dog to break?" says he with meanin'.

"The first lesson I would teach that dog," says she, "is how to keep his own place."

"Faith! you know how dam' well," says he. "Anything else?"

"The dog in your mind is too long a rogue," says she.

"Break a rogue," says he, "and he's yours for all time, tide an' eternity."

"An' eternity plain hell, maybe," she comes back at him.

And so they went at it, sparrin' with words, clever as you like, thinkin' me mintal capacity no more'n the hound's; but I had me tongue in me cheek, an' after a time I remarked careless kind to the lady.

"Speakin' o' dogs, ma'am, I often noticed that the dog askin' for breakin' is a'ready broke."

The captain went off then, but he got into the habit of often meetin' us after that, and it was always the same betune them: fri'ndly enough but sharp-pointed, runnin' the knife o' their tongues into each other be way of fun in airnest, an' she the master o' the game. In no time at all I seen that bould Owen Terrie's goose was cooked; his name was mud; drowned deep as in a well he was; tied an' tangled like a fly in a spider's web—him that used be a big yalla wasp smashin' webs for divilmint. Becripers, sir! he was prepared to go up to the altar rails with Una Loftus, a widda-woman. An' listen to me! When a man like that is ready to go as far as that with a woman, you an' me an' all men can cry salt tears for the downfall of the last man to stand up for the indipindence o' the breed. Amn't I right? Carried unanimous!

Boys, oh boys! that was a great summer we had

wance the track season started in earnest. I raced that Magpie hound with a judgment that trackin' men talk of to this day. An' me lady left me to me own devices.

I began slow and ord'nar'. I entered Magpie for the three-thirty-yards puppy stakes at Tralee, an' he was beaten a length after goin' wide at the last turn an' gainin' four. I put him in for the three-twenty-five sprint at Ballydowd, an' his own brother Brian Boy beat him two lengths aisy. An' then I entered him with two-year-olds for the five-hundred oblong at Limerick.

We had our bit o' money on him that time at four to one, an' he came out o' the ruck in the back stretch an' at the last bend it was as if th' other dogs had stopped dead. After that we won the long course at Cork, an' then I took him to headquarters, right up to Dublin, an' he won the Jubilee Junior Cup in four heats. We made a pile—only I lost meself for four days in The Liberties with Davy Hand. Davy, the scut, brought along a Inglish buyer, an' he offered me a hundred quid for Magpie an' a single ticket to London, an' then two hundred, an' jumped to two-fifty, but at the last minit I remimbered the widda's curse, an' directed the hated Saxon to where Mrs Una Loftus was stayin' in the Shelbourne Hotel. The lady wouldn't sell for the crown o' Ingland. I mind runnin' Davy round four corners into *The Brazen Head*, where we was so exhausted that we had to have two pints each afore settlin' our difficulty—amiable.

After that we took Magpie on the south circuit, an' at the end of it Brian Boy beat him one length in a sprint at Ballybunion. We took him home to Vesey then, an' it was there the trouble betune the widda an' the captain came to a head an' a show-down. I'll tell you.

It was an evenin' late in the season, an' I was sweatin' meself in the kennel-yard at Dromo rubbin' down the dogs after a scamper. Una Loftus was sittin' on the palin', the reins of her colt in her elbow, and Owen Terrie was leanin' at her side as near as he could without touchin' her. He daren't touch her, an' he knew it. They were at the tail-end of a talk that had started somewhere else, an' I could see that the iron was twistin' in the captain. They took no notice at all of me. I was no more to him or to her than the dog I was groomin'. Men like me has no ears whin their betters are confabbin'.

"You don't hould out much hope, do you, Una?" says he, sullen.

"Not a hope, Owen. I was unlucky with one man, and I'm afraid. Day an' night I'm afraid." Her voice was not too steady.

"Afraid of what?"

"Afraid of another man that might not be so unlike the first—if all tales be true," says she.

"You might give me a chance to——"

But she stopped him sharp and hard.

"No. That sort o' chance is all on one side." She pointed her ridin'-crop to where I was rubbin' down Brian Boy. "Look! For my own sake I could give you no more chance than that dog of yours has of beating my Magpie."

"He has beaten your Magpie twice this season," comes back the captain.

"In sprints. Try them the full course and see. You never have. Were you afraid?"

"Is that a dare?" says the captain, fast.

96

"It's a challenge."

"Does my chance go with it?"

"Don't be a dam'—don't be silly," says she, stirrin' on the palin'.

"Dam'd or not, silly or not," says he in a timper, "will you marry me if my Brian Boy beats your Magpie?"

"Marry you on a dog race! My eternal soul on a dog race!" She was wantin' to feel insulted, but he stopped it.

"Who started it? 'No more chance than that dog of yours,' says you. All right! I'll take that chance. You won't. You're a coward."

"A coward?"

"It is time I called you that, begod!"

She faced him sudden, an' nearly fell off the palin'.

"And if you lose?" she put to him.

"Then," says he, his voice stern, "as sure as God made me I'll stop troublin' you, except in my dreams —and yours," says he.

"It's a match," she cried. "Name your day, Owen Terrie."

"Next week at Castleinch, the last meetin' of the season," he answers prompt. "The full distance, and let the judge o' the course decide."

"It's a match," she cried again, flamin' mad to be called coward. She snapped her ridin'-crop on her boot and went from the palin' on to her colt easy as a cat; and as she clattered out o' the yard she called back somethin' about God maddenin' people before puttin' the kybosh on them.

The captain stayed where he was, leanin' on the palin', an' I cocked an eye at him over Brian Boy's shoulder.

"Maybe I am mad at that," says he. "You heard some o' that, Thomasheen James?"

"Not a dam' word," says I, puffin' away at me work. "You'd not like your dog to win, I wouldn't doubt?"

"Be funny with me, me bucko," says he, "if you want a crick in your neck. Go on! I need a bit of action."

He could use his tongue on me to his heart's contint. I didn't mind, if it relieved his feelin's.

"Maybe you think Brian Boy has a chance?" says I.

"You should know," says he.

"I do so," says I. "The chance of a snowball in hell, as the Yankees say."

"You've tried them out?"

"Three lengths, an' the gap widenin' after five hunderd."

"Does Una—Mrs Loftus know?"

"I wouldn't put it past her," says I. "She was holdin' the watch on them at the time."

"Women are the very divil," says he, sad. "I thought she was a taste quick in takin' me up. Ah well!"

"A bit late to draw on your expayrience," says I, "but still an' all, Brian Boy might win."

"Win?" says he.

"It could be," says I, me head down an' me hands busy. I was tryin' him out only. "There's no dog," says I, "can't be shortened a few lengths at a pinch— as well we know," says I.

"Say that plain," he invites me.

"You heard me," says I. "All's fair in love an' war."

He was silent so long that I took a peep at him sideways, an' 'twas well I did. For as I turned me head he hopped the palin' without puttin' a hand on it, an' I fell over Brian Boy evadin' the flyin' root he made at me. He lifted me off the ground as if I was a tarrier dog, an' there was his fist within an inch o' me eyeball, an' his teeth grindin'.

"You dam' Dublin Jackeen from the County Wicklow!" says he; "would you play divil, an' temptin' me so aisy? I done many a foolish trick in me time, with dogs," says he, "and with bitches," says he, "but I'm in this for me sowl's sake, an' I'll win fair or I'll lose dacent. Whisper here, you varmint!" says he, "an' mind me words! If you do anything, any least dam' thing to slow Magpie, Ireland, all of it, will be too small to hould you, and England not big enough, and Wales," says he, "and Scotland itself will not have a mountain tall enough to come between me and you. For," says he, shakin' me, "I'll find you, an' I'll pluck your gizzard of a heart out of your carcase for a pumice stone; I'll boil your livers and lights four hours for a hound's mess; I'll take the hide off of you an' tan it for a saddle-cloth. Are you listenin' to me?" says he. "I'll—I'll——"

"Aisy, Captain, aisy!" says I, houldin' me temper. "In another minit you'll be threatenin' me. The dog is not me dog, an' he's not your dog neither. I'll take me orders from Mrs Una Loftus."

An' at that I twisted me shoubleder out of his grip an' le'pt the palin'.

"I'm feelin' grand now," says the captain, and I left him there grinnin'.

I never stopped to draw me breath till I was in the yard at Vesey an' knockin' at the back door.

"Take your freckled gob out o' here!" says the housekeeper, an outrageous slut of a woman with her tongue.

"Why don't you say the same to your fri'nd the divil?" I tells her. "Is the lady-o'-the-house within?"

"Is that you, Tommy?" says her voice within in the hall, and out she comes herself, shapely and fine-drawn in a white dress. We went across the yard together.

"Anything wrong, Tommy?" says she. "You look like you seen a ghost."

"The divil himself, ma'am," says I. "Could I be askin' you a plain question?"

"Why not you, Tommy?" says she. "Two if you like." But be the way she straightened herself I knew she knew what was on me mind.

"Wan is all I'll ask," says I. "Do you want Magpie to beat Brian Boy in that match?" A straight enough question, though hidin' the prime one. But she did not answer it straight. What woman would?

"Magpie can't lose, can he, Tommy?" says she. But I would not let her off.

"That's no answer, ma'am," says I, "or if it is you'll have to be enlightenin' me a bit more."

She stopped then an' looked at me, an' kept on lookin', an' a trouble grew in her face, an' for the first time the secret she hid in her heart was plain to be seen.

"I don't know, Tommy. I don't know at all." An' her voice was no more than a whisper, an' wan hand was holdin' the other.

"In that case, ma'am," says I, "'tis meself knows dam' well."

"Life hurt me too much, Tommy," says she. "I have no luck, an' I'm afraid night an' day."

Right enough, she had no luck with her first man. He was the infayriour article, a cruel divil by all accounts, an' the things he done to his young wife I heard whispered, but no one will ever know the full of it. Jealous he was an' with no reason, an' a cruel man gone jealous is not fit for hell even. In the end he got out of Ireland two jumps ahead of a warrant for manslaughter an' came to a bad end in South America—Peruvia or some consarned wild place— some says be a man-killin' horse, an' some says be one of them gowjoes slippin' a knife in his ribs for a good reason. He was dead for sure, wan way or another, an' his widda thought she had l'arned her lesson for good an' all. But here she was at her ah-bee-sees over agin an' feart as hell she'd blot her copybook.

"I must win, Tommy," says she, confidin', "mustn't I?"

"Don't say another word, ma'am," says I. "Leave it all to me."

"I always left Magpie to you, Tommy," she says, her eyes watchin' me. She gave a hopeless throw to her two hands like she was drownin'. "I'll grasp at a straw, Tommy," says she, "an' trust to your judgment."

An' without another word she left me, an' I did not speak to her again—or even see her—till the very day o' the match.

Back I went to Dromo, slow enough o' foot this time, an' quare thoughts in me mind, an' be the time I got there I knew that there was only wan thing to be done. I didn't want to do it. I was a traitor to me sex. I was like wan o' these fellas we read about in holy books that takes a delight in flagolatin' themselves. I met the captain at his own gate.

"Where were you, you fox?" says he, suspicious.

"On your business, Captain Terrie," I tells him, an' I was so mad at him an' meself that I was fit to be tied.

"Damn you!" says he. "I'll attend to me own business," and he strode at me.

But if he did, I rammed my hat on the ground an' me coat was off in wan twist.

"Put a hand on me now, Owen Terrie," says I, "an' I'll take a fall out o' you if you was as big as Finn MacCool."

He stopped an' looked at me in wonder. An' I will say that he was gintleman at the back of all. He knew that he could lick me to glory with wan hand tied behind him, an' he knew that I wouldn't back down no more. What else he knew I don't know. Instead of puttin' his fists up, he brought a hand to the salute, an' says he:

"Sorry, O'Doran! Let's forget it." An' he turned on his heel and walked slow up the drive, his head down.

To make a long story short, we entered the two dogs for the Crowner Plate at Castleinch, a small place for size but packed with enough roguery to fill a bolster. I trained the dogs faithful, the captain pretendin' he wasn't watchin' me, an' by the fatal day I had them fine as a silk thread. The four other dogs in the race might as well be at home for all the chance they had. You could get any price you wanted on 'em.

On the day of the match Magpie was six to four on, for his qualities as a distance dog was known; Brian

Boy was twos, even if he had bet Magpie twice. No wan can fool a Kerryman in summin' up the final result. But I had a sum added up in me own head, an' ten minits before the race I took the track kennel-man to wan side.

"Take that," says I, "an' spread it on Brian Boy as far as it will go." That was every last farthin' I had in the world, an' it was a nice little pile.

"Brian Boy!" says he, consternated. "Are you out of your mind, Thomasheen James?"

"Do what you're told, you Kerry bog-trotter," says I, "an' if you have a shirt don't be feart to risk it." I had the same fellow under me thumb for a reason or two, an' anyway I had to trust him.

He put me money on all right, for in about two minits the bettin' came down to evens on Brian Boy, an' there was a hullabulloo of suspicion among the knowin' gints. Moreover, the word had somehow gone round that this was a made match with more than money at stake; an' here was someone in the know pickin' Brian Boy to win. A minit to go and both dogs were evens.

As soon as the dogs went out to parade I slipped round to the far side o' the track, for I didn't want to be contag'ous to the captain—or to the widda either. Mind you, be this time I had no fear for the result. Brian Boy was bound to win. But all the same, me heart was in me mouth while the dogs paraded round the track, for Magpie walked a bit on the soles of his feet, his head up as if takin' the air, an' I didn't draw an aisy breath till the six dogs was in the startin' trap.

Then, clatter-clack, the tin hare gave a start an' came scootin' round, hell for leather. An' bang! up went the trap-doors an' out le'pt the dogs like a shot out of a gun. I needn't tell you, Magpie was a length behind an' his tail barely clear o' the box. He was more than that behind at the top swing, an' a'ready Brian Boy was in the clear an' huggin' the turn slick as a eel.

"Cripers!" I says. "I overdone it, an' the crowd'll be after skinnin' somewan."

But wait you! The race wasn't over yet. Sorrowful day it wasn't over! Wance again Magpie was givin' us a taste o' his customary performance. Slow, slower than ever from the trap, he began closin' the gap up the back stretch. Hand over fist he was closin' it, an' in spite o' everything I found meself roarin' with the crowd, an' they were liftin' the sky as Magpie came up on the outside o' the ruck. It was agin nature, an' me two eyes were out o' me head watchin'. For at the last bend Magpie, game as a pebble, let go in his whirlwind finish, an' no wind out o' hell ever came faster. He drew dog after dog back to him, an' there he was at Brian Boy's shoulder—an' there was the winnin' post. There was only a nose in it, and it no more than a pug's nose. I couldn't tell the winner till the numbers went up, an' I had to blink the tears out o' me eyes to see. An' when I did see I blinked me eyes again in astonishment an' dismay. Yes! Magpie had won—won be a short nose.

I couldn't understand it nohow. But there it was. Magpie had won; I had lost me little savin's; Owen Terrie had lost a wife; an' what Una Loftus had won or lost I don't know. It was me usual misfortunate disaster, an' that's me whole story for you. An' if 'tisn't worth another bottle o' beer to take the dryness out o' me throat, say so.

Thomasheen James stopped his narration and shook his head, an introspective look still in his eye. He had gone into the past and briefly resurrected an old romantic urge that I thought he could not be capable of. After a time I said quietly, as if to myself:

"In a spirit of, shall we say, sacrifice, you had arranged for Magpie to lose the race?"

"Didn't I say that, dammit?"

"Not directly. What came undone?"

"I suppose I'll have to tell you. I didn't mean to. I couldn't dope the dog because I wouldn't, an' I daren't touch a toe-nail with the captain watchin' an' his eyes peeled. But when the kennel-man went off to lay me money I fed Magpie a bowl o' soggin' wet rice I had hid in the covers—two pounds o't; an' on top o' that, a minit before the parade, I poured a bottle o' soda-water down his neck, an' a second bottle to make sure. The weight an' the wind will slow any dam' dog as much as a second—or more. 'Twas a invintion o' me own."

"Yet Magpie won, you scoundrel, in spite of that?"

"He did not. I fell over meself in tryin' to make sure. I tried to be too dam' sure altogether. With all there was at stake I overdid the sartinty, like many a man before me. It was that second bottle o' soda-water that cancellated me virtue an' cooked our goose. For Magpie got powerful sick on that overdose inside the startin' box, got rid of his handicap, an', though still squeamish, pulled off his final devourin' finish to win be a nose. That's it all for you now."

"And so the young widow remained a widow?"

"Did she so?" said Thomasheen James sardonically.

"Didn't I say at the beginnin' that you couldn't know what a woman would be up to next? The widda had the game won, an' renaged the last fatal trick. Listen! She was so tarnation sorry for her poor ould forlorn captain that she up and married him the next week. I came away."

"They threw you out?"

"They did not. They wanted me to stay, but I came away," said Thomasheen James in his quietest voice. I did not taunt him any further.

CHAPTER V

THOMASHEEN JAMES AND THE
OPPROBRIOUS NAME

I

As he himself would put it, I had seen neither hair nor hide of Thomasheen James, my-man-of-no-work, for two whole weeks; but I was not surprised. The season —early June—entailed honest work with a dutch hoe, and he had a habit of disappearing into the misadventurous unknown with the burgeoning of the weeds. I could do nothing about it even if I wanted to. Thomasheen James was no wage-chattel of mine. He was a free agent, coming and going when the tinker-gipsy blood so moved him, and we continued to tolerate each other for our own purposes. And yet! I missed the scoundrel.

And then one fine Thursday morning I heard indirectly from Thomasheen James. I was standing at the french window looking across my garden, smoking my first after-breakfast pipe, and trying to make up my mind between a dutch hoe and a writing-pad, when I saw a short tubby figure coming up the garden path. The figure wore a bowler hat, and though the morning was already warm, a black overcoat was tightly buttoned over a round paunch.

I knew the visitor at a glance. He was Davy Hand, team-mate to Thomasheen James in nefariousness, a friendly, rather lovable little wastrel out of the slums of Dublin. His wife was a char-lady, and kept Davy and six or ten children on a small but steady income. Davy provided an occasional largesse for luxury and betting by his activities as a dog-fancier. They were one happy family.

I went down the path to meet him out of my wife's hearing, for his style of speech was, if anything, more robust than Thomasheen James's.

"God spare you the health, sir!" he saluted me. "Isn't it grand you're lookin'."

"Hello, Davy! Are you after Thomasheen James with evil intent?" I queried, coming directly to the point.

Davy, whose round face had looked unusually glum, brightened up wonderfully.

"Don't tell me, sir, that he has the bloody luck to be here with you this blessed an' holy mornin'?"

"I haven't seen him for a fortnight, Davy," I told him.

"You haven't heard from him be any chance, sir?"

"No, and I don't want to."

"Ah! I was feart for that." Davy shook his head sadly. "I was dam' feart for it. That's why I come up to see you so airly, sir. Wait till I show you what I got here."

He extracted from a tight pocket the soiled and greasy sheet of an old newspaper, opened it raggedly, and stabbed it with a forefinger.

"'Tis only be a miracle I found out," he explained. "Me wife's brother, Nedeen Lowry, a keeper down the country, sent us up a brace o' rabbits last night an' they was wrapped up in this. 'Tis the *Ard-na-Righ Observer*, sir. I looked it over careless to see how the country cawboons was behavin', an' the sight was quinched in me eyes when I saw this iotem. Read it for yourself, sir. There it is. I don't sca'sly believe it."

He shoved the ragged sheet under my nose and again stabbed at one paragraph. The startling item was there in all its journalistic baldness, with a blotch of grease across one corner:

> Yesterday at Ard-na-Righ, before District Justice Kerins, Thomas James O'Doran, jobbing gardener, of no fixed residence, was charged with a dangerous assault on Bernard Doony, a travelling showman from Limerick. Doony was unable to appear, his injuries being such as to necessitate medical attention in the local infirmary, and the District Justice remanded the accused in custody until the next District Court at Ard-na-Righ.

I read it twice, pausing on the name and description of the accused. I was completely astonished, for the Thomasheen James O'Doran that I knew was no warrior, and here was a redoubtable one.

"Maybe 'tisn't our Thomasheen James after all," said Davy half hopefully. "But that's his name all right, Thomas James O'Doran; an' since he sucked up to you, sir, he calls himself a jobbin' gardener, with respects. An' another thing! If he has any fixed residence so has a bloody cuckoo."

"But a showman, Davy? You know the calibre of an Irish travelling showman?"

"The what, sir? All I know about a showman is that I could take the meanest o' the breed an' tie his elbow to his ankle, an' the same fella 'ud belt Thomasheen James into the middle o' next week."

"This showman couldn't," I said.

"Mind you," said Davy on a fresh slant, "Thomasheen James was rale handy with his mawleys when he was a nipper, but that was long ago. Still an' all, he might ha' got in the first wallop wit' a pavin'-stone or a pint-pot. Have you noticed the date on top o' that rag, sir?"

I had. The paper was more than a week old.

"The first thing I done whin I got me senses agin," said Davy, "was to run an' borrow a Ould Moore's Almanack from Tim Mulvey the fancier, an' be it I l'arned that the District Court is held in Ard-na-Righ twice a month, the first an' third Thursdays, at two aclock p.m."

"The first and—— Wait! This is the first Thursday in June, is it not?"

"As sure as you're born'd. Me wife, who has schoolin', the poor crathur, calc'lated be an almanack an' the date o' that paper that this here is the very idintical Thursday, whin Mr Thomas James O'Doran Esquire, whoever he is, gets it in the neck for stampin' the face o' plain Barney Doony. That's why I'm here this mornin', sir."

"What are you suggesting, Mr Hand?" I enquired coldly.

"Nothin'! Nothin' at all, sir!" The flat of his hand urgently denied all ulterior motive. "Dam' the thing! Thomasheen James, if that's him, will be gettin' his sixty days in Mountjoy jail without the option, an' me, or you naither, can do nothin' about it."

"Then why are you here?"

Davy tilted his bowler hat over his nose and scratched under it.

"'Tis a sort o' fire insurance I'm takin' out," he said, with an ingratiating grin. "'Begobs!' says I to meself, 'if the boss don't know about this, an' if by wan chance in a million Thomasheen James gets the option of a fine, who's to pay it? Not Thomasheen James. An' if 'tisn't paid,' says I, 'I'm straight for hell betune the

pair o' them for keepin' me trap shut.' So up I come.
You don't know this District Justice Kerins be any
chance, sir?"

"No. And I'm not paying any fine either, after
corrupting justice."

"The Lord be good to us! I never said nothin' o' the
sort," protested Davy. "Not another word, sir! Me
duty is done an' I'm off. God bless the work!"

He turned hastily, and actually squattered out of the
garden. Usually his visits lasted a couple of hours and
were terminated with beer, but now, having cunningly
placed any responsibility there was on to my shoulders
he had played Pilate with the utmost despatch.

I stood looking down at the greasy tattered sheet and
wondered if the goddess Chance did not really use an
intricate method in her work. A ragged fragment of
a country newspaper, a careless habit of Davy Hand's,
and the goddess was whispering in my ear: "What
are you going to do about it?"

"Damn the thing!" I said, and armed myself with
a hoe.

Thomasheen James was or was not in custody.
Thomas James O'Doran was, and he would get a jail
sentence without the option of a fine, or he would get
the option of a fine and, if unable to pay it, undergo
the same jail sentence. It was jail either way, so why
worry?

The soft first warmth of summer had brought on my
seedlings nicely and the weeds profusely; golden-ball
turnip needed thinning; a row of peas needed staking;
the time was ripe for a sowing of scarlet-runners—
heaps of work that I liked infinitely better than
scribbling. But I disliked my garden that morning.
I was only a drudge driven by the seasonal spawn.

I was only blindly following my customary rut. I had not even the will to pitch the whole thing to glory and go fishing. To the devil with Thomasheen James anyway! And as for Davy Hand, that little slum schemer——!

Finally I went into the house and put the whole thing to my wife, knowing exactly what she would insist on, even knowing that she would volunteer to let me have her car for the afternoon. . . .

II

I drove across the market square of Ard-na-Righ a few minutes after two that afternoon and parked my wife's car before the columned court-house in the centre. A tall Civic Guard, holding the door for Justice, looked at me with an observant eye, and let me through without remark. I slipped unobtrusively into a far-back bench behind the broad shoulders of a yawning citizen. The business of the Court had already begun, but I was in plenty of time for the case that interested me.

The new District Courts of Ireland have lost most of the unique drama and character of the notorious old Petty Session Courts of the British period, when every man was agin the Government and swore accordingly. With freedom has come responsibility and same, unhumorous justice. An Irish Court is no longer the best show in town. Consequently not more than two-score mildly interested citizens were scattered down the sloping forms of the spacious room.

The District Justice, on his Bench, a youngish man, with a smooth, strong, ironic face below his black Dogean head-dress, lazed forward in his chair, his

112

arms at ease on the desk before him; his registrar sat below him busily writing; half a dozen members of the legal profession and two or three Guard officers lolled on leather-covered chairs at each side of the broad low witness-stand directly facing the Bench; and a row of litigants and witnesses occupied the front seat outside the Bar. Craning my neck, I could see one bandaged head in that front row.

The proceedings were ordinary and uninteresting. Ard-na-Righ was a peaceful small town. Some applications for dance-hall licences, a few small infringements of the Liquor Acts, a case or two of trespass, and the way was clear for the criminal offences. After a race-meeting, a cattle-fair, and two markets, there was only one case of near-mayhem. That was the State *versus* Thomas James O'Doran.

As the Court Crier called out that name I sank well down in my seat and fixed my eyes on the railed edge of the Dock to the left of the Bench. In the silence I heard the clack of shod feet on the stairs leading up from the prisoners' room; and in that very moment I resolved finally that if the prisoner was my Thomasheen James (which was unlikely), and if he got the option of a fine (which was more unlikely), and if that fine did not exceed twenty shillings (and it probably would), I would pay it; but that if it exceeded a pound by as much as a shilling Thomasheen James must serve his just period in Mountjoy jail. And that was that.

Then the accused's head appeared above the railings of the Dock, and there was doubt no longer. There was no mistaking that close-clipped, sandy-haired dome. It belonged only to Thomasheen James, and there was not a mark on it.

The prisoner was followed into the Dock by two uniformed Guards, and their height and width made him leaner-necked and wirier than ever. The white of his skull showed through his close-cropped hair, his red ears stood out, the freckles had faded on the ridge of his sharp nose, and his china-blue eyes were as calm and as cold as the sea. He was not a furtive scoundrel. Nor was he licking his chops. He was just a plain and unfortunate man. He faced the Bench, gave the Justice a half-military salute, turned slowly and surveyed the court-room. Those cold eyes flitted past my secluded seat, and I was certain that they never rested on me. Indeed, during all of the subsequent proceedings, his eyes never once came in my direction.

A Superintendent of the Guards in a neatly-tailored smoky-blue uniform rose lazily by the side of the witness-table.

"I prosecute for the State, your Honour."

The Justice nodded and looked at Thomasheen James.

"Is the defendant represented?" he asked impersonally.

"No, sir, your Honour," spoke up the high hard tenor of Thomasheen James. "I'll conduct me own offence."

"There's a proverb about that," murmured the Justice, and looked at the Superintendent.

That prosecutor was dispassionate, brief, and, I thought, more than fair to the defendant.

"A case of undue assault, your Honour," he said, his mouth in a slight quirk, "and unprovoked as far as I can learn, which is rather surprising. Briefly, the accused, Thomas James O'Doran, assaulted—and

114

battered—Bernard Doony, present to-day in Court, within and upon the licensed premises known as *The Short Grass Bar* in this town. As the State witnesses will place the case fully before your Honour, I shall not waste the time of the Court with further details. My first witness will be Patrick Kelleher, the proprietor of *The Short Grass Bar* in question. Mr Kelleher!"

Patrick Kelleher, a tall, semi-bald, dignified man in a black morning-coat, rose from the front bench, mounted the witness-stand, was sworn, and took his seat on the windsor-chair facing the Bench. Evidently he was a much respected man in the community, for the Justice nodded and smiled, and the Superintendent's tone was almost deferential.

"You were witness to this assault, Mr Kelleher?"

"It came under my observation, sir."

"Please tell his Honour what you observed," requested the Superintendent, and sat down.

Mr Kelleher turned slowly to the Justice, and every movement betokened an innate dignity; his voice was cultured and of a resonant timbre; and his words might have been chosen from Lord Macaulay's Essays.

"The accused, your Honour, known to me for some years as Thomasheen James, was a customer on my licensed premises on the afternoon in question (here he gave the date and exact time). He was sitting on a stool in the partitioned alcove at the extremity of the bar furthest from the front entrance. To an eye of some experience he showed no signs of inebriation. I had served him with a pint of plain porter. The only other customer at the time was Michael Guilfoyle, builder's labourer, of Pound Lane. For him I was drawing a medium of half-and-half at the other extremity of the bar when Bernard Doony, subsequently injured but then intact, came in by the front entrance. He proceeded upwards, without the customary salutation, towards the alcove, and there I heard his voice lifted in address to the accused."

I was keeping an eye turned on Thomasheen James while my ear enjoyed that rich voice, and at this juncture the blood flamed to his brow, and if he were capable of embarrassment I would say that he was suffering that feeling acutely.

"Intent on my own business," went on the dignified publican, "I did not catch the actual words employed by Bernard Doony, but the tone of delivery was certainly amicable or even jocose. I was consequently astonished when a sudden commotion ensued. I turned hastily and proceeded in the direction of the commotion, and in the alcove I discovered Thomasheen James, the defendant, severely punishing Bernard Doony. The weapons employed were his fists, a pewter pint-pot, and a three-legged stool. Michael Guilfoyle aided me in separating the combatants and in keeping a restraining hold on the defendant. Bernard Doony was in a semi-comatose condition and wedged in a corner of the alcove. In the circumstances I thought it necessary to call in the Guards, who forthwith removed the parties to the assault. The fracas, your Honour, was extremely sudden, and quite inexplicable in view of the usual peaceful nature of the accused, with whom I am pleasantly acquainted for some years. That is my evidence, your Honour."

"And very clear too, Mr Kelleher," complimented the Justice. "You are certain that you did not hear any of the words employed by Doony in addressing the accused?"

"Only that blatant tone assumed by members of his class in playful mood, your Honour."

"Did the accused say anything in reply before launching his assault?"

"His reply was the assault, your Honour, and it was entirely wordless," said Mr Kelleher with suspicious smoothness.

"Did the accused say anything after the assault?" queried the Superintendent on his feet.

"Just the usual meaningless ebullience customary to the occasion."

"Could you give us a sample, Mr Kelleher?"

"It consisted entirely of expostulation with Michael Guilfoyle and myself for interceding before the removal of Doony's internal organs."

The Superintendent sat down overwhelmed, and the Justice looked at Thomasheen James.

"Any questions, O'Doran?"

"No, your Honour. Patsy Kelleher has related to you how I am a peaceful man—an' all Ireland knows the sort Barney Doony is."

Mr Kelleher stood down, and Michael Guilfoyle, builder's labourer, of Pound Lane, took his place. His evidence was in less elegant language, but more pointed and picturesque.

"I was watchin' Patsy Kelleher, so he would not put too much head on a medium he was pullin' for me, your Honour, whin Barney Doony come in. He went up be the bar after wan look at me out of the corner of his eye, for he reco'nised that I was no mark for a pint. I heard him salutin' Thomasheen James up above in the alcove, but I wasn't payin' no attention, only I said to meself——"

"Never mind what you said to yourself!" the

117

Superintendent interposed. "You saw the assault committed?"

"Some of it. It broke out so sudden that I missed the best o' it, the partition interruptin' me view. Whin I got there Thomasheen James was combin' Barney's hair, the pewter in wan hand an' the stool in the other, an' after a while—whin I saw that maybe we'd have to be spoonin' Barney's brains back out o' the sawdust, your Honour—I helped Patsy to haul Thomasheen James off of him."

"You are certain that you did not hear what Doony said before the assault?" The Justice was interested in this.

"Not a word, your Honour, barrin' somethin' about a drink. Maybe he was suckin' up to Thomasheen James——"

"You heard the threatening language after——"

"There was no threatenin' language at all, your Honour. Divil the word! Only I was houldin' Thomasheen James be the two arms, and says he to me, 'Le' go o' me, Mick Guilfoyle! Le' go o' me, an' God love you,' says he, 'an' I'll spread his livers an' lights on the flure for you.' Sure it was only be way of talk."

"Your Honour will decide if any threat was implied," said the Superintendent, and directed the witness's attention to the accused.

Thomasheen James asked only one question:

"Mick, will you tell his Honour why you wouldn't stand Barney Doony a drink?"

"I stood him plinty in me time——"

The Justice tapped sharply on his desk, and Guilfoyle saluted with deference. "Barney is only a scrounger for drink, your Honour," he said, and Thomasheen James had got his point.

Two members of the Civic Guard then gave formal evidence. The next important witness was the young house physician of the local hospital. He gave his testimony smartly and with some inner satisfaction.

"On the evening in question Doony was brought to the accident ward by the Guards. He was not unconscious when admitted, but was in a dazed condition, and was under the impression that a roof had fallen on him. It might have, your Honour. Both eyes were swollen and beginning already to colour; his nose was flattened—absolutely; there was a scalp wound that necessitated seven stitches, and three of his ribs were floating loose. He complained that one knee was broke in four places, but it was only out of joint; and he insisted that his kidney—he claimed one only—had got shifted to the region of the spleen; but after a week's observation I am satisfied that his injuries are entirely superficial—but well-intended."

That young doctor, I gathered, did not care for Doony. Thomasheen James did not cross-examine him, but a gleam of satisfaction lit his face as the injuries of his victim were detailed. I myself was astounded and had a faint feeling of apprehension. Had I been nurturing and not infrequently goading a slithy tiger that at any moment might turn and rend me with his venomous fangs?

Doony, the victim, was then called to the stand; but his evidence did little or nothing to explain the sudden violence of the attack. As he moved with an exaggerated limp to the witness-stand, I saw a bullet head below a bandage, a short massive neck, and the firm shoulders that bespoke the old soldier; and I understood less than ever how such a warrior had been so disastrously vanquished by one whom Thomasheen James himself would describe as a "skinamilink."

When Doony turned to take his seat on the windsor-chair I saw his face, and I knew that he was one of that ignoble and humourless clan that have fallen far and live unashamed on the tattered fringes of society. Thomasheen James could never fall as far as that— or could he not, given time? I also saw that a sound job of work had been done. One eye was still closed and the other was a fine blue-black; a long strip of plaster crossed the flattened ridge of his nose, and another strip showed under the bandage on his fore-head; and as he eased himself into the chair he placed a broad paw over his ribs and grimaced painfully. Seated, he gave one glance at Thomasheen James, and I saw his thick shoulders lift and twitch. He gave his evidence with a dishonest straightforwardness.

"Your Honour," said he in a hoarse strong voice, "I went into *The Short Grass Bar* in the heel o' the after-noon for me first drink that day—or many a day— an' I interfered with no man. I went up to the cubby, an' there I seen Thomasheen James sittin' on a stool over a solitary pint all be himself. I was glad to see him, your Honour. We was ould acquaintance, we bein' at school together, an' I hadn't set eyes on him for a donkey's years. An' when I seen him in Kelleher's pub that evenin' me heart ruzz, an' all I done was to clap him friendly on the shoulder. 'Thomasheen James, me ould —— bucko!' says I, 'is it yourself is in it? Put it there! an' drink that down. You'll take another pint with me—or a quart,' says I— 'for the sake of ould times.' Them's me very words, your Honour. And there an' then, your Honour, he turned round an' off the stool, an' stepped back from me, an' without a word out of him let go wan welt of a sidewinder at me, an' his fist, your Honour, hopped fair off the bridge o' me nose—an' I heard the bone go. An' on top o' that, with the sparks blindin' me an' me guard down, he clouted the pewter pot on me lid, an' I thought me last hour had come. Ne'er another thing do I remimber, your Honour, until I was stretched on a table above in the infirmary an' Doctor Doyle sayin' over me: 'This spoils the poor b——'s chance for ever in a beauty show.' At death's-door I was for a whole week, your Honour, an', whatever the doctor says, I have a weakenin' dead sort o' pain in me insides. Here, your Honour! In there! That's the truth, your Honour, no more an' no less."

The Superintendent put him no questions, but the Justice, holding him with a cold unbelieving eye, put him one.

"Are you sure that you said nothing else to the accused?"

"Dam' the word, your Honour! Jest greeted him like ould times an' offered to stand him a drink."

"He's a bloody liar, your Honour," said Thomasheen James promptly, glaring down at Doony, who kept his eyes straight forward.

"Careful, O'Doran!" warned the Justice. "Any questions?"

"I wouldn't perjure his sowl worse than it is a'ready, your Honour," said Thomasheen James quickly; and I thought he was foolishly losing the chance of a ripping cross-examination.

Doony limped back to his seat, and the Superintendent, half-rising and sitting down again, said:

"The case for the State rests, your Honour."

The Justice sat back in his chair, eased his Dogean head-dress, and looked dubiously at Thomasheen James.

"The defendant has our attention," he said laconically.

Thomasheen James placed his hands on the rail and looked across and up at the Justice.

"Your Honour," he said, "I haven't no witnesses. But what am I sayin'? Wasn't most o' the evidence on me own side? Sure, me charackter is well known, an' Barney Doony hasn't as much as would light his pipe for him—if he had anything in it——"

"Will you take the witness-stand?" the Justice put to him.

"I will not, with respecks to your Honour. But I would like to make a small statement from where I stand, an', sure, 'tisn't the first time a Irish patri't made a speech from the Dock."

"And was hanged thereafter," murmured the Justice.

"Thim was the days, your Honour, before strick justice was dissipated in this misfortunate island. Before I begin I would ax the Sup'rintendint to certify that me repitation as a breaker o' the peace is noted be its absence?"

"There is no record," said the Superintendent after a pause, "that the accused has been before prosecuted for breaking the peace."

He was more than fair. I knew, and he knew, and probably the Justice knew, that Thomasheen James had once spent ten days in jail for daylight poaching.

Thomasheen James placed his forearms on the rail and leant to the Bench confidentially. The crisis had come, and, despite the damning evidence against him and his refusal to take the stand, I had confidence in him still. He had victimised me so often from untenable positions that I could not see him lose now with his liberty at stake.

"Listen to me, your Honour, an' I will not keep you long from your tay—or whatever it is. I was down the country a bit recoverin' a small debt was owin' to me, an' I was hurryin' me way back to Dublin where I have a steady job as a gardener to a gintleman in the lit'ry line these last coupla years; an' passin' by I took a quick turn into Patsy Kelleher's to restore me energy for the last lap o' the road be a pint o' plain. I was sittin' peaceable, takin' a sup out o' the pot an' plannin' the week's work ahead, when all at wanst I got a prod in the small o' me back, an' a voice bust the drum o' me ear. 'Is that yourself, you ould so-an'-so, suckin' a lone pint in a corner? Come on! Order another for me or I'll shove the pot down your windpipe.' It was Barney Doony, your Honour, an' no fri'nd o' mine, young or old, though I know him these twenty years. 'Come on, me ould so-an'-so!' says he—an opprob'ious name, your Honour —an' all I done was to give him a small push in the face, an' he staggered back till his head hit the edge o' the partition."

"A small push!" wondered the Justice, glancing at Doony of the ruined features aslouch in his seat. "Go on, O'Doran."

"That's all, your Honour. The pewter was in me hand unbeknownst, an' the damage was done be the time I got a rehould o' meself."

I sat up. Thomasheen James was letting me down. Having brought off an almost impossible feat of derring-do he was now failing to justify it, his only hope. On a promising foundation he had set the anticlimax of a feeble lie. He had made no shadow of a case. There would not even be the option of a fine.

The Justice leant forward over his desk and tried to help him.

"Tell me this, O'Doran. Was it the demand for a drink that led to this—complicated push in the face?"

"No, sir, your Honour. I wouldn't mind the drink——"

"Then it was the opprobrious name he called you?"

"It was, sir. I couldn't stand it no longer."

The Justice nodded. "Yes, I can understand Doony using a name that might cause mayhem." The Justice sat up and glanced round the court-room, and I knew that he was making sure that no ladies were present before putting a leading question, the horrible answer to which might win leniency for Thomasheen James.

But Thomasheen James forestalled that question. Once again the flush came up to his sandy-red hair, and there was embarrassment and urgency in his voice.

"Don't ask me, your Honour! I wouldn't soil your Honour's ears. I couldn't say it, your Honour."

The Justice looked surprised, and then shrugged his shoulders.

"Very well, O'Doran! My imagination—even my experience of language—fails me. Is that all?"

"Me last word, your Honour, if I was to hang for it."

"Not quite," said the Justice. He leant back in his chair and rubbed his hand on the back of his head below his Dogean head-dress. He was sorry for Thomasheen James, but justice had to be administered. He was brief and to the point. He sat up.

"The evidence in this case is too conclusive for leniency. Accepting the accused's statement, this Court cannot condone grievous bodily injury in reply to an unidentified opprobrious name thrown out half-jocosely in an Irish public-house." He tapped his desk sharply. "I am determined, in this Court, to put an end to brawls of this nature on respectable licensed premises like Mr Kelleher's—where I partake of an occasional refreshment myself. While I regret that I have not Doony before me for gross language, I sentence you, O'Doran, to six weeks in jail with hard labour. The case is concluded."

And that was that. Thomasheen James was shocked into silence, but not for long. He lifted up his voice in desperate appeal.

"Holy God, your Honour! Wouldn't you give me the option this wance?"

"If I conscientiously could."

"But me first offence, your Honour—o' this nature —an' sure the world knows that the father an' mother of a batin' was comin' to Barney Doony. An' listen, your Honour! I'll lose me fine gardener's job with a dacent gintleman."

"That is a plea that appeals to me." The Justice hesitated. "If I thought you had steady employment——"

"I can prove it, your Honour."

I started in my seat. Had Thomasheen James seen me, and was I to be called on to lie valiantly on his behalf? But no! The Justice decided for himself promptly.

"Very well, O'Doran. I'll accept your plea, but the fine will be big enough to restrain what my friend Mr Kelleher would call your future ebullience. I give you the option of a three pounds fine, to be paid into Court."

It was a staggering fine for Thomasheen James, and I saw his Adam's apple jerk up and down as he swallowed.

"Gi'e me time to pay, your Honour, an' God love you!"

"Paid into Court, I said. What time do you want?"

"Three hours," said Thomasheen James with astonishing promptitude. "Only three hours to gather me little resources."

"Oh, certainly!" The Justice was surprised at the moderation of the demand. "I give you till six o'clock this evening."

I was left wondering as to the nature of Thomasheen James's little resources.

III

The door of the Dock opened, and Thomasheen James, stepping down into the body of the Court, came up the aisle towards the entrance. He passed the end of my seat, but he never looked my way. I was sure that his china-blue eyes had never rested on me. The Guard at the door let him through, and a second Guard slouched easily after.

The work of the blind goddess was over. People moved out laughing among themselves, but the Justice sat on, busy scribbling at his desk. I sat on too, hard-thinking. Three hours to gather his resources! If he had any I was prepared to eat my hat. Who then . . .?

Let me say at once that within two minutes I recognised the inevitable. If he had any resources I was them. I was not impelled at all by charity, or friendship, or any of the other admirable virtues. There was the thought of what my wife would say, a lesser thought of my garden, and there was curiosity. Anyhow, in about two minutes I sighed, rose to my feet and walked down the aisle to the clerk sitting below the Bench.

"I'm paying that fine," I said sourly.

"Whose—O'Doran's?" He lifted brows at me.

"Whose else?" I was in a temper. "A dam' shame to give him the option! There are three pounds."

The Justice looked down at me and grinned without majesty.

"I thought our friend had a little resource somewhere," he said. "I'd give a sovereign to know the opprobrious name that would soil the ears of a District Justice."

"You're on, Mr Kerins," I said. "I'll claim that sovereign by six o'clock."

I turned and moved away. Barney Doony, the victim, was still slumped in his seat, waiting, possibly, for his final gloat, possibly afraid to go out too close behind Thomasheen James. His half-shut steely eye was on me, and his lips moved silently; and I knew the imprecatory words his lips formed.

Thomasheen James was waiting for me at the foot of the court-house steps. A tall Guard lounged carelessly against a near-by column. Neither would know that I had paid the fine.

"You took your time in there," said Thomasheen James. "Who told you?"

"Davy Hand, darn him!"

"An' blast him as well!" added Thomasheen James. "'Twas he got me to go down the country to investigate a bull-tarrier bitch before he stole her."

"You're an ingrate," I told him.

"Whatever I am, me heart lifted in me when I seen you hidin' in a back seat."

"Ah, I see! And you hoped to gather your little resources off me in three hours—a pound per hour."

He did not even attempt to deny it.

"Couldn't you be deductin' it from me bit o' wages?"

"Wages?"

"Manalive! think o' the weeds neckin' the cauliflowers, an' the lawn fit to feed a cow a blazin' shame before the neighbours. Oh, very well! very well! The garden can go to hell an' all, and six weeks in quod won't kill me, maybe. Have a small piece of a heart anyway an' advance me half a dollar."

"You'll not need it where——"

"I know that dam' well, but I better get a good linin' inside o' me for a start. There's a good could snack to be got up the Main Street in Patsy Kelleher's bar."

"Not Kelleher. He'll throw you out, and me with you."

"Divil the fear as long as we got a bob to spind. He's a dacent ould blatherumskite, Patsy. An' you needn't let on you know a condimned prooletariat wance we're inside the door."

Mr Kelleher, dignified as ever in a white apron, received us quite affably, and expressed his polished regret that his evidence, given on oath, might be adduced inimical to Thomasheen James, whereas he was, in fact, gratified that Doony had at last received a much-needed castigation.

"Cripers!" said Thomasheen James in my ear.

"He'd be suggestin' a free pint if you wasn't here. I'll mind that."

We went up by the long zinc-covered counter guarding the tiered shelves of brilliantly labelled bottles to a partitioned alcove at the end of the bar opposite a side-door to a laneway.

"Behould the scene where I pasted Barney in his own blood," boasted Thomasheen James. He patted the partition with spread fingers. "There it is! You can feel the dint I made with his skull, an' will you look at the new leg on the stool? Mr Kelleher, sir, this is the gintleman I garden for in the metropolice, an' he is goin' an' about to reg'late me with a pint o' two ex, a plate o' cold beef, a bit o' lettuce, an' a biled spud if there is wan—or two."

We had all these—each of us. I had had only a hurried bite of lunch, and Mr Kelleher's fare was excellent as the man himself. We ate amicably together, and I made no protest when Thomasheen James requested "wan more skivver with the blood in it." I was treating him tactfully, hoping to get my curiosity satisfied, but I was not yet telling him that the fine had been paid.

"Six weeks were about the least you could get," I said for a strategic opening.

"I got them."

"Anyone paying your fine would be seeking to defeat justice after such an unprovoked assault."

"That's all you know."

"But a mere opprobrious name——!"

"'Twasn't the first straw broke the camel's back," said Thomasheen James cryptically.

"But I have called you opprobrious names?"

"And will agin. That's different. Psha!" He

shrugged his shoulders resignedly and surrendered un-
conditionally. "You'll have your own way with me,
as often before. I know fine what was at the back o'
your mind in fillin' me with cold mate, but thank you
all the same. I can see you cogitatin' the best way to
tear me little secret out o' me gizzard for the edifyca-
tion o' your public. I don't mind. Gi'e me another
pint to extrack a piece o' lettuce out o' me windpipe
and I'll be tellin' you what I never told no man.
It'll be time for me private apartment at public
expinse when I'm done, an' the divil mind me."

IV

When I was a young chisler of seven risin' eight
(began Thomasheen James) I was left a poor little
lonely orphan in the heart o' The Liberties, an' me
as happy as Larry sellin' papers up an' down the streets
o' Dublin. Ay, sir! happy as the day is long till some
interferin' society of ould women grabbed me be the
slack o' the pants an' rammed me into Barnaby's
Orphanage out the Bray road.

Mind you, I have no dam' word to say agin the
Sisters in Barnaby's. They treated me as if I was a
Christian, an' gev me the start of a useless eddication,
as well as the rudyments of a trade with a sweepin'-
brush an' a garden-rake. But me very first night up
in number ten dorm't'ry a thick block of a lad, older'n
I was be a year or more, faced up to me, an' says he:
"Hullo, me ould so-and-so! I'm cock o' the dunghill
in number ten, and this is to remind you of it." It
was an opprob'ious name that he called me, an' a
puck in the nose with it. His name—you're right!
his name was Barney Doony. It was our first encounter.

He was too mature for me, an' I was frightened of him, an', besides, wake with lonesomeness. He cowarded me before all them young bastards o' divil's brats, an', worse than all, the name he called me stuck —an' so did the fear he put into me. Ay! the name stuck for five years. No! I'm wrong. Four years. Barney was thrown out the fifth year, an' after that, if any young guttersnipe as much as opened his gob at me, I took him back o' the chapel an' welted the stuffin' out o' him. I did so. That was a prime year.

Whin I was let loose on the popylace agin I circulated back to me ould newspaper beat in Lower Abbey Street fornint the Abbey Theatre. But lo an' behould you! me very first evenin' I got a prod betune the shoulder-blades, and there wance more for the second time agin was Barney Doony, a grin under his nose where his front teeth wasn't.

"There you are, me ould so-and-so!" says he. "Hook it! or I'll cut the daylights out o' you. This is my beat."

The ould fright wakened the legs under me, an' though I had me aim fixed on the middle o' his nose me hands betrayed me. There wasn't a blow struck—not be me—an' I had to resort to an infayriour clienteley down be the Quays. But you know how a nickname sticks; an' the name he called me stuck to me all over Dublin an' in the Belvedere Newsboys Club, till Barney went on the tramp, an' after that I took the hide off of many a young whipper-snapper I had marked down for recantation. I was rale handy with me dukes be that time.

After that I grew up to me inches, an', after a bit of sanguinity with a peeler, I made me escape to the wilderness o' the country. I consorted with a tribe

o' tinkers for a while—the Shurridans o' Kildare—
an' l'arned about dogs an' horses; an' me eddication
complete, I took a job as kennel-man with a Captain
Terrie—but I told you all about that, an' the way I
left. For six months then I tried it out with the
farmers o' Tipperary, God help us, till I was only a
shadda o' me former self; an' then wan Saturday
evenin' in Clonmel I ups an' j'ined Daly's two-pole
circus as a roustabout.

Daly was a tough, rough man with a notion o'
echo-nomics that paid dividends. He would come
into a town an' set up the tent, provide his roustabouts
with the makin's of a blind drunk, pitch them out
without no pay, an' engage a new lot. I was wan o'
the new lot.

He didn't succeed in pitchin' me out. I was never
a hard drinker, an' Daly had to keep a few hands he
could trust. I stuck it out that season an' part o' the
next, an' Daly put me on the pay-roll reg'lar. The
stories I could tell you, but I won't. Meself an'
Foley the Clown got to be rale fri'ndly. He was a
great clown, an' me duty was to put him to bed drunk,
an' sober him up dacent for the show seven or eight
nights a week. Wance or twice in a emergency I
took a turn with him in the ring an' got a laugh all to
meself. Do you know? I had me mind made up to
follow the powder 'n paint the rest o' me days when
one night in Birr as I was beddin' down in me own
quarters at the back o' the monkey-cage—meself and
the monkeys used be talkin' together like Christians,
an' there was wan blue-nosed boboon had more sinse
than a archbishop—as I say, I was beddin' down
for the night, me back turned, when I got a root of
a kick in the tinderest place; an' round I come rarin',

me left on guard an' a tent-peg swingin' from me heel up.

"Hullo, me ould so-and-so!" says Barney Doony. Ay! who else? Not tall, but thick as a post, an' life had left its mark on him. Daly'd recruited him that very evenin' in the ordinar' way. Someway, the Injun sign came out on me then an' there; an' though I had me eyes fixed on the ridge o' his nose the tent-peg misbehaved itself an' fell out o' me hand. The blue-nosed boboon was hoppin' up an' hoppin' down, hootin' an' expostulatin' me to belt Barney one on the snout—sure as hell! I heard him plain—but before I could gather me courage to the explodin' p'int Barney gave me an' aisy short jolt in the split o' the breast-bone an' I sat down hard, me wind an' me courage evaporatin' like a busted tyre. An' there I was agin under his thumb.

Me only hope was that he wouldn't last long—same as others like him—and I held on. But so did he, for you couldn't make him drunk; an' worse than all, the name he called me got known, an' was customary applied on every dam' occasion. In the end, Foley the Clown took to usin' it in the ring itself to make the country bogtrotters laugh. That was more than I could stand, so I up sail in the black of a wet night, an' left a week's pay behind me an' my curse on Barney Doony.

The Big War was on at the time, an' for a whole year I reproved the timptation I had to go out an' fight gallant for the dividends o' the capitalist class; but wan day in a unguarded condition I j'ined up with the Dublin Fusiliers, me martial nature floatin' high on noggin o' rum—an' I repinted next mornin' too late, as is prevailingly the case.

Listen! whin I stood to attention that mornin' in Beggar's Bush Barracks for squad drill, me heart melted dead away whin I set me eyes on the drill-sargint—no, a corporal he was at that time. Barney Doony! It was himself, with a jowl on him. His eye was on me a'ready.

"Hullo, me ould so-and-so!" says he, grinnin'. "Are you for l'arnin' to be a swaddy? You're in the right shop for it, an' 'tis meself will l'arn you, soon an' dam' soon."

He had me in the hollow of his hand, an' squeezed his fist on me, so that every bone in me carcase was wrinched in its socket be the time he let loose o' me, an' that was not till we was ordered to France. An' the same ould name he called me was a preva'lin' method o' address in all D Company.

We got our share o' the front trinches, I guarantee, and went over the top twice, an' I mind wance in a bit of a dog-fight at Messines I had an itch in me trigger finger to absquatulate Barney from the rear, an' him leppin' in front o' us bould as a line, the Jerries runnin' away at the time. But I put the timptation behind me, an' anyway, the captain was lookin' my direction, an' before it got another chance to waylay me, me turn came for ten days' furlough in Blighty.

Back to Dublin I came, tin helmet, rifle an' all, but the rifle didn't last long, for a coupla Sinn Feiners persuaded me agin me will to loan it to them permanent for two quid the second night. I mind the last night leanin' agin the bar below in Murray's at the Metal Bridge, standin' alternit pints to a Navy stoker, an' bemoanin' me hard luck; an' says he:

"W'y the bloody 'ell, Mick! Wot ya grousin' abaht?

J'ine the Navy, an' 'ave a clean shirt to yer bloomin' back every Satahday night!"

"An' be shot for a bloomin' deserter out o' hand?" I says.

"A bloomin' needle in a bundle o' 'ay," says he, temptin' me.

An' I did it. I j'ined the Navy. We borried a suit o' civvies out o' the Iveagh Lodgin' House from a man not wearin' 'em at the time, bein' sound asleep in his cubby, an' next mornin' I j'ined the Navy down in Amiens Street under the name of Doyle, all questions answered prompt. An' in a matter o' two days I was safe an' snug in H.M.S. Pembroke. Take care, the Pembroke is not a man-o'-war. 'Tis the name they give to the naval barracks at Chatham outside o' London.

That was the life for me. Me luck had turned at last—or I thought it had. A gran' fri'ndly shop, the ould Pembroke. Every second Saturday afternoon, an' the sheet clane agin you, your pay an' your pass in your pocket, your hair slicked, an' your ribbons ironed, off you betook yourself to London for the week-end; an' after two pleasant nights in the Union Jack Club near Waterloo, back you come on Monday mornin' to another fortnight o' light duty among fri'ndly sailor men, with a hammock all to yourself an' four good meals a day. I'm tellin' you.

That heav'nly time lasted for most o' two months, an' then me fate overtook me. Wan Saturday night I was imbibin' a quiet drink in *The Red Line* down the Strand with a coupla marines whin a hand was clapped on me shoulder. Right agin! In all o' London an' in wan pub out o' ten million there was Barney

Doony runnin' up agin me. Barney Doony on furlough from the Front with the bars of a sargint on his sleeve!

"Hullo, me ould so-and-so!" says he, like a cat purrin' over a naked mouse. "So this is where you hid yourself?"

"Hexcuse me, swaddy," says I, after swallowin' me palate an' coughin' it up agin, puttin' on an Inglified accent. "Your hidentity is mistook."

"Like hell it is, you ould so-and-so," says he, his eyes takin' in me ratin' badge an' the name round me cap. "Open up, me bucko, or I'll——"

"Doyle, laddie," says one o' the marines—Doyle was me cognomin on the ship's muster—"Doyle, laddie, is this pie-faced mud-digger for cockin' his bonnet at you? Lat's tak' him ootside an' see what mak's his gadgets circulate."

Twa hefty lads frae the Broomielaw o' Glasgow, an' good with hand an' foot. Barney stepped away quick with a gratifin' grin on his clock.

"My mistake, gintlemen," says he. "I took Stoker Doyle o' the Pembroke for an ould friend." An' he dodged away among the crowd after wan knowin' look at me.

I knew, as sure as this pint is empty—thank you!— I knew that me bad luck was home agin. There was a weight on me all that followin' week an' most o' the next. But nothin' happened, an' my mind aised on me, thinkin', maybe, that Barney, back at the Front, had interposed himself with a six-inch shell inclusive. But Saturday noon, an' me shinin' me shoes, a whistle in me teeth an' a pass in me pocket, the Master at Arms came stormin' down the Armoury.

"Doyle! Stoker Doyle to the front!"

Me heart stopped. I knew. Dam' well I knew! He had two armed marines with him.

"You are under arrest," says he. "The Commodore will interview you in the wardroom."

Yes, sir! I was court-martialled then an' there, standin' to attintion, the two marines on aither hand, baynets at shoulder, an' the Commodore sittin' across the table, his officers about him. There was no sign o' Barney Doony, him havin' spiked me guns from a distance.

"Stoker James Doyle?" says the Commodore, his face an' voice smooth as milk.

"That's me name, Commodore, your Honour," says I, brazen.

The Commodore laid a hand on a paper before him.

"It is here alluded to," says he, "that you are in fact Private Thomas James O'Doran——"

"What's that, sir?" says I.

"O'Doran, dem' you!" He wasn't angry at all. "A deserter from D Company of the Tenth Dublin Fusiliers."

"Who, me, sir?" What else could I say?

"Quite right, me lad!" says he, agreeable as you like. "That is your proper attitude if you are not guilty. Stick to it. But," says he, "if you are guilty and you impel me to bring two of your company from France to identify you, listen!" says he, "better for you that a millstone was shoved down your neck an' you sunk into the bottom o' the sea. Now, let us start again. Are you or are you not a deserter from the Dublins?"

"I amn't no deserter, your Honour," says I. "'Tis how I lost me mimory."

"That's better," says he, grinnin'. "Any explanation you care to make will be welcome."

A gran', easy-goin' man Commodore Sampson, the fill of a door, with a face on him like the settin' sun. It was boasted of him that he drank the messroom under the table six nights a week an' twice on Sundays. He had mercy in the roots o' his heart, and I knew that. So I collected me brains inside me head for the credit of ould Ireland an' spread 'em agin the Saxon foe.

"When I was a young chisler, your Honour," I begins, "I had always a taste for the say—the sea, your Honour."

"And a sound judge too," says he, pleasant.

"An' when the war broke out, your Honour," I goes on, "me determination was to j'ine the Navy, only I got circumvinted be a recruitin' sargint in Mooney's Bar, an' when I woke up I was in Beggar's Bush Barracks, number 7651 R.D.F. 10th Battalion. There was nothin' I could do, your Honour, but the fancy for the Navy never left the back o' me mind. Out at the Front I got a bit of a shell-shock at Messines, an' me captain sint me home on ten days' furlough to restore me mimory—back to Dublin, your Honour, rifle an' pack an' all. An' there, your Honour, I got inveig'led be two Sinn Feiners in fri'ndly disguise with a bottle o' Red Biddy, an' next mornin' I found meself inclosed in a suit o' civvies—an' me rifle was gone, an' me identity badge as well. An', your Honour, the Red Biddy buzzin' in me head, I couldn't as much as remimber me own name—barrin' a hazy sort o' notion I had that I was in the fightin' forces wan time or another. An' it was then, your Honour, that me youthful proclivity came to the fore, an'

138

fearin' that I might get the name of a deserter an' a cowardly man, I decided that the best thing to do was to up an' j'ine the Navy. I did it, your Honour, that very day, an' when me mimory came back here I was in the Pembroke where I belonged. What would you do yourself, your Honour, in a case like that?"

"That's a leadin' question," says the Commodore, laughin', an' he turned to his officers. "Gintlemen," says he, "truth or her half-sister out o' the bottom of a well"—whatever he meant—"that's as cast-iron a statement as we ever invinted in the middle deck."

They talked back an' fore betune themselves, an' I could see that though they didn't believe wan word I said they was impressed be the quality of me mind. An' after a time the Commodore promagated his sintince.

"Your offence," says he, "technally amounts to desertion, but not in the face o' the enemy, lucky for you. Considerin' the nature of your explanation, an' in view o' the fact that you j'ined the Senior Service without delay, we will give you the binifit of all our doubts and not return you to your regiment. Misfortunately for yourself you will lose your pension rights in the Army, an', furthermore, you will be confined to quarters for a month, an' thereafter disposed of on a sea-goin' ship. Dismiss!"

I got off light, but there was murdher in me heart, an' I swore be me ten crossed fingers that if ever agin I met Barney Doony this side o' hell—or in hell itself —I would break an' pulverise his nose into a million halves.

There's me past history for you now, as far as Barney Doony goes. I never sat eyes on him agin till ten days ago in this cubby, where I was takin' a sup out of a pint same as I am now. A prod in the back I got that cracked a tooth on the rim o' the pewter, an' says he in me ear:

"Hullo, you ould so-and-so! Suckin' a pint in a corner!"

An' when I saw who it was, his face like a rotten swade turnip with drink an' depravity, all me past life rose up before me, an' all me misfortunes, an' the shame o' the name that he stuck on me like a stickin'-plaster. But, let me tell you this, me dear sir, it was the thought o' you waitin' for me in your garden that gave me timper its edge like a razor. It was so. For the ould fear was beginnin' to reduce me when the thought came to me mind that Barney Doony would stick to me—an' he would—till we got to Dublin, an' that you might see him an' hear him, an' if you wance reco'nised the wreckage o' company I was keepin' you'd up an' drown me in the Liffey—for all the times you threatened to do it an' didn't. That gave me the courage of a ravin' line.

"This is where we cross the river o' sticks, Thomas James O'Doran," says I to meself, grindin' me teeth.

"Mine'll be a quart," says Barney, an' they was near his last words.

I never opened me mouth to him. No, sir! I set me aim for his nose, stepped back for distance, an' brought me fist circlin' up from the floor. It lepped like a sledge-hammer off the ridge o' his nose, an' the force I put in it wheeled me round like a top, an' as I come round I pivoted him under the ear. That's the time his head bumped the partition there. He ducked his head down then, an' I gave him the rabbit punch with the pot, an' straightened him agin with a knee in the ribs. He staggered blind agin the stool, an' I caught it as it fell an' set to to combin' his hair in that corner. An' after that I started to paste him in rale airnest. Do you know, if Patsy Kelleher an' Mick Guilfoyle hadn't incommodated me I'd ha' done the poor divil a injury. That's me whole story for you now. The rest of it is the property o' the public accordin' to evidence.

V

Thomasheen James finished abruptly and turned a shoulder to me. I said:

"You should have told that story to the District Justice, you blame fool."

"That's right! Call me out of me name. Would you be likin' me to expose me wounds to the public? Not never."

"By the way," said I, assuming indifference, "as regards this opprobrious name——?"

"I knew too dam' well you'd come to it," cried Thomasheen James desperately. He hopped off the stool, and again the blood came up to his brow. He swallowed twice. "I can't—I can't put me tongue to it. Don't ask me—I can't, I tell you."

He swung on his heel and was out the side-door before I could say a word. His pint-pot was not more than half-empty, and that, more than anything else, brought home to me the enormity of the opprobrious name inflicted on him by Barney Doony.

I sat on, musing on the malicious two-edged way Chance had of restoring the balance of Justice, and on my folly in stepping in and dulling the edge for one of her victims. I used think Thomasheen James a basically freer man than I was, for he carried freedom under his hat and was outside all castes without being in any sense debased or untouchable. And here he was with an Achilles heel, and his inner security could be shattered with a phrase. There is no such thing as Freedom.

I had heard no one enter by the side-door, but I was unpleasantly roused from my musings by a low rasp of a voice behind me.

"The fine gintleman that robbed a man be playin' god'llmighty!"

Bernard Doony was standing within the mouth of the alcove. His half-shut bloodshot eye estimated me malevolently, and there was a sneer about his bruised lips. Out of the side of his mouth came a hoarse, low-voiced, turgid stream of language. The publican serving a customer at the far end of the long bar could not hear. I know some language, thanks to Thomasheen James and Davy Hand, but he used four words of Dublin vituperation that I had never heard before.

Sitting round on my stool, I did not move or speak. I just watched the slightly-moving twisted mouth. I knew the breed, and I knew the one and only way to treat this sample of it: smite him summarily on the crown with the pint-pot and heave him out in the gutter. I didn't. The thought in my smug middle-class mind was that one could not touch pitch without being defiled, that, outside my own class, I had to fall back on the blatant thing called dignity.

And then another figure appeared round the corner of the partition.

"Me dear friend, Barney Doony! Take a look at

me, Barney." That was Thomasheen James using his most coaxing voice.

Doony whirled, one shoulder already hunched protectingly.

"Jasus!" he cried. "The divil'll kill me dead this time."

"Go on, Barney!" Thomasheen James coaxed him. "Keep on insultin' a dacent gallant man. Go on, I tell you! Open your pig's mouth now and say a few more ch'ice words."

"I was sayin' nothin' at all," cried Doony, his voice lifting queerly.

"All right so! Suppose you say two words to me? Just two words, Barney! Come on! Say them!"

"I'm sayin' nothin'."

"You are not. An' you will not—not never again. For after you'll be lickin' this gintleman's boots I'll rip your tongue out be the roots, you misbegotten poltroonious remnit o' humanity."

With what seemed one smooth motion Thomasheen James's coat was off, his shirt-sleeves up, and his wiry freckled forearms weaving patterns.

Doony proved himself a coward, and cowed for evermore.

"Le' me out o' this!" he screeched, ducked his head under folding arms and made a rabbit-like bolt under Thomasheen James's flying fists.

One of those doughty fists made a mighty swoop over the ducked head, and Thomasheen James's legs tangled on themselves jointlessly.

And there Patrick Kelleher showed what a sterling cool quick man he was. He had vaulted the counter with astonishing grace and ease, and now he had the side-door open for Doony; and as Doony bounded through he was timed perfectly by a pithy sixty-yard punt that turned him clean over in the air. He came down on his back, rolled, scrambled on all-fours, yelled and fled yelling, never looking behind.

The cool publican shut the door quietly and turned to face Thomasheen James, who was expressing clamorously a desire for sanguinary pursuit. I thought for a moment that there would be a second aided projectile through the door, with the possibility of myself making a third; but Mr Kelleher merely placed a hand on Thomasheen James's breast and said with soothing dignity:

"Restrain your pugnacity, Thomasheen James." He looked over my varlet's head and addressed me. "I apologise, sir, for permitting that scoundrel to incommode you."

An admirable, cultured, widely-read man, Patrick Kelleher. He is now one of my best friends.

Thomasheen James came back into the alcove.

"Look at me!" he demanded, striking his breast, the flare of battle still about him, and in his voice and eyes the pride of Alexander after Gaudemala. "Look at me! John L. Sullivan 'ud be jealous o' me his best day. Becripers! there is wan man I can put the fear o' hell in, anyway."

He came closer and his voice changed.

"It is a gran' thing to have a fri'nd. When I saw you me heart lifted, an' was me heart wrong? No, sir! Come away home now, me gallant man, an' you'll see me makin' the weeds an' the daisies bow their heads like—like Barney Doony."

He came closer still, and his voice again changed and lowered.

"I'll tell you, though it tears me heart. Whisper

here! an' don't use it agin me. The name Barney Doony put on me was 'Snotty Nose.'"

I have called Thomasheen James many names since then, but, though often sorely tempted, I have never called him by that opprobrious name.

CHAPTER VI

THOMASHEEN JAMES AND THE
BLIND PENSION

I

THOMASHEEN JAMES, my-man-of-no-work, draped his breast with medals (out of pawn for the occasion), touched me for two half-crowns, and took a bus to Phoenix Park to attend the memorial service on Armistice Day. He came back quite early in the evening, reasonably sober and in the best of humour.

"A Gineral," said he, "who batthered his way through the Big War bitterly from the rear got up on his two hind legs, an' says he: 'These is hard times, me fellow-sogers, and we deserve well of the State. Let me an' you sink our hellish pride,' says he, 'and if want an' destitation stares us in the face let us apply ourselves to the proper constituted authority.' It is the first time in all me careerin' that I saw nose to nose with any rank higher than a full private. Ay! these are hard times right enough, an' a hard winter before us."

"Am I to understand," I enquired, "that you are about to apply yourself to the proper constituted authority?"

"Why not I?" he declared boldly. "I am not wantin' a bite or a sup, an' I admit it, but a coupla weekly half-dollars in me pocket won't hurt me."

Forthwith to acquire these dishonest half-dollars he applied to some Society of ex-Soldiers and Sailors, and an eminently just committee, after brief investiga-

146

tion, decided that he neither deserved nor needed assistance. The decision was communicated baldly to Thomasheen James.

He went straight up in the air and let loose a burst of temper that astonished me. What rankled in him was that no opportunity had been given him to display his powers of chicanery.

"Look at me!" he cried, striking his bony breast. "Take a good look at me! Be land an' say, be might an' main, fair an' foul, mornin' an' night, before an' after meals, for four long years I belted the Prooshan and the Rooshan and the Turk—not forgettin' wan or two Inglishmin in the bygoin'—an' what do I get? What do I get?"

"What you deserve—nothing."

"Very well so! From now on, wakin' an' sleepin', drunk an' sober, I am agin the Governmint."

"The Government had nothing to do with this."

"Dam' the hair I care. 'Tis a constituted authority, an' I'm agin it as me fairest mark. You are lookin' at a convicted communist—a line in wolf's clothin'— an' the powers'll be rueful o' the day they tangled with T. J. O'Doran prooletarian. Mark me words!"

I treated his declaration of war with derision. He had, in his time, out-manœuvred me and my wife, Davy Hand, and even Detective-Sergeant Joe O'Dowd, but he could not hope to bluff a hard-hearted and bowelless Government Department. I told him so.

"Keep your eye on me," he said, "and warn me when you see foul play, an' if I call on you to testify, don't forget that blood is thicker'n water."

All that winter Thomasheen James battened on me, but with the first signs of spring he disappeared without warning. The trace of tinker-gipsy blood in him grew dominant when soil had to be delved. An empty wheelbarrow and a yard sweeping-brush were his favourite implements of industry, and, as he himself put it, he could not sleep a sound wink if there was a spade under the same roof.

I was chagrined, though I should have known what to expect. I had two sprouting boxes of early potatoes ready for planting, the drying March winds had left the ground in perfect condition for drilling, and under the impetus of tongue and fork-handle Thomasheen James had acquired a fairish method of distributing fertiliser and spacing seed-setts. So I cursed him warmly as the first perspiration of spring moistened my brow.

And then on a fine morning in late March the early post brought me a long official-looking envelope.

"Income-tax returns again," said my wife sadly over her tea-cup.

The document enclosed was certainly official, but it had nothing to do with income-tax. Having read it, my first feeling was mirthful.

"Listen to this, will you?" I said.

As near as I can remember, the following is what I read aloud:

> In connection with a claim by Thomas James O'Doran, the Model Lodging-House, Lord Edward Crescent, Ard-na-Righ, for a Pension under the Blind Pension Act, 1934, the claimant has referred me to you, and I shall be obliged if you supply the following information:—
> 1. How long have you known the claimant?
> 2. Has the claimant been in your employment, and, if so, during what periods?
> 3. To the best of your knowledge and belief, is the claimant's eyesight so defective as to incapacitate him from following his stated occupation of jobbing gardener?

A paternal Government had recently enacted legislation conferring a weekly pension of ten shillings on blind persons or on persons so defective in eyesight as to be unable further to follow their ordinary occupations.

Thomasheen James had at last tangled with a Government Department, and had called on me to remember that blood was thicker than water.

"Does that really mean that our Thomasheen James is claiming a blind pension?" wondered my wife.

"Not at all!" I said. "It is really an indirect application for sixty days in jail."

"I often noticed that he was short-sighted," said my wife, who has a habit of making excuses for a lame dog.

"He is, when contemplating a job of work," I said, "and he is certainly short-sighted this time. He is not going to fool the trained officials of a Department used to the wiles of the non-blind and half-blind. That claim after investigation will be sat on by a local committee of taxpayers whose first allegiance is to the taxpayer. Jail stares him in the blind face."

"How are you going to answer that document?"

"I have a duty as a citizen——"

"Duty!" said my wife witheringly. Women have no civic conscience.

But back in the quietness of my own den I found that I could not testify against Thomasheen James. He had impelled or compelled me to share in so many of his nefarious misadventures that I could not now, at his own invitation, help to rub his nose in the mud. I could reply to that document in three ways: by the brutal truth, by oracular equivocation, or by straight lying. The second appealed to me. I could so easily say that Thomasheen James could not see a job of work under his nose, and let the Pension Officer infer what he liked. I toyed with the idea and rejected it. What then? Finally I went into the kitchen and consulted my wife. She laughed at me. That did not help. I said:

"Lend me your car for the afternoon?"

"Will you bring him back with you?"

"As far as the first deep pool in the Liffey."

"Your garden is behind," hinted the woman.

That was so true that I lost my temper, and had to apologise before getting the car.

II

I motored down to Ard-na-Righ that afternoon and discovered the Model Lodging-House in Lord Edward Crescent. A model lodging-house is, technically, one that is subject to police regulations and supervision.

Lord Edward Crescent, notwithstanding its genteel name, was a winding slum lane off the Main Street, and it had a twelve-foot roadway between ancient, tumble-down, one-storey, rabbit-hutch, stone houses. A gang of bright but not-too-clean urchins clustered to the car and led me, noisily as jackdaws, to the door of the lodging-house, the only two-storeyed building in the lane.

"A gintleman to see you, Francy Lawson. Come on out!" my escort yelled jointly and severally through the open door.

"To hell ou' that!" shouted a voice casually, and Francy Lawson appeared in the doorway.

He was a tall and venerable man with a fine white beard and eyes invincibly peaceful. He was the proprietor. For one modest sixpence he provided a straw mattress and a pillow in a cubicle; for a third of that sum he provided dormitory accommodation and a communal pillow. That pillow was a stout taut cable hooked from wall to wall a foot above the floor; and at seven o'clock each morning it was Francy's custom to unhook one end of the cable, bump the sleepers to vociferous wakefulness, and coil away for the day. Bed-making was then complete.

"Thomas James O'Doran! Could I see him, Mr Lawson?" I enquired politely.

"Thomasheen James! Are you wantin' him?" Mr Lawson was a wary man.

"I have a few words to say to him," I said.

"Maybe 'tis business you have with him?"

"Yes. About his blind pension."

That drew him. "Ach! the poor fella! He's after bein' investigated to hell an' all, an' him as blind as a bat."

"Is he available?"

"Available! No, then. Davy Hand led him up the street a small while ago. If they're anywhere they'll be in Patsy Kelleher's bar, but if there's the price of a pint between them they hid it well from me."

I knew Davy Hand. Any time that Thomasheen James ran a scheme in double harness the other member of the team was sure to be Davy Hand. A pleasant, likeable little wastrel of a dog-fancier, one small fraction of a degree less improvident than Thomasheen James.

I thanked Mr Lawson and moved towards the car. He called after me:

"A whole week's lodgin' I have on the slate agin 'em. You'll be givin' him the pension, maybe?"

"I'll give him what's comin' to him," I called back.

"God spare you the health!" prayed Francy Lawson.

I brushed a cluster of brats off the scrabbled bonnet of my wife's car, distributed a largesse of coppers, and backed out on to the Main Street. It was a long, straight, narrow street, and the houses framing it were coloured red, pink, ochre, yellow, blue, and green, with no least attempt at harmony. Patrick Kelleher's saloon—*The Short Grass Bar*—was near the far end, and I could see the porch of it jutting on to the pavement.

As the car approached, a round bowler hat projected itself from a column of the porch, was set attentively towards me for two seconds, and disappeared. I knew that bowler hat.

Patrick Kelleher was glad to see me. He has been one of my best friends since that notable day when Thomasheen James was fined—and I paid—three pounds for battering one Bernard Doony, a travelling showman. A dignified, widely-read man, Mr Kelleher, and his rich-voiced grandiloquence straight out of Macaulay's Essays. He expressed his gratification at the comeliness of my appearance and felicitated me on the elegance of my health. Thereafter he gestured a thumb over his shoulder.

"Your arrival has been anticipated and your presence arranged for."

"So I noticed," I said.

At the far end of the long bar was the historic shallow alcove that I remembered, and I moved slowly towards it. I looked in on Thomasheen James and

Davy Hand. Each leant an elbow on the high zinc-covered counter and rested one foot on the brass rod, two leisurely plutocrats at ease over a careless drink. Davy was a short, tubby man under a bowler hat, and his black overcoat was buttoned tightly over a round paunch. Thomasheen James, lean as a lath, an old tweed hat of mine on the back of his red poll, his eyes—but I could not see his eyes. His wary china-blue eyes were hidden below big dark-blue spectacles—those ordinary sun-glasses to be acquired for a shilling in any cheap stores. I could not tell whether he was looking at me or over my head, and his lean, bony, freckled face was as still as a mask. He did not recognise my presence by word or gesture, but Davy was effusive enough for both. Davy insisted on shaking my hand warmly.

"Ah, sirr! is it yourself is in it? Come away up to the counter an' have a drink with us. Dammit, you will so! Many's the pint you stood meself an' Thomasheen James in your time, an' you'll gi'e me the option on this pleasant occasion. What'll it be, sir? A ball o' malt an' a small soda?"

I looked at the zinc counter. On it stood two empty glasses showing traces of beer froth.

"Jest after finishin' our second," explained Davy in some haste. "Care for another, Thomasheen James?"

"Go to hell, Davy Hand!" said Thomasheen James unamiably.

I was not unacquainted with this bread-on-the-water ruse that Davy was trying out on me. I played the game.

"Thanks, Davy! I'll have a glass of lager with you."

"Hardly worth your while, sir," said Davy, "wake

stuff like that, but whatever you say. A glass o' lager for the boss, Mr Kelleher, an' take it out o' that." He slapped a lone sixpenny-bit on the counter.

"Lager beer is customarily another twopence," remarked Mr Kelleher, "but never mind, Davy!"

"At your pleasure, me good sir! I won't ask you to change a pound note for me so airly in the evenin'."

Patrick Kelleher poured my drink carefully, and Davy Hand, watching the golden amber of the liquor, could not keep his tongue from his dry lips.

I savoured that beer slowly and maliciously, taking all of ten minutes to it. We talked, Patrick, Davy, and myself, of weather and of crops, of dogs, of horses, and the chance a certain two-year-old had at the approaching Ard-na-Righ Races. Thomasheen James took no part in the conversation. He and I ignored each other. His blue-black glasses goggled into vacancy, and his mouth was a stiff line in the stiff mask of his face. Finally I put down my empty glass.

"Thank you kindly, Davy!" I said. "See you again some time," and strolled slowly out of the bar.

An emphasised word or two of a low-voiced, bitter altercation reached me as I went, and I gathered that Davy Hand ran the imminent risk of having certain parts of his viscera spread before the hounds of the street.

A wooden bench ran along the wall of the open porch right of the doorway. I sat at the far end, filled a pipe and waited. The long street was somnolent in the spring sunshine. Now and then a citizen slipped furtively down the lane by the porch on his thirsty way to the side-door of the bar. Some distance on my left a donkey drowsed in the shafts of a cart, and the cart was slewed across the road to the danger of motor traffic—but there was no motor traffic. On my right an empty hay-waggon congested the Dublin road, and the horse's head was deep in a nose-bag. A dog or two slept peacefully in the gutter, and one on the very crown of the road beyond the hay-waggon. Everything was as still and lonesome as in a siesta hour in Spain.

I had not long to wait. Hands fumbled on the doorpost, and Thomasheen James came pawing his way into the porch. He felt for the bench as only a blind man would feel for it, and for a moment I wondered. Then he sat down with a tired sigh, and the blue glasses stared straight ahead across the street.

"Are you there?" enquired Thomasheen James in a weak voice.

I merely grunted as I scraped a match alight.

"You're there, an' fine for you to be able to see the smoke," he said dolefully. "Smokin' is no dam' use to me since this infliction come on me like a clap o' thunder."

"It will leave you just as suddenly," I said.

"Do you think so?" He spoke eagerly. "Thim is the first hopeful words I heard in ten days. Do you think it will?"

"Yes. Not that you'll need much eyesight picking oakum in jail."

"I was feart you'd be prejudicial," he regretted.

"I always knew you were a rogue." I began to limber up. "Now I also know that you are a blind idiot."

"Mind you, I'm not dead-blind," he explained.

"Blind as a bat," I insisted. "Do you know what you are up against?"

He was nettled. He gestured wildly.

155

"Every impedimentia is scattered before me attack."

"Has the Pension Official interviewed you?"

"Hasn't he so? An' askin' as many crooked questions as ever you consaved your own self. Becripers! he was as tough as Saint Matthew the taxgatherer, but I answered him prompt to me own satisfaction."

"And to his? When do you face the local Pension Committee?"

"Friday with the help o' God. Sure, every dang wan o' them is watchin' me the whole week an' Davy Hand leadin' me round like a lapdog. Only yesterday evenin' the chairman himself gave me a hand across the street. 'Me poor fella!' says he. 'Keep your heart up, an' I'll make it right for you Friday.' A dacent, simple ould buffer!"

"Have you been medically examined?"

"From A to X, an' me sartificat' safe an' sound."

"Nonsense! You could not fool an oculist?"

"Whatever you call him—an' he's plain Doctor Doyle—and I didn't fool him. I didn't fool no one. He sint me a dispatch to call at his house Monday mornin', and so I did, Davy Hand steerin' me. His car was in front o' the door an' he came down the steps himself to invent'ry us.

"'Tis the poor blind man, T. J. O'Doran, Doctor,' says Davy, retrievin' me out of a holly bush. An' he only shoved Davy well away from me.

"'Come down to me sudgery,' says he. 'Get into the back seat o' that car. Quick! In you go!'

"'Twas wan o' them two-door Ford cars an' he watchin' like a hawk for me to open the door an' tilt the front seat. But did I? He had to hook me cursin' off the top o' the raddiator an' shove me in head first. An' off we scooted like a cat out o' hell, with Davy

Hand scratchin' his nose with his bowler hat on the pavement. Down below in the sudgery he flattened me out in a chair an' blasted a flash o' light into the back o' me skull out of a tin tube.

"'A little as-astigmanism,' says he.

"'Heaven's me bed, Doctor,' says I. "'Am I bad as that?'

"'You'll be a dam' sight worse, me lad,' says he, an' I could hear him rubbin' the bristle of his jaw.

"They was a big white chaney bowl on a table, an' he held it up in his hand across the room from me.

"'Look this way,' says he, an' me eye fixed. 'Do you see that?'

"'Have you anything there, Doctor?' says I.

"'I have,' says he, hot. 'What is it?'

"'The divil melt me! I can't scc a stim,' says I. 'Bring it closer, if you plaise.' An' he brought it half-way.

"'Do you see it now?'

"'I see the shine o' something,' says I, 'but it'll have to be, maybe, a foot closer.'

"An' he stuck it within a foot o' me nose.

"'Ah!' says I. 'I see it plain as a pin now.'

"'What is it?'

"''Tis aither a two-shillin' piece or half a dollar,' says I, an' I thought he'd ha' busted the dish on the roof o' me skull.

"'Get out!' he bawled at me. 'Sling your hook out that door. Out with you!'

"An' I bashed meself into a corner an' brought down a frame with big ah-bee-sees on it off the wall. He had to lead me to the front door rough as a chucker-out in a low pub, an' he heaved me down the steps straight into Davy Hand's waitin' arms, an' off we went, Davy oxterin' me an' the doctor scratchin' his poll behind us. 'Tis all plain sailin' the rest o' the way."

"Is it? There is still a rock in the channel."

"A rock in the channel!" said Thomasheen James ruminatively. "You're not meanin' yourself, are you?"

"Right, first time! Myself, exactly."

"Thunder an' turf! an' we like brothers for three years or more," expostulated Thomasheen James splutteringly. "Manalive! Didn't I make you me referee, an' how could you renage me after that?"

"I could and I will."

"Listen to me for a minit!" implored Thomasheen James. "'Tis not for meself I'm doin' this work o' charity. 'Tis for poor ould Davy Hand."

I mocked him with mirthless laughter.

"Laugh at me good intint if you want to, but I'm tellin' you the eyetarnal truth." He spoke so intensely that I knew he was making it up as he went along. "Davy, the poor little gom, is in a bad way with his ould woman temp'rally in the Coombe, an' a houseful o' kids besides, an' his best blue tarrier killed dead a'most be the dint of a chokin' it got from a bull-bitch."

"Why then was not Davy afflicted?"

"The ignorant crathur! He hasn't me contrivingness in the face o' the foe. Look now! Gi'e me three months to set him on his feet agin, an' as I hope for a happy death I'll drop the pinsion, an' return to me allegiance faithful an' true."

"Allegiance?"

"You'll be missin' me."

I took that opportunity to dilate inadequately on his shortcomings and his morals; and in reply he wagged a hand impatiently.

"I heard all that before with no witnesses present. Laive it be! Sure I know I can trust you through thick an' thin." His tone changed suddenly to confident appeal. "As wan fri'nd to another, an' I hate to ask you, would you have the price of a coupla pints loose in your pocket?"

"Not loose. Go in and get Davy Hand to change his pound note."

"I would never doubt you," said Thomasheen James commendingly. "Did that little mealy-mouthed tub o' dirt think he could put that wan across on you after bein' me best student in years? I tould him so beforehand an' he coaxin' me last tanner out o' me. 'What's the good o' wan tanner betune the two of us?' says he. 'Let us float it on the river for the boss, an' it'll come back to us immediate in the shape o' two pints o' stout.'" He grew indignant. "Me last tanner an' the tongue stuck to the roof o' me mouth! Me bloody last coin o' the realm till I draw me first pinsion on Friday! Do you know? I got a dam' good mind to go in an' take the windpipe out o' him for belittlin' the both o' us."

He rose to his feet, sidled to the door, and peered into the bar, lowering one side of the blue spectacles to see more clearly. I saw the live keen eye of the scoundrel. Then he grinned at me wickedly.

"I got him the exack place I wanted. Take a peep o' this if 'tis a laugh you're after. It'll be worth your while."

What followed was certainly worth while.

Thomasheen James disappeared into the bar and I stepped softly to the open doorway and looked after. He was sidling cat-footed along the outside of the long counter. Patrick Kelleher was talking to Davy Hand and some other occupants of the alcove. Davy was sitting far back on a three-legged stool. I could see half the stool projecting outside the edge of the partition, and the rearward black-coated curve of Davy as he sat leaning forward.

Thomasheen James reached the partition silent as a cat, lifted a foot, balanced himself, and suddenly hooked the stool from beneath his victim; and as the victim thudded and bounced off the floor Thomasheen James gave him a contemptuous side-footed heave that tumbled him over on his face.

There was a bellow that would do credit to the wildest auroch bull. The fallen man rolled, scrambled, bounded to his feet with the resiliency of a rubber ball, and whirled, arms swinging, to face the attacker. And my mouth opened as I blinked and stared.

For the victim was not Davy Hand. He was a short stout man, indeed, and he wore a tight-fitting black coat; but he was never Davy Hand.

There followed an explosion that should have blown the roof off. The short stout man flamed, roared, leapt straight and nimbly into the air, and before his feet again touched ground his right arm launched itself. Thomasheen James, not a whit less nimble, got out from under. He whirled wildly on his heels and came streaking for the door. If he had gone up the bar light-footed as a cat, he now came down, in his own simile, with the celerity of a cat with a tarrier dog on its tail. As he went by me for the great outside he yelled anguishedly:

"Hould him! Hould him!"

I might as easily have held a black panther. A dark streak went through my hands, air lashed my face, a bellow lagged behind. Such a display of unleashed temper I had never imagined.

My wife's car was by the pavement kerb. Thomasheen James, wily as a fox, retarded himself with the sudden ease of a Chaplin, and swooped round the bonnet in the nick of time. The short man, astoundingly agile, circled on his tail. They rounded the car twice, and then Thomasheen James straightened out and went up the street towards some distant horizon. The short man, yelling his abundant energy, straightened out behind him.

Thomasheen James ran well, with the loose long action of a greyhound, but the short man's action was shattering, and his short legs had the very drive of piston shafts shuttling furiously.

Thomasheen James was doomed, I thought, his jacket tails already within reach. But even in that extremity he did not lose his cunning. Up the street the donkey-cart was still askew across the road, and Thomasheen James, in the very act of bounding by, doubled as a hare doubles, missed the tail shafts by an inch, swished round the donkey's head, and came back in his tracks with a renewed burst of speed.

The short man, agile though he was, lost many yards by that tactic, but his rending urge never failed him. He simply refreshed himself with another yell and came scuttering on the quarry's traces.

The street had come alive by now. The ordinary week-day in Ard-na-Righ is made up of long somnolent periods between sudden dog-fights. Here was something better than any dog-fight. Men and women tumbled out of doors, youngsters came flurrying like sparrows, cheerful exhortation echoed from wall to wall, dogs barked and fled. But no one, not even a Civic Guard lounging at the barrack door opposite the public-house, tried to apprehend the flying Thomasheen James, though his pursuer was the leading citizen. Such was not the technique.

Thomasheen James went loping by me, fear and despair in the rolling eyes he cast at me. He had shed his blue glasses somewhere.

"Hould him! He'll strang'late me." There was despair in his appealing yelp. It would take a traction engine to hold that short stout man.

The horse under the empty hay-waggon, frightened by the pandemonium, had slewed round and backed the waggon tail against a lamp-post, thus blocking three-fourths of the road. The driver wrestled with the nose-bag. Thomasheen James, again losing ground, again brought craft to his aid. He took the hub of a wheel in his stride, and with a vault and a roll tumbled over the high side of the waggon. He had a fortalice now. His long neck reared above his battlements; he had lost his hat, and his sandy-red head was like an oriflamme.

That astounding short man bounded on the road below and in a mighty voice invited Thomasheen James to come down and be kilt; and Thomasheen James tried to placate him with an urgent patting of the air.

"Come down to me!" roared the short man. "Come down, I tell you!"

"I will not—gi'e me time," shouted Thomasheen James.

"I'll come up so," roared the valiant short man.

He laid hold of the wheel and essayed the assault. Would Thomasheen James play king-of-the-castle? He would! He would not! He would! No! His morale was gone. As the head of the enemy appeared above one side of the waggon Thomasheen James vaulted the other side and proceeded up the Dublin road at an accelerated rate of knots.

The short man bumped back to the road, circled the waggon, and was minded to resume the chase. But the inevitable must be recognised even by the most furious. Thomasheen James was a distance runner; the short man was a sprinter, a remarkable performer, indeed, but still only a sprinter. He had wind left for just one final yell. Standing on wide-planted feet, he shook a strenuous fist after the fugitive and let loose that yell. And, forthwith, Thomasheen James added a foot to his stride.

The dog asleep in mid-road waked up lazily. It was used to sudden explosions and did not recognise the insecurity of its sleeping-place until too late. As it yelped and leaped for safety it took Thomasheen James's flying kick, and went out of town ahead of him, emitting "whelps" at every bound, as Thomasheen James subsequently put it. It was accompanied by a dozen other yapping curs; and all, including Thomasheen James, disappeared over the crown of the railway bridge.

Patrick Kelleher spoke calmly at my shoulder.

"I concede you tactics for Dublin, but Ard-na-Righ holds the stricken field."

"Every problem carries its own solution," I said sententiously. "I came down to get Thomasheen James out of Ard-na-Righ. He's out."

"Here comes the unslaked victor," said Patrick warningly. "Take him placatingly."

The short man came striding back. He stopped facing us, blew great breaths, mopped a red handkerchief on a redder brow, glared at us. His temper was no more than down to seething stage.

"Did you see what that tramp did?" he shouted. "Did you see the indignity he put on me?"

I fear that my effort at placation was malicious.

"His eyesight, sir!" I said. "He's half-blind, and mistook——"

"Blind!" he yelled. "Blind! Did you see the way he went round that dam' car? Did you see the way he dodged the ass-and-cart? Did you see him mount the wheel? Did you see him kick Tom Purcell's dog? Did——? Blind! I'll blind him!"

Patrick Kelleher's effort fared even worse.

"The finest display of agility since Adam was a boy!" he said. "The poor fellow was insane, Mr Doherty—a sudden cerebral storm——"

"Bah-h-h!" roared Mr Doherty. "Your bad whiskey! You keep a disorderly house, Patsy Kelleher, and by the Lord! I'll oppose the renewal of your licence."

"The circumstances would appear to justify it——"

"Shut up, you ould blatherskite!" barked Mr Doherty, and striding furiously away switched into a shoe emporium, apparently his business premises, some distance down and across the street.

With his disappearance the little town began to settle back into its customary week-day somnolence. Dogs began to trickle back over the railway bridge, tongues hanging. Thomasheen James did not trickle back, but, no doubt, his tongue was hanging.

"A dam'd ould bully, Tom Doherty!" said Patrick, forgetting his Lord Macaulay.

We went back into the bar and he shook his head in mystification.

"I don't understand this cyclonic event. Your henchman must certainly be suffering from a sudden insanity."

"He was. He mistook your Mr Doherty for Davy Hand."

"But Davy was back in the kitchen imbibing bread and tea."

I explained Thomasheen James's seeming madness, and my friend draped himself over the counter, clasped his hands over his semi-bald crown, and sought to restrain his mirth within the bounds of dignity. After a time he straightened up and wiped his eyes.

"You and your henchman should visit us more frequently," he said. "This community needs stirring up occasionally. Come upstairs now and we'll partake of the cup that cheers but not inebriates."

He left the bar in charge of his cellarman, and we went upstairs to Patrick's book-cluttered bachelor's quarters. There we discussed tea and buttered scones, books and the characters therein, for a pleasant hour.

Davy Hand was waiting for me when I got back into the bar, and I recognised the futility of abuse.

"Hello, Davy!" I said. "Want a lift back to Dublin?"

Davy scratched doubtfully under his bowler hat.

"Maybe we'd be overtakin' Thomasheen James on the road," he said hesitatingly.

"Yes, he mentioned something about extracting windpipes."

165

"The last man he kilt was home before himself," said Davy, "but all the same I'd better wait for the bus—if——" He lifted a diffident eye at me.

I said nothing about his pound note as I put hand in pocket.

"They's Francy Lawson o' the Model as well," said Davy quickly. "While you're at it, sir, could I be bould enough to touch you for a small loan be way of pacificatin' Francy?"

He got a ten-shilling note off me. Also he had two pints of stout.

"Wan for meself," he said with laughter, "an' wan be proxyin' Thomasheen James, the poor blind man."

I considered that the afternoon was well worth the money.

I drove my wife's car slowly on the home road, and kept a weather eye lifting. Just as well that I did. A long league out of Ard-na-Righ, round a sharp bend, I overtook Thomasheen James, head-down, stubbornly plodding the middle of the road. The motor horn blared in his coat tails, and, like an antelope, he jumped twelve feet into the heart of a furze bush. The car stopped at the side of the bush, and I opened the door invitingly. He looked at me frigidly, extricated himself painfully and climbed in. There was nothing left in him but plaintiveness.

"Hasn't enough happened me this misfortunate blasted day without you chokin' me at th' ind of it with me own gizzard? Long enough you kep' me waitin', me tongue like a rasp, an' you full o' Patsy Kelleher's beer!"

"Davy Hand had your pint as well as his own."

"I hope it won't rind him till I get me hands on

his windpipe," said Thomasheen James, a spark of life returning.

I drove steadily on. You cannot keep a good man down. After a while Thomasheen James cleared his throat and made everyday conversation.

"Tell me, is the spud seeds sprouted?"

"They is."

"Have you the drills open?"

"Some."

"Wait till the mornin', then, an' you'll see me makin' the dirt fly. I'll have them down for you be the week-end."

"But you have to attend that pension meeting on Friday?" I suggested smoothly.

He gave me his pale glance sideways.

"I suppose Patsy Kelleher told you?"

"Told me what?"

"Didn't you see that chunk o' mud I rooted off the stool in the cubby?"

"I saw a smaller man chase you out of town."

"I gev him wan good root anyway. Do you know who he is?"

"A Tom Doherty."

"He is the chairman of the bloody Pension Committee," said Thomasheen James.

CHAPTER VII

THOMASHEEN JAMES AND THE
GUM DROPS

I

I THINK that I have said before now that Patrick Kelleher is one of my best friends. He is the proprietor of *The Short Grass Bar* at Ard-na-Righ, and a man of parts: a sane, sound, inveterate bachelor, with the salt of humour savouring an innate dignity, versed in life and letters, and pleasantly afflicted with a style of diction acquired in a youthful flirtation with Lord Macaulay's Essays. But even though he is an inveterate bachelor, he recently ran the imminent risk of losing that admirable status—admirable, I mean, for certain men, of whom Patrick is one.

Thomasheen James, my-man-of-no-work, with some little assistance from me, played god-out-of-the-machine, and nearly wrecked three households as a consequence.

It began by Thomasheen James and I having one of our not unusual parting of brass rags—or is it brass rings? I had gone across to Lough Corrib for the may-fly fishing, and on my return, after an all too brief three weeks, found my tomato plants wilting in their boxes, my early peas tangled and unstaked, the potato-shaws unearthed, and the weeds choking my young vegetables. I would not mind, only that I had fondly thought that I had, by this time, trained my-man-of-no-work to rake and hoe and even digging-fork.

168

I spoke to and at him with justifiable warmth, and found him recalcitrant.

"Blame the missus," he said, bending over in a cramped attitude. "She kep' me plantin' out antherntynums till the crick in me backbone 'ud disable a richinorous."

I spoke still more warmly, and he reacted just as warmly. He was shouting before long.

"All right! If that's the way I'm to be miscalled in seed, breed an' generation I'll not stand it no longer. Small right have I to be spillin' me sweat for a grudgin' half-dollar wance in a blue moon, an' a good job waitin' for me first time o' askin'. 'Twas in the paper last night."

"A good job!" I said derisively. "I'd eat my hat if you held a real job down for a week."

"I've a dam' good mind to make you ate it so," he threatened.

"Go to your fine job!" I was shouting too. "Go to it! And don't let me see that freckled façade of yours inside that garden gate ever again."

And so, after a brief twenty minutes of altercation, Thomasheen James and I parted for ever. But, then, we had parted for ever on at least four previous occasions.

I thought, at the time, that it was merely the seasonal tinker-gipsy urge that was driving him, and that he would be back as usual when the garden work slackened. But as week after week went by I began to wonder rather uncomfortably if he were really holding down a job somewhere. In fact, Thomasheen James had become so much part of my life that I was jealous at the thought of another householder as his victim.

And then, after the lapse of two months, I received a letter with the Ard-na-Righ postmark. It was from Thomasheen James. I had not before seen his handwriting, and was surprised at its neatness. But he was no literary artist with the pen. Here is a copy of his letter:

Dear Sir hoping this finds you well as it leaves me well paid and cared for I take my pen in hand to drop you a polite hint that a friend of yours that you know Patcy Kelleher of the short grass bar this town is at the present making the biggest fool of a jackass of himself in all Ireland, if something is not done for him soon and sudden he will be worse in a short time forever and a day amen, There is nothing no one can do about it me or you either but after this if we meet as strangers you will not be able to blame me for my silence in face of insulting language hard to forget. Come down if you can. Yours remaining with respects T. J. O'Doran esquire.

I cursed Thomasheen James. His letter was not illuminating but it was disturbing. I gathered from it that my friend Patrick Kelleher was contemplating an act of folly the effects of which would be permanent; and, though it stated that nothing could be done by me or Thomasheen James, that final sentence, "Come down if you can," gave me a sense of urgency and hope.

But what folly could Patrick Kelleher be contemplating? He could not make a fool of himself even if he tried. And all the time, I refused to contemplate the one possible folly that would fill the bill. The only thing to do was to go and see for myself. So I borrowed my wife's car and went down to Ard-na-Righ that very afternoon.

170

I manœuvred the car round the foot of a ladder set against the porch of *The Short Grass Bar*, and looked up at a leisurely artisan renewing the ornate foot-high lettering on the long signboard: PATRICK KELLEHER TEA WINE AND SPIRIT MERCHANT. Patrick was a publican first and foremost, but, like most Irish country publicans, he was also a grocer.

Before stepping inside the porch I glanced down and across the street and noted that another craftsman was engaged on the sign of Thomas Doherty's Boot and Shoe Emporium. I seemed to remember that name Doherty coupled with Thomasheen James's.

Patrick Kelleher, who was alone in the bar—the inveterate evening thirst had not yet assailed the citizens of Ard-na-Righ—greeted me with decorum and, as was his custom, began carefully to draw a cool tankard of lager. But my opening gambit towards conversation he countered with silence, as was not his custom. This usually equable, long-worded man was heavy-browed, disgruntled, almost shamefaced. He hesitated to meet my eye, and I was close enough friend to make rude remark.

"Anything biting you, Patrick?"

"Biting me? Oh, yes! a colloquialism, and quite expressive," he murmured weightily. He lifted and dropped his shoulders as he placed the creamy tankard before me. "Well! there is no fool like an old fool."

He was not more than middle-aged, and the years had not commenced to draw lines on the healthy pallor of his face. In fact, he was a good-looking, dignified, youthful man, with a fine half-bald dome of brow.

"Are you calling me names?" I said. "You are not old?"

"Old enough to have acquired my modicum of common sense."

"Meaning you haven't?"

"You might think otherwise," he said, smiling palely. His eyes met mine and his jaw squared. "I may as well be your first informant, before some individual with a perverted sense of humour gives you a garbled version. In brief, I am contemplating joining your happy family of Benedicks."

"Good heavens!" I blurted before I could restrain myself.

"I am somewhat astonished myself," said my friend.

"I know what a happy Benedick is," I said, "but let me get this straight. Are you telling me that you are thinking of getting married?"

"The straightforward question can seldom be answered in like manner," he answered solemnly. "No man is a free agent where certain impressions have been produced, and matrimony would seem to be an inevitable conclusion."

Was he ponderously trying to tell me that he had been philandering? And with whom?

"I don't know the lady, I suppose?" I hinted broadly.

"Not to my knowledge. Mistress Catherine Byrne of Elm Vista——"

"Mistress Catherine Byrne?" I emphasised the mistress.

"Generally known as the Widow Byrne, and a highly presentable member of her sex, with more than her due share of the world's goods."

"You are not marrying the lady for her money, are you?"

172

"Money finds money," he said obliquely.

"My congratulations," I said then, and belatedly.

I was disturbed. Patrick Kelleher was one of the few natural celibates that I had ever met. One could not visualise him in double harness, nor a team-mate to suit his own particular pace. But what disturbed me was that feeling of shamefaced reluctance I sensed in him. Matrimony in such circumstances might be disastrous for my friend, as disastrous as matrimony might be for another celibate of my acquaintance— Thomasheen James—but in a totally different way. The thought of the sandy-haired wastrel gave me a way out of a rather awkward silence.

"Seen anything of him whom you designate my henchman?" I enquired in Patrick's own language.

"Thomasheen James? A meritorious working citizen at the moment."

"Get out! He's never holding down a job?"

"With might and main. Remarkably enough, he is seasonal gardener to the lady who intends to be Mistress Kelleher."

"My congratulations again," I said, brightening up. "She must be one kindly and forbearing lady——"

Patrick gestured towards the door.

"Withhold adverse criticism! We speak of his satanic majesty."

There was a clatter in the porch, and Thomasheen James himself made a dramatic entrance. The evening was warm and he was minus jacket and vest; his bare wiry forearms were speckled like the sides of a brown trout; his neck had the polished gleam of new copper; his long nose under an old tweed hat, once mine, was peeling unpleasantly; he was a fine (but surely false) sample of a toiler indurated to labour under too much sun. One elbow was hitched in the loop of a large wicker basket covered with a white cloth.

He saw me and his eyes lit for a single instant, and again quenched to their customary wary washed-clean blueness.

"Good evenin', sir!" He saluted me with a nice shade of aloofness.

"Good evening, Mr O'Doran!" I copied him.

He lifted the basket on the counter, drew away the cloth to disclose many empty bottles, and addressed himself to Patrick Kelleher.

"Two dozen strong ale, Patsy, two bottles of gold label whiskey"—he emphasised the two—"an' the widda's reg'lar weekly for groceries, not forgettin' the quarter-pound o' gum drops."

"The good lady used order in more moderate quantities not so long ago," remarked Patrick for my information.

"They's a man in the house now," said Thomasheen James, "an' isn't the toilin' an' moilin' wage-slave intitled to his little imolumints this blisterin' hot weather? Becripers! me tongue spinds its time in the roof o' me mouth."

I took the hint for my own purposes.

"Have a drink with me?" I invited amiably.

"Thank you kindly, sir!" he accepted readily. "A pint o' half-an'-half, Patsy, an' not too much froth."

I had to take Thomasheen James carefully. He had sent for me with some urgency, but if I aroused his ignoble ire he might shut up like a clam; and he was the one and only individual who could enlighten me on my friend's intended fall into matrimony. In a town the size of Ard-na-Righ he would already know the history, open or secret, of every man, woman, chick or child; and if taken the right way might impart the discernible truth wrapped up in scandalous imaginings.

Patrick Kelleher, having served Thomasheen James with a brimming pint, had gone to the grocery end, and I made as tactful an opening as I could.

"I came down to see you," I said. "I got your SOS."

"It wasn't my SOS, was it?"

"No. When that comes I hope to let bygones be bygones."

"It takes two to make a bargain," he said, and addressed himself to his pint.

"But only one to pay the piper," I said, forgetting myself.

"I'm lettin' bygones be bygones, meself, for longer'n a minit," he hit me.

We waited in silence until Patrick Kelleher came back with the weighted basket.

"Two dozen, an' two bottles o' the hard stuff?" enquired Thomasheen James.

"Not forgetting the gum drops, my friend."

"Good for the dygestion, thim gum drops," remarked Thomasheen James, and I wondered if the lady was a dyspeptic as well as a widow.

Thomasheen James burthened himself with the basket and spoke over his shoulder.

"Put the account in the ledger, Patsy, an' the widda will settle as per her usual at th' end o' the quarter." His tone grew casual. "Be the way! how long is it to th' end o' the quarter, anyway?"

"August-September! Oh! some six weeks yet."

"God is good!" said Thomasheen James. "I'll be seein' ye."

He gave me a twitch of the head that I understood, and took his departure, one side straining away from the weight of the laden basket.

I nodded to Patrick Kelleher and followed slowly after Thomasheen James. He was waiting for me in the porch.

"Will you look at that?" He pointed his chin down and across the street. "Tom Doherty decoratin' the face o' his boot-shop agin Patsy Kelleher. Isn't it damawful what the revelry o' love'll do to two ould buckeroos?"

"The revelry of love! You mean rivalry, don't you?"

"Isn't that what I said, dammit?"

"What? Is Doherty a suitor of the widow's too?"

"He is, whether he suits her or not. So Patsy was tellin' you? Himself an' Tom Doherty 'ud give you a pain in your belly."

"Doherty!" I said. "I seem to remember that name. Something to do with you?"

"Your mimory is the best o' you, an' that's hell," said Thomasheen James hotly, and strode away from me up the long street.

But I walked firmly at his side, and after a time he looked aside at me out of a sea-cold eye.

"I know—I know—I know!" He made a song of that. "'Tis information you want out of me—all about bould Patsy an' the bloody fool he's after makin' o' himself."

"Has he made a fool of himself? Who says so?"

"I do. The head an' tail an' interals of a fool! But how the divil can I argyfy the question an' this

176

brute of a basket tearing the showlder out of me? Come up this way!"

He switched up a laneway and round into another that ran behind the gardens and outhouses of a row of detached villas. Some distance along he opened a wicket-gate in a big double-door and led into what had once been a coach-house but was now a motor-garage.

"In this way!"

He opened another door at the side into what had once been a harness-room: a tidied brick-floored apartment showing evidence of his handiness with a sweeping-brush. It was occupied scantily by a sagging basket-chair, a few empty butter-boxes, an odd collection of garden tools, and a lawn-mower; and it looked over a half-door on to a long kitchen garden, beyond which was a veranda and a french window.

"Welcome to me domain!" said Thomasheen James pleasantly. "Rest your legs in that chair while I arrange me appearances."

He threw a wary rapid glance over the half-door, unlocked a wall-cupboard, and began swiftly storing away bottles from the basket. I also looked with curiosity over the half-door to see the ruin that had been wrought in that garden. I was surprised. The lawn at one side of a concrete path had been shaved to the last quarter-inch; the vegetable patch at the other side was planted to the last foot; and there was a notable absence of the grosser weeds.

"I see this lady, Mrs Byrne, employs a gardener," I said.

"Out o' your own mouth you said it," he said triumphantly. "A gardener! an' that's me."

Having replenished the cupboard, he carefully

counted the bottles remaining in the basket and re-arranged the white cloth over them.

"I am pleased as bedam to see you here as me guest," he said, a real note of sincerity in his voice. "You'll take a bottle o' bitter out me hands?"

"Yours to offer?"

"Don't let us be muzzlin' the ox that thrashes out the corn, me good sir, as Mark the Evangel said—though how the divil would a ox thrash corn bates me! Sit down there! You wasn't bad yourself at drawin' an odd cork, an' I'll say that for you agin all comers."

I sat down cautiously in the sagging basket-chair, and he poured me a bottle of beer into a clean glass. He poured another for himself into a mug without a handle, and took his seat on an upturned butter-box. From where he sat he could look over the half-door by leaning forward, and during the subsequent discussion he never once forgot to keep a wary eye lifting towards the back of the house. He sampled his beer and gestured towards the garden.

"All me work—every blasted spade of it. You said you'd ate your hat if I held down a job o' work for as much as wan week. I won't ax you to do it, considerin' the nature o' the hat, but your words, leadin' the direction o' manslaughter, wrangled in me, for, I'll admit it, I was feelin' the sting o' truth at the bottom o' them. I was beginnin' to fancy meself manicled to a diggin'-fork when you clouted me fancies in the mud, an' I left the place swearin' nex' door to a bible oath that I would up an' show you. An' I have. Two months I am holdin' this job down in conditions contrairy to union rules; and do you know what is in me mind all the time? You do not. I'll tell you.

Six—no! five more weeks I'll stay by me servitude for good measure, an' thin I'll be slippin' up to Dublin to see a gallant fri'nd o' mine with a preposal that he sees his way to instigate me into a reg'lar job at a reg'lar week's wages—say twenty-five bob all found. Would that be fair to me an' him?"

"He would have to be a dam' gallant friend," I said. "Look here! I didn't come down from Dublin to discuss jobs with you——"

"Very well so! wan thing at a time." He waved a condescending hand. "What do you want to know, me honourable sir?"

"Patrick Kelleher is apparently contemplating marriage with your lady employer——"

"Wait there!" His finger stabbed at me. "You got it dead wrong from the start. Patsy Kelleher is contimplatin' nothin' o' the sort. But—an' listen to me—me lady employer is doin' a bit o' contimplatin' on her own, an' what she contimplates is as good as tied an' bound an' hamstrung an' poleaxed—an' safely in the bag till death do us part amen. Now you can raysume where you left off."

"But, surely, if Patrick were not agreeable——?"

"Too agreeable he was, the spry ould roosther."

Suddenly he gave his thigh a resounding slap.

"Be the powders o' war!" he cried, "that is dam' funny."

"I don't see anything funny——"

"It was yourself started the whole thing——"

"Don't be a dam' fool!" I said startledly. "I don't even know the lady."

"But you started her all the same—in abstenshia. Raycall to your stickin'-plaster of a mimory that day in spring you deprived me of me blind pinsion."

He was referring to the notorious occasion when he made a fraudulent claim for a pension for the blind and spoiled his chances by an unwitting assault on the chairman of the local Pension Committee.

"I could not deprive you of what you never had," I said patiently.

"You was a ack-sessory behind the facts. You're not forgettin' that block of a man I rooted off the stool in Patsy's bar?"

"And the little man chased you straight out of town."

"I gave him a good root all the same. That was Tom Doherty of the boot-shop."

"Ah! I thought the name was familiar. Does he threaten to resume the chase?"

"We made it up in the arms o' neutrality. But let that be. The thing is that Doherty took it into his fat head that Patsy Kelleher filled me to the gunn'le with drink that disastrous day an' sicked me on him be way of a joke. He wasn't to lade or drive a whole month, an' threatened Patsy with all the proceedin's of the law of licensin' a disorderly house. In the ind, Patsy, a patient ould slob mostly, got rale hot under the collar, an' raytorted by takin' a honest-to-god rise out o' Tom. He's a gay-minded ould stick-in-the-mud, Patsy, behind that gablend of a physiogamy, an' is partial to a bite in a bit o' fun—same as yourself. But, be cripersjoe! he picked the wrong bit o' fun for wance, an' got the bite took out o' himself. Ay! an' the whole swally of a whale starin' him in the face.

"I mind you accusin' me wance the way the pagan gods had of makin' a loony out of a man before destroyin' him for good an' all. That's it? Well, Patsy Kelleher destroyed himself be his sinse o' humour.

180

He knew—we all knew—that Tom Doherty was after the Widda Byrne for her money. In the height o' desperation he was after her for business purposes connected with his boot-shop in a bad way. An' there was the widda, her stockin' full—in more ways than wan—an' she half agreeable, bein' o' that youthful age when a second victim comes natural as daylight. And there was Patsy, knowin' the financial relations an' blind to danger, organisin' to cool Doherty's bad timper by givin' him the fright o' the divil an' his gran'mother. What do you think the poor omadhaun done?"

I shook my head sadly. This had happened so frequently to other men, and, yet, men remained blind.

"You got it! Be way of reprimandin' Tom he made up to the widda himself. Only on the edges you might say, but the edge was like a razor an' cut the feet out from under him. When it comes down to a ch'ice between Tom Doherty the man an' Patsy Kelleher's balance in the bank, what need I be talkin'? An' besides, Patsy has a sootherin' style about him that might be amiable to the sus-pectabilities of a female woman o' the opposite sex. He assailed the widda comin' out o' the chapel on a Sunday, an' walked home with her, makin' himself agreeable like a tuneful ould blackbird; an' he went an' took tay with her an evenin' through the week. An' there you have it.

"In no time at all she had her tin-tackles bedded in him. I heard you often alludin' to the eyetarnal triangle, and 'tis only now I know what you was drivin' at. There was Patsy Kelleher reprovin' Tom Doherty be stickin' his own head out for half a brick, and Tom after the widda for her tin, and the widda after Patsy for his tin, an' the result Patsy headed straight for hell be way of the altar rails. Have I got it right?"

"I hope not. If money is the driving force, has not the widow plenty of her own?"

He hooted at me. "Has she? Have you? Has anywan? How did she get it? Be addin' wan penny on top of another, an' skinnin' a flay for its hide. An' that's the only way money is made high or low, an' the disease is chronic."

"She has kept you for two months," I said, "and I note no lack of generosity." I lifted my beer-glass and nodded towards the cupboard.

"What doesn't lie in her road won't break her shins —till the end o' the quarter, anyway."

"Another point," I said. "Could not Patrick Kelleher have withdrawn, if he wanted to, when he saw danger ahead?"

"He tried. I'll say he tried. But tell me this out o' your own expayrience? Did you ever, ever at all, know any woman, an' 'specially any widda woman, extricate her tin-tackles out of a man this side o' the altar—or at the other side of it an' she suited? Did you, on your affidavy?"

"I did."

"You did not. 'Tis agin nature. Patsy is a polite, mannerly sort of a glugger-head, an' she tackled him his own way with a inside grip on his seven deadly sins same as her mother before her and her gran'mother —an' little ole great-gran'mother Eve her own self. Let me tell you somethin' you don't know about women but ought to—oh! all right! The conclusion is that she has Patsy like a bird sittin' stupid on a bough an' the scorpion crawlin' up on him on a hunderd legs."

"Your zoology is a bit mixed."

"What harm? The result is identic. If nothin' happens in the matter o' two weeks your friend Patsy is led to the halter; an' me conscience is clear now that I have it off me chest."

"But even if the affair is as bad as you make out —and it can't be—what can we do?"

"Nothin'. But still an' all I had a sort of a notion that the two of us together might bring home the flitch o' bacon as we often done before. Haven't you no notion at all?"

"I could take him a fishing trip to Scotland. We planned one last winter."

"You could so," he derided. "But he'd be back, wouldn't he? An' the widda would be here waiting for him, wouldn't she? But you could drownd him in the say, an' be hanged for a work o' charity. No, sir! His goose is cooked."

"Is Doherty completely out of the running?"

"A mile behind as long as the balance in the bank is in favour o' Patsy——"

He stopped dead. His eyes widened. His mouth gaped and snapped. He looked at me with awe.

"Cripersjoe! The sound man! You' given it to me. Wait! gi'e me time to take a peramble about this." His voice sank to a monotone as in communion with himself. "Mind you! Mind you! I never did care for Tom Doherty, the bloody little fly-off-the-handle. An' a dacent ould buck, Patsy Kelleher, for all the knots he ties in his tongue. Many's the fri'ndly pint he stood me when times was bad, an' yourself has a consate o' him that touches me fri'ndly feelin's."

"There wouldn't be many free drinks with a close-fisted wife in charge," I put in.

"You said it. Gi'e me time to think, will you? I got a glimmer o' daylight like the schreek o' dawn. Tom Doherty an' Patsy Kelleher! There they are like me two fingers, an' swop 'em across. Where are we then? Leave me to it."

He went deep into thought, and I watched him, wondering in what sink of roguery his mind wallowed. I myself did not see any way in which we dare interfere in Patrick Kelleher's matrimonial affair.

Thomasheen James did not get much time to evolve one of his nefarious schemes. Though deep in thought, he of sheer instinct still kept a watch over the half-door, and suddenly he started to his feet, emptied his mug in a single gulp, snatched at my quarter-full glass, thrust mug and glass into the cupboard, locked the door, gave a searching glance round and dropped back to his seat on the butter-box.

"Stay where you are," he whispered urgently, "an' take your bill'ard cue off me. Kepp your eye away from the door. Listen!"

I stayed where I was and listened. Light footsteps sounded faintly on the concrete path. They grew fainter as they approached, and ceased just beyond the half-door.

"Man-oh-man! Don't ask me to swallow that bit o' news!" The disbelief and astonishment in Thomasheen James's voice were almost too real. "I wouldn't never believe it of Patsy Kelleher. The soundest man in town!"

He winked at me, and I had no compunction in following his cue where a stealthy eavesdropper was concerned.

"There are the facts," I said. "Take them or leave them."

Thomasheen James's voice lifted in indignation.

"But are you askin' me to believe that he wouldn't settle your account for a measly hunder' quid?"

"He couldn't," I said with truth.

"Balderdash! Look here! If Patsy was sunk an' Tom Doherty set on foreclosing on the house, wouldn't the whole town know it? Wouldn't the bank know it?"

He looked at me hopefully and I had an inspiration.

"Playing the stock markets through an English bank is no game for an amateur."

"Bedam! that's the truth anyway. But what'll happen to poor Patsy? Do you think Tom'll keep him on as bar-tender?"

"He might. But I got a whisper to-day that Kelleher is hoping for another solution."

"Becripers, you're right!" cried Thomasheen James in surprise. "So that's it! Wo—wo—wo! this'll be news."

"Not a word," I warned him. "Give the poor devil a chance to pay his debts."

"But there's me duty to me employer?" said he doubtfully.

The sinking sun cast a shadow over the half-door and a hand clicked on the latch. A lady stood in the doorway and I rose to my feet, hat in hand.

She was not the widow? Or was she? She was younger than a widow should be—but many widows are. She was handsome in a blonde way, plump but shapely, and fashionably attired in a flowered teagown —but so are many young widows. And then I encountered her eyes, and the blue of them was clear and hard and discerningly cold. She must be the widow. Thomasheen James was on his feet too.

"A first cousin o' me own, ma'am," he began volubly, "a whiskey traveller from Belfast. Do you know what he's after tellin' me——?"

She stopped him promptly, with a hard polish to her voice.

"I do not care for gossip—or visitors—during your working hours, O'Doran."

Working hours! It was then eight o'clock in the evening.

She walked straight to the basket, lifted the cloth and looked calculatingly at the contents. I caught Thomasheen James's eye, and he winked at me. The scoundrel was a born gambler, and loved to play a game on a thin edge. He led another high card.

"They's a rumour in town, ma'am, about Tom Doherty foreclosing a mortgage he has——"

"Store these away in the pantry," she ordered sharply. "The lawn needs another cutting to take it over the week-end, and you haven't picked that pail of peas for lunch to-morrow. After that, don't forget to water the tomatoes and the hydrangea. Your supper will be waiting for you on the scullery shelf."

"To be sure, ma'am! to be sure!" said Thomasheen James agreeably, but the glance he turned on me was utterly virulent.

She went, not again glancing in my direction, and left behind in me a something approaching male abasedness. I felt, I knew, that my temerarious friend, Patrick Kelleher, was as good as lost unless Thomasheen James could produce a scheme that might involve mayhem, arson, felony, bribery, corruption, chicanery and the suborning of the State's lieges.

"That's the widda for you now!" said Thomasheen James with some warmth, "an' she has every dam' wan of us in her trousers pocket."

"You poor fool!" I mocked him. "You'll not convince that lady that Patrick Kelleher is only after her money."

"Continued droppin' wears away a limestone," misquoted Thomasheen James, "an' I dropped a gallon a'ready. You're not off, are you?"

"You heard her orders?" I said, moving towards the door. "Get on with the good work!"

"I don't object no way to a bit o' work in the cool o' the evenin'," he brazened. "After me apprenticeship is served, gintlemin o' me acquaintance'll be fallin' over aich other offerin' me twenty-five bob a week all found."

He led me out into the laneway and walked with me to the opening into the Main Street. His head was down and he was in deep thought. I found, not for the first time, that I had unreasoning confidence in his strategy, but I was careful to say:

"Don't you get us all into trouble. Good evening!"

"Wait a minit!" He laid a hand on my arm without raising his head. "I sort o' see the dawn o'er moors an' windy hills as the song says—but you'll ha' to advance me a small loan for expinses."

"Don't you get any wages?"

"All wages an' bills at the end o' the quarter. Le' me see! ten—fifteen bob would cover it." He thrust his other hand at me and was almost imperative. "Fifteen bob! gi'e it to me. 'Tis not for meself. Put it there an' ax no questions. I'll not be gettin' you into no trouble, for 'tis me own consarned windpipe I'm puttin' under the gullantine."

Without further protest I handed him over a pound note.

"You'll get your change—five bob," he said carelessly, but he still kept a retaining hand on my arm. "You wouldn't happen to be down this way agin next week?"

"Do you want me?"

"Nex' Widnesdy is the Big Fair at Ard-na-Righ. Could you be handy with the car in the heel o' the evenin'?"

"Why?"

"When I was in the Big War I kep' me lines open front an' rare——"

A clear sharp voice shrilled up the lane, and we both jumped. Mrs Byrne stood outside the wicket-door beckoning peremptorily. Thomasheen James and I went our separate ways hurriedly.

III

I borrowed my wife's car on Wednesday and went down to Ard-na-Righ in the heel of the evening as Thomasheen James had suggested. All during the week my interest and curiosity had been mounting up, and could now be described as eager.

The Big Fair had long been over when I got to Ard-na-Righ. An Irish cattle-fair starts at dawn and is over by midday. The streets were now empty, but showed many traces of the fair. The ladder was gone from the front of *The Short Grass Bar*, and I glanced up to see how the sign looked in its new paint. I blinked and looked again. I had to believe my own eyes.

That sign should have read: PATRICK KELLEHER, TEA WINE AND SPIRIT MERCHANT. It did not. A strip of canvas had been neatly fitted and tacked over the long board, and on its grey-white surface I read in staring black capitals: THOMAS O'DOHERTY, BUSYNESS AS PER USUAL.

I shut my mind against all surmise, and hurried into the bar. The front portion was without customers, but the sound of voices came from the partitioned alcove at the far end. I strode down there and looked in. Patrick Kelleher was drawing on the beer pulls behind the high zinc counter. Thomasheen James and a short, stout man in a tight-fitting black coat sat on stools outside. I thought for a moment that this second man was Thomasheen James's nefarious friend, Davy Hand, but when he turned his head I saw that he was a stranger, though I had seen his face somewhere before. Thomasheen James greeted me with a nonchalant gesture of head and hand.

"Where the carcase rots the magpies is gathered together," he said out of his varied and inaccurate reading. "I knew I could trust you, but 'twas a false alarm. The widda still loves me, but not Patsy no more. Come away in! Patsy's standin'."

"Make the acquaintance of my friend, Mr Tom Doherty!" introduced Patrick.

So this was the new proprietor? Perhaps. I remembered him now. He was chasing Thomasheen James out of town the last time I had seen him, but since then they had made up their quarrel "in the arms of neutrality." I made my voice cordial.

"I beg to congratulate Mr Doherty, and I am glad that he is keeping you on as a barman, Patrick."

Thomasheen James snorted and Doherty grinned sheepishly.

"A temporary arrangement—until the times do alter," explained Patrick Kelleher. He was doing his level best to look shamefaced, but the old dignified aplomb was breaking through in patches. I faced him warmly.

"Do you think this will get you anywhere, you old donkey?"

"Why not it?" Thomasheen James spoke up. "The rumours was goin' through the town the whole week same as a fire in shavin's. They was drink in saycret, an' bettin', an' stocks an' shares, an' a privit establishment o' depravity up in Dublin, an' every dam' thing. Becripers, sir! it'll take poor Patsy a year to live it all down."

"I can survive a year where I dreaded a life-sentence, my friend," said Patrick.

"An' when the sign was changed for the whole fair to behould with their open mouths in the mornin' the last coffin-nail was clinched an' there wasn't a doubtin' Saint Thomas o' Coventry to let a peep out o' him," said Thomasheen James. "Do you know what? I'd give a pound note—if I had it—to shake the hand o' the darin' man that pulled off that wan."

"Heaven help all poor women!" I said. "But I don't believe you've pulled off anything on a certain lady."

"I assume you'll change your mind when you cast your eye over that formal communication," said Patrick Kelleher.

He drew a folded note from his breast-pocket and presented it with a flourish. The communication was brief and formal indeed, but it barely suppressed violent recrimination.

> Mrs Catherine Byrne informs Mr Patrick Kelleher that his *interested* and gross advances are completely distasteful to her, that she desires to ignore him except as an example of what no gentleman should be, that all relations business and otherwise are to cease from this date, and he is hereby requested to furnish his account for the current quarter immediately.

Thomasheen James, trying to peep over my shoulder, was murmuring in my ear:

"A whole pound it must ha' cost the darin' fellow—in paint an' canvas, not forgettin' the tin tacks."

"Spell business!" I said in a low voice.

"Bus'ness! Why not I?"

"Go on! Spell it!"

"B-u-s—busy-ness. One s in the middle and two at the end. There you are!"

"The serpent always leaves a trail," I said, and turned to Patrick Kelleher. "Patrick, re this communication, have you furnished that account as requested?"

"Certainly—immediately."

"What account?" yelped Thomasheen James, leaping six inches off the floor.

"Mrs Byrne has withdrawn her custom——"

"Pokers o' hell, an' them rid-hot! Holy St Patrick, preserve us this day! Patsy Kelleher, an' God love you, don't tell me you sent the widda her account."

"An hour ago."

"Oh! You—you—you cuckoo in a wran's nest!" Words failed him. "After all I done for you! I'm ruinated past redimption."

"The widow still loves you," I said.

He whirled on me and gripped the lapel of my coat.

"Have you the car handy?"

"Why the hurry?"

"Let's be on the road," he urged, pulling at me. "The state of your garden is botherin' me the whole week."

"It can wait another five minutes. Finish your drink."

He abjured strong drink for ever with a flung palm.

"You'll give me time to have one," I said, firmly recovering my lapel.

"Very well so! Fill yourself to the back teeth. I'm off! I'll have an eye out for you on the road."

He smashed his hat down over his brow and made for the door long-striding.

He took a single step into the street, reared back on his heels, and stopped dead. Then he took a cautious step backwards, a second and a third, until he was again in the bar. He placed a hand on the counter as if about to vault it, but he was too late. The serpent's trail had led home.

A lady appeared at the entrance of the porch. This was exactly as it should be. The lady was Mrs Catherine Byrne, handsome, plump, younger-looking than ever. Behind her shoulder towered a uniformed sergeant of the Civic Guard.

The lady came forward with decision, and her pointing finger was no more pointed than her voice.

"There he is, Sergeant. Arrest him!"

The sergeant bore down on Thomasheen James, who retreated backwards with celerity.

"Keep your hands off o' me," he yelled. "I got me resources here."

I knew too much about Thomasheen James's resources, and began a hurried estimate of the cost of his weekly thirst. Good heavens! Jail was the only thing. I would never foot that bill.

Doherty crouched out of sight in a corner of the alcove, swearing softly to himself. I stood half-hidden by the partition. Patrick Kelleher thumped firmly on the counter at Thomasheen James's shoulder, and took control of the situation.

"Sergeant!" His voice was commanding. "Don't you dare arrest that man on my premises!"

The sergeant hesitated, and Thomasheen James moved back out of reach until brought up by the outside of the partition.

"What damn'd nonsense is this?" demanded Patrick sternly.

"Damn—Nonsense!" cried the lady. "I'll show you, Mr Kelleher. Don't let him evade you, Sergeant."

She jerked open her fashionable handbag, extracted a many-folded document, unfolded it stormily on the counter, slapped a gloved hand on it.

"There is your account. Look at it! On seven several dates you have charged me with a quarter-pound of something called gum drops. I don't use the things. Who does?"

I could not believe my ears. Gum drops! That is what she said. Patrick Kelleher looked surprised but remained in control.

"Gum drops! Most astonishing! Surely some mistake."

"Not mine."

"Permit me to verify this, madam."

He took the account to the front window where his big ledger lay open on a high desk. He flicked the leaves over and his voice carried.

"Yes-yes! Here it is. Mistress Catherine Byrne, Elm Vista." His finger ran down the page. "Gum drops—good for digestive purposes! No gum drops! Strange indeed!" His finger sought the opposite page. "Could it be that I interpolated an item from another folio? Dear me—dear me! a most reprehensible mistake. Mistress Byrne does not use or *need* these sour confections." His fountain-pen was busy for half a minute and he brought the account back to the lady. "Sorry, madam! There is your correct statement. Do you take discount for cash?"

She snatched the document and glared at him.

"Such business methods! No wonder you find yourself in your present plight."

"I shall not seek to change it, madam."

The lady was at a loss. She did the only thing possible. With a final glare round, she turned, and in a flurry of skirts left some chastened males behind her —and one stern one.

The sergeant was towering over Thomasheen James where he leaned fordone against the partition.

"A narrow squeak that time, Thomasheen James!" he said. "Watch out or I'll get you—in spite of your friends." He turned to Patrick Kelleher. "You can't throw dust in my eyes, Kelleher."

"Mister to you, Sergeant," said Patrick coldly.

"I am surprised at you treating a perfect lady like that."

"Our civic defenders should be always chivalrous. You would be more surprised if you had attempted a wrongful arrest. Anything else?"

194

"Not at present." The sergeant stalked out like a stiff-legged fighting Airedale terrier.

Thomasheen James was painfully trying to swallow his Adam's apple, and the blank unbelief on his face wrecked my composure. He turned up a feeble head to his saviour.

"Am—am I blind-deaf, Mr Kelleher?" he enquired weakly.

"Intermittently, my friend, but not on this occasion."

"But—but—she said nothin'—you heard her—not a dam' word about—about anything else."

Patrick laughed richly.

"You know the parable of the unjust steward?" he enquired.

"I might—wance. I'm thinkin' o' takin' to religion this very dam' minit in rale airnest. Was that the fellow that offered outrarg'ous wages?"

"'Take your pen and write twenty!' Something of a grafter, my nefarious ally! Thus I did. Wherever I saw two in a certain connection I took my pen and wrote one. Cheap at the price in the circumstances. But I was not aware of your own predilection for gum drops. Why did you not inform me?"

"They was for me dygestion," said Thomasheen James, and wiped his brow.

"Try another quarter-pound?" invited Patrick.

Mr Doherty hooted, and I slapped Thomasheen James's limp shoulder.

"You are losing your grip, my poor old gum drops," I said. "You had better come back to the simple life and straight abuse."

"True for you," he agreed with a transient humility. "Take me away with you an' put a spade in me hands."

And that is all.

But perhaps I should say that Mr Fly-off-the-handle Doherty failed to win the widow "for business purposes connected with his boot-shop in a bad way." Instead, she took that Civic Guard sergeant to husband, and made him an Inspector.

CHAPTER VIII

THOMASHEEN JAMES AND THE
BIRD-LOVER

I

A RECENT issue of a provincial Irish newspaper featured half a column under the following caption:

TREASONABLE ACTIVITIES ON THE
CARLOW BORDER;

and went on to relate how Sir Gaspard Guilcoyne, the famous bird-lover, and his nephew, Edward, on furlough from Burma, had captured the notorious Commandant Muldoon of the I.R.A.; how the commandant's brigade, some hundreds strong, had rescued its leader, nearly hanged Sir Gaspard, and maltreated the nephew with rifle-butts; and how the authorities, provided with several useful clues, hoped to make some arrests in the immediate future.

The Lord forbid!

My republican friends laugh at that half-column. They say that there were no activities on the Carlow border at that time, and that there was never a Commandant Muldoon in that or any other area. And yet, though my name is not Muldoon—! But I had better begin at the beginning.

I had been to London on business; only for a week, but I was mighty glad to get home. London, with its narrow streets twisting and turning so aimlessly about its helpless millions, afflicts me always with claustrophobia; and it was good to get back to my own airy lift above Dublin, with the plain of royal Meath spreading away to the far horizon below me, and the brown hills rolling behind into the welter of the Wicklow mountains.

That was the last week of October. I got home by the early morning boat, and my wife treated me to woodcock on toast for breakfast.

"Ha-ha! the cock are in again," I said in some excitement. "Where did these come from?"

"Oh, a friend in the country," said my wife carelessly. "Some more in the pantry—and a brace of pheasants."

"Colonel Sandys's coverts should be well stocked," I said. "To-morrow I'm going down to Celbridge to see."

The woodcock were in, and the great winter shooting of Ireland had begun. The first drift of them comes with the October moon all the way from Norway, over the grey North Sea, down through tumbled Scotland, and south and west all across Ireland to Bantry Bay; and there at the very extremity of the Old World the gallant small birds go seeking fifty miles out to sea before turning to drift slowly back to their breeding-grounds in Scandinavia.

I filled a pipe and sought my den with the intention of doing a little work, but I merely fingered through a pile of correspondence before unlatching a wall-cupboard and lifting out my battered leather gun-case. I opened it, looked inside, and stilled as if frozen, my mind blank for a moment.

My twelve-bore fowling-piece was old, but good as the best, with beautifully-chased barrels, a stock specially built to my left-handedness, and a balance as perfect as that of a Castle Connell trouting-rod. But at that breathless moment I was looking down at black steel barrels and a stock of poorly-grained elm. It was never a gun of mine.

I came alive with an explosive exclamation. I snapped stock and barrels together and knew the worst. The infernal article was clumsy, an inch too long for my shoulder, and if it weighed an ounce it weighed all of a dozen pounds. I recognised it for what it was: one of those mass-production Continental atrocities to be acquired for a fiver in any cheap ironmongery, and likely to blow the user's head off at the first discharge.

I jerked open the breech, looked, sniffed, and got my first clue. Streaked smudges of burned cordite showed on the polish of the bore; the thing had been recently used and hastily cleaned. Already I knew where to prosecute disastrous enquiry, and I did not hesitate. I went to the door and shouted. A good savage bark gives the attack a moral advantage from the start. I barked three times in as many seconds, and my wife came hurrying. She checked guiltily when she saw the gun in my hand.

"Dead Injun!" she said. "I'll be good after this."

"Where is my gun?" I was loudly calm.

"In your hands."

"This is not my gun."

"Of course it is your gun," insisted the woman to whom one gun was much the same as another.

This was leading nowhere. I swallowed some words and they burned all the way down. I began again.

"Is that incredible tough—is Thomasheen James about?"

"He was—before breakfast."

"He has been away?"

She hesitated, but I pressed her.

"When did he get back?"

"Two days ago—and slept the clock round."

"I will now cure him of his sleeping-sickness," I said, and started for the back door.

"Don't be a brute!" the woman called after me.

"Of course not," I shouted. "This rotten butt will go at the first lick, but wait till I get my hobnails on."

I did not find Thomasheen James, my-man-of-no-work, at once, which was lucky for him, but I was careful not to command his presence by shoutings. If I shouted, and a passing guilt weighed on him, he would slink into cover like a fox. So, after a hurried bustle through garden and orchard, I let some of my temper evaporate, and began a fairly patient search of the outhouses and his sleeping-quarters over the stable; and was finally rewarded by catching the soft rub of a shoe from the lean-to potting-shed at the back of the garage. I opened the door quietly and had my man cornered.

He sat under the skylight on one of the butterboxes I use for tomato plants, an old tweed hat of mine on the back of his sandy-red head, and smoke from an old pipe of mine curling about his prominent ears. He was meticulously painting his wheelbarrow, and, after one rapid glance in my direction, kept on doing so. He was loosing all his artistic urge on that unfortunate barrow. His favourite colour scheme is green, white, and orange—but he calls orange "yalla." The body of the barrow was vivid green, the rim and hub of the wheel a brilliant orange, and he was now picking out the spokes in staring white.

I contemplated him statically for half a minute. Then I drew in a long breath, and began.

"You lean, wiry, red-polled, quarter-tinker, ex-soldier, ex-naval stoker, but not ex-scoundrel——!"

"Cripersjoe!" he exclaimed admiringly. "You didn't laive your tongue behind you in London. Is the Caeff Royal still addicted be poets an' poetasses?"

"To hell with the Café Royal!" I said.

"A dam' dear place, o' course, for the likes o' us." He gave a passing glance at the gun in my hand. "I see your appetite is wetted be the taste o' woodcock. You'll be for Celbridge an' a crack at 'em. An' if you are, 'tis time we started—the barrow can wait."

He was about to rise to his feet, but my carefully temperate words glued him to the butter-box.

"You took the wrong gun out of pawn this time."

I was hinting at that notorious occasion in our early relationship when he had tried to pawn my new waders, had been made dance to a lively tune, and I had paid the piper.

He looked more closely at the gun I held up, and his eyes and his mouth widened. Thomasheen James knew about guns, and he knew as well as I did that the gadget in my hands was the worst sort of changeling.

Never before had I seen him struck so completely dumb. Surprise, dismay, perplexity knotted and spread on his face, and I could see his mind plunging into depths where there was no anchorage. For a time he wasn't even breathing. Then he moved his head forlornly from side to side, turned away, and resumed his painting with the same meticulous care. But his hand betrayed him, and he splashed white on the orange of the wheel-hub.

"So Mullarkey got the better of you once again?" I probed him.

He shook his head as if to clear it, and I knew that he was seeking desperately for inspiration. He played for time.

"You know dam' well I got a wake heart," he complained plaintively. "You hadn't no right to spring a thing like that on me unless they's murdher in your intintion."

"There is."

"A dam' pleasant disposition to bring home with you out o' London." He was grasping at straws fast as he could. "Off you wint as gay as a lark—an' you a fam'ly man—an' here was I with two thruppenny pieces to slip through the hole in me pants. What could I do but recapture me former occasion, an' me ashamed to approach the missus with me penuriosity? Women is forbidden ground to me. Wait! I will not ask you to raylint an' your temper the way it is for the nex' two days; but if I had two days, an' two days is all I want, you would have your gun back—out of Mullarkey the pawn."

He kept his head turned from me, and I knew that he was lying, and clutching on the rope I had thrown at him. He knew about my missing gun, but he did not want to tell me what had befallen it, or he had forgotten.

I set the black steel barrels against the wall; I moved the paint-pot into a corner, took the brush out of his lax fingers and thrust it deep into the pot (whereat he yelped anguishedly); and then I kicked out another empty butter-box and sat facing him. I knocked out my pipe and began to refill it, merely to keep hands and temper in place; and he sank his head between his hands and groaned. I said firmly:

"You will now tell me what you did with my gun?"

I gave him time, and after a while he lifted his head, placed his hands on his bony knees, and sighed deeply.

"I'll tell you all I know," he said resignedly. "I suppose 'tis the only way. The only way! I mind me seein' a play be that name once an' Martin Harvey doin' Sidney Cartoon. Says he——"

"Sidney Carton was guillotined at the end," I hinted grimly.

"So he was, the poor omadhaun! Many's the good man suffers for another's fau't, an' here am I sufferin' from Davy Hand."

"Was Davy in this with you?"

"He was the head an' tail of it, but, an' mark me words, his careerin' is now drawin' to a conclusion, for—an' you can throw it in me face if I fail you— the minit I clap me two eyes on him I'll prisint his windpipe in a knot to you you couldn't take out with your teeth."

Davy Hand was a Dublin Jackeen and a breeder-cum-stealer of fighting terriers. He was Thomasheen James's side-kick—or "butty" as Thomasheen James called it—and when the two were allied in a campaign it was time for all honest citizens to take cover.

"Go on with your complaint," I ordered.

II

Wait you now! (began Thomasheen James, again master of the situation, and his wits beginning to run in their greased grooves). Me mind was addled on me be dint of astonishment, an' if the truth has to be told you'll have to let me recapture me recollections

203

me own way. Lend me the loan o' that pouch, you'll get your gun back.

You had woodcock for breakfast—I smelled 'em. Meself is the universeal provider in this house, but I wouldn't gi'e a hoot out o' hell for all the woodcocks that ever flew out of a sally bush. Good sport all right! but gi'e me a chunk o' fat bacon an' a forkful o' greens—— Take it aisy! Tell me, did ever you hear of the Gasper Guilcoyne? Sir Gaspard Guilcoyne as you say, the bird-lover. That's him, and sich is his natural disposition; an' if wan o' his own cock-sparrows picks the two eyes out o' his head—but what's the use o' talkin'?

You don't know where the Gasper lives? Somewhere in the country! Somewhere in the country is right. Fifty murdherin' miles from where you're sittin' this minit on that box, be the side o' the Walsh Mountains on the Carlow border. A darlin' bit o' ground. The Gasper Guilcoyne owns maybe a thousan' acres of as nice a bit o' grouse moor as you'd get out o' Scotland, an' the side of a country of oak-woods covered for cock and pheasant, an' a track of arable land with partridges thick on the ground as spuds in a drill. The sort o' place to make a sportin' man like me an' you sell our sowls to the divil. But if the Gasper caught you lookin' at a bird crooked inside his boundary you'd find yourself lookin' straight through a gratin' in a cell wall the nex' sixty solid days.

A bird-sancshery he calls his place. Sancshery me eye! Every two or three, or maybe ten, years half o' the grouse die off be disease, an' the ground over-crowded; the magpies steals half the pheasant's clutch; the foxes an' stoats think 'tis heaven they're

204

in; an' from September on, the handy boys o' the counthryside enj'ys the risk o' jail an' a charge o' shot be draggin' a net over the coveys in the dark o' the moon. It stands to reason that a little judicial shootin'——

Right—all right! I am comin' at it me own way. Listen! Last Widnesday as ever was the Gasper went across to Rosslaire Harbour to meet a nephew o' his comin' home from Burmay or Ramgoon or the road to Mandalay—one o' them Eastern parts. The young lad has a good job beyant there, stampin' on the face o' the naygur for the glory o' the Impire an' a tidy salary. The Gasper went to Rosslaire be train, for the young rajar was bringin' his own car across, an' the both o' them was takin' a jaunt into the Wicklow mountains—two days.

Listen agin! On the same fittin' occasion the Gasper's gamekeeper—Nedeen Lowry—the Gasper is a mane oul' skinflint and does most o' his own keepin' with the sole help o' Nedeen—Nedeen Lowry, as I was sayin', borrowed the Gasper's car unbeknownst an' away up with him to Dublin to see his sister.

Pay heed to me now, for this is where history begins to relate itself. Nedeen's sister is a married woman, an' you wouldn't never guess the remnit of a man she's married to. Becripers! You have it. Davy Hand. Davy Hand, that little tub o' mud his own self, doomed to dismimbermint o' his windpipe this blessed an' holy day. Davy, I'll say that for him this last time, has a bright idea under his bowler hat wance in a while. He sint wan o' his guttersnipes up with a message to me, an' in the heel o' the evenin' me day's work done, an' well done, an' the timptation raysisted a resonable time, I wint down to meet him in *The Brazen Head* off the Quays with the intintion of arguin' him out o' the proposal in hand. His brother-in-law Nedeen Lowry was there too, an' Davy had a'ready softened him round the edges with two pints o' stout. Meself an' Davy had a word on the side, an' sure you know Davy, an' after that he introduced me to Nedeen. A honest sort o' *bosthoon* from the County of Mayo, with a sinse o' duty contrairy to the laws o' God an' man. It took us another two pints to make him amiable to the preposition we crowded on to him, the same bein' that meself an' Davy go down to the Walsh Mountains with him in the mornin' an' blast our destroyin' way through the Gasper Guilcoyne's covers. We kep' at him an' we kep' at him, an' after his fourth says he:

"Right ye are, me dacent buckos! Ye can come down, an' ye can blatther away at the woodcock, for that'll be no great harm an' they only passin' through. But," says he, "if I see wan or t'other o' ye, an' you're me own brother-in-law, Davy Hand—if I see ye as much as liftin' a barrel in the gineral direction of a cock-pheasant," says he, "I'll blow the eyetarnal daylights out of ye," says he, "if I see ye," he says.

"You won't see us," says Davy.

"I promise you that," says I. An' there we had him.

Well, sir! Nex' mornin' bright an' airly we went roarin' down be Baltinglass— What's that you say? I didn't, neither. I never stole your gun. I axed the missus for it fair an' dacent. Mind you, at the first she didn't take to the notion, but after a few remarks on your partic'larity for a woodcock on a slice o' gravy toast she relinted.

"If he ever finds out, Tommy," says she, "there'll be no livin' with him in this house."

206

"If he finds out, ma'am," says I, "he'll be a witch o' the deepest dye, for who's to tell him?"

Wo-wo-wo! Amn't I the misfortunate gran'son of a Wicklow tinker? Here you are a bare hour off the mail steamer an' you grindin' the saycrit out o' me gizzard. The saints preserve me till I lay me claws on Davy Hand. I'll rind——

Very well so! To make a long story short, we got down to the Gasper's place, an' we wasted no time on the road or later. It was a gallant day we had, I promise you, an' as nice a bit o' rough shootin' as ever you seen. I wouldn't let your gun out o' me hand for safety, and Nedeen Lowry gave Davy the Gasper's ould blunderbuss of a gun. I reco'nise it now. There it is standin' agin the wall, an' how the bloody wars it got there bates me unless 'twas the divil himself. I never laid no hand on it wance. The Gasper keeps it for shootin' an' missin' foxes an' poachers an' similiar varmint. Davy said it wasn't sich a hell of a bad weapon at all wance he got the hang of it, takin' a full sight an' allowin' four foot north an' be west. It knocked him flat on his back the first time he let loose, but on in the afternoon he was gettin' rale handy with it. I kep' well away from him all the same.

Manalive! I was in nate form that day. The bit of a gun knew it was in capacious hands at last, an', as sure as I'm tellin' you, I could feel it lift in me fingers. Right an' left, over the top of a holly, round the belly of a scarth o' briars, under the hang of a sally bush, it was all the wan to me, me bird came down same as you hit him with a cannon ball. Nine brace o' cock to me own gun, an' I wiped Nedeen Lowry's eye twice. That was prime shootin'.

Oh! the pheasant? Oh, well! them was a mistake,

as it might be. You know the way wan is apt to mistake wan bird for another gettin' on for dusk? You can so! size an' all. I did it meself—four times —an' Nedeen round the other corner of a plantation. "They might be a new breed o' cock," says I to meself. "They're runnin' big this year, an' I better make sure." They was cock a' right—cock-pheasants, an' a brace o' them seasonin' in the panthry this minute.

It was evenin' be this time, an', do you know? I finds meself up agin a heeautus. They's a blank spot in me retintiveness. It is a strange thing, an' I often noticed it before—I should see a doctor about it— but me adventures of an evenin' often escapes me retintion——

Whiskey! Who said anything about whiskey? Me! Me sleep twenty-four hours o' drunken reprose? Was it your wife told you that? Look you here to me! I said it before an' I'll say it agin, an' this is what I'll say: no man can put his trust in a woman, any woman at all, as long as he leaves the tongue in her head. Very well so! if 'twas a guess. It was a dam' good guess.

They was only two bottles, an' what is two bottles betune three? They was maybe a quart o' poteen as well that Nedeen got from his uncle in Mayo— harmless lookin' as spring water, an' a week old, an' a bite to it as if a mule kicked you in the pit o' the stomach. Maybe that's what done the damage! It could be, an' Davy Hand not used to it——

Wait! Wait now! Becripers! my mind is beginnin' to work, an' I got a glimpse here an' a glimpse there. . . . I have somethin'. . . . Let it come. . . .

There we are, the three o' us, in the Gasper's office-lib'ry. We got in be a frinch window accustomed to the blade of a knife under the latch. Th' ould butler was away to his bed down a mile o' stone passages an', besides, him deaf as a post. He's the only wan sleeps in the house, the Gasper havin' at laist enough sinse to be a bachelor man an' predilicted agin women. A girl from wan o' the lodges comes in every mornin' to rayconstruct the beds and brush the floors. Yes! there we was. . . . I see meself—or was it meself?—a seegar, one o' the Gasper's, in me eye-tooth an' me warblin' "*Me Uncle Dan McCann*" out o' th' other side o' me mouth. You know how it goes:

> "Have you seen Me Uncle Dan McCann?
> A typical bit of a Galway man,
> He landed in the U.S.A. in the year o' sixty-wan.
> Where he is sure I don't know.
> I searched him high, I searched him low,
> But back to Galway I can't go
> Without me Uncle Dan."

I was in tip-top tune, an' Nedeen Lowry liftin' the turn be throwin' a few grace-notes out of a mouth-organ—a great spud Nedeen under the mollification o' a ball o' malt. An' Davy Hand! As sure as I'm tellin' you, Davy was embracin' the Gasper's gun-case —I seen him puttin' the gun in it, canvas it was. There he was, a hand above an' a hand below, waltzin' the gun-case round a big desk in the middle o' the room in a complicated invintion o' his own betune a slip-jig an' a single reel. I took the case off of him, an' he on the floor, an' hung it up on the wall where we got it—a hook betune two presses o' ould books. And what is more, at the end o' the proceedin's, an' everything empty, I brought your leather case out the frinch window, in me two arms, like you'd be holdin' a baby, so careful I was. Nedeen Lowry whipped us down to Carlow on two wheels, an' we come home be the mornin' milk train——

Amn't I tellin' you I had your leather case in me two arms the whole time, and will you be tellin' me that that there ancient blunderbuss was inside it? What did I tell you? Davy Hand! Would you rather I prodded his backbone up through the roof of his skull, or would you be havin' him cheepin' like your canary an' he without a windpipe——?

Cripes'llmighty! Am I to be tellin' you all day? Didn't I see Davy, the blind crathur, puttin' a gun in the Gasper's canvas oul' case—an' what gun was it? An' didn't meself hang it on the wall betune two presses o' ould books? That's where your gun is, safe an' sound, this very minit. That's me story for you now, an' you are as wise as meself.

III

There was a silence then, weighted, and I sought in my mind for something really adequate to say. There was nothing really adequate, but before I could say anything Thomasheen James spoke with a fine disinterestedness.

"Maybe it would be better for you not to start killin' anywan till you get your gun back."

"How am I to get my gun back?" I shouted.

"Aisy—aisy! If that's all that's troublin' you, leave it in me hands." He brightened up. "If a man is ginerous enough to forgive a little bit of a blunder it will be no trouble for me to get Nedeen Lowry to slip in through the frinch window an' swop the guns."

"If my gun is still there!"

"Why not it? The Gasper never touches a trigger till the hin-pheasants begins to lay in springtime. Say the word!"

After a pause I said:

"When do you start?"

"Any minit you like." He lifted to his feet under the skylight and peered out and up into the clear October day. "I could be takin' the midday train to Carlow—if I had the price o' the fare—an' after that I'd ha' to foot it the seventeen miles to Guilcoyne House—an' foot it back as well, seein' Nedeen couldn't borry the car an' the ould Gasper at home. You'd ha' to gi'e me three days—maybe four——"

"Four days——?"

"Man—man! don't make me swally me heart that way! Sure it can't be helped now—an' you'll miss the first flight o' the cock." Again he looked up into the high October sky. "A gran' day, glory be! an' if we had a car handy we could do the job under five hours."

I confess that this thought—probably telepathic—had entered my own mind.

"Mind you," said Thomasheen James, "I am not suggestin' nothin'—only I thought you might like a wallop at the cock to-morrow, an' wan in every bush. An' besides, if I know anything, there wouldn't be as much as wan cheep of an objection to the loan o' the car—as a sort of a pacificator."

What I said after that does not come into the story. But Thomasheen James nodded approvingly.

"Fine—fine! Get it off your chest. I'm used to it be now."

I calmed down then and grumbled morosely.

"A pity, but I suppose I'll have to postpone your decapitation."

"My what?"

"Your decapitation."

"Becripersalive!" he shouted heatedly. "I'll allow no man to interfere with me organs."

My wife, indeed, loaned me her car with unusual readiness, and that afternoon Thomasheen James and I motored down by the flanks of the Walsh Mountains. The road along the foothills was winding and narrow, but we did the fifty miles in under two hours.

It was a perfect day in the late fall. The heather on the Wicklow hills had gone a ruddy brown, the beeches were browner still, the birches a pale gold, the aftergrass in the meadows a brilliant green; and the small white cloud islands floated high against the fragile, austere, sun-full sky. I was almost ready to forgive Thomasheen James.

Sir Gaspard Guilcoyne's wide estate is on the first swell of the Walsh Mountains, a lovely and a lonely country. It is backed by the easy lift of the rolling moors, clothed in ancient oak woods, and enclosed in its whole area by an eight-foot limestone wall. In its thousand and some acres there are only the old mansion-house, four gate lodges, and a row of workmen's cottages across the road from the main gates.

At five in the afternoon, the sun shining orange in our eyes, I drew up before the row of cottages, and Thomasheen James climbed out.

"Nedeen Lowry lives his lone with an ould wan to look after him," he explained. "I won't keep you long."

I watched him go up the garden path between berry bushes, tap at a door, and try the latch. Apparently the door was locked, an unusual thing in the country, for he stiffened up and rapped with sharp knuckles. Then he turned and nodded reassuringly in my direction, and the door opened at his shoulder to frame an old lady in a check apron.

They talked and gestured for ten minutes. I could stand that. In country Ireland, as in country Scotland, no business is ever done without a preliminary gossip lasting any time up to half an hour. In ten minutes Thomasheen James came leisurely down the garden path, and the old lady stood watching him from the doorway, calling a few final items. He got in beside me, his lean face seriously calm, and his washed-out blue eyes as cold as china.

"Drive on a piece," he said in a low, even tone. "I have something to tell you. Go slow!"

Without a word I let the car slip forward until a curve of the road took us out of sight of the cottages. I was fully aware that something had come undone.

"Stop here!" he directed, and I drew into the side of the road.

Opposite us the demesne wall turned away at right angles, and a grassy drive, paralleling the wall, made a long vista under overhanging hazels.

"What is it?" I enquired temperately.

"There is no dam' use at all losin' your timper twice in the wan day." He was taking precaution.

"What is wrong?" My tone lifted.

"Aisy now! Nothin' is wrong past mendin', only people do be dyin' at the wrong time—blast 'em! Nedeen Lowry is west in the County of Mayo buryin' his gran'mother. He'll be gone four days——"

"Four days!"

"Maybe a week," said Thomasheen James.

I did not lose my temper, or, rather, I did not loose it. I leant across him and flung the door open.

"Get out! Out you go! Four days or a week or four weeks, I don't mind, you'll hang about here till Lowry returns, and you will get me my gun by hook or by crook. Out you get! and take that dam' blunderbuss with you."

"Whatever you say," he agreed with resigned humility. He extended one foot over the running-board and looked aside at me. "You wouldn't be wantin' me to take a bit of a risk?"

"Risk your neck and break it. Certainly!"

"If I was to go down on me two binded knees would you listen to me for jest wan minute?"

"Fire away! I have the evening before me."

He drew in his foot but left the door open.

"I been thinkin'. Often enough, the Lord knows, I do be thinkin' for more than meself. Maybe I'm wrong, an' whether I am or not you'll say so; there's Nedeen out o' reach in far Mayo, but they's the big house over that wall an' only half a mile from where we are. That's plain fact for you."

"Go on!"

"They's the big house then, an' divil the wan in it but the Gasper Guilcoyne an' the Hinjoo nephew—for we can forget the ould butler an' him deaf as a post. You mind me tellin' you the way we got in last week? a frinch window at the side with a catch handy to the blade of a knife! Are you gettin' me point?"

"Do you mean——?"

"I do. What's to prevent me slippin' in the idintical same way agin once more an' rescuin' your gun off the wall? I ask you? I just ask you?"

"Housebreaking in broad daylight?"

"Restorin' an exchange o' property an' not a thing else—and who said anything about daylight? This has to be done circumspeck. Listen! The moon will be three-quarters full comin' on midnight, the butler will be asleep as well as deaf. That's number two. Number three, the Gasper is hard o' hearin' himself——"

"Number four is the nephew, and he's not deaf, is he?"

"No, but after the way o' the Impire builders amongst the infayrior races he'll be addicted to orderly habits be poundin' his ear between stated times for eight hours. It would be no trouble at all to me, I tell you, an' if they's a risk, who's takin' it? An' they's the cock waitin' on you to-morrow."

"Do you suggest that we are to hang round here till midnight?"

"For the whole world to see an' remimber? No, sir! I amn't that bloody foolish. We could run across to Carlow for a bite—and a sup, an' there might be a picture-house as well as our ch'ice o' pubs. An' we could daunder back this way be eleven, ready an' willin' an' full o' fun. Look! they's that grass track on be the wall an' a hazel bush to shove the car under while you gev me a leg-up to the copin'. You'd have your gun in your arms in less than half an hour. Better that stratagim if you can."

"I can, and I should have thought of it before now. I can drive right up to Sir Gaspard Guilcoyne's front door and explain the whole business to him——"

"You can. Becripers! but you can. And poor Nedeen Lowry to suffer for it in an' out o' jail."

"As he deserves."

"Very well so! That lets me out of it, an' fareyou-well." Again he extended a foot over the running-board.

"Shut that door!" I barked, and stamped on the self-starter.

IV

We were back from Carlow by lonely roads shortly after eleven, and had the car snugly parked under a hazel a safe distance up the grass drive.

The night was fine, with a shrewd breeze out of the north-east, and only the filmiest of clouds drifted across the stars pale in the light of a moon so full and bright that one might almost read a printed page.

Thomasheen James opened the car door, thrust out a long neck, and looked at the moon over the tops of the half-bare trees. His voice, communing with himself, was soothing, pensive, and resigned.

"A gran' night, glory be to God, for a expert honest bit o' poachin'—an' no wan in all the world but deaf an' sleepy people! A cock-pheasant roostin' on a branch ten feet up, an' you could count the feathers in his tail! A quarter-charge o' powder an' three pellits o' number four, an' the puff of it wouldn't wake a wran! I found a few ca'tridges in me pocket be accident, an' prepared wan or two in the lavattery beyont in Carlow——"

I pushed him forcefully and got out behind him.

"None of that!" I whispered violently. "Do you hear me? None of that!"

"Only talkin' to meself I was. Laive be!"

"I'll give you half an hour. Not more! Half an hour, and after that you can tramp it to Dublin—if you are not in the lock-up for poaching."

"Have it your own way! Come on, an' give me a leg-up."

I heaved him to the coping of the eight-foot wall, and reached him the Guilcoyne gun wrapped in an old sack. Sitting astride, he peered into the wood beyond, and then leaned down to whisper to me, an easy confidence in his voice. I had to admire the nerve of him.

"The goin' looks dead aisy. Gi'e me that half-hour good, an' thin laive me to me own deevices—if that's your way. If the worst comes to the worst don't be feart, I'll keep me trap shut. An' listen! try an' rimimber a forgot prayer for me sowl in torment." There followed a rustle and a thud where he dropped into the dead leaves on the inner side of the wall.

I went back into the car and switched the dashboard light on and off. The panel-clock showed 11.25. I would give him till midnight, and not a minute longer. I filled a pipe slowly and smoked, and I slowly realised the folly of letting Thomasheen James loose in stocked coverts, a gun in his hand. I should have searched him for those prepared cartridges.

After what seemed a long time I again switched on the light. The time was 11.40; and later, 11.50. Something must happen soon. I opened the door carefully and set an ear to the opening. There were no sounds but a far sighing of the breeze and the muted rustle of dying leaves.

But even as I listened there came to my ears out of the heart of the wood a small explosive puff "that wouldn't wake a wran"; not a detonation but a softened smack that I might not have noticed at all had I not been intently listening.

"Heavens! the scoundrel is at it."

217

Two minutes later came a second small explosion, then a third, and, after a longer pause, a fourth. But that fourth, coming directly down-wind, was either close at hand or it was the detonation of a full charge at a distance.

I got out of the car at that juncture. I began to seethe. I slipped across the grass to the shadow of the wall, and felt over the rough stones for a finger-purchase. I found one and then another, and with the energy of anger clawed myself on to the coping. There I crouched astride and glared into the wood. The oak trees, wide-planted and still in half-leafage, cast heavy shadows under the moon, and the scattered clumps of cover were crouching black monsters. Nothing moved across the patches of moonlight, and there was now no sound other than the wind in the leaves.

For minutes I watched and listened, and slowly anxiety began to oust anger. If Thomasheen James had fired that last shot he should have been with me long ere this. It had sounded like a good hard explosion close at hand, and if he had been using that dangerous Guilcoyne gun—! I had to do something. I don't suppose that at any time I had intended leaving Thomasheen James in the lurch, and though he was a mutinous tough I could not help admiring the cool daredevilry of him as a poacher. And yet, he was not physically brave.

I slid down the back of the wall, which was not more than five feet high on the demesne side, and after reconnoitring the ground ahead ventured across the open towards the trees. That was not the first time I had been in a wood on a moonlit night, and I had a fair-enough technique in the way of procedure.

The moon and the breeze gave me my line, and the clumps of undergrowth provided splendid dodging-points.

I flitted forward from one clump to another, crouched in the deep shade, examined the ground ahead, and again flitted forward: and as I crouched I whistled softly a bar of a tune that Thomasheen James would at once recognise: "*My Uncle Dan McCann.*"

And then it happened.

The two men stalking me were adepts in game-watching and thief-catching, and one of them knew the ground like the palm of his hand. Careful though I was, they manœuvred about me so that I walked right into their ambush. I had backed into a thicket of pliable sallaghs and was scrutinising a patch of open ground when the branches swished behind me and two strong tentacles pinned my arms to my sides.

"Got you, my lad!" A crisp voice snapped above my head, and, forthwith, I was lifted off my feet and swung out into the moonlight. That crushing lift and wrench apprised me of the quality of the muscle that held me.

We were out in the full moonlight, and I twisted my head to look up and over my shoulder. My captor was young and very tall, bare-headed, and the moon glinted on his light eyes and shone through his tossed light hair.

Another voice spoke behind him.

"Let me have a look at him, Ted!"

A second man, also tall, came round in front of me, and bent to peer into my face. An oldish man with rugged features and shadows under the strong bones.

"No! he's not one of my men," he said. "I don't

know him—he's not a native of this place." His deft
hands went over me quickly. "Not armed either!
Where is your gun, fellow?"

"I hadn't a gun." I tried to hold my voice steady.

"He shot—at least twice," said my captor over
my head.

The older man kicked round in the base of the
sallaghs, and swore at me.

"Where is your gun, damn you?"

"I have no gun—damn you!" I said, not so cool
as I intended, and got a savage shake.

"Very good!" he snapped. "We'll find it in the
morning. Let's take him up to the house, Ted, and
have a good look."

"Right you are, Uncle!" said my captor cheerfully.
"Get along, my little dacoit!" He smartly changed
his grip to the back of my neck and thrust me forward
at arm's length.

It happened as quickly as I have told it, and I knew
that I was in the hands of Sir Gaspard Guilcoyne, or,
rather, physically in the hands of his nephew—Ted
his name—from the East Indies. I had met that
word dacoit in Kipling. It is, I believe, Burmese
for robber.

The young man treated me with unnecessary rough-
ness as he pushed me along, driving his knuckles into
my spinal column and tightening my shirt-band so
that I had difficulty in breathing. I began to dislike
him. If only Thomasheen James would erupt from
somewhere we might try our native toughness against
brute strength. But where was Thomasheen James?
Where in heaven was that—that—— But no! I must
not get hot under the collar—though it was choking me.

The thing I had to do now, while I had time, was

to decide on my attitude in the immediate future. Such was the formula I had read somewhere. Living a rather sheltered life, until the advent of Thomasheen James, I had often wondered how I might react in circumstances not unlike this. Here was my chance to make good. The thing to be done immediately was as clear as the moon: play the game close to my chest and not look too far ahead for a new deal. Later on—— But what would my wife say?—and Thomasheen James?

We came out on the drive before the house, and the moonlight glinted on a double row of blank windows. It was the usual type of Irish Georgian country mansion: a great, ugly, four-square block of rough-cast with a columned portico jutting meagrely over the front entrance.

Young Ted thrust me up four stone steps under the portico, and Sir Gaspard opened a huge door that led into a high wide hall dimly lit by a hanging lanthorn. He led on down a long, echoing stone passage and round a corner into a large room that I recognised from Thomasheen James's description as the office-library. There I was thrust into a corner beyond the big desk, swung smartly round, and released. Sir Gaspard turned up a paraffin-lamp on the desk and glared at me with malevolence.

"Small but tough-looking!" remarked Ted.

I am not big, and at the moment I was attired in rough homespun, but, while making no claim to gentility, I do not think that "tough-looking" was quite fair. I was disliking this young proconsul more and more.

"An absolute stranger to me," said Sir Gaspard. "Anything to say for yourself, my man?"

"Not at the moment," I said, "but I was not poaching."

"A straight lie," said the nephew. "He was poaching, and with a gun."

The old man nodded his head.

"Let him reserve his defence if he wants to. It will not serve him."

"What shall we do with him, Uncle?"

The uncle was prompt and experienced in dealing with poachers.

"Get him off our hands as soon as possible," he said. "I'm used to this sort of thing, Ted, in this damn'd country. I'll get the car out and we'll run him across to the Guard barracks at Elton Cross. I show no mercy to dam' scoundrels disturbing my coverts."

"Only a dam' fool," I said.

"Tell that to the Justice. Sure you can hold him, Ted, while I get the car out?"

"Just let him try anything," said Ted confidently.

"Give me three minutes," said the prompt old poacher-fighter, hurrying from the room.

I leant against the wall, realising that the game was going dead against me. My guard stood facing me by the desk corner. He was big—too big—with high square shoulders and a jaw like a paving-stone.

I looked round the room. The flat-topped desk was scattered with papers, there were estate-maps on the wall, shelves holding black-japanned boxes, several book-cases, and—yes! between two book-cases a canvas gun-case hanging from a hook. It was not a stiffened case, and I could see that there was a gun inside it. That gun was mine, almost within reach, and I could do nothing about it. The young man was talking.

"Care to try anything?" he invited.

"No hurry," I said.

"Three minutes only. Too dam' smart, weren't you? Went dacoity, and thought you'd make a killing while Lowry was away, what?"

"Dacoity! That's Burmese?"

"Knowledgeable sort o' cuss, ain't you? We know how to deal with thugs like you out there."

"You are in Ireland now, you know?"

"Fine! Let's see what you can do."

"You will," I said, with a confidence I did not feel.

Behind his high shoulders, in the side-wall, heavy drawn curtains reached the floor, and I assumed that the french window mentioned by Thomasheen James was behind them. For no reason at all I had something definable as faith in that accomplice of mine, and my eyes would keep straying to those curtains. Once, and my pulses stirred, I thought I saw them shiver.

I let my eyes move carelessly about the room, and, again, brought them carelessly back to the curtains. Even as I looked they tremored as in a draught, and softly moved apart by a single inch. This time I had sense enough to turn my eyes up to the cornice and keep them there. My heart I felt high up in my breast.

The strain that was in the room was getting my truculent young guard. He swore irritably.

"Damn that old bus! Slow as ever to start!"

"It might not start at all," I said remotely.

"No hope, sonny! It always does."

"Not to-night, you poor mutt."

"Damn you! be careful——"

And there, and dramatically right, a cold voice spoke behind him—cold and quiet and deadly.

"Put them up! Up with them!"

The young man whirled and his hands went up. They surely went up, and they stayed up.

I brought my eyes down to the french window. A truly formidable desperado out of the night filled it. A red handkerchief, tied cowboy fashion, hid the lower part of his face; a tweed hat was pulled low on his brow; and between the two one cold and pitiless eye looked out. The other eye was shut. I knew that red handkerchief, the hat had once been mine, but the steel eye belonged to Thomasheen James and to no one else. It was looking unwinkingly along the double barrels of a shot-gun, and the muzzle was pointed unwaveringly dead on young Ted's midriff. I could see the two black rings, and they did not once waver. And his voice coaxed me with cold savagery.

"Say the word, Commandant Muldoon! Say the word an' I'll blow his interials through his backbone! Say the word for me! One—two——"

My name is not Muldoon, and I am not a commandant in any army, but I took the hint.

"No, Sergeant! Not yet. He doesn't know Ireland, and must have his one chance. Have you a guard on Guilcoyne—in the garage?"

"He's locked in it, sir. The boys are looking for a bit of rope to hang him. I've a squad in front an' wan behind me. Let me spatter the legs of the Hinjoo anyway."

"Not if he keeps his hands up. Set a guard on the window. We'll hold this lad for an hour. After that he can go to—Burma."

I had to go within the young man's reach as I sidled round the desk, and I watched him carefully. He had grit in abundance. I saw his hands twitch and fling for my shoulders. His idea, no doubt, was to grapple me as a shield and hurl himself on the gunman.

But Thomasheen James was no slouch. As the young man's eyes left his, Thomasheen James came forward in two long strides, his weapon at the lunge, and the muzzle dunted fair on the young man's midriff. He grunted like an ox stricken. His head came down, his hands were already touching my shoulder, and I brought my left up for all it was worth. I used have a useful left hand, and that paving-stone jaw was an easy mark. His head jerked, he folded over, went down on his knees, clasped himself with both arms, and began to whoop like a chicken in a struggle to get his wind back.

"That'll hold the naygur," cried Thomasheen James. "Let us out and hang the Gasper."

We went. There was no need to spread ourselves further. The curtain swished behind me, and Thomasheen James had hold of my arm.

"This way!" he hissed. We skirted the corner of the house into the moonlight. "Let us trot." We trotted.

As we loped past the arched gateway giving on the out-premises a clamour and a clanging came to my ears. A door was being furiously kicked somewhere to the accompaniment of a stentorian bellow.

"The ould fella," said Thomasheen James. "I banged the door on him an' threw the kay over the roof. He'll be some time gettin' out, an' the window barred. Let us keep trottin'."

But at the first of the trees I stopped in my tracks and exclaimed warmly.

"What is it this time?" he enquired peevishly.

"My gun! We left it hanging on the wall."

"Haven't you eyes in your head? I have your gun in me hands. That was the first thing I done. Run on, an' I'll overtake you in half a jiffy."

There is hardly anything more really worth the telling.

We got home safely by devious roads through the glens of Wicklow, and safely stabled my wife's car at four o'clock in the morning. The moon was low then and shone weirdly through the stripped orchard trees, and all the world was wan and dead and burnt out all round us. A sad and careless peace came over me, and I knew that revenge and anger and resentment were dust in the mouth.

Thomasheen James sighed not unhappily at my shoulder.

"Well—oh, well! That's another little misfortunate adventure put by us. We're a good team, me an' you. They had me cornered in a holly bush when you took their attintion to yourself, an' after that I was able to bring up the horse foot an' artillery, Gineral Muldoon. Haven't we the gay life sometimes!"

"It is life anyway," I said mildly, smoothing a hand on the barrels of my nearly too-precious gun. "Let it go on. Come into the kitchen and we'll have a last drink."

"Me gallant man! I wouldn't never doubt you. Lead me on!"

In the kitchen I switched on the light and looked round at Thomasheen James. He was carrying a sack under his arm, and it was not empty.

"Hell!" I exclaimed. "You've not brought that brute of a gun back here?"

"Only a souvenoir."

He threw the sack on the table and heeled out its contents. There were four cock-pheasants in full plumage.

"I'm a bit of a bird-lover meself," said Thomasheen James.

CHAPTER IX

THOMASHEEN JAMES AND THE DEEPSEA-PILOT CAP

I

IT was my wife's sense of the ridiculous that gave a first impetus to this misadventure of Thomasheen James, my-man-of-no-work. It reached its inevitable conclusion as far as I was concerned.

She and I had gone far afield at last: as far as Boston and New York and Philadelphia, and even Washington its very self; and after a long six weeks we had arrived back home, she purring, and I vowing that for the next ten or two-score years a team of wild horses could not tear me away from my own Dublin foothills.

We got home on a fine hot June morning, and found Thomasheen James using extraordinary energy on the lawn-mower. He was giving our small spread of grass a second run-over, but the colour and texture of the sheared surface told me that that small lawn had been cut the previous day for the first time in weeks. He lifted his hand aloofly at us and went on pushing at the rate of knots.

"Really, he is a disgrace," deplored my wife. "If our American friends saw him now! Just look at him!"

"Your eye is out of tune," I said. "That's his usual hot-weather rig."

But he was, indeed, a disgraceful spectacle. His

clipped, congested, sandy poll gleamed in the sun above a neck of copper; he was without jacket or vest, his braces looped to his knees, and his shirt-sleeves had been stagged off at the shoulders; one wiry, freckled forearm was tattooed with a blue heart pierced by a red arrow, and a dancing-girl rippled nakedly on an inadequate biceps; also he was barefooted, his ragged trousers were folded to below the knee, and the rather flamboyant legs of an old pair of pyjamas, substitute for underwear, hung to his lemon heels. Otherwise he was presentable enough, and everything was scrupulously clean.

"I will *not* have him going round like that before the neighbours," said my wife definitely. "You must speak to him."

"Not our first day home—oh, all right! I'll drop him a gentle hint later on."

That very afternoon I ran him down in the kitchen garden. He was sitting on the tail of his empty barrow in the shade of the privet hedge, his chin propped on the handle of a yard sweeping-brush, and one foot holding down his enemy the digging-fork. The garden was surprisingly clear of live weeds, but the ones slain by a dutch hoe had not had time to wither in the sun.

"Did you bring it home to me?" he enquired promptly.

"You ragamuffin! You would disgrace any respectable scarecrow," I began, dropping my gentle hint.

"Glory be! The Yanks left you your tongue anyway. You brought it back with you in prime order. But did you bring back the deepsea-pilot cap you promised me? Oh! You have it there behind

your back? I wouldn't never doubt you, me gallant
man! Gi'e me a peep at it!"

Before leaving for the States I had idly and foolishly
enquired if he would like a piece of New York, and
he had promptly answered:

"I tell you what I would like. A deepsea-pilot
cap—you can't get 'em in Dublin nowhere."

"A deepsea-pilot!"

"What else? Thim shape o' caps has been me
fancy since me days in the Navy beltin' the Turks—
but mostly gettin' belted. You know? Black cloth
not too flat in the crown and not ejectin' too much
over me ears, satin braid for trimmin's, an' a silk
coard looped in a kiss-me-quick knot. An' whatever
you do, don't let no Yankee robber saddle you with
a shiny peak. I wouldn't be seen dead in a shiny
peak. Half a dollar it will cost you, not more, size
six-a-half. I've a small skull."

A deepsea pilot! That was a new genus to me,
and I am still wondering if there is such. A friend in
New York had no doubts, and with the aid of a marine
outfitter invented me an article to the required specifications. It cost four dollars.

I now handed this creation to Thomasheen James,
and waited silently for his devastating criticism. I
expected nothing less out of a long experience.

He said nothing for quite a time. He turned the
cap this way and that, twisted his head at all angles
to get different perspectives, felt it over, smoothed it,
tried his teeth on the peak, frowned in the deepest
consideration. And then his china-blue eyes lit up,
and I breathed freely.

"Be the powders o' war! Me gallant fri'nd! This
is the identical bloody article. This is the elegantest

affair in caps since Noah sailed the sea, an' will you take a feel o' that cultured material? See that peak! That's the dead downright slant—steep but not too steep—I had in me mind's eye. I wonder how does it fit me?"

He placed it carefully aslant over one eye like a certain famous admiral, and the simplest sailor that ever sailed the sea would have known him for a fraud.

"Dammit! 'Tis half a size too big for me. But what harm? Me head is swellin' a'ready. How do I look?"

"The cap is fine," I said, "but you look like the wrath-to-come, and your pants would disgrace Noah."

He looked down at himself and nodded, holding his cap on.

"I'll not deny it. An' if I am wearin' a shamefaced pair o' pants, who left me a whole six weeks in a state of dishability? Do you know this? Thim pair o' pants you're lookin' at with contimpt cost me the chance of a good dinner last week. Davy Hand was takin' me to the Metropolitian Bird-fancier's Annual Banket at *The Frozen Head*, but when he saw me best pants he mutinied an' took his wife instead. Maybe it was as well I didn't go, for Davy was in bed three days with inframation o' the stumach. I was down to see him. 'Two knifes an' two forks they gev us,' says he, boastin', 'an' three varieties o' mate—bacon an' beans, pork an' napplesauce, an' ham an' greens.' An' says I to him, jokin': 'You'll be tellin' me next they gev ye napkins?' 'They did,' says he. 'What did ye do with them?' says I. 'We ate 'em,' says he. The poor ig'orant Jackeen! Speakin' o' pants——"

"I can let you have another old pair of flannel bags."

"What's wrong with 'em? No wan but yourself 'ud think o' matchin' a pair o' flannen pants with a genteel cap the like o' this. 'Tis not done, me dear sir. If you want to know, I have suitable trouser wear marked down a'ready in Mullarkey the pawn's window. To look at 'em you'd say they was dyed and decorated to go special with this cap o' mine." He took the cap off and smoothed it affectionately. "The same exack cultured black material, and the same two strips o' braid down the seam, an' you could shave yourself with the split in 'em."

"Evening-dress trousers, probably."

"Let 'em! They'd fit aiqually well of a Sunday mornin'. With the cap and pants an' that black half-mornin' coat the missus wouldn't let you wear at Donovan's weddin', becripers, sir! you wouldn't be ashamed o' me at a Castle Ball. Mullarkey has a ten-shillin' ticket on the pants, an' they're cheap at the price—if I had it."

"If you haven't the price you haven't the pants," I said heartlessly. "My wife objects to your present rig, but she'd throw a fit if she saw your sartorial ambitions satisfied."

"If you didn't use langwidge to hide plain talk," he said disgustedly, "you wouldn't be worth listenin' to."

But when I told my wife of Thomasheen James's sartorial ambitions her sense of the ridiculous submerged her respect, such as it was, for the conventions.

"Oh, glory!" she chuckled. "I can see him—I must see him. Dress trousers, ancient morning-coat, and that ridiculous sailor cap——"

"A deepsea-pilot cap," I corrected her.

"Please—oh, please! Let him have that ten shillings."

"That's a good coat yet for a funeral or two——"

"If you don't, I will."

"In that case I don't," I said.

But I did. I found Thomasheen James in the tool-shed wrapping his deepsea-pilot cap in tissue paper. I tendered him a pound note. He accepted it and subjected it to careful scrutiny. Then he turned an oblique eye in my direction.

"I am not making a mistake," I answered that oblique look. "That is a twenty-shilling note—the smallest I have, unfortunately. Get your black pants out of the pawnshop, and bring me back ten shillings change."

"I wouldn't doubt the missus!" he said. "She'd know the ettikwet o' fashion. There'll be the price o' the bus fare—an' a hot day an' all——"

"Ten shillings change," I said firmly, "and absolutely no explanations accepted."

"Very well so! You know you can trust me."

I knew that I could not, and that my ten shillings were in extreme danger. As a matter of fact, I meant him to have the pound, and merely insisted on the change hoping to get him back reasonably sober. Well, I had provided him with the sinews of war and was due what I richly deserved.

Next morning Thomasheen James went to town, and I saw him off with a final word of warning. He was still ragged, but scrubbed and shaven, his deepsea-pilot cap jauntily atilt over one eye, and his boots black-glistening in the sun. He could put a shine on leather to make a New York bootblack envious, and that is saying some.

He waved a hand at me as he went out the gate, and called cheerfully:

233

"I'll be back to water the tomatoes in the early evenin'—laive them be."

He was not back early or late that evening, and I watered the tomatoes myself.

But two o'clock in the morning our bedroom phone rang and kept on ringing. I pretended to be asleep, and my wife took the call. I heard her exclaim, and then the receiver punched me between the shoulders.

"You are not asleep?—it is for you. Sergeant Joe O'Dowd!"

"Had you your car out to-day?"

"No. Joe is laughing."

He was still laughing, right into my ear.

"Nice hour for a joke, Joseph," I growled. "What is it now?"

"It is on you," said Joseph. "Do you know a couple o' gents named David Hand and Thomas James O'Doran?"

Detective-Sergeant Joe O'Dowd is a friend of long standing, and he knows Davy Hand and Thomasheen James about as well as I do. When I heard their names coupled I knew that peaceful citizens somewhere had suffered catastrophe. I said cautiously:

"I don't know them any more."

"Davy is here, and wants me to send you a message. He's afraid the phone'll bite him."

"Where is Thomasheen James?"

"He's pulled."

"He's what?"

"Pulled! In the lock-up at Store Street Station."

"Manslaughter?"

"Oh, the usual—nothing at all! Drunk and disorderly, speechifying to the obstruction of traffic, resisting arrest, and a few little things like that."

"Nothing at all, as you say. Was he wearing a deepsea-pilot cap and evening-dress trousers?"

"He might be coming home from a ball right enough."

"Is Davy Hand pulled too?"

"He's thrown himself on my mercy, but whatever you say. He's been in the wars all right."

"Give me his message first!"

"He says that you are the only gintleman in all Dublin or the three counties round it that'll swear blind to the peaceability of Thomasheen James in normal occasions. That's right."

"Does he expect me to go in and bail Thomasheen James out—at this hour?"

"He is much safer in Store Street for the night. Leave him. The Police Court is in the morning— Green Street, eleven a.m.—and Davy intimates that Thomasheen James is broke."

"Broke!"

"Dead broke—not a wing on him. Twenty shillings fine—or twenty days hard! You'll be in?"

"He can go to ——"

"You are to blame giving him money to make an exhibition of himself."

"You can accompany him, Mr O'Dowd."

I slammed the receiver on its rest and explained hotly to my wife. She said almost gleefully:

"You did not foresee the extras when you paid four dollars for that silly cap."

"And who started the extras?" I demanded bitterly.

There followed some recriminations, and I finally turned my back, consoled by the knowledge that for the next twenty days Thomasheen James would be exactly where I wanted him.

Eleven of the clock found me on a yellow pine bench at the back of Green Street Police Court, still cursing myself a little. I will not detail any of the considerations—nor any of my wife's—that impelled me to be there. They would sound too lame.

Before entering the Court I had seen the tubby figure of Davy Hand in the distance, but he had seen me first and switched round a corner with celerity.

Dublin is no longer, if it ever was, a drunken and disorderly town, and there was not much doing in Court that morning. A couple of draggled ladies, a few minor motor-car offences, some petty larcenies, two or three drunks, and Thomasheen James. The proceedings were brief and laconically just. A name called loudly, a worse-for-wear figure appearing above the Dock rail, a few stereotyped words from the police, the beginning of too many from the victim, and the Justice, eye and ear cocked, interrupting with: "Ten shillings or ten days hard." Occasionally there was the Irish flash of wit and the ready retort, but the fine or jail sentence never varied until Thomasheen James broke the sequence.

I sat there remembering a day at Ard-na-Righ when he was fined three pounds for demolishing a showman, and I had paid it. I was prudent enough now not to make a resolution at the risk of breaking it within ten minutes. I just hoped for the best.

I heard his name called, and watched for the appearance of his sandy poll from the stairs leading up from the prisoners' room. The head emerged and it was bare, and unmarked except for a slight graze above one eye; the eyes that took in the whole Court-room at one sweeping glance were washed-out but shameless; his shirt collar was torn, and his pants—what I could see of them—were disreputable as ever. There was no sign anywhere of his deepsea-pilot cap or those evening-dress trousers, but I hoped that these might be downstairs. He did not look directly at me, but I knew that he knew that I was there.

Two police witnesses gave their evidence without stressing in any way that the case was out of the ordinary, but the evidence was damning. There was drunkenness but not incapableness, there was disorderly conduct, there was speechifying from a soap-box, disturbance of traffic, abusive language, resistance to arrest verging on riot, and injury to a policeman's night helmet. How he was to explain away these things to me later on I could not imagine, but he would. He would even try it on with the experienced Justice.

The Justice looked indifferently at him, and Thomasheen James accepted the inevitable.

"Guilty, your Honour." Every tenor inflection carried resignation, self-accusation, repentance, and surprise at an unaccountable lapse from customary virtue. "I hadn't much more than two pints o' plain porther, your Honour, an' it wint to me head on a empty stomach. You see, your Honour, I hadn't ate a bite for three whole days due to knot in me guts be dint of pushin' a lawn-mower under a boilin' sun in a gintleman's garden where I'm reg'lary employed. Your Honour——"

The Justice smiled faintly and interrupted him.

"Judicious fasting is best for that kind of knot. I recommend twenty days of it——"

"What's that, your Honour?"

237

"Thirty shillings fine with ten shillings added for injury to State property, to be paid into Court, or twenty days hard labour. Stand down!"

"Thank you, your Honour," said Thomasheen James with dignity, and with dignity took his seat on a side bench. A placid policeman lolled at his side.

It was then that Thomasheen James's eyes met mine in an unrecognising stare, while his lean face did not twitch as much as a mouth corner. Slowly, very slowly, he moved a hand into a trouser pocket, drew it forth again and opened it emptily downwards. Thereafter he lay back on the bench and looked up and far away through a high-set window. Plain as speech he had said to me: "Your move. I have no further interest in these proceedings."

I sat on until there was a pause in Court. Apparently the scales had finished the morning's weighings. The Justice was busy over his case-book; his clerk, at a table below the Bench, was accepting a fine or two; and after a time I moved reluctantly forward between the empty forms. The clerk lifted head at me.

"O'Doran!" I said.

He glanced at his book.

"Thirty shillings and ten shillings charges."

I looked up at the Justice and he looked down at me, one eyelid flickering. We are members of the same Sunday foursome at the Hermitage Golf Club. I said:

"Your Honour, I regret the leniency that gave this individual the option of a fine."

I slapped two notes before the clerk, bowed truculently to the Justice, said over my shoulder: "Watch out on Sunday!" and stumped for the entrance. I would get two pounds off that fellow or bust a niblick. I never looked at Thomasheen James, but at the foot of the stone steps outside his voice spoke temerariously at my shoulder.

"You would have your bit o' fun, an' you're welcome to it. I dipinded my life on you, an' the Lord He knows, I'm sca's'ly worthy o' your ginerous nature."

I faced round at him, and he fluttered a weary hand before his face.

"Whatever you say is only pilin' the evidence agin me an' you not knowin' my side. You can kill me dead if you like this blasted minit, but as you hope for a happy death laive wan stem o' life in me till I meet up with Davy Hand that misleader into timptation."

I looked up and down the street. There was no sign of Davy anywhere. Davy knew his strategy.

"Cripersalive!" Thomasheen James exclaimed suddenly. "I wonder did we drownd him last night? I rimimber me sound-man Jock wrastlin' him towards the Quay wall. Wo—wo!"

I did not know who the sound-man Jock was. I did not want to know. I turned and left him without a word, and my anger made me so energetic that I walked all the way round by the Quays to the home bus at O'Connell Bridge.

Thomasheen James was in the bus two seats ahead of me, and I ignored him. The conductor was an old acquaintance, and knew something of the strange but not strained relations between Thomasheen James and me. He was at my shoulder for the fare.

"Two, sir?" he said.

"Two, Michael," I said. Thomasheen James was broke, and I would be no party to a petty squabble in a public conveyance. Damn! I was still his privy purse. Then the ludicrousness of the whole affair struck me and I smiled, and from smiling went on to silent sniggering, and had to hold handkerchief over mouth to hold in laughter. I felt better after that. I noticed that Thomasheen James was still bareheaded, and that he was carrying no parcel. Where were his deepsea-pilot cap and dress trousers? Curiosity ousted the last of my grouch.

I did not have a show-down with Thomasheen James until that evening.

It was a warm evening and I was in the front of the airy summer-house at the garden foot leisurely filling a pipe when Thomasheen James brought his barrow down the path and across the grass patch before me. The barrow, for once, was meagrely loaded with lawn-cuttings which he would scatter between the rows of raspberry canes. He looked aside at me, was about to go on, hesitated, and stopped, still gripping the handles.

"Are you makin' up your mind to gi'e me the sack at last?" he enquired in the tone of a man resigned to his fate.

"You never had a job," I said.

"'Tis a hell of a apprinticeship so," he said, with a small return of vigour. "They's wan char'table mimber in this house, whatever, an' that's the missus, before you think I'm coaxin' you with flattery. She's after givin' me a good dinner an' a schooner o' beer on top—an' a few kind words."

"Which you richly deserved," I said.

He had drawn me. He put his barrow down, cleared his throat, and made the first move in his campaign.

"But mind you, I did meself no manner o' justice this mornin' on a empty stomach, an' me throat like the back of a hob. I got two roots in the ribs last night an' a mug o' wake tay this mornin', no sugar in it—an' I'd rather another root in the ribs the sort o' tay it was. But now! will you have a heart in your bosom for wan two minits an' listen to me?"

I looked him up and down, and he bore the scrutiny with difficult hardihood.

"Where is your deepsea-pilot cap?"

"With me black pants."

"And where are the black pants?"

"With me deepsea-pilot cap."

"Where then are cap and pants?" I pinned him down patiently.

He tried to be facetious, but only for a moment.

"They're both together." Then he groaned resignedly, scratched the bristles at the back of his neck, and sank slowly into the grass-cuttings in his barrow.

"I s'pose there is no gettin' away from the horrible occasion, but isn't it a pity o' the world that a man, an' I won't mintion names, can't be a Christian for more than a minit at a time; an', anyway, what is a few shillin's betune you an' me?"

"A few shillings!"

"Right—all right. I'll tell you the whole thing from beginnin' to ind, an' if you're not satisfeed I was the innocent victim o' wholesale timptation we can leave me cap an' pants where they now raypose. An' I'll get on better if I ha' me pipe in me teeth to keep me from grindin' 'em down to the gums with timper whin I think o' Davy Hand. You have your pouch in your hand. Wup! Well held! Thank you!"

I'll be above-board with you in me gallant attimp's to evade timptation (went on Thomasheen James). Like a bad drame it is, with a patch o' pleasantry here and there. I began well—I began too dam' well.

You saw me lift sail yesterday mornin'—or was it yesterday mornin'? me heart light, me deepsea-pilot cap at the Beatty angle, an' your poun' note rayposin' in me hip pocket. I was so light on me feet that I cruised wide an' han'some every foot o' the three miles to the Donnybrook tram an' saved thruppence for you in bus fares. An' whin I got in be the Quays adjacent to Mullarkey's I says to meself:

"It'll be no credit to me if I don't play the clane potato be the boss an' knock that Irish-Jewman—manin' Mullarkey—a shillin' down in the price o' the pants."

It was thin I rimimbered, or the divil himself rimimbered for me, that Davy Hand was a bit of a blood-relation be marriage with Mullarkey an' might have a pull in notagations. So without warnin' meself o' the soart o' sarpint Davy is I padded it round to Winetavern Street an' found Davy sittin' in his vamps, his feet cocked, an' his missus scrubbin' the floor, havin' a holiday from charrin' that day—a clane woman with a houseful o' brats an' fightin' tarriers. I gave Davy the specifications, an' says he, shoutin' at the missus to put a shine on his boots:

"You're losin' whatever scrap o' sinse God gave you, Thomasheen James. No wan but yourself would think o' givin' oul' Mull more'n half the ticket on a pants. Ten bob! We'll give him six at the outside, an' have four left for—for contingencies," says he.

"Don't desaive yourself," says I. "They'll be no sich contingencies. Make your mind up to that, me bucko, an' if you can't," says I, "stay sittin' there on your hunkers out o' timptation like a monyment o' sin," I says. I had to speak gintlemanly, the missus listenin' an' sayin', "Thu! thu! thu!"

"Forget I mintioned it," says Davy agreeable. "Come on an' see me down Mullarkey!"

Well, sir! we tackled Mullarkey, horse foot an' artillery, p'ison gas an' inframatory bombs, high an' low, collar an' elbow, a hand over an' a hand under, an' recrimatory langwidge free as air. You should ha' been there. Tough as a hake he was, an' slippery as a eel, but we batthered him down an' we batthered him down, and three times turned our back on him for ever, till on in the day we inched him to eight bob, an' there he stuck, both heels in bedrock, and wouldn't lade or drive. I saw that. I slapped seven bob on the counter under his nose.

"Take it or lave it!" says I short.

"Get to hell out o' here!" he roared, "an' take the pants with ye."

So away we came, the black pants handy in me oxter wrapped in a *Irish Times*. Not a scratch on' 'em, even if pulled about a bit between Mull an' meself, an' a dead match for me deepsea-pilot cap, braid an' all. I was happy as Larry savin' three bob for you, an' the divil put it into me head to say jocose-like to Davy:

"That's a bob you owe me, Davy Hand! Six you said, an' seven he took off us."

"I'll owe it you," says Davy, "an' I'll pay it when I sell Juno's nex' litter." Juno is his blue bitch. "On wan condition," says he.

"What's that?" says I, suspicious.

243

"Bind the bargain on me with wan solit'ry pint o' stout," says he.

"Timpt me, divil!" I roars at him, "the hot day that's in it, an' me hoarse as a crow from softenin' Mullarkey."

"The boss wouldn't mind—even if you told him," says he, "the dacent man!"

"Maybe that's what you think," says I, feelin' a soft spot in me.

"I know he wouldn't," says Davy. "I mind the day Tom Doherty run you below in Ard-na-Righ."

"Mintion that agin!" says I, tightenin' me parcel under me oxter.

"Two pints the boss stood me, wan for meself an' wan for you, an' a third if I wanted it."

"You was borned to be hanged," says I, "since me curse didn't kill you."

"Moreover, haven't we the price o' four pints in that buckshee three bob," says Davy, never relintin', "and after a pint apiece you could show him a han'some profit on the transaction."

"Becripers! but 'tis true for you," says I.

"Well, then?" says Davy, an' he after leadin' me footsteps be devious corners. "Here we are at *The Frozen Head*!"

In he turned, an' me feet turned me in after him in spite o' me iron resolve. I had no control over 'em, an' I was wonderin' if I was losin' me sinse o' direction like a man in a sunstroke.

"Wan pint apiece," says Davy, "an' not a drop more if you was to shove it down me neck."

We had our pint apiece and it barely wet us round the edges. An' after a while Davy says:

"Do you know what I'm thinkin, Thomasheen James?"

"I do well," I says, "but I dare you to say it, Belleezabub!"

"'Tis a great pity a bird can't fly on wan wing," says Davy.

"I know that," says I, "but are you alludin' to anything in partic'lar?"

"Not a thing," says he, "only how could the boss find out about that buckshee three bob?"

"You don't know him!" says I. "They's a contrack betune us, an' it is me rule in life an' death to put me cards face down on the table before him. I ingaged him out of his sight ten or, maybe, eleven times, an' 'tis me proud boast that I never deceived him wance. He always found out." An' so you do, out o' me own flannen mouth, as often as not. "Mark me words," says I, "he'll find out about this solit'ry pint before another day is over me head," and there was prophetisin' for you.

"If he does," says Davy, "an' I'll not deny he might, he'll be as hard on you for the wan wing as the two—if I know him," says he.

"You have your facks," says I. "He don't know the difference betune a venal an' a mortial sin."

"Very well so!" says Davy, hittin' the anvil. "We might as well be hung for a sheep as a ha'porth o' tar. Here, Danny! Fill 'em up agin."

An' before I had me mind made up to crown Davy with the bottom o' the pewter, Danny had a full pint under me hand agin me better judgment.

We spread thim two pints out slow, for Davy couldn't see his way to the infringement of your ten-shillin' note, an' we just talked this way an' that leadin' round an' about the subjeck in hand.

Be this time the bar was fillin' up for th' evenin',

but we held down our two stools till a sailor-man came in an' edged his way betune us.

"Beggin' yer pardon, skipper!" says he in a polite way, lookin' at me deepsea-pilot cap. Ay, faith! skipper he called me.

"You're welcome, mate," says I. A big hard-faced buck-sailor with a Glasgow accent.

"What ship?" says he.

"The *Clytie* out o' Stamboul," I tells him, that bein' me last ship an' port I dunno how many years ago.

"Stamboul!" says he. "We passed it on the port ten days back. The *Ellen Jean* out of Odessa, grain an' hides."

"What do you think o' me fri'nds the Bolsheevicks?" I says, makin' talk.

"They ha'e their p'ints," says he in a circumspeck way.

"So has a mangy yalla pup," Davy comes buttin' in.

"Don't mind Davy Hand, mate," says I. "He's only a totalisator—or are you agin the Soviets yourself?"

"I'm open to conviction, in a way," says he.

"Very good!" says I. "I'll soon convict you. Will you have a drink with us?"

The words was out o' me mouth before I knew I spoke; an' I couldn't swallow 'em back, could I?

"I'm no' the man to insult twa Irish gints be refusin'," says the sailor boy. "I'll ha'e a pint an' a chaser."

We tried that variety o' nourishment the three of us, an' then the sailor stood his hand like a spunky lad. A Jock he was be the name o' Campbell, but sure you sometimes get dacent men 'o that name an' nation.

After that second drink he cast an eye in Davy's direction, an' Davy nudged me in the short ribs; an' for the honour o' oul' Dublin I couldn't do less than slip him a half-dollar to stand his turn. An' it was about then I noticed that me judgment o' future contacks was scattered be the power I felt to prove to any man that black was no more than a dirty white.

Yes, sir! me reasonin' powers was as clear as spring water, an' I had the bar listenin' to me while I made a convicted fellow-communist o' that sailor-man in a matter o' two hours. I pulverised the whole capital system into smithereens, an' had the Bank o' England tucked away like me black pants under me oxter. The Jock laddie stood out for his share o' the Bank as a swore-in comrade, an' I had to let him have it; an' Davy said he wouldn't mind j'inin' the cause if we let him in on the vault floor, but we ejected him for a base motion.

Time was gettin' on then, as time will in brainy collogin'; an' I mind Davy proposin' to invite us home to supper only the missus would be in bed with the childher an' a hard day facin' her to-morrow. An' Jock, a dacent spud, ups an' says:

"I could be doin' fine wi' a humploch o' sausage an' mash. Let's gang awa' oot an' stoke up."

An' he sunk his paw in his pants an' excavated a sixpenny bit—wan lone solit'ry tanner—an' a bawbee.

"Sorry, mates!" says he. "Ye behold a sunk prooletarian."

"This is on me, comrade," says I, explorin' me own resources.

Do you know? Some thievin' robber must ha' been pioneerin' in me pocket, for all I could dig up was a thruppenny bit. We couldn't have nohow consummated twelve bob an' as much from Jock Campbell. Dam'd if we could!

"A bob a head we need," says Davy, "across at Mother Mitchell's—the complatest sausage an' mash this ind o' the village. Suppose ye laive this to the only mimber o' the financeer class in the company, meanin' meself?" he says.

"Have you sacret raysources, you varmint," I says.

"No," says he, lookin' hard at the parcel in the *Irish Times* secured under me oxter. "But, as you say yourself, the raysources o' civilisation are inexhausted. Mullarkey's is still open."

"God reward you in the parish o' hell!" I says.

"I want to stand ye two blind bolsheevicks a platter o' sausage an' mash," says Davy. "Will you lend me the loan o' four bob, Thomasheen James, an' I'll pay you back to-morrow with the other shillin' I owe you?"

"How will you?" says I. "With what?"

"I've a good thing in the 3.30 at the Curragh to-morrow," says he. "The genuwin article! An' I'll scrounge half a dollar off the missus."

"Is it a good thing?" says I, prudent.

"A dead-sure snip, an' no wan on to it but meself," says Davy. "Ten to one at a liberal estimate," says he.

"All right so!" says I. "We'll go round an' borry the four bob from Mullarkey—a dacent thief."

Round we went an' found Mullarkey puttin' up the shutters—just in time. He loaned us the four bob all right, but the mistrustful Yid persisted in holdin' me black pants as sicurity—an' he first of all tore a hole in th' *Irish Times* to make sure the pants was inside. An' even at that we had to root hard to lift him to four bob.

"Don't be in a hurry to bed, Mull," shouted Davy up the street. "We might be needin' you."

After that, in the langwidge o' the sea, we made a long leg an' a short leg by an' wide to Mother Mitchell's, an' enclosed ourself in her notor'ous sausage an' mash—three powerful plates of it, an' a second helpin' for Davy. Powerful is no name for it —the sausages spiced an' the mash peppered to the inginderment of an all-fire thirsht.

"Bedom!" says Jock, blowin' through his gob to cool it, "a' the guid o' the beer is evaporated oot o' me. Is there a few bawbees in the checker ava?"

"A tanner an' a ticky," says I, "the price o' wan betune three of us, and what good is that? Let's toss for the lucky man."

"Do you know what I'm thinkin', Thomasheen James?" says Davy Hand to me, an' be this time ould Satan himself must be feart for the usurpin' o' hell.

"Don't ask me to do that, you remnit," says I, ready to go on me two knees to him. "What'll the boss say to me?"

"All the same," says he, "you shouldn't be wearin' that iligant new cap without you had a pants to match it. 'Tisn't ettikwet nohow," he says.

"To hell with that!" says I.

"An' moreover," says he, playin' his ace o' hearts, "the way you are now, the cap would be safer with the pants in Mullarkey's."

"I will not differ with you for half a minit," says I. "Tell me, is that a dead-sure thing you have in the 3.30? What horse is it?"

"You might lift the market on me if I told you," says he. "Twelve to wan in the bag, and that's

249

thirty bob for the half-dollar investment. Hurry up, an' we'll catch Mullarkey!"

"Very well so!" says I, trottin'. "We'll deposit me deepsea-pilot cap with the matchin' pair o' pants —for safety," I says, "an' the boss'll understand the care I'm takin' o' them."

We got Mullarkey out o' bed be dint o' kickin' a loose board in the door that was used to kickin', an' he irrupted in his shirt, cursin' down Moses on us. But business is business, an' me deepsea-pilot cap plaised him. He gev us first-hand value for the pleasure o' holdin' it. Two half-dollars he gev us. What? Four dollars! How much is that in Inglish money? Oh, thim Yankee robbers! An' we thinkin' we fooled Mullarkey. Two half-dollars is what he gev us.

I'm not denyin' it, we circulated back to *The Frozen Head* agin once more for the secon' time, an' there we stayed till they thrun us out ten minits past closin' time. It was about then I noticed that Jock—a dacent spud—was yawin' a bit in the fairway, so we concluded to convoy him aboard down be the North Wall, so as he wouldn't be drownded in the Liffey—an' if he wasn't drownded he'd be worse, p'isoned dead. You heard o' the man that attimp'ed to commit suicide be drownin' himself in the Liffey. He was dead anyway, an' up above Saint Patrick forgave the suicide, but Saint Pether packed the poor fella off to hell till the tang o' the water dried out of him— an' he's in hell yet. Moreover, Jock intimated that wan o' his mates had a quart of vodky under his bunk that evaded the Customs.

But when we got to wan end o' Butt Bridge over agin the Custom House they was a young, hungry-lookin', telegraph-pole of a lad holdin' down a cluster o' down-an'-outs from Liberty Hall be recountin' the evils o' the age on top of a soap-box: powdery noses an' painted lips, an' toe-nails sunk in blood, an' no retycences anywhere—you know the usual. We listened a piece till I couldn't stand it no longer.

"Lids o' hell!" says I. "The joker is lookin' at it from the wrong triangle. 'Tis the capital finance that distorts nature, an' not the plain pleasant inclination to sin. Let me put him right peaceable."

So I heeled him off the soap-box, an' Jock ran him into Abbey Street. In tip-top form I was, an' nothin' or no one could stand up to me demolishment. I nailed down the first planks of a Soviet, Jock supportin' me be challengin' any son of a sea-cook to throw half a brick—an' Davy Hand hailin' Hitler from the presinks o' the crowd that was gatherin' to be converted—or not, as the case might be. I mind Jock trying to induce Davy to jump over the edge o' the quay be a lift o' the pants, an' disrimimber the result. Poor ould Davy! I'm sorry if he's drownded, for I want to exercise the divil out o' him be laivin' him no windpipe to talk with—to-morrow as ever was.

"Well, sir! I'd finished off Montagu Norman and the Jew finaseers, an' was dilatin' a few negatious remarks on the power o' the Church, when a young country cop came surgin' through me fellow-citizens.

"That's enough!" says he. "The meetin' is adjourned."

They's no use at all bein' rough with a peeler an' two more o' them watchin' from the corner. I took him aisy.

"Go back home, you Kerry bog-trotter," I says. "They's still freedom o' speech in this island o' saints an' sellers."

"Not where you are and I am," says he. "Sling your hook or I'll pull you for obstructin' the traffic."

"Young fella," says I, "I'll be patient with you. Go an' wipe the buttermilk off your County Cork gob, an' while you're at it take a wisp o' straw to the cow-dung on your number tens. An' what's more," says I——

He had me off that soap-box like a herrin' off a tongs, an' me sound-man Jock hopped him. His helmet went scatterin', an' the beans wor spilled. It was hot while it lasted, some for me an' some agin me, an' we doin' our dam'dest to execute a disorderly retreat, which is the first and last object agin three peelers o' Civic Guards. The Jock got away in the gineral rucus, an' Davy too—if he wasn't drownded at the time; an' I'd ha' got away meself only I hesitated makin' a football o' the cop's helmet. I got me first kick in fair an' square—an' a poor ten bob's worth—but I miscalculated me second, an' fell on me face. It was thin I got the two roots in the ribs. What else is there to tell? The three murdherin' cops frog-marched me into the lock-up in Store Street, and there I was. An' here I am, an' you know the best an' the worst o' me without a word of a lie.

IV

Thomasheen James finished, looked at me with a sort of truculent diffidence, and awaited my reactions.

"You took a roundabout way to answer a simple question," I said. "Ignoring all the rest, I gather that your cap and pants are in pawn—"

"For safety's sake—the cap anyway."

252

"—and that you need about ten shillings to redeem them?"

"That's the total li'bility, but am I askin' you to cover it? No, sir—not yet! Don't forget Davy Hand's good thing in the 3.30 at the Curragh—an' becripers! that was this very day——"

"There were no races at the Curragh to-day," I told him.

"To-morrow it might be," he said, but doubtfully.

"The next race-meeting at the Curragh is in three weeks' time."

He took it mildly and with a resigned gesture of head and hand.

"I suspected as much when I came to me everyday sinses. An' anyway it makes no differ to the things I have in store for that——"

"Shut up!" I barked. "That deepsea-pilot cap cost me four dollars to begin with——"

"A nice cap! But you was robbed——"

"It cost me a pound yesterday——"

"Dammit! That was for the pants."

"It cost me two pounds to-day——"

"For the upholdment of free speech——"

"But if you think that I am going to——"

"Wait—wait—wait!" he besought me urgently. "You're startin' to get hot under the collar, an' in a minit you'll be gone too far to recant. Look at it this way! If me deepsea-pilot cap cost you as much as you say be implication, what's the good o' chokin' over a measly ten bob at the ind o' the day? I ask you?"

There was no use talking any more. I gestured him away, and he went, saying over his shoulder:

"An' besides, you have me full permission to slander

me little misfortunes for the good o' the ol' firm. That ten bob is the same as a loaf o' bread in the water for us."

I wonder.

Last Sunday he sported black, braided trousers, and deepsea-pilot cap, but there was a hiatus between, for I had not the temerity to overtry public opinion with an ancient morning-coat. Some day . . .!

CHAPTER X

THOMASHEEN JAMES AND THE
DANGEROUS AGE

I

AN afternoon late in August I sought out Thomasheen James, my-man-of-no-work, in a shady corner of the garden. I found him sitting on the tail of his empty barrow, an old pipe of mine in his teeth, and his chin propped on the handle of his sweeping-brush.

"Just after takin' a small piece of a rest to dry the sweat out o' me," he explained.

I ignored that.

"We're off in two days' time," I said.

"Who? Me an' you——?"

"No! My wife and I—Kerry this time, for all September."

His eyes lit up.

"Ah! I was feart it might be Scotland. Kerry! You'll need a safety-pin in your pocket, an' you better take me along to guard you from the rear."

I swept a hand round the garden.

"You will give the lawn and the hedges two final clippings, lift and pit the last of the second-early potatoes, give the celery a third earthing, pull the keeping onions for drying, plant out four rows of savoy, strip the plums, store the carrots in sand-boxes, tidy away the pea-stakes, keep watering the tomatoes, gather the refuse for burning, and—well! that's about all."

"Just as you say," he said agreeably. "Anything else at all at all?"

"You can take your own holidays then," I told him unwisely.

"Like the birds o' the air, an' grow fat on daylight an' spring wather! Let it be! I'm used be this to subjugation."

I let it be, and in two days we left house and garden to the mercy of Thomasheen James. He might do none of the things that I had enumerated, but the house and all in it would be perfectly safe in his charge. Plain, petty pilfering was never within his compass; rather was he in the diplomatic class of scoundrel, for he always had a stake on the board and generally lost it—or I did.

The first morning in the last week of September found my wife and me at our final brief anchorage at Bally-bunion on the Kerry coast. In the shade the air had a crisp edge, but the sun was comfortably warm and the water had that wonderful tang and perfume that comes with the ripening and bursting of the bladder wrack.

My wife was lounging and reading on the ruin-crowned promontory that noses out into the bathing-strand, and I, after a swim, was taking a sun-bath on the dry sand below. Under the leaf of an old panama I looked down my nose and over my bare toes at the sun-shimmering green waters of Shannon Mouth, and at the bold black cliffs of Clare six miles away across the estuary; and, for no reason at all, the thought of Thomasheen James leaning on a hoe in the arid suburbia of Dublin came into my mind. I was lazily sorry for him.

A shadow fell across my feet, and a voice that I knew made insulting speculation.

"Cripers! I wonder is there a touch of the Chinee in him? The sun couldn't do that to no man."

I lifted the flap of the panama. Yes, that was the satan of my thoughts, Thomasheen James himself, aslouch within three paces. He was wearing a cast-off, but sound, homespun suit of mine, and his deepsea-pilot cap was set aslant over one eye. His lean face was as speckled as a brown trout; his china-blue eyes were alive, youthful, bold, and wary; he was in the very pink of hard condition, but I knew it had not been acquired in any garden of mine.

Having given me one quick appraising glance, he turned his eyes aloofly towards the cliffs beyond the Lady Strand, and got the first blow in.

"I'm on me holidays—same as you told me."

After years of experience I was wise enough not to bandy words with Thomasheen James on work not done. He was no chattel of mine, and the tie between us, while close enough, was never that of employer and employee. He carried freedom under his hat, and came and went like the rain or the wind or a visitation of Jehovah. And secretly I was a little flattered that he had sought me out in the wilderness of Kerry.

I let my head drift back on the sand, snuggled my shoulders into ease, and enquired nonchalantly:

"How did you get this far?"

"Be me usual method—perambulatin' on me two round feet."

"Not all the way?"

"Every dang foot—except for a short bit of a lift I got between Ard-na-Righ and Castleinch."

That short bit of a lift covered at least five-sixths of the total two hundred miles.

"Oul' Matt Shurridan the tinker an' his Kildare

band o' chicken-stealers was bringin' down six vans for the Listowel Races," he went on to explain. "I picked them up at Ard-na-Righ an' dropped 'em at Castleinch. Matt is a dacent oul' puckaun in his own way."

"You were in good company—one tinker with another."

"And that's not much of a lie for you," he agreed surprisingly. He sank cross-legged at my side, turned one shoulder to me, watched a handful of dry sand trickle in a yellow spray through his bony fingers, and went on half-musingly. "'Tis true enough, I have a drop o' the tinker blood in me, as you pointed out more than wance, usin' strong langwidge. Me gran'-father was a Ward from the County Wicklow, tinker to the core. That was on me mother's side, an' we'll leave me unknown father rest at peace in his own hell. Oul' Matt Shurridan says that wan drop o' the blood sinds a man to the road late or airly, an', mind you, 'tis a life I could be doin' with. A tilt van painted green, white, an' yalla, with a stove an' a coupla bunks, no work to speak of, and food in your mouth reg'lar! What more could a man want?"

"A woman to cook the stolen food."

"An' that's the bloody snag, I admit," agreed Thomasheen James. "A woman to cook an' wash, an' her oul' granda attached, mendin' tin cans through the country an liftin' a chicken here an' there. I know tinkers, for I lived with 'em many the day an' night, an' you only think you know them because you wrote about 'em. Thim tinkers o' yours never spit in a man's eye nor tanned a woman's hide for divilmint. Moreover, I never cared for the red hair you're always draggin' in be the gory locks."

"Nor for black hair?"

"I never said nothin' agin black hair," he protested too warmly. "Since that time in the Big War beyant in Stamboul I have a prediction for the brunetty wans in a gineral way. You know the sort? Black as a crow's wing in the hair, an' blue-black in the eye, an' the dusk o' the sun redd'nin' her cheeks, an' shapely bones well padded—if you get me?"

"That sort does not exist."

"I seen her."

"Not amongst the Sheridans," I led him on, marvelling. "I know that tribe of tinkers. Lean as a pole and ragged as a bush——"

"You never seen Peg Kate, oul' Matt's gran'-daughter. You'd be puttin' her in a book an' changin' her past knowin'." He lapsed into his half-muse. "An' there's no dam' need to change her neither. Risin' twinty an' nice in her ways. I used to be cuttin' sticks for her, an' fillin' her can o' water—an' watchin' the white hound's teeth an' I gettin' a laugh out o' her. Young, young! an' 'tis the pity o' the world to see her gay at the beginnin' o' the road the tinkers travel. Ay! an' her own cousin sidling up to her every chance he gets. A black pug of a lad an' a mean streak in him—Mick Andy. May the divil meet him!"

I lifted the flap of the panama and considered Thomasheen James from a new angle. His gaze was lost in the shimmering green sea, and the blue of his eyes was hazed with dream. I was filled with wonder. Was the dangerous fire of autumn aglow in him? Had Romance, to show her dominion, tackled her most unpromising subject? Never once in all our dealings had he failed to rail contemptuously at woman with or without provocation, and here he was dwelling fondly on the attractions of one Peg Kate! And at his age! But what was his age? He hid his years well, but he must be approaching forty.

Forty! No, that was not old. It was worse. It was the dangerous age. And at that dangerous age had Thomasheen James done one of the really dangerous things: made advances to a tinker maid? A maid of the wild gipsy tribes that ramble and riot over the roads of Ireland, mending cans and pans, huckstering donkeys, coping horses, drinking, fighting, stealing only occasionally, going to jail often, and beginning again the same old round. A tinker maid! Lovely at twenty, draggled at thirty, dead at fifty, worn out by child-bearing and man-handling! My poor Thomasheen James!

His eyes came down aslant to mine and looked hastily away, and, as I live, the rare flush of embarrassment came to his lean face. He changed the subject hastily. Like most Irishmen, he hated to be caught in his own secret dreamings.

"You was easy traced. A word in a hotel bar or a Guard barracks, an' there was your trail leadin' on dead straight with a coupla bends on it. One week you was at Glengariff an' a second at Sneem, an' a week fishin' at the back o' Waterville, an' you caught a fi'-pun' trout—be a stroke-all so 'twas said —an' here you are takin' the say at Ballybwingan. How's the missus? I see her up on the Castle Green watchin' us."

"Fine. Were you looking for me all these weeks? My garden——"

"I was not. Our circulations co-opted be accident.

Tell me, are you goin' to the races at Listowel to-morrow?"

"Ah! I'm getting you. You're going?"

"I'll be somewhere contag'ous."

"And you're dead broke?"

"Don't misdoubt me. I've a mornin's job sellin' race-cards for oul' Matt Shurridan, an' later twirlin' a rowletty wheel. 'Tis only pure fri'ndship directed me footsteps to your vicinity. Are you goin' to the races, I axed you?"

"Too much racing in Dublin."

"But manalive! Listowel! The best three-day meetin' in all Ireland!"

It was one of the best certainly, a nice blend of fences, sticks, and sprints. Listowel was only ten miles away, and we were going the first and second days; but on the third day I had an appointment at Killarney that I would have to keep.

"O' course you're goin'," said Thomasheen James. "I'll have something good for you—an obsolete dead-sure snip."

"Same as Davy Hand had at the Curragh?"

"I knew you'd bring that up agin," said Thomasheen James regretfully. "You keep on doin' it. An' blast it all! Haven't I worked off them few shillin's in blood an' sweat an' abuse."

"You'll need the lives of a cat to work off some things," I said. "What is this absolute dead-sure snip?"

"I haven't it yet— Wait! Wait, won't you? Gi'e me time to eluciate! Comin' down through Kildare we called in at the Curragh an' dug up a piece o' information."

"How dead was it?"

"Will you listen to me or won't you?"

I listened. The Curragh is the headquarters of Irish racing, and any real information therefrom is worth considering.

"Oul' Matt's sister has a great-gran'son a stable-boy with Tom Kent the trainer. Turn up your nose if you want to, but a cute lad of a stable-boy knows more about the capacity of a horse an' the misintintions of a trainer than the owner himself. It stands to reason. So oul' Matt had a talk with Seumaseen in passin'. Seumaseen is the lad's name. Look here! Did you ever see a tinker lose money on a bet? You did not. I know—I know! But I'm only a fraction of a tinker. Did you ever get a tip from a tinker? You did not. They keep it betune theirselves. Listen to me now! Tom Kent, the trainer, is bringin' down a string o' four horses to Listowel, an' wan o' them is earmarked to win; an' whin Tom Kent earmarks a horse to win, that horse retaliates be winnin'. It'll be wan o' two, but which wan will depind on the state o' the goin'. Are you attendin' to what I say? Tom Kent will win a good race an' the race will be in me pocket on the mornin' of the day—or maybe the evenin' before. That's all."

"Not quite. How much are you demanding in advance?"

"Betune me an' you? The Lord forgive you! Listen! To-morrow, up to the first race, I'll be sellin' race-cards at the near end o' the foot-bridge across to the Island Course. You'll see me an' I'll see you, an' if any information is goin' you'll be welcome to it—so long as you keep your thumb on it. The meetin' is now adjourned. I'll be seein' you."

262

He got limberly to his feet and started to move quickly away. I sat up and called after him:

"Wait! Sure you're not broke?"

He made a lordly gesture with his hand.

"Keep your money—this time. I'll make me own killin'."

He went on three paces, wavered, paused and turned back, his eyes on the ground. I had expected this sort of tactic before the final inevitable touch. But his words surprised me, and their hesitating diffidence.

"I'm often wonderin' what wan o' thim caravans 'ud run a man in for. You might know?"

"You mean the price? A motor-van?"

"No dam' fear! A horse for me. I'd want to navigate slow an' renconter the resources o' the native. A green, white, an' yalla van, with a stove and a bunk—or two bunks—you know?"

"I know. A horse—you'll need one with a full set of legs—say thirty pounds; the van about eighty; fittings, twenty——"

"Cripers! that's a power o' money——"

"But there's a final item much more expensive."

"What the hell could that be?"

"A dark-haired tinker girl named Peg Kate."

Thomasheen James did not explode; he did not even protest mildly. His eyes met mine and his mouth opened.

"You was takin' it all in," he said gloomily. "Amn't I the bloody fool at my age?"

He turned and plodded away head down, and this time he kept going. His hard-bitten misogyny was fighting hard against the autumn fire in his blood.

My wife and I went to Listowel Races on Tuesday and Wednesday. The weather was perfect, the track in fine order—if on the hard side—and the racing first-class. I am not describing that racing, or the crowds, or the games, or the daredevil gambling cheerfulness of the men of Kerry. This chronicle is devoted to Thomasheen James.

I purchased two race-cards from him on Tuesday morning at the foot-bridge crossing the Feale River to the Island Course. I looked the card over while my wife, who is a born gambler, questioned Thomasheen James for a gambler's tip. He gave her two horses that might have "a chance an' a half."

"Tom Kent has a horse in the third," I suggested.

"Put your shirt on it an' be arrested for inclemacy," said Thomasheen James deridingly. "Don't touch a horse o' Tom Kent's till I say the word!"

Nevertheless, I had a small bet on that horse and lost it. My wife, plunging on Thomasheen James's two horses, had no better luck.

On Wednesday I ignored Thomasheen James, or, rather, he ignored me. Again Kent had a horse running, and again I lost a little on it. I am more interested in horses than the gamble thereon, and never bet heavily—a good rule for a man unlucky in gambles. Still, I had some of the luck that was going at Listowel, and at the end of the second day was ten pounds to the good. My wife, who does bet, had varying fortune and was five the other way—which was better than her average.

"That finishes Tom Kent as far as I am concerned," I said, "or need we go to Killarney to-morrow?"

"We must," my wife said, and added slyly, "You could make Thomasheen James your agent?"

I maintained a dignified silence and we left it at that.

We were slowly shouldering our way across the crowded foot-bridge when I saw a well-known deepsea-pilot cap ahead. Thomasheen James's sandy-red poll was below it. He was not alone. A girl was holding his arm. He was a tallish lath of a man, and her bare black head barely reached up to his limber shoulder. Black, indeed, was her hair, and the sun of twenty summers had not rusted the gloss of it. Over her shoulders and low on her neck was the gay-tartaned tinker shawl, and her neck, between hair and shawl, was round and the perfect colour of old ivory. She was busily, gaily talking, and when she turned her head up to her swain I saw the dusky richness of her cheeks, the impudent tilt of her chin, the side-glint of white teeth.

I remembered Thomasheen James's words: "The dusk o' the sun redd'nin' her cheeks, an' the shapely bones of her well padded." That described her. She was as bonny as—as a tinker lass. For half a minute I commended Thomasheen James—perhaps envied him—in my own mind, and then I remembered her breed and was sorry for him.

At the bridge exit, where the crowd splayed out, he turned head and saw us. He said a quick word out of the side of his mouth to the girl, and I saw the unaccustomed blood touch his cheek-bones. At once she dropped his arm and, never turning a glance in our direction, twisted her lithe tinker's way through the crowd; and as she went she called back encouragingly:

"Never you mind, Tommy boy! To-morrow for luck!"

"Goodness!" exclaimed my wife. "What a lovely girl! That is never our Thomasheen James?"

"Only the end of him," I said.

He waited for us. He glanced at my wife shamefacedly and touched the peak of his deepsea-pilot cap.

"I want a word with the boss, beggin' your pardon, ma'am."

"Too late, Tom!" she said. "We are not racing to-morrow."

"I'd like a word with him all the same, ma'am," he said stubbornly, "if 'tis no incommodation to you."

She looked at me firmly.

"We are going to Killarney to-morrow," she said. "I will wait for you at *The Listowel Arms*. Do not be too long." And she in turn made her more sedate way through the crowd.

Thomasheen James led me away, and I went without protest. He did not pause till he had me round the quiet flank of the old Desmond Keep that towers over the placid reaches of the Feale. It was the last keep in Ireland to fall to Cromwell.

"Let me show you," said Thomasheen James briskly.

He extracted from breast pocket the race-card for the following day, thumbed two leaves over, and brought his hand smack on a page.

"There it is! The fifth! For three-year-olds and upwards that never won a race value 100 sovs.! Weight for age. That's right! Put on your specks. See that wan! Number 2, *Caroline Hot*, owner an' trainer T. Kent. An' down here below, No. 11, an' bottom weight, *Rushes Green*, trainer T. Kent. That is our wan—*Rushes Green*."

"Why not Kent's own, *Caroline Hot*—or is it hat?"

"'Tisn't hot, anyway, an' I'll tell you why. 'Tis only a mud-larker. An' that's Tom Kent's cuteness. He has a double string to his bow an' arrow. *Rushes Green* runs only on top o' the ground, the harder the better, an' to-morrow the ground'll be as hard as that oul' castle wall—barrin' the sky falls, an' it won't. We have it in the bag, I tell you."

"You heard what my wife said?"

"I wasn't payin' no attintion," he lied. "What was it?"

"We are not racing to-morrow."

"What differ is that?" said Thomasheen James with a confidence that I knew was superficial. "Can't you trust me to put your money on for you? Wo—wo! Keep your hair on! This is straight out of the horse's mouth, I tell you."

"All right! You back it. I'm not interested."

He sighed deeply, and came to his real object.

"Very well so! I've another engagement, an' I'll not waste your time. Will you advance me two quid?"

"Advance!——"

"Call it anything you like. I'm broke as bread."

"You've been broke all the time?"

"No, only a bloody fool same as always. I had five quid in me hip this mornin', all me own an' won honest, an' I'm after backin' five losers with it wan after the other."

"And you want me to finance that sort of luck? You are mistaken. Cut your losses and run—and run hard. You know what I mean, you poor moth."

"Cripers! You got a new name for me agin. Alludin' to the two quid——"

"You'll find them waiting for you in Dublin," I said, and strode away.

I strode a dozen paces and looked over my shoulder. Thomasheen James was standing forlornly, head down and a hand rubbing the cropped hair at the back of his neck. I should not have fallen; it might have been better for him if I had not. I probably did owe him a pound or two, and I had some winnings on me. Having beaten him into the last ditch—for his own sake—I walked straight back and pulled him out of it.

"Here! It is bookmaker's money and unlucky."

"Becripers!" exclaimed Thomasheen James in warm surprise. "Two fi'-pun' notes! I always knew you were a man back of all."

"Five o' that is yours, and you can put it to any foolish use you like. The other five is mine and you will put it for me on *Rushes Green*."

"What else would I do with it?"

"Many things. I know you. Absolutely no explanations accepted. That fiver goes on *Rushes Green* and on nothing else."

I had no faith in that horse, and I had no faith in Thomasheen James. I knew that he would not cheat me directly, but I knew from experience that he might change his mind, with or without reason, and back another horse for me. So I insisted on *Rushes Green* to save my future.

"On his nose it will go," proclaimed Thomasheen James with finality. "Dog, god, man, or divil will not make me swop that darlin' bet. 'Tis as safe a'ready as the Bank o' Ireland. I'll be seein' you to-morrow night, me pockets full o' tin."

I knew that I was a fool, and I left him without another word.

III

We went to Killarney next day. I did not want to go, but I went.

The weather had changed overnight, as weather does change in the South, without warning. There had been no rain for three weeks, and any weather sign that I knew was set fair, but I was waked very early on Thursday morning by rain pelting on my window. And it pelted and poured and cascaded and sheeted all day. The sky fell indeed.

But we went to Killarney, and all the lovely hills were shrouded to the feet, the silken waters were grey, and the trees drooped and dripped chillily; but we kept our dull appointment, and ate dull food, and talked dully of dull things. And in between whiles I looked out at the pouring rain and wondered what the going was like on the Island Course at Listowel, and what chance *Rushes Green* had of racing on top of the ground. Now there was *Caroline Hot*!!

The rain was turned off as by a stop-cock before set of sun, and we motored home through a perfect evening, with the mountains royal in purple, and the waters serene in their silken sheen, and all the leafage brighter than emerald and ruby in the glow of the west.

At our hotel in Ballybunion I went straight across to the desk-clerk, an old friend.

"What won the fifth, Bill?"

"The fifth! Were you on it too?"

"I had a small interest in *Rushes Green*."

"So had I—the decaiver!" said Bill feelingly. "So

269

had every man, woman, an' child with a tanner to bet. Favourite at six to four on."

"And lost?"

"Mind you, he might have won," said Bill with deliberation, "if they turned on their tracks half-way round. He'd have a forty-length start the second half. Came in some time before the sixth race, slithering in the mud."

"What did win?"

"His stable-companion, *Caroline Hot*. Larruping home in the mud—at tens, and you could have got twenties till some stable-money went on at the end."

"Ah, well!" said I resignedly. "A good thing to have a double string to your bow and arrow."

"What? Had you a saver on *Caroline Hot*?"

"No, Bill. I very carefully cut that second string last evening. To hell with it, anyway!"

I did not see Thomasheen James that night—his pockets full of tin. I did not see him next day either, because next morning early we left for Dublin. When I saw my garden I really did want to see Thomasheen James—to immolate him in his own autumn fire.

I did not see Thomasheen James for four weeks. Often enough in the past he had disappeared for longer periods, and I had never given him a thought; but now I discovered that I had a friendly interest in the scoundrel. I was worried about him. The wild strain in his blood might send him back occasionally to the gipsy life without much harm, but if the autumn fire had really immolated him on the altar of Peg Kate, the tinker girl, that would be harm in plenty. There was in him too much tame blood ever to mix adequately with the tinker strain. The blend could only result in disaster to Thomasheen James and the girl—to a moral and physical degradation. And Thomasheen James was not yet degraded. So I was worried about him.

And then, one brisk afternoon at the end of October, Thomasheen James turned up. It was a clear, brilliant day in the fall, with the sun shining brittle as glass, and a brisk breeze blowing and veering. I was in the vegetable patch burning garden refuse—a job I like, for it is pleasant to watch the flames flicker and lick, to dodge about the curl and eddy of acrid smoke, to sniff the fine earthy perfume of burning weeds. And Thomasheen James turned up.

I had got a wisp of smoke into my eyes and was giving utterance when a voice that I knew made remark close at hand:

"Cursin' won't help without you have sinse to keep win'ard."

I wiped the tears out of my eyes. That was Thomasheen James. He had been away for a mere month or so and was now back. That was all, and there was nothing to do but behave according to code. Already he had a spare fork in his hand, and a single dead cabbage leaf impaled for sacrifice. I cleared my throat carelessly and said:

"Had a nice long holiday?"

"If you'd call it that, an' me trampin' the roads o' Ireland like a sowl out o' hell."

Here, as well I knew, was an indirect intimation that he was prepared to be questioned and had all his answers ready. While busily forking I took occasion to consider him out of the side of an eye. At the end of September he had been brown-freckled and lean and fit; but now the brown and freckles had paled, his cheeks had grown sallow under tight-skinned cheek-bones, and his eyes were washed to a colder blue. His old homespun showed stains of wind and weather, his shoes, that used to shine with my polish, were scuffled grey as the grey dust on them; but his deepsea-pilot cap still retained a little jauntiness. Wherever he had been for the last month he had not enjoyed life, and now he wanted to tell me about it for some purpose of his own. He would too, and I could not stop him; nor would I aid him, for all my curiosity.

The fire was going well now, and I leant on my fork handle, out of the smoke but near enough to get the pleasant warmth. Thomasheen James shuffled to my shoulder.

"Hot work!" he said. "I'm not used to it yet. I saw you calculatin' the weight on me mind."

"Can't weigh the imponderable," I said.

"That don't mane nothin' to me no more than to yourself," he said, sighing patiently. "Do you know? the divil out o' hell is timptin' me the whole week to tell you a straight honest lie. 'Keep your trap shut,' says he to me. 'I never could,' says I. 'I'll ha' to tell him somethin'.' 'All right so!' says he. 'Tell him what he'll believe.' 'He'll not believe it,' says I, 'after I tell him.' An' so we went. No, sir! I never told you no lie—not never."

"Not never is hardly right, though you never told me much else."

"You know what I mane. Them bits o' lies be way o' business or divarsion don't matter a ha'porth. Don't you live be lies yourself an' you callin' it ficshun? Haven't I caught you twistin' me own little prevari-catin's? That's nothin'. But when it comes down to the rock, an' what's expected from you to me, I have cause often enough to curse the tinder nature

272

o' me own honesty. Listen, while I have the spunk! Do you remimber bein' at Listowel Races—an' may the divil drown the same Listowel an' ten miles round it?"

"I believe I was there—one day, or was it two?"

"'Tis the third I want to forget. An' you well remimber handin' me a fiver to put on an animal called *Rushes Green* in the fifth? You remimber that?"

"I do."

"An' you remimber shovin' your fist under me nose warnin' me that I was to back *Rushes Green* an' nothin' else?"

"Well?"

"I didn't do it."

"Didn't do what?"

"Didn't back *Rushes Green*," said Thomasheen James, and sighed. "I got it out at last—but don't you have no hopes, I'm warnin' you."

I grasped his arm and stopped him.

"I'll have no fears either," I said forcefully, "and I am warning you. As far as I am concerned, that fiver went on *Rushes Green*, and I refuse to be responsible for its later adventures."

"Just as well," said Thomasheen James, brightening up a little. "I ran away meself. I better tell you all about it."

"Be brief!"

"If I had a stem o' sinse," cried Thomasheen James bitterly, "I'd be brief to the p'int o' extinguishment."

He went round the fire forking furiously at half-burnt twigs, and then quieted down. All during the subsequent narrative he emphasised his misfortunes in the same way, and in his calm periods I collected more material for his fork.

Ay! I'd be dam' brief (went on Thomasheen
James). Me privit divil says to me: "*Rushes Green*
lost, so keep your trap shut!" But could I? I can't
—damn'd if I can! The Lord knows, maybe I am a
fool, but I respecks the footin' on which both of us
stand an' fall. It gi'es me a sort o' place in me own
mind, a sort of a feelin' that I'm a peg above all
them heirs to the throne except the heir himself. If
I done the dirty on you on the heads of a measly fiver
I couldn't never look you in the face agin. I'd be
as bad as a politeecian. Thim's my sentiments, take
'em or leave 'em!

Gi'e me time, me dear man! for this is comin' out
o' me with a corkscrew twisted in me interials. Where
was I? The third day at Listowel. Yes, becripers!
It started to rain after the turn o' the night, and in
bucketfuls it came down. The weather set out to
quinch hell, and the course went along. Two horses
came down at the regulation fence first time round
in the steeplechase, an' in the third—a flat mile—the
jockeys came in mud to the eyeballs. "If this bastar'
Rushes Green goes on top o' the ground 'tisn't in Listowel
he'll go it," says I to meself, an' I whirlin' the rowletty
wheel.

I had your fiver in me inside pocket ready to slip
on when the time came, an' I was grossly consarned
for it, an' a bit for me own as well. So I bundled
up the wheel—'twas too wet for play anyway—an'
took a quick turn round to get a hould o' Peg Kate.
You didn't hear me mintion Peg Kate—Peg Kate
Coffey, oul' Matt Shurridan's gran'daughter? Oul'
Matt the Kildare tinker—Oh! you did? You'll

hear more of her from this on. I knew where to find her.

"Peg Kate, *agrah*," says I, "is *Rushes Green* still the goods?"

"I couldn't rightly tell you, Tommy," says she, for she has an honest drop in her. "Me gran'dad is away round to see Seumaseen"—that was that stable-boy o' Tom Kent's.

"Will the Oul' Wan tip us the wink?" I asks her.

"He'll tip it to me, anyway," says she, "and I'll pass it to you, Tommy, but they mustn't see me doin' it."

You know the underground way thim tinkers has. Their infromation stays at home. Though I was a piece of a month with thim, an' thick as thieves with wan or two, divil a word I'd ha' known about *Rushes Green* only for Peg Kate, an' it took me a week to ameliate her be collogin' in a corner.

"Where could I meet you on the quiet, Tommy?" says she.

I knew the spot. "Down below at the las' turn, Pegeen," says I. "You'll see a bit of a hedge flankin' the post at the river-side. We'll meet under it out o' sight while the fourth race is on. Run now an' find the oul' puckaun!"

Off she wint, an' as I turned round there was Mick Andy givin' me a dirty look close to hand. He's her own first cousin. I told you about him! An ugly thick pug of a lad, an' makin' up to Peg Kate.

I met a fri'nd then, an' we had a pint in a markee an' another on top, for I needed courage to decide not to obey orders, as it might be. Wan thing an' another, the fourth race was over whin I got down to the hedge. Peg Kate was not there. There was no

275

wan there, though they was millions round the corner. I wasn't none disturbed at first. There was lashin's o' time, and I could dipind my life on Peg Kate. I gave her five minits. Thin I gave her two more, an' began to bite me tongue.

"Blasht her! the rashpeen!" I says out loud.

An' at that I heard a squeak at the other side o' the hedge. A choked kind o' squeak—like a rabbit in a brass loop, but with a touch o' the cat an' the female about it. There was a hole in the bottom o' the hedge, and through it I wint like a fox. Behind, there was a tree or two growin' on a narrow patch o' grass, an' then the bank o' the river fell straight down five or six feet; an' below was a spit of stones an' gravel with the shallow water washin' the edge of it.

Listen! As sure as I'm tellin' you, Peg Kate was down there, an' so was her cousin Mick Andy. He had her throttled agin the bank with wan hand, an' th' other hand was over her mouth; an' she was doin' her dam'dest with her teeth an' her feet, an' gettin' an odd squeak out betimes. He was as strong as a wake mule, an' she couldn't do much, the crathur.

"Aisy! Aisy there!" says I up above, an' he let her go an' jumped clear. An' she jumped th' other way an' let a screech out of her.

"Tom! Oh, Tommy! He's after tryin' to break me windpipe so I couldn't pass you the word."

"Mick Andy, you tinker's scut," says I, humourin' him for the occasion. "You shouldn't man-handle no woman less she's your wife."

"Near enough," he yelps at me in a timper. "Come down here, you Dublin Jackeen, an' I'll l'arn you man-handlin'. Come on down!"

276

"I don't want no trouble with the likes o' you, Mick Andy," I says, peaceable be intent, "an' far be it from me to shame you before your own cousin, Peg Kate."

He hopped on the ground like a magpie, an' his coat was off in a twist.

"Come down!" he bawled, "an' I'll show Peg Kate the colour o' your liver. Come down, you deludherer! Or I'll come up."

I don' mind admittin' that I was a bit discreetly frightened of him. Tinkers is dirty fighters—kick an' gouge an' bite—an' he was a thick, strong-built chunk of a young lad.

"Clear out o' here, you chicken-stealer," I says, doin' me best to pacify him. "You heard what happened the last man I hit?"

"I did." He let a bellow out of himself. "He got two months for mistreatin' a—a snotty nose."

Wherever he got that approbious name I don't know, but he hadn't it out o' his gob before I landed on top of him an' scattered him to the gravel. An' as he come up under me I gev him the right. You saw that blow I hit Barney Doony in Ard-na-Righ? You did not! I mane the blow I hit him whin you wasn't lookin'! That's the wan I gave Mick Andy —from me heel up. It turned him round like a tee-toe-tum an' I stopped him with a left under his ear. Ay! but he was indured to corporeal beltin' an' he comes at me, his head betune his shoulders an' both hands thrashin'.

"I'll take you to bits, you so-an'-so," says he.

But I circulated away from him, jeldy-footed, an' he near wint into the river. I abetted him with a root in the right place, an' he wint in knee-deep. He come out agin be main force, an' we had it.

277

I had a couple or more inches on him in reach, but he had it in weight be a stone, an' me eyetarnal sowl depended on the way I could stand off an' bombinate him with long fire. I did that, an' hot an' heavy for five minits, Peg Kate enj'yin' herself hoppin' round us an' gettin' out o' the way. An' then the drink began to tell on him, young as he was, for he was full o' bad porther an' had been for three days. I had him gaspin' for breath in no time at all, an' then I set about returnin' him proper to his native mud. I would, too, in another minit, only me foot turned on a stone, an' he got his hands on me. It done him no good. He was too done to get me down, an' whin he tried to get his thumb in me eye I propped his head agin the bank, an' started to gi'e him the double roll o' kettle-drums in the short ribs. At that he let a final yell out of himself.

"Peg Kate, don't let him kill your cousin! Hit him a chroosht with a lump o' stone."

Busy as I was, I saw her out o' wan eye leverin' up a lump o' rock as big as me head, an' I tried to shake meself loose; but he had the strangle-clutch o' death on me. You know what tinkers are, or do you? Did you ever insinuate yourself betune two o' them in a puckin' match? You did not, an' don't never. 'Tis dead fatal eleven times out o' ten. They j'ine forces an' rip your hide off.

I remimbered that with Mick Andy tangled on me, and Peg Kate comin' in at us with the stone up in her two hands. An' I could do nothin' but dodge me head down an' shut me eyes—an' I had no time to think o' the falsity o' the sex. An' then! Ker-r-lump! An' Mick Andy wint limp in me arms an' slipped to the ground under me. Think o' that, will you?

"Did I kill him dead, Tommy?" she screeches, pullin' me off him.

"You did," says I, "less his head is iron."

"I better hit him another to make sure," says she. "I'll never get a better chance."

But I held her off. The three C's fits me to perfection—calm, cool, and collected. In all the ruckus the business in hand never took a back seat, the same bein' the investment o' two fi'-pun' notes to the advantage o' the oul' firm—me an' you.

"Peg Kate," says I, shaking her, "what's the latest?"

"The latest what, Tommy?" says she, the sinses scattered on her. So I gev her another good shake to settle her.

"*Rushes Green*? You *onshuch*!" says I.

"Oh!" says she. "Seumaseen says *Rushes Green* has no chance no more—not in the mud."

"What has, then?"

"Things is betwixt an' between. I dunno, Tommy! The goin' is too soft for wan, an' maybe not soft enough for another, but Seumaseen says that *Caroline Hot* is the best out o' the bag as things are."

"Best out o' the bag is good enough," says I, an' I made a drive to top the bank. But she caught me.

"You can't, Tommy!" she schreeches.

"Le' me go, you rip," says I, me hand up to her.

"But if you saw yourself? Like a stuck pig you are, your nose the way it is. An' where's your collar an' tie? Put your head round the corner an' you'll be arrested for manslaughterin' Mick Andy."

She was right too. No man can fight a tinker for five minits an' come out of a band-box. I felt wan eye shuttin', an' me own blood tasted salty in me mouth. But did I lose me sagacity? No, sir! There was only wan thing to be done an' I done it. Me hand in me hip, the two fivers slapped into Peg Kate's hand, an' her fingers down on them—like that!

"Run, you divil!" says I, givin' her a shove towards the bank. "Run! an' put thim two fivers on *Caroline Hot* at any price you can get. Our bit of a van is in it." We used be talkin' of a van all to ourselves an' we alone together. "Run!" says I, givin' her a hoist, "or I'll tear every hair out o' your head. Meet me at the usual place at the fall o' dark." We got into the habit o' comin' together for a bit of a collogue in a quiet place at the back of oul' Matt's van. "Run, me darlin'!" says I, "an' remimber our own nate bit of a van an' our travellin' shop. Run, you imp o' hell!"

I thrun her on top o' the bank in a last heave, an' she wint through the hedge prompt as a cat in haste. After that I turned round to Mick Andy. He was sittin' up blinkin', an' rubbin' the goose egg that was laid be the rock on the roof o' his skull.

"We'll raysume the argyment where we was interrupted," says I.

"The conclusion is clinched for the time," says he.

"Only wan nail to drive home," says I, liftin' me foot—an' he lay down agin.

I left him there watchin' me out o' wan eye, an' after gettin' a bit o' the blood off me face an' shirt I circulated round be the river an' got off the course. . . .

You know what won? You do! *Caroline Hot* at tens. Me good intintion was to meet Peg Kate in the usual spot, collect our spondulicks, take the last bus out to Ballybwingan an' heave a rock through your winda to joyful awakement. No, I didn't heave no rock. I wasn't in Ballybwingan at all. I'll tell you. 'Tis all I can do.

That evenin' comin' on dusk I wint round to the back o' the tinkers' camp a mile outside the town—in a bit of a plantation. There was a nice shady sally bush there between two scarths o' briars—only it was damp be that time. Peg Kate wasn't there yet. I waited for her. I waited an hour. I got a start of a fright wonderin' if she was late gettin' our money on, an' maybe herself afraid to face me now—an' well she might. I waited on. There was no Peg Kate.

I crept close in an' looked through the wheel of a van. There was a big fire in the open, an' a melodeon goin'. The tinkers, men and women, had a good day be all appearances. Some o' them dancin', an' some singin', an' two o' them havin' a quiet puckin' match to theirselves in a corner—an' the kids scurryin' like chaff—an' all o' them takin' turns at a slug out of a five-gallon jar. But there was no sign anywhere of Peg Kate, or oul' Matt—or Mick Andy aither. I daren't go in. Desprit an' all as I was, I had sinse enough to keep out. Go in among a band o' tinkers ravenin' in drink, an' me after malafouxterin' Mick Andy! You could bury me remnits in a cigar-box.

I crept up on me belly as near as I could to oul' Matt's van—the green, white, an' yalla wan I told you about. He had a brindle dog, a cross betune a bull an' a hound, that slept under the van, an' that same brute-baist 'ud tear the throat out of his own mother after the fall o' night. The van was dark an' the curtains down, but in betune the varses of a song beyant by the fire I thought I heard snorin'. That would be oul' Matt, blind drunk. Pegeen, as I knew, had not reached the maturity for sich wholesale music.

I wint a bit closer in an' gev a small whistle, an' the dog growled. I stuck me ground an' whistled agin—louder—an' after that I left there knockin' sparks out o' the ground, an' the dog hell-for-leather after me. I bate him to the road an' turned him with a rock hoppin' off his rump. I gev in for the night.

I slept in a horse-box with two stable-boys, an' waked up nex' mornin' the sun shinin' bright into me good eye; an' me heart in me boots. What would you do then? Curse your bellyful an' cut your losses, an' maybe you'd be right too. I cursed sure enough, to break an ass's back, but I did more.

I know tinkers, an' you don't, for all your talk in print. I wint up to the camp an' marched straight in, drums batin' an' colours flyin'. It was on in the mornin' then, an' most o' them were at a late breakfast round the fires. You'd 'a been in bed with a could bandage on your head, but the tinkers, after a tearin' night, was wolfin' down bacon an' sausages an' eggs an' strong tay. The perfume made me mouth water, an' me stomach agin me backbone.

Let no man miscall a tinker where I am. In their own camp, an' sober, they are the fairest, hospitablist set of bastar's in all Ireland, an' a few belts an' kicks given an' partook in drink is only considered as a bit of divarsion—till next time drink is in 'em. I knew that, an' staked me carcase on it.

They hurrooed when they saw me an' gathered round to speculate me black eye, for, as I soon l'arned, they knew 'twas me busted Mick Andy. Did they mind? Not thim! His own brother slapped me on the back. "I'd give the sight o' wan eye," says he, "to be able to trim him so han'some. He's beyant in the tilt, a poultice on his head an' a yard o' stickin'-

282

plaster holdin' his ribs on. You're a ragin' terror, Thomasheen James."

I ate with them an' kep' wan eye liftin', for, as you may guess, there was no sign o' Peg Kate anywhere— or of oul' Matt. An' all the time I was wonderin' how many o' the facks was known to the band; for I caught some o' them grinnin' an' winkin' behind me back. So after a last cup o' tay I says sort o' careless:

"Where's the Oul' Wan?"

"Over in the van," says a lad, "havin' a late sleep to himself."

"I'll over an' bid him good mornin'," says I.

"Why not you?" says he agreeable.

So over I strolled, an' becripers! if the whole crowd didn't follow me, nudgin' an' showlderin' each other. The van door was shut at the top o' the steps, an' before I could climb up, the whole jing-bang o' them, men and women and childer, lets a yell out o' themselves to wake the dead.

"Ould Wan! Ould Wan! Here's Thomasheen James to bid you good mornin'."

At that the door opened, top an' bottom, an' there stood oul' Matt, mild as milk, sober as a judge, an' his beard white as the dribblin' snow. An' oul' man he was, an' noble-lookin' as a bishop; an oul', white-livid puckaun with a white smeg in a caroline hat, an' you'd think, to look at him, that butter wouldn't melt in his mouth; but he had a weight o' sin an' expayrience behind him to sink a battleship. In all Ireland there wasn't the likes o' oul' Matt Shurridan.

Tinkers haven't no leaders—they won't stand for no leaders—but in every band you'll find a charackter that goes be the name th' Oul' Wan. He hasn't a ha'porth o' power, maybe, but nothin' worth mintion is done till he vets it, an', even then, it might not be done or done contrairy. 'Tis a dam' quare office.

Oul' Matt was the Oul' Wan o' the Shurridans. I seen him at work. A lad might have a turn-up with his wife a batin' wouldn't settle, or a double-crossin' bargain on the tape, or a difficulty about a horse or a girl, or a thing like that, an' he'd sidle along careless-like in Matt's gineral direction an' start a indifferent collogue; an' the two o' them would go at it talkin' about an' along an' over an' under the subjeck in hand, an' not wan plain word o' the subjeck direct; an' after a while the lad 'ud withdraw himself cursin' the oul' divil, his head moidhered; but after another while a word here an' a word there might come to his mind, an' puttin' two an' two together he'd have a hell of a notion o' his own smartness.

Oul' Matt sat down on the top step above me, an' never let his mild deceivin' ould eyes rest on me down below. He looked out over all our heads an' started to cut a plug o' tabbacy for his pipe, an' I tried to get a peep up into the van behind him. I took him judicial to start with.

"Me hairy oul' puckaun!" says I, "where's Peg Kate this mornin'?"

He took no notice at all but went on sawin' at the plug. I kep' me timper.

"Do you want me to come up an' take the whiskers off of you like I'd pluck a goose?" I says reasonable. "Where's Peg Kate, I asked you?"

An', at that, the pack o' divils behind me let a yowl out o' them.

"Where's Peg Kate? Come on out, Peg Kate!"

An' becripersjoe! Peg Kate herself came out of a

corner o' the van, an' stood up above the Oul'
Wan. You saw her wance. She's nice. She was
nice then, her mouth all atrimble an' her eyes big
with the tears she unsh'd. An' her voice trimbled
as well.

"Tommy! Oh, Tommy!" says she. "They done
it on me."

I didn't ax what they done on her. I wint up
three steps, an' the Oul' Wan stopped me with the
p'int o' his knife firm agin me breast-bone.

"Peg Kate," says I soft over his head. "Did you
do that?"

"I did," says she, "every farthin'. I got twelves,
an' a minit sooner I'd 'a got twenties."

"An' what then, you tinker's brat?"

"Wo—wo!" says she. "'Twas all your fau't,
Tommy, not to let me hit Mick Andy another peg.
He was only half-kilt, an' heard every word. An'
whin I got me winnin's—the full o' me two stockin's
—off of Jack Larry the bookie, an' before I could
move a foot, I was surrounded be Mick Andy an' the
crowd o' them there."

"They took it off of you?"

"Not where it was, but they ran me home to
camp."

"An' that was th' end of it?"

"No, Tommy, no! Me gran'da here has it—every
penny. Don't be hard on him, Tommy, an' he
mightn't see us wronged."

I looked up at him, an' he wasn't lookin' at me,
but over me head, and the p'int o' his knife not movin'
agin me breast-bone. I wasn't none hard on him
outside plain tinker langwidge.

"You sepulchrous oul' ruffeen!" I said. "That's

285

me honest-won money—wan hunder' an' thirty solid quid—and I'll have it out of you if it was hid in your gizzard itself. Come on, you——!"

The p'int o' the knife bit me, an' I took a buck of a jump backways that landed me on me heels with agility.

The lads gave a hurroo, an' the Oul' Wan lifted his hand to stop them, an' they hurrooed agin before givin' him silence. Not once, mind you, did he let his deceivin' oul' eyes come down my way.

"A strange thing," says he, addressing his remarks to a tree across the way. "A strange thing how a drop o' the blood'll tell! I mind as well as the day before yesterday the mornin' this girl's father"—he put a thumb over his shoulder—"Black Tom Coffey, a dacent man, God rest him, but wake in the skull-bone, he was killt be the kick of a jinnet at Puck Fair. I mind that first day he come into me camp near Scartaglen. His great-gran'father, a farmin' man, poor fella, on the Cork border, stole away wan o' the black Carty rips out of a band o' Kerry tinkers, and here agin was the wild drop comin' out in the third ginera-tion——"

"Will you shut up, you oul' gandher," I roared, "an' talk turkey?"

"I mind the day well," he keeps meandherin' on calm as a jail, "when in walked Black Tom in desp'ra-tion. A prosperous travellin' tinsman I was at that time with two vans o' me own an' me only child Kate growin' up around me. 'Matt Shurridan,' says he, 'I can't sleep no longer under a thatched roof an' the moon shinin' in at the winda; I can't get up at five in the mornin', day in day out, to milk the cows an' wather the horse; I can't sit down to three square meals a day at the same kitchen table. Damn your sowl, Matt Shurridan!' says he, 'will you let me go the road with you for a piece of a year, an' I might come to me sinses an' marry a thick-hocked agricultooral girl from the North o' Kerry.' I was a soft-hearted man, an' I did it——"

"I'll soften it agin for you, you ould blatherskite," I roars up at him.

"Kill or cure, I did it. Man dear! he took to the life like a duck to the wather, an' in no time at all I made a good tinsman out of him. He could bottom a can with a nateness of judgment so it wouldn't leak a drop till our next round was due. An' after a time he saw me daughter Kate for the first time—an' he after seein' her every day for months, an' she lookin' at him her eyes like a dyin' duck. She scatthered the sight on him, I tell you, for she was a purty armful. But he was a honest *bosthoon*. He comes to me. "Tis this way,' says he stutterin'. 'I know,' says I, 'you want Kate, can you keep her?' 'If she'd stay—' 'You blockhead!' says I. 'I mane can you feed her an' the mouths to come?' 'There's me bit o' land on the Cork border,' says he. 'She'd die on it,' says I, 'but if you had a van of your own or the price of it—' 'I could sell the bit o' land,' says he. 'Very good!' says I. 'Listen! when you meet her to-night in that bunch o' sallys betune the scarth o' briars tell her that you are ready an' willin' to jump the budget with her. I won't have her wronged,' I says. He did, he told her, an' they jumped the budget in front o' me eyes, an' I gave the pair o' them me second van at a bargain. Ah well! they are both dead now, God rest them, an' I won't see their daughter wronged naither."

287

That was all he said. He got up on his lively ould feet, and turned towards the door. I let a yell out of me.

"What about me money, you white-liveried oul' finaceer?"

He turned agin an' looked over me head.

"I never wronged no man," he says, "an' I'll not begin now, wan foot in the grave. A gran'daughter's bet is a gran'father's bet till she has a man of her own an' a van of her own. I am wrongin' no man, an' I will not. I will not tear any man's windpipe out be the roots as long as I have a dog to do it. Here, Paddo!"

An' there was Paddo, the half-bred bull, on top o' the steps, grinnin' down at me, pleased with anticipatin' me windpipe.

Oul' Matt turned into the van, pushin' Peg Kate in front of him, but not before she took two handfuls o' wool out of him. The whole band hurrooed me in a mockery, an' for wan desprit minit I had a notion of assailin' the dog. But me madness evapirated observin' his bare teeth.

I made a silent retrate. What more could I do. I wint down to the river bank an' considered su'cide an' murdher an' a bit of arson on the quiet, an' after a while I raycalled a few o' the scatterin' remarks the Oul' Wan had vintilated. There was the van at a bargain, an' jumpin' the budget—which is the tinker's method o' matrimony—an' there was that sally bush in the scarth o' briars. How the divil did the oul' puckaun know o' the sally bush an' meself an' Peg Kate circumspeck as weasels? That stuck in me mind, an', be way o' investigation, I crept round there that evenin' at the fall o' dusk.

You guessed it! Peg Kate was there before me, an' her arms round me neck like a—a octopus.

"The luck o' the world we have, Tommy darlin'," says she, makin' me ear tickle. "Everything is right agin. Look what I have for you?"

I thought 'twas me money she was rubbin' agin me cheek, an' me heart lepped; but it was only a square o' white paper with writin' on it—she could write handy—an' a stamp at the foot.

"What the hell is that?" says I jumpin'.

"A receipt," says she.

"A receipt?" says I, an' you could knock me down with a feather.

"Yes, Tommy," says she happy. "A receipt for wan hunder' an' twinty quid marked be me gran'da be his own mark. We're grand, Tommy! He sold us the van horse, budget an' fittin's for wan hunder' an' twinty—a dead bargain. All he asks is a shake-down in a corner an' a bite now an' then—an' he says he'll taich you to bottom a can for nothin'. But we'll ha' nothin' to do with a tinker's life no more, Tommy darlin'. We'll have our own little travellin' shop. Isn't it grand?"

I swallowed me heart an' palate, an' tongue an' tonsilatus, an' after a while I coughed up me tongue.

"They was another ten pounds," I said in a wake voice.

"Here it is," says she, "an' th' Oul' Wan said it was for our honeymoon—Killarney an' the bed of honour itself. We can jump the budget to-morrow if we have to, an' then go off be ourselves an' get married decent be a priest, for I'll be a tinker no longer."

An' she shoved the two fi'-pun' notes into me hand,

an', as I live be bread, they was the same two identical notes you pushed at me the second evenin' o' Listowel Races. An' there you are, back where you started.

v

Thomasheen James sighed deeply and was so long silent that I ventured to prompt him.

"So you married your Peg Kate?"

"I had no bad intintions agin her that way. She was a dacent bit of a girl—an' strong as whalebone. I won't deny that any little things I might be whisperin' in her ear at the butt of a sally bush could be half-true—at the time—an' sure a man can ha' fancies o' his own. But, on the other hand, when a man comes face to face with bein' tied an' tethered an' bound to a female woman over the budget or before the altar rails it is time for him to stand off an' consider the jurisdiction of the whole affair. It was that time with me, an' whin I got me sinses agin I says:

"'Good enough, Peg Kate! But they's an oblige-ment on me with a gintleman up in Dub—Belfast,' I says, 'an' I must see him first.'

"She tightened her hould on me an' began to ullagone.

"'Tommy, would you fool me? If I let you out o' me sight now I'll never see you agin, an' I'll be goin' the roads o' Ireland with a double-barrel gun full o' buckshot to blow your stony heart into the dust o' the road.'

"I gev her a hug an' a wallop at the same time, an' the wallop was meant.

"'Me honour is consarned in this,' says I. 'You

wouldn't have me wrong a gintleman that is like a brother to me?' meanin' yourself.

"But still she cried—as the song says.

"'Look, Tommy! They's honest blood in me the same as yourself—me father's blood—an' I hate this livin' in bands an' stravagin' through the country for roguery. Let us go off in our own van an' start our bit of a travellin' shop.'

"'But there's oul' Matt,' says I, weakenin' a bit.

"'He's good at the bottom,' says she, 'an' odd times we could park him with his sister an' Mick Andy.'

"An' so we argyfied back an' fore, till she near melted the heart in me. It was only the thought of you, an' what you'd say, that held me up to me guns, an' I was softened so much that in the ind as a token of me faith I caught a grip of her hand an' agin for the secon' time put the two fivers in her palm an' shut her fingers on them.

"'There!' says I. 'Thim's for our honeymoon. Take good care o' them or I'll belt the hide off of you.'

"'I'll take care o' them,' says she, 'till they melt in me bosom.'

"'I'll hould this receipt,' I says, 'an' you stick to the van. P'ison Paddo for me, but nourish the Oul' Wan, for I want to strang'late him to me own specifications.'

"And there I left her," said Thomasheen James, his tone strangely desolate, "an' I have not been near her since. I been wanderin' the roads o' Ireland like a sowl out o' hell wonderin' whether it would be safer for me to go back to her or vinture me tale for your

291

misunderstandin'. Here I am now, me tale told, and you have a rake in your hand."

I was tempted to clout him one. He had indeed escaped matrimony with a tinker girl, but I was not in the least happy about it. I had seen that girl once and the picture she made remained in my mind; and Thomasheen James himself had subconsciously given her an attraction of her own. I was just being romantic. I moved to the other side of the fire out of temptation.

"Where is this poor girl now?" I asked restrainedly.

"Don't take it into your head you can find her," he warned quickly.

"Does she know where to find you?"

"With a double-barrel gun! You mus' take me for the dam'dest fool in the world." He sidled towards me. "You better keep this here docyment, since it contains your sixty solid quid."

He handed me a folded and draggled scrap of paper. I opened it carefully so that it would not fall apart at the creases. It was the neatly written receipt of one "Matew Sherdan X his mark for one hunderd and twenty pounds the price of van, horse, budjet, fitings painted green white and yelow as well as the dog paddo sold to Margaret Catherine Coffey and Tommy J. Doran gettin' marrid."

I refolded that document carefully and put it in my pocket; and I had a queer psychic unfinished feeling about the whole thing. I was not vexed, or inclined towards anger; I was just resignedly sorrowful.

"That is the way in real life," I said. "Winter is upon us and the autumn fire is dead."

"They's wan warmin' our shins this minit," said Thomasheen James, not comprehending.

I looked at him with distaste.

"But sometimes an old tree blossoms again in spring, and you may find that out to your cost."

"Ah! I have you." He cheered up at some thought of his own. "Becripers, you're right! An' I am no old tree neither. You've took a weight off me mind an' I knew you would. Do you know what we'll do? We'll give spring another chance at me. How long do you think it would take for two fivers to melt in a warm bosom?"

I then hit him with the rake handle.

CHAPTER XI

THOMASHEEN JAMES AND THE
ALMOST POSSIBLE

I

IT was spring again for the million millionth time, and again Thomasheen James, my-man-of-no-work, was restless. Often before, in the many years I had known him, I had noted that spring restlessness. With the burgeoning of the May blossom and the first surge of garden work the quarter-strain of gipsy-tinker blood had stirred in him, and always with the same result. He had fought against the wandering urge for days, and, then, my garden had not known him for many weeks.

He was fighting against it now this pleasant spring morning, and fighting harder than usual for some reason that I dimly understood. To hold his itching feet in one secure patch of ground he had enlisted even his inveterate enemy, the four-pronged digging-fork; and I sat under the new sunlight in the doorway of my summer-house and watched the losing battle. And a losing battle it must always be, with a gradual sinking of his standard until he no longer had a standard to lift. That thought often worried me, for I liked the man, and I will admit it here for the first and last time.

He was delving a trench for a row of maincrop peas, delving deep and delving well, but not for long at a time. After about two minutes of real effort he slowed down, paused, wiped a freckled forearm across a meagre brow, rested his midriff on the fork grip, and gazed up into the sunful, cloud-flecked, fragile spring sky. In another two minutes he resumed digging for another brief spell. He reached my vicinity and paused to contemplate me.

"Not a word wrote since you lit your pipe! Do you know what I'm thinkin'?"

"I do."

"You don't?"

"The call of the bad blood in you."

"Cripers!" His eyes widened. "I'll be afraid to think wan o' these days. Sure enough I got the bad drop in me. Me father, so it is said—and the divil has him—was a sailorman out of Arklow, an' me mother, peace to her sowl, was a gran'daughter o' Patsy Ward, the Wicklow tinker. An' isn't that a dam' nice mixture in me misfortunate veins?"

"You believe in heredity?"

"I wish I had your langwidge to addle me intelleck. Maybe I am a bit of a heretic, but small right have you, above anywan, to be throwin' it in me face."

"I mean that you blame your parents for your own sins?"

"Why not I, an' their blood in me carcase? But, be the powers! I'm waterin' it down with me own sweat, an' here goes!"

He finished the trench in a final burst, dropped his fork carelessly as will a bad gardener, and brought his wheelbarrow squeaking across the green patch before the summer-house. He sat on the tail end.

"I'll restore meself with a few draws o' the pipe afore I tackle the parfume o' the cow fertilisator," he said, producing an old briar of mine. I threw my pouch at him.

"Thank you. Do you know? I haven't a bad life of it. A bit o' pleasant an' useless work, a bite an' a sup three times a day not inclusive o' beer, a roof over me head at night, an odd half-dollar when not forgot, an' only the or'nary pastimes o' timptation pleasin' to the human frame. What more can a man want, I ask you?"

"The thing that you want."

"T' hell wi' that! Yes, sir! This gard'nin' occipation is the life for the thinkin' an' considerate man, an' I'm stayin' with it as long as I get fairplay. You wouldn't think o' offerin' me a reg'lar weekly wages, say twenty-five bob all found?"

He had mentioned this before. I looked round the garden where a reasonable portion of the work was to his credit for the first time, and I was tempted. But in the end I shook my head.

"Don't let us fool ourselves," I said.

He took that without protest, for he understood.

"I s'pose I'm no spadesman at the back of all?" he said with a touch of dolefulness.

"And never will be. Neither can you stay put. You'll either mellow or rot."

"Under six foot o' solid mud——"

"That's the place to do your rotting, after growing and ripening for threescore years and ten. I have noticed signs of decay in you this last year——"

"Decay! an' me doin' two min's work."

"You are deteriorating."

"Cripersjoe!"

"Your moral fibre is slackening."

"Go on! I'll have you in a minit."

"You will. You've had some misadventures in your time and survived them with a certain debonair spirit, but this last year you have done one or two things that you are ashamed of — one thing especially."

"An' you got out o' bed the wrong side this morning."

"Next year and other years," I went on inexorably, "you will do worse things and you will not be ashamed."

"Listen! Haven't I kep' out o' jail, anyway?"

"Keeping you out has not been easy."

"Very well so! Talk o' rottin', you can let me rot in jail next time!"

"If you compel me to; and that will be an end between you and me."

"I see—I see!"

And he did see. He is no fool in the uptake. He rubbed the back of his neck, his head turning from side to side disconsolately, and I watched him, feeling oddly sympathetic.

"I get it," he half-mused. "I suppose I get it —an' me thinkin' I was settlin' down like a Christian."

"Look here!" I said. "Have you any notion at all, any dream of something you'd like to do and keep on doing—something almost possible? Tell me."

"You're takin' me apart this fine mornin', an' if 'tis for me own good it feels like hell." He pulled at his pointed nose and gazed up at a drifting cloudlet. "All right! I got a notion, an' I don't mind tellin' you, me dear father confessor. Let me see! Let me see now. You know how I likes a bit o' discussion back an' fore with th' other party not buttin' in on me; an' I likes people comin' an' goin', an' a bit o' coin movin' from hand to fist, an' a buckeroo tryin' to do me down an' I not bein' done down—that sort o' thing."

"You don't mean politics?"

"What do you take me for? The thing I had in me eye was a small bit of a huckster-shop."

"A shop!" I knew what he was driving at now.

"What's wrong with it?" he said aggressively. "I started off me fancy with a lock-up shop, not in the country nor yet in the town neither. A sort o' terrytorial area like this, with a coupla dacent rows of artisan cottages convanient."

"What would you sell—illicit whiskey?"

"Don't put bad thoughts in me head, I'll take a note o' 't. What would I sell? I'd sell the daily an' weekly papers, especially *The Kerryman*, an' pins an' ink an' notepaper with a piece o' red blottin'-paper, sugar-candy an' chocklates an' gum drops—ay! gum drops, luminade an' ice-cream, pipes an' tabaccy an' fags, tape an' galluses, an' a hank o' huss'ife thread, studs an' cuff-links an' dimon' rings, penny pincils with a rubber top an' a gadget to p'int 'em that would bust the lead from stem to stern, an' noranges an' apples—not forgettin' the winner o' the two-thirty. What wouldn't I sell? I've a list somewhere I made out in a fancied hour. But what's the use o' talkin'? All them things with shop an' fittin's would take capital, wouldn't they?"

"Some."

He grinned at me possessively and went on.

"Mind you, the capital mightn't be outside me capacity, an' I can see meself takin' a pride in me organysation, customers reg'lar an' content, an' money in the till. But over agin that I up an ax meself: 'Would you stay with it, you tinker's get? Would you? Some fine mornin' like this, the birds singin' an' the air leadin' out along the country roads, would you up sail an' leave yourself an' the boss bank-rupted?'"

"Leave whom bankrupt?"

"I was thinkin' of you as me partner—fifty-fifty."

"Mine the capital and yours the profits?"

"Any divide you like. Sure I was only havin' the notion, an' I wint on addin' trimmin's for fun. 'No,' says I, 'a lock-up shop would tie a man to the ground, but couldn't I take advantage o' me little proclivity for the loose foot an' make a virtue out of it?' So I decided I'd kill two birds with wan welt of a stone an' keep a travellin' shop. What do you think o' that?"

"A shop on wheels—motor-car and trailer?" I led him on.

"No dam' feard! No contraptions for me. A tilt van painted green, white, an' yalla in strips, with a black stove-pipe stickin' out o' the top an' a coupla bunks, an' shelves galore, an' a tailpiece for counter—all drawn soft an' aisy be a fifteen-hand geldin' horse. An' in the four hard months o' winter we could park the horse an' van in your two-acre lot, usin' me present quarters as a store-room, payin' a fair rent an' givin' you a hand as required."

"Anything else?"

"To be sure. Them's only the everyday workin' parts o' me outfit. I kep' on embroiderin' me fancy in me idle hours—an' them not many. I'd have a double-barrel gun an' a fishin'-rod, a long-handled

gaff an' a otter-board, a stroke-'aul, twinty yards
o' net and a bundle o' brass-wire snares, an' sich-
like injines o' the sportin' gint. That'd be about
all."

"No. There is another small item."

He looked at me out of the side of an eye, and gave
a careless throw to his chin.

"It don't matter, a small iotem. What is it?"

"Peg Kate Coffey, the tinker girl."

He brazened it out, and gestured a hand carelessly.

"Oh, that one! Me mind wasn't within a million
miles o' that tinker's brat."

"She has been in your mind all winter, and now it
is spring again, and the old tree is blossoming. You
speak of a van painted in three colours, and a travelling
shop, but behind all is the thought of the tinker girl
who is keeping two five-pound notes warm in her
bosom—till they melt——"

"She'd melt 'em."

"Also she is looking through Ireland for you with
a double-barrel gun to blow the thing you call a
gizzard into the dust of the road."

He grimaced painfully, and his hand urged me not
to go on talking nonsense.

"You don't know tinkers, me dear sir, an' I do;
an' I can tell you now that last October I put all that
about Peg Kate to wan side forever. I buried it
deep an' two fi'-pun' notes along with it. I knew I
was doin' it, an' maybe I was a dam' fool. She was
a nice girl an' nice in her ways, an' many's the time
we talked of the van and the travellin' shop. I admit
it. It could be that I missed the tide—an' for good
an' all. Ay, sir! When all is said an' done Peg Kate
is a tinker girl, young and purty, an' her cousin Mick

Andy after her, that I broke the nose of, an' well able to melt two fivers his own way. Listen to me last word. If I know tinkers, and I do, Peg Kate jumped the budget with Mick Andy months and months ago."

"Why then dream of the van, and the trimmings?"

"Why drame at all?" He got to his feet smartly. "Don't let us be wastin' me time, an' work waitin' on me. This diggin' an' delvin' is me job, an' I got a strangle-hold on it forever an' a day."

He worked with fury till sunset, and then hid himself in his own quarters. Next morning he was gone, and I knew that he would not be back for many weeks. Later on I might get an S O S from him, as I had got often before, and, doubtless, I would answer it; but some day, some year, soon now, he would make no appeal to me—or I would not answer. The gulf would have widened beyond bridging. I felt strangely melancholy.

II

On an afternoon early in June my wife found me reclining in a hammock in the summer-house, a handkerchief over my eyes to help inventiveness.

"Wake up! An old gentleman at the front door looking for Thomasheen James." She removed the handkerchief.

"I am not asleep," I said, suppressing a yawn. "What did you say?"

"An old gentleman looking for Thomasheen James."

"He is no gentleman."

"He is venerable, at any rate. I suppose our Tommy is in trouble again."

"He is. You didn't give the complainant any information?"

"Of course not."

"Damnation! I s'pose I'd better see him."

I went round the house to the front door, and the old gentleman came down the steps, lifting a brown caroline hat off a mane of venerable white hair flowing into a more venerable white beard. What I could see of his face was unwrinkled and weather-brown, and his eyes were as blue and as mild as the sky. He wore a tail-coat of rusty brown cloth, one of those mid-Victorian cut-aways with side-flaps and two buttons in the small of the back.

"Good morrow, sirr!" he greeted me in a rich baritone. "I was wonderin' if I could see me ould friend, Thomasheen James?"

For a moment I considered denying all knowledge of that individual, but then thought I had better prosecute an enquiry of my own. I said non-committally:

"Thomasheen James! Did you expect to find him here?"

"Just be accident, sirr, but it don't matter a hair. We chanced to be passin' your gate in the van, an' I thought I'd look in an' pass the time o' day with an oul' friend."

He was passing the gate in a van. That was my first hint. I turned and looked across the lawn towards the road. The van was there. I could see half of it above the clipped privet hedge, and surely I had heard Thomasheen James describe such a van: "A tilt van painted green, white, an' yalla in strips, an' a black stove-pipe stickin' out o' the top." That fitted, except that the yellow was really orange. And then and there

302

I recalled another word-etching of Thomasheen James's: "An oul' white-livid puckaun with a white smeg in a caroline hat, an' you'd think butter wouldn't melt in his mouth." Thus he had described Matt Sheridan, the Old Man of the tinker tribes; and here was a man that fitted that description—hair, beard, caroline hat, and mildness. But, also according to Thomasheen James, "he had a weight o' sin an' expayrience behind him to sink a battleship." He was speaking again.

"The bit o' fire is out in the stove, sirr. I wonder would the missus boil a kittle for me at the back door?"

"Certainly. Go round and the maid will get you some hot water."

I guessed that he wanted to do some prospecting on his own, and that suited me. I waited till he had disappeared round the corner, and then I walked across the lawn to the front gate. The van was a little distance beyond and I could not see the driving-bench.

A brindled lurcher dog, half bull-terrier, half hound, lay somnolent, jowl on paws, under the front axle of the van. It opened one eye at me, kept that eye fixed steadily, but made neither move nor growl. A shapely brown gelding, neatly groomed, something over fifteen hands, lazed, hip aslant, in the shafts.

I walked up to the front of the van, and the girl seated on the driving-bench under the jut of the tilt started and flushed, and a light lit in her dark eyes and went out again. I did not know if she knew me, but I knew her. That was no wonder. Having seen that tinker girl once, few men would readily forget her. She was young and fresh and bonny and vital as only her breed can be; black-haired, ivory and bronze, sparkling, full of young blood, and not yet debased. A varicoloured silk-muslin kerchief was loose about her shoulders, and a red ribbon held her raven hair loosely at the back of her neck.

"How are you, Miss Peg Kate Coffey?" I saluted her, and the light lit in her eyes again as she smiled.

"Fine, thank you, sir. I hope you're well yourself!" Her voice was softly husky, not yet with the tinker harshness.

"I saw you at Listowel Races last year," I said.

"Maybe you did, sir."

"You were with Thomasheen James O'Doran—Tommy you call him."

I was watching her carefully, and at mention of his name her eyes flickered and became guarded. I would not play cat-and-mouse with her.

"He was here, but he is not here at present. How did you know he was here?"

"Francy Lawson o' the Model at Ard-na-Righ told us, sir."

"You were looking for him, then?"

"'Tis the Oul' Wan, me gran'da, sir," she answered quickly.

"I had hoped he had gone looking for you?"

"When, sir?" she snapped.

"Some three weeks ago."

"No, sir." She shook her head and was definitely glum. "He could find me in three days if he wanted to find me. He knows the way."

"Perhaps he was afraid of that double-barrel gun

full of buckshot," I said. I wanted her to know that I knew.

"What gun, sir? What would I be doin' with a gun? Och, that!" She lifted her limber shoulders, started to smile, and then had a flash of the tinker spirit. "Maybe a coupla grains o' powder an' shot wouldn't hurt him. He was only talkin' *rameis*,* all the same."

"Have you those two five-pound notes still?"

"I have them." She flushed, and her hand moved towards her breast. "I have them here to throw in his face."

She frowned and grew sullen, and I saw that she would close up if I pursued that line.

"Your grandfather is looking for Thomasheen James. Why?"

But that question was too direct. She said, but not impudently:

"You're askin' a lot o' questions, sir. You'll have to ask the Oul' Wan that."

"That onnatural rip hasn't no more manners than me foot," said a deploring baritone voice behind me.

Matt Sheridan had come quietly down by the grass-edging, and stood in the gateway, a steaming kettle in his hand. I do not know how much he had heard.

"Did you find him?" I asked, and he saluted me with his free hand.

"I wish I had a friend like you, sirr. I wonder where he'll be hangin' out at all?"

"Do you want him?"

He took his Old One's way of answering. He pointed accusingly at Peg Kate.

* nonsense.

"She has the melt broke in me, that wan. I dunno what to do with her at all at all, an' she with the bad drop in her. Her da, the poor fella, an' God rest him, was a honest soft slob of a farmer's son from the Cork border be the name o' Coffey, an' a good tinker for all that he had a wake bone in his skull. An' there she is, a throwback in spite o' me to ginerations o' soft bog-trottin' farmers. I'd be 'shamed o' me life, sirr, if anywan was to find out the latest notion she's took into her head, the poor *onshuch*. Don't ax me, sirr!"

"They's no shame in it," cried Peg Kate with spirit. "What shame is there in keepin' a shop?"

"A shop!" I cried. "A shop on wheels?"

"Wo—wo—wo! Did you ever hear the likes?" lamented Matt Sheridan. "Seed, breed an' ginera-tion the Shuridans is dacent travellin' men and tins-men, an' she talks of a shop—a huckster's shop sellin' to bog-trotters——"

"'Tis honest, anyway," cried Peg Kate.

"'Tis worse. 'Tis a tarnation disgrace—an' in me own van too."

"It is not your van, an' you know it."

"Who says so?"

"I do," I said. "That van, horse, dog, and fittings belong to your granddaughter and Thomasheen James. I hold the receipt."

"Very well so!" said Matt Sheridan, showing no surprise. "Let her find her own mud-foot fancy an' run her consarned shop. I'm finished."

He put the kettle on the ground and made as if to mount the step of the van, had another thought, turned to me, and went off in one of his indirect statements.

306

"You didn't know me young brother Andy, sirr. You did not, for he kilt himself with bad whiskey ten years ago, an' how he did it I dunno, for he was rank p'ison himself; an' what was worse, he left a pup behind him that bangs Banagher an' Ballinasloe for drink an' divilment. That's Mick Andy, an' there's the girl he's after——"

"I'd rather drownd meself first," said Peg Kate.

"'Tis a fair choice—mathrimony or hell," said her grandfather grimly.

"Could not the girl run her own business without interference?" I demanded, getting warm for this pretty tinker girl who did not want to be a tinker girl all her days.

"I don't want no false man at all, so I don't," cried Peg Kate, near to stormy tears. "All I want is me own rights in me own van."

"There she goes agin," deplored her grandfather. "Till she has a man of her own she's a tinker's daughter, an' the tinkers can hould their own in spite of an Ould Wan his feet in the grave."

I came to a sudden decision.

"Let us get to the bottom of this," I said. "Suppose you two people come up to the house and talk it over with my wife? She is wiser than I am, Peg Kate. Come on!"

"Your wife, sir?" Peg Kate was suddenly shy. "I'd be 'shamed before a lady."

"Come down off that perch, you farmer's brat!" roared her grandfather. He turned to me and was direct for once. "We'll come, sir. Disgrace or no disgrace, I want to do the fair thing be this crathur of a girl. She's all I got, an' if we don't get a hould of her own mud-foot soon she'll be married the tinker's

307

way in spite o' me to Mick Andy, and he's the lad 'll drink the van an' the pony an' the pony's tacklin' same as a cat lappin' crame. Come down, Pegeen Kate, you rip!"

III

The best-laid plans o' mice and men—and of women——!

My wife made a plan and baited a trap. And nothing happened. Once or twice a month for three months Peg Kate Coffey, her grandfather protestingly under her thumb, called on us; but the other party, unknowingly in the scheme, to wit Thomasheen James, failed to co-operate. He had vanished for a longer period than usual, and no murmur or appeal came back from that wilderness full of wolves where he loved to lie; indeed, I was beginning to wonder whether that wilderness had finally claimed him.

In those three months my wife had discovered an admiration and affection for this steadfast Peg Kate. So had I, but I did not say so. The girl was a unique throwback to the settled strain in her, and, now more than ever, hated the wild, drifting, ungoverned life of the tinker tribes; and, strangest thing of all, she had an unquenchable affection for Thomasheen James. He had come to her out of what she took to be a respectable world, treated her with a gallantry that she was not accustomed to, was her one scrap of high romance in a sordid company as materialist as hell; and she cherished that simulacrum with all her tough young might, so that we, out of sheer sympathy, were impelled to help her.

But for three months nothing happened. And then, about the first week of September, my wife received a letter from Peg Kate. She wrote a neat hand, and expressed herself quite clearly.

Dear lady,

I take my pen in hand to write you these few lines hoping they find you well as they leave me at present so that you can tell himself that he need not go to no more trouble about me as my granfather Matt is after telling me that Mick Andy Sheridan and his mother and her lot is making plans to marry me on Mick Andy the last night of Listowel races the end of the month.

I can not get away by myself no more they all of them keep a watch on me day and night and lamed the horse on me with a nail in the frog of his hoof, they will make me jump the budget drunk and brave with Mick Andy the last night of the races and after that what am I but a tinker all my days till I get a chance to drownd myself or my dog Paddo tears him for lifting a hand to me.

You and himself did all you could for me and I will not forget it for ye the longest day I live. Do not tell no one when it is all over, no one at all and god bless you with respects to all Margaret Kate Coffey.

"Oh dear! Oh dear!" said my wife, not hiding her distress. "Her heart is breaking and she cannot say it. Can you do nothing—nothing at all?" She flared at me. "You that could do what you liked with that man-of-no-work of yours——!"

I left hastily and kept going till I found my friend Detective-Sergeant Joe O'Dowd. Joe was very pleased to exhibit for me the efficiency of his branch.

"Nothing at all!" he said. "Haven't we this bit of an island plotted like the palm o' your hand? Give me three days and I'll have him earthed for you."

"You will not," I said.

"Three days! Will you have half a dollar on it?"

"I will," I said, for I am unlucky in bets and I wanted to be unlucky then.

But I won that small bet, doubled it and won again, offered to redouble it, whereupon Joe, accusing me of a new racket, called all bets off. He had found a stale scent many weeks old, followed it up, lost it, found it again, and alarmed the quarry, who forthwith popped out through his bolt-hole, dived into another burrow, pulled it in after him, and made no fresh trail for three weeks. And three weeks brought us to Listowel Races.

The famous races were on Tuesday, Wednesday, and Thursday of the last week in September. On Wednesday afternoon, all hope gone, I had a visit from Davy Hand, sometime-partner to Thomasheen James in schemes of extreme dubiety. Davy's visits were only occasional, and they invariably had something to do with Thomasheen James. I immediately became interested and wary, especially wary. I hid both under boldness.

"You're welcome, Davy," I said, "but if you are looking for Thomasheen James he is not here."

"I knew that, sir," said Davy.

If he knew that much he might know something else. And why was he here? I was bold some more.

"And another thing, Davy Hand! If he is in trouble and you are here looking for help you can go straight to hell!"

"Oh megod, sir!"

"I'm sick and tired paying fines for him, and he can go to jail this time. What's he done?"

"Dam'd if I know, sir! But he might be in jail all right. The p'lice was lookin' for him a month ago."

"How do you know?" I barked at him.

"I know all right, sir," said Davy, starting his own game.

Knowing Thomasheen James and knowing Davy Hand, I now knew that the latter knew where the former was hiding out; and I knew that Davy Hand was visiting me at Thomasheen James's behest to find out if I knew anything and what it was; and I also knew that if Davy found out that it was I who had set the police on Thomasheen James he would shut up like a clam.

It was then and for the first time in my life that I bluffed Davy Hand right up my alley.

"You say that the police were looking for him a month ago?" I queried, moving closer to him.

"They was, sir."

"A month ago!" I shook my fist under Davy's nose and bellowed. He is a small tubby man and not valorous. "You dam' little Dublin Jackeen! He'll be in jail now past help. Why did you not tell me before?"

"Wait—wait, sir!" he cried, starting away. "He can't be in jail yet. Sure 'twas only yesterday I got the letter."

"So you got a letter? Why didn't you say so at once? How the devil can I help him if I don't know where he is?"

"Do you know the Nyer valley, sir?" Davy capitulated.

"In Waterford? I fished the lower Nyer last year."

"He's at the top-end, sir, under the mountains,

311

workin' the harvest with a hill-farmer be the name of Martin Kennedy."

"Let a mountain fall on him," I said, calming down, "and if he needs help let him ask for it. Have some beer, Davy?"

"Whatever you say, sir. I wonder what'n hell he's done now? But he's safe enough where he is."

I did not enlighten Davy. He had two bottles of beer, groomed the canary, and departed.

I went in and told my wife. She said:

"How far is it to the Nyer?"

"A hundred-odd miles."

"And to Listowel from there?"

"The same again."

"You could get there in time——"

"To get myself killed in a tinker's camp?"

"Think of the good work! Think of Peg Kate!"

"The work might not be so good—for her or Thomasheen James," I protested finally.

But she was determined to fulfil Peg Kate's romance or break a bone—my bone.

"You could take my car," she said.

That was how I ran Thomasheen James to earth next morning before nine o'clock. He was stooking oat sheaves with a long mountainy man in a scrap of cornfield in a secluded valley below the heathery swell of the Comeragh mountains near the head-waters of the Nyer. Down below the young stream chuckled over clean pebbles, and across the valley a great hillside was one smooth sweep of polished-green rhododendron.

Thomasheen James was toiling within fifty yards of the clay-fenced, sandy hill-track, and he watched the car to a standstill. I touched the horn, and saw his head and shoulders jerk. Then he rubbed a sandy poll below his deepsea-pilot cap, and walked as if dragged across the stubbles. His braces looped to his knees, his stagged shirt-sleeves showed his wiry, freckled, tattooed arms to the shoulder; his stringy neck was raw copper; his eyes were as clear and as blue as blue china. I had never seen him in harder condition. He put one leg over the clay fence and sat astride.

"Was it you put the cops on me?" he greeted me.

"Blast you and Davy Hand!" I said. "What have you done this time?"

"I done nothin', an' I didn't send for you naither. Becripers! I'll demolish that Jackeen the minit I lay eyes on him." Then his eyes lit up. "I'm sorry in me heart to bring you this far for nothin', you're a loyal man."

"Don't flatter yourself," I said, and added not untruthfully: "I am prospecting the southern waters for a late run of sea-trout and thought I'd look you up in passing."

"Ay! I see you got the rods in the back o' the car."

"I suppose you'd want to join me but for the harvest work?" I said. "Don't let me keep you from it."

He looked distastefully over his shoulder at the half-stooked field.

"I been holdin' the job down for a whole month, bent on provin' to all consarned that I can take a job an' keep it." He grinned at me. "You're not after temptin' me to forsake the best part of a week's wages?"

"Not at all! Get back to the good work! See you next month probably."

313

I took a chance and put a hand on the gear lever, whereat he yelled sharply:

"God'llmighty! don't forsake me that way. To hell with your hurry, an' to hell with me wages as well. Wait wan minit!"

He trotted across to a stook for his old tweed jacket, and said a few words in the general direction of the lean farmer; and that man lifted up his hands and his voice in a protest that carried across the valley of the Nyer. Thomasheen James merely wagged a hand at him and came away.

"I'm the only free man out o' captivity," he boasted. "Whin me jacket is on I'm outfitted to explore the South Pole." He scrambled in beside me. "You better hurry, or Tom'll come across an' explore us with a two-prong fork."

I worked the car round on the narrow road and departed rather ashamed of myself.

It was as easy as that to lure Thomasheen James away from work. I knew it would be, outfitted as I was for fishing and loitering. But, having lured him, what then? I had no detailed plan of campaign and was merely concentrating on getting him to Listowel that day. After that!!

"We'll take a look at the Blackwater and Feale tributaries," I said.

"Fine! That'll take us all day. You'll find the water stale with the drouth."

I drove fast and merely glanced at the streams in passing, agreeing that the waters were too slow and sluggish, until we came to the fast-flowing Feale, and that I decided was just worth a trial. We were then at the small town of Abbeyfeale, a bare ten miles from Listowel, and the time was shortly after noon.

"We'll try a pool or two after a bite of grub?" I suggested.

"As well fish a bucket o' spring water," said Thomasheen James, "but let us ate anyway."

I bought a sporting edition of a Dublin paper, and while waiting for chops in the little hotel we sat at the bar and drank cool lager. I looked casually over the sporting news, and, after a time, exclaimed suddenly:

"Hello! Do you know the day it is?"

"Thursday in the Nyer, but I could aisy miss a day or two in that same place."

"Thursday, the last day of Listowel Races," I said.

Thomasheen James looked at me for a long time, and I kept a still face.

"I knew that all along," he said. "What's in your mind?"

"You could fish a mile up and a mile down, and I could run across and see three or four races."

"You don't want to take me?"

"Would you dare?"

"Why not I dare?"

"Every tinker in Munster will be there," and I added boldly: "You might run across Peg Kate Coffey with her double-barrel gun!"

After another considering pause he spoke half-ruminatively.

"I been puzzlin' me head about you all mornin'. 'Tis in me mind that some gint not a million miles away set Joe Dowd on me, an' for why I don' know. An' here we are approachin' Listowel Races, an' the name o' Peg Kate in a man's mouth. Is it to the races he's takin' me?"

"If you care to risk it."

"Mind you, I dunno!" he said rather plaintively. "I was never no more nor a lump o' cobbler's wax in your hands, an', indeed an' indeed, you didn't never mistreat me if you could help it—an' you couldn't." He struck the bar sharply with a forefinger and reached an open palm to me. "Lend me ten bob an' I'll risk it. All the rest is ould history now in a tinker's life."

Again it was as easy as that, and I began to worry at the easiness of it.

IV

We got on the open Island Course across the Feale while the second race was being run—a mile-and-a-half hurdle.

"Just me bloody luck!" lamented Thomasheen James, watching the horses lean over for the straight. "I had the winner o' that race taped. See the cherry jacket, wan leg over the rails? Thim's Tom Kent's colours, an' I always folly Tom at the South meetin's. Cripers! he's bet. Are you goin' in the Ring?"

"Not in this suit."

"You'll do as well with the prooletarians, an' I'll give you two winners, not forgettin' to restore you your ten bob."

For the first time in my life I was not interested in horse-racing. I do not even remember if Thomasheen James gave me two winners or four losers, but I do know that he did not refund me any ten shillings.

The third day at Listowel is not the crowded day on the open course, and so it is not difficult to find a sought-for individual in the bookmakers' avenue. The tinker tribes were there in full strength, Cartys, Coffeys, Briens, Sheridans, Wards and all; and after the third race I picked out the caroline hat above the white beard of Matt Sheridan. He was drawing money from a betting-man. Peg Kate was not with him.

"Be the powers! there's oul' Matt!" cried Thomasheen James. "Wait till I pluck a fist o' goat's wool out o' him for the sake o' oul' times."

He slipped forward between wide country shoulders and gave the old man a solid clap between the shoulder-blades; and the old man whirled, quick as a youth, his gnarled old fighting fists coming up on guard. Thomasheen James slapped the bunched knuckles.

"Me whitened oul' sepulcrit! Put your hand there!"

"Me man, I rimimber your thievin' countenance well, but the name on it escapes me mimory," said the shameless old liar.

"Oh, cripers! Listen at him, after unloadin' a secon'-hand van on me only a year ago! Is it so you have resould me green, white, an' yalla van, you ould——?"

"Thomasheen James!" cried old Matt. "I'd never known you from Adam. Manalive! the years are tellin' on you, an' 'tis no wonder."

He shook Thomasheen James's hand mightily, and looked across at me, no recognition in his guileful old eyes.

"This gintleman is a fri'nd o' mine," Thomasheen James told him, "an' you'll have nothin' to do with him for his own sake."

"Glad I am to make the acquaintance o' wan

gintleman anyway," said old Matt, and pumped my hand with dignity.

We moved out of the press. Thomasheen James had something on his mind.

"Did you hear me, you oul' billygoat?" he persisted. "What did you do with me van?"

"Your share o't is safe an' sound up at the camp," old Matt told him.

"Oh! Me share of it!" said Thomasheen James, a little deflated.

"To be sure! Th' other half belongs to me gran'-daughter Peg Kate—you might rimimber her? Look here, Thomasheen James!" put the old tinker quickly, "what'll you take for your half—you'll not be needin' it now?"

Thomasheen James looked at him suspiciously.

"What do you want with me half, Oul' Wan?"

And Matt Sheridan answered him promptly:

"I want to make a weddin' present o't to Peg Kate."

Thomasheen James stepped back as if someone were making ready to hit him. His mouth opened and shut. He looked from Matt to me and back again, and there was speculation in his look.

"Didn't Peg Kate jump the budget yet?" he asked curiously.

"To-night when the clock strikes twelve," Matt told him.

"To-night! With Mick Andy?"

"The very fella—Mick Andy."

Thomasheen James looked round him.

"I didn't see Peg Kate about?"

"She's up at the camp gettin' ready for the jollifications."

318

Thomasheen James narrowed his eyes at him.

"She wouldn't be tied to the wheel o' the van, be any chance?"

Matt Sheridan moved his massive head weightily.

"They's wan or two watchin' her, an' I won't tell you no lie."

"Maybe you are tellin' the truth for wance in your life—be a mistake."

"Don't let us say no more about it now," said Matt. "Will you two gintlemin have a drink on me?"

Thomasheen James looked doubtfully at me and I said:

"Thank you, Mr Sheridan. Certainly."

"He was never slow to stand his hand, an' I'll say that for him," said Thomasheen James.

We went across to the big marquee at the back of the betting-pitch, and found an empty end at the temporary bar of rough pine boards.

"Put a name to it, gints?" invited Matt Sheridan.

Thomasheen James sampled his mug of beer and ruminated. I hopefully saw that he could not get away from a certain subject.

"So the Oul' Wan wants me share o' the van for Mick Andy?" he speculated.

"What use is it to you, Thomasheen James? I'd give you ten—twenty pounds for it."

"Ten—twenty pounds! Becripers! You got a ginerous nature, Oul' Wan! Maybe me share is no use to me, but wouldn't I be the dam' fool to make a bad bargain till I have to. Listen, Oul' Wan!" His chin jutted. "Whin Peg Kate is over the budget with Mick Andy, talk to me then."

"That's the talk I like," said the Old One.

"But get ten—twinty out o' your head," said Thomasheen James. "It'll be nearer eighty." And he lifted his mug and drank deeply.

A loud half-angry bellow was lifted behind us, and Thomasheen James's shoulder was thumped so forcefully that his breast struck the counter, his teeth clacked on the mug, and beer splashed into his face. He slapped the pot on the boards and turned, the light of battle in his eye. And then the light died down, and the hostile expression was wiped downwards off his face with the hand that wiped the beer.

"Behave yourself, Mick Andy!" he said surlily.

"You've no bloody manners, you tinker's vomit!" said Matt Sheridan more adequately, stiffening up into real pugnacity.

"Look what the cat brought in!" said Mick Andy.

I had not seen this Mick Andy before, and I examined him with interest. He was a short, powerfully-built, youngish man gone sadly to evil flesh. He had a blue jowl over-full, a broken bridge to his nose, a head of crisp black curls, and the devilish tinker eyes. A dangerous-looking customer whose youth was on the brink of inevitable debasement. And only a year ago Thomasheen James had belted the daylights out of him. So Thomasheen James had said, but Thomasheen James was usually more than fair to himself. I began to wonder, with this squat warrior before my eyes.

"What brought you out of your hidy-hole, you yalla fox?" He was jeering at Thomasheen James.

"That's me own business," said Thomasheen James distantly.

"And mine to-day. You heard the news about meself an' Peg Kate?"

"You're welcome to her," said Thomasheen James with cold generosity.

"Yerrah! Why would you say that, me darlin' lad? Come on! Be a sport, an' fight your corner. Last year over beyant you kicked in three o' me ribs an' I down from a peg of a stone. I forgive you, but 'tis another day now, an' wouldn't you like to cock that navy cap at me for half a minit? Wouldn't you, me dacent bastar'?"

"I don't want no trouble with the likes o' you, Mick Andy," said Thomasheen James with dignity.

"Dam' well you don't! Change your mind an' I'll accommodate you. So-long now, me yalla canary!"

He gave Thomasheen James a playful prod in the shirt-front and went off, laughing uglily. The prod was so suddenly sharp that it made Thomasheen James grunt gaspingly and fold a hand across his midriff.

"I kep' me temper well," he said with difficulty.

"You did so," agreed Matt judicially. "He's dam' handy with his mawleys, Mick Andy."

"I wouldn't never hit a man in the worse o' drink," amplified Thomasheen James.

"He didn't touch a drop for two whole days—or a day an' a half anyway," said Matt.

"Moreover, I wouldn't deface him on his weddin' day." Thomasheen James was never short of an excuse, as I knew.

"You'll have it your own way," said Matt agreeably. He tossed off his neat whiskey. "Excuse me, gints! I got a bit o' business——"

"Is it a good thing, Oul' Wan?"

"'Tisn't at all." He took two paces away and turned round. "I wonder would this gintleman like to come to the weddin' to-night?"

"I should be delighted——"

Thomasheen James interrupted me quickly.

"Would we be welcome, Oul' Wan?"

"Me honourable friends, who would put a hurtin' finger on ye? You ought to know that, Thomasheen James! The oul' camp across the river, eight o'clock till the drink gives out. I'll be on the look-out for ye."

He hurried off towards the betting-pitch, and Thomasheen James grumbled.

"The tinker all out! A good thing in the fourth, an' he wouldn't give it to us." He turned to me. "Him an' you know aich other?"

"You introduced us," I prevaricated.

"You know what I mane. I saw ye speculatin' one another an' avoidin' intercoorse. I dunno——"

I changed the subject.

"So that was the notorious Mick Andy?"

"You saw the best o' him, and thim's his manners."

"That was the man you belted last year?"

"As prime a beltin' as ever you saw."

"He seemed to give it a different complexion."

"Cripesman! You couldn't expect to pacificate a tinker with wan beltin'."

"And he is marrying Peg Kate?"

"Are you excusin' me to give him a second goin' over? Have another drink?"

"No! I will not drink with you," I said sternly.

"Whatever you say. 'Tis in me heart to get thorough drunk this blasted day."

322

I had now no smallest hope of doing anything to save Peg Kate, but some unconscious purpose in me kept nagging at him.

"Mick Andy took a long time to get round Peg Kate—a full year."

"'Tis cause for wonder right enough."

"She was waiting for you all that time."

"It could be. I missed the tide——"

"The tide will be full again, to-night."

"For Mick Andy—'tis him she's marryin'."

"She is being forced——"

"She is. An' that settles it. Whin the tinkers makes up their minds to a thing they'll make no change this side o' hell except for a better man."

"Damn you!" I swore exasperatedly. "Aren't you the better man?" I knew already that he was not.

He looked at me underbrowed and shook his head.

"Mick Andy is fifteen years younger'n me."

"And drink-sodden?"

"He has a coupla stone weight over me."

"Adipose tissue."

"Whatever it is he has it. All right! Let me shame meself. Whisper here! Last year, back yonder, he was leatherin' the stuffin' out o' me till Peg Kate hit him a chroosht with a lump o' rock, an' even so I had to root him in the ribs to hould him down. What have you to say now?"

"Only this," I said. "I am seeing this thing through right up till the budget is jumped."

"'Tis a pagan custom, but you needn't be wan bit afraid."

"You are, and you can stay away."

"I am afraid. You can bet your last bob I am afraid. But I am comin' with you all the same, an' 'tisn't to see no Peg Kate jump no budget. No, sir! I'm comin' to squeeze your sixty quid out o' oul' Matt Shurridan, an' not a penny less. It is the laist an' last thing I can do for you, an' if 'tisn't done to-night it won't be done at all—not with Mick Andy in possession. Come on! I want to see this race."

v

The tinkers' camp was a mile out of town in a grassy, furze-scattered common backed by a grove of sycamores undergrown with briars and sallaghs. Thomasheen James and I walked out there that night before ten o'clock.

The festivity was in full swing when we arrived, and we had been hearing it for the last half-mile. We skirted a clump of furze on a hosting that is growing rarer every year, even in Ireland: a full meeting of the tribes for a budget-jumping. All the tinkers in Munster, many from Leinster, some from Scotland, were milling there in that clearing. Night had fallen, but there was a full harvest moon in a clear sky, and, besides, a big bonfire of peats and bog-pine as well as some cooking-fires blazed across the trampled grass; and each van—twoscore or more along the margin of the grove—carried its paraffin flare.

"You could pick a pin off the ground," said Thomasheen James.

The fronts of the vans were to the clearing, the shafts had been removed, and the wide driving-benches made convenient perches for the too old and the too young for wassail and footwork; but the bulk of the motley crew, men, women, and a multitude of children, were circling and shifting about and between the fires, drinking, eating, dancing, figuring, singing, embracing, not yet fighting. The high tinker yells, the wail of fiddles, the skirl of pipes, the drone of melodeons and mouth-organs, made a heady and blood-stirring blend and medley of sound. I felt it stirring in my own tame or tamed blood.

The ragged children were having the time of their lives. Tinkers, especially the men, are notably fond and inconsiderately considerate of children. More than once that night I saw a wild tinker, who would brutally fight anything on two legs or on four, with a child on his back throttling him, a younger child in the crook of an arm, and a tin mug of beer in his free hand; and, before himself drinking, he would lift the mug over his shoulder to the child's ready mouth.

We were half-way across the clearing towards the Sheridan green, white, and orange van before anyone noticed us. Then a man shouted: "Thomasheen James, by hell!" and within ten seconds we were surrounded by men and women.

They were entirely friendly and even enthusiastic. Little notice was taken of me, but Thomasheen James was thumped and hand-pumped and shouted at broadly by everyone. His popularity—and it was real—astonished me, and gave me a fresh aspect of the man.

And then the press about us broke apart, and there was the squat powerful figure of Mick Andy driving through. He bellowed cheerfully, and there came a sudden hush. Everyone there knew of the bad blood between the two rivals, and looked for a show-down—drink and meat to a tinker.

325

"Thomasheen James, me bould cur dog! Are you for tryin' me out after all?" Mick Andy hallooed again and swept open the buttons of his vest.

But there, before Thomasheen James had time to show the yellow, Matt Sheridan's huge old figure came heaving through ; and with a savage hand-thrust that was almost a blow he drove Mick Andy backwards. His baritone roar drowned all other sounds.

"Aisy, you scut! This gintleman and Thomasheen James is me guests of honour, an' that goes in earth or hell."

"Hurroo the gintleman!" someone shouted.

"Up, Thomasheen James!" yelled several.

Matt shook his knuckly fist under Mick Andy's nose.

"Listen to me, you botch's brit! Make trouble here to-night an' I have ten min to lave you so you won't jump no budget in a month o' Sundays. D'you hear me?"

Mick Andy, grinning wickedly, struck the fist aside.

"Take it aisy yourself, Oul' Wan. They'll be no trouble if the yalla canary don't make it."

"Maybe he might then," said Matt. "This way, me friends!"

A woman clapped me on the shoulder as I followed Matt and said: "You're welcome, sir, whoever you are."

But I knew that Thomasheen James would make no trouble.

Matt led us to the green, white, and orange van; and there was Peg Kate herself, young and bonny in her bright shawl, sitting alone on the driving-bench at the head of the let-down steps. She came down slowly to meet us. The blood had ebbed from the smooth old ivory of her cheeks, and her eyes were blazing black. Yes, she was vitally young and even lovely, and if Thomasheen James had a heart in him anywhere it must be turning over.

She looked at me, and I moved my head negatively from side to side, for it would not be fair to rouse any hope in her.

"Two fri'nds o' mine, Pegeen," Matt said. "You'll be knowin'——"

"Wan o' them is welcome." Peg Kate gave me a strangely graceful, slow bob of the head.

She gave Thomasheen James a level blaze.

"Th' other is no fri'nd o' mine."

"Peg Kate! the night that's in it!" protested her grandfather.

"I been a bad fri'nd, I admit it," said Thomasheen James with humility.

"No fri'nd at all—but a traitor! The wan man I trusted to take me out o' ways I hated! The coward that failed me! Here now to see me part of a bad bargain."

Thomasheen James hung his head and was dumb. Peg Kate looked at that down-hung head, her mouth barely under control, and to keep herself from breaking down she whipped her temper. She thrust a hand inside the folded shawl down into her bosom, and brought forth a creamy envelope that crinkled in the crush of her fingers. She thrust it at him.

"Take it!" she said with low violence. "Take it! it is yours—two five-pound notes. I won't have nothing that belongs to you. Look to see if I didn't rob you! Go on! Take it!"

He took it, smoothed it, lifted it towards his face.

"'Tis warm," he said in a whisper.

"Why not it? where it was over my heart I tore you out of." She flung a hand over her shoulder. "That van—all of it—is yours too, but you'll not get it. Th' Oul' Wan here will pay you back what he took off of me——"

"Lids o' hell!" exploded the Old One.

"Every penny he will pay you." Peg Kate stamped the ground. "And after that you can go down to hell your own way, an' I'll go down to hell me own way."

She swept by us and out towards the blazing bonfire, where tinkers were furiously dancing furious eight-hand Irish reels.

"Begobs!" exclaimed Matt Sheridan, blowing an astounded breath. "You're well rid of her, Thomasheen James. She has the sour, bad-timpered Coffey drop in her."

"Maybe I am, an' maybe she has," said Thomasheen James wearily.

Matt Sheridan sat us on the driving-bench of the van and ministered unto us in princely fashion.

I am not going into details of that night. There was eating and there was drinking, and we had our share of both; but I was prudent enough to pour most of the strong liquor that was pressed on us round the corner of the driving-bench. Thomasheen James did not object. Drunk, he loses all discretion and at the same time becomes physically innocuous.

After a time I left him and sought Peg Kate among the crowd. She came to me herself, smiling.

"Will you dance with me, sir?"

"I was casting round for a good-looking partner," I said, "but you'll do, Peg Kate."

We danced an eight-hand reel and a set of jig

quadrilles, and in between times we said a few words.

"I am sorry, Peg Kate," I said.

"You done your best, sir, but 'tis too late now. Mick Andy'd make smithereens o' him—an' no stone handy to me hand."

"You don't want him in smithereens?"

"I don't, thin, an' that's quare."

"Could you not slip away with me? I have the car in the hotel yard."

"They's four o' them watchin' us, an' they'd rip you as soon as look at you."

"This jumping the budget is not legal, Peg Kate. I mean, it will not bind you."

"It will bind me enough this night," said Peg Kate steadily, not blinking the fact. "An' what am I after that? Only a tinker girl, an' I wish I never was borned."

I had no more to say. I went back to Thomasheen James and sat down by him.

"I wouldn't doubt you!" he commended. "You batthered a few tricky steps in that reel."

"The tightness in my throat made my shoes too tight also," I said.

"It would. You've a soft heart."

He was sober enough, but the drink was crawling in his secret places. He leant his shoulder against mine, and I sat still.

"Ay! You're near as soft-hearted as your missus. I knew that from the start, an' played on it many's the time. We had our bits o' fun, hadn't we? I won't do it agin."

"You will."

"I won't! Not never! I'm sunk. Me name is

mud. I missed the tide. I'm on the down road for hell—an' so is Peg Kate. Poor Pegeen! I'm not wan dam' bit sorry for meself—an' maybe I am too—but I'm sorry to the heart for that bit of a girl. She was nice, an' nice in her ways, an' many's the evenin' last year—or was it the year before?—I cut sticks for her fire, an' filled her can o' water, an' we both collogin' an' makin' fun; an' many's the good clout she ga' me behind the ear for her own good. An' look at me now, an' look at her, an' what can I do for her?—only get meself masacreed before her eyes, an' what good would that be?"

"Pity you didn't turn up three months ago when she came to Dublin looking for you."

"Lookin' for me?"

"Yes. We have been looking for you ever since."

"I knew you was lookin' for me—an' the divil keepin' me hid in a hole. An' I knew where you was bringin' me when we set out from the Nyer, an' here I am failin' you and Peg Kate in the last pinch. I have no stigma in me to fight me corner no more. 'Tis me own fau't. You warned me I was rottin', an' here I am rotted before your eyes. Oh God! What a mess I ha' made o' me life all me days because I thought I could take the aisy way an' keep me sowl alive with me tongue!"

VI

Matt Sheridan came, serious-faced, up the steps and we moved apart for him.

"Ten minutes more, an' the dirty deed is done," he said.

He opened the door of the van and drew forth a heavy, iron-clasped, scratched leather bag. He put

330

it down in front of the bench and sat down between us. He gave the bag a touch of his toe.

"Me budget, an' me great-gran'father's afore me."

The budget is the traditional bag in which the tinker carries his tinsman's kit: soldering-irons, anvil, vices, hammers, pincers, shears, files, solder, fluxes, tin-plate, and so on. Some of these bags have been handed down for generations and become almost a sacred possession.

Matt Sheridan placed his hands on his knees and looked out over the heads of the milling tribes. With his white hair and flowing beard and eagle nose he looked the genuine old fighting patriarch. He spoke remotely, as if to some listener that only he could see.

"Me gran'da gev me this budget the day I jumped it and caught a hould o' me first wife; an' before that he had l'arned me all he knew. But he never l'arned me the thing me father l'arned me. I rimimber wance we had a young mare with a buckin' vice, an' 'twas me ambition to fork her, only I was young an' feart. 'The thing you're feart of you must face always,' says me da. 'Up you go!' An' he thrun me on her, bareback. Sirr, oh sirr! She shot up in the air an' down again, an' I thought me backbone was through the roof o' me skull; an' she went this way, an' she went that way, an' up with her agin sudden, an' there I was above under the sky with nothin' betune m' legs an' nothin' to hang on by. So I kem down on dome an' didn't wake up for two whole days. ax never be able to stay on her, da,' says I. 'D led me.' 'I'm axin' you nothin',' says he. ''Y it'll wance, an' if you don't fail twice or te Come be because you'll be kilt-dead or on top

on out!' says he. 'If it has to be that way,' says I,
'I'll die on her or under her. Hould her a bit!'
An' do you know what I done? You don't. I tied
a strong piece o' himp rope from me wan ankle to me
other ankle under her barrel. 'Let the bitch go now,'
I screeches, 'an' I'll see ye all in hell.' An' when I
woke up I was still on her back an' she sweatin'
whole water. I rode her many a day after, sober as
a ould mule. The geldin' I have now is her great-
gran'son. Ay, faith! The thing you fear is the thing
you must face. Boys, oh boys! the times that was, an'
the times that is, an' the time is up."

"And the tide at the full," I said.

Matt Sheridan lifted slowly to his feet, man-handled
the heavy budget, and went down the steps. Thomasheen James cursed him savagely.

"May all the black divils out o' the pit o' hell
sweep you an' your parables, Oul' Wan!"

As soon as their Old One appeared in the open
lugging the budget there was one wild yell from the
merrymakers. Men rushed here and there shoving
and shouting, and brought some sort of order out of
chaos. Two small fires had been built not more than
two paces apart and some twenty yards out from the
van. Matt placed his budget midway between the
two fires; and the tribes made a wide ring with the
circumference of it lapping along the row of vans.
There they sat, knelt, crouched, and stood, their
wild eyes and white teeth agleam in the flames, silent
last, all their attention fixed on their Old One.

"Let us begin in the name o' the wan God," boomed
eat voice of this ancient High Priest.

"the name o' the wan God," thundered the
from the men, for only the men responded.

I wondered whether that one god was Jahveh or Bel or Ammon-Ra.

Mick Andy detached himself from the ring and went into his mother's van. Peg Kate came up the steps, not looking at Thomasheen James or at me, and went into the van behind us.

The High Priest opened the budget so that it lay out flat showing its medley of tools. Amongst that medley he stood two small vices upright, side by side, and fixed two short wax candles in the gripping jaws. He scraped a match on his pants and lit the candles. Then he towered up, both hands thrust forward, and the pointed flames, in the still night air, seemed to strain upwards to his fingers.

He lifted his right hand and his voice boomed.

"Meehaul Andra Shuridan?"

Mick Andy sprang to the ground from his mother's van and strode across to the old man's right side. He had drink taken, but he moved smoothly and lightly as a cat. He was bare-footed, bare-headed, and naked to the waist. In older and starker days he would be completely naked. His squat, massive, paunchy, hairless torso and heavy short arms looked delicately white in contrast to his red-brown neck and black-brown hands.

Again the celebrant's voice lifted.

"Mairgead Caith Coffey?"

The door of the van behind us opened, and I turned sideways to see Peg Kate, frame of it, young and vital and her petticoat, bare-footed and bare hair loose on her white shoulder covering her firm budded breast our heads with wide dark eye

333

deeply, and went down the steps and across the grass to her grandfather's left hand. Her steps did not falter.

The three figures stood there very still before the pointed flames of the candles, and there was a waiting hush all round them. The wash of flames over white skin, the gleaming ring of eyes, the wild dark faces, made the setting entirely pagan.

It is a pagan ceremony older than history, and it is forthright. The woman, at the command of a phrase in old Gaelic, jumps over the budget and her candle, making as sure as she can not to quench the feeble flame; the man does likewise; the priest says, "*Ta sib posta anois*"—"now ye are bound"; and forthwith the new-married man lifts his wife in his arms and carries her over the threshold of his darkened van, the whole congregation storming round them. That is all, and it is as binding on a tinker as any ceremony can be.

The Old One's figure towered over the two young ones, and his powerful baritone bellowingly intoned:

"Before the word is given—before the budget is jumped—before I bind them, has any man in this place anything to say? Let him say it now, and make the man's challenge."

"Oh God!" said Thomasheen James at my shoulder. "Why was I ever borned?"

Some power stronger than his fear wrenched him to his feet, and words were torn from him harsh and loud:

"I have a thing to say."

Out of the satisfied aglleam in the wide circle came a that filled and weighed the night.

334

This was meat and drink indeed—raw meat and warm blood. Gooseflesh ran up and down my legs and back.

Thomasheen James stumbled down the steps, and went across the grass as if forced from behind. I knew that he was not drunk, but I knew that he was mad.

The three between the fires had faced round, and Peg Kate was staring at him, her mouth open. Mick Andy grinned wickedly, and his clenched fists looked like blocks of oak at the end of thick white arms. Matt Sheridan was as dignified as a High Priest should be, and everyone heard his rich calm voice:

"Do you make the man's challenge, man o' the O'Dorans?"

But Peg Kate brought her hands up to her face and cried between them.

"Don't make it, Tommy! Don't make it! He'll kill you dead——"

The High Priest brought one hand down on a naked shoulder, and slapped the other firmly across her mouth.

"Men at their own business! Wait on it!" he said fiercely, and fiercely thrust her away. A growl of approval rose from the men round the ring. The women were dumb.

Peg Kate came staggeringly and at a run across towards the van, and I came down the steps to meet her. I caught her or she would have fallen against them. Her shoulders were smooth and cold.

"Mother o' God! He's dead on me," she whispered

I put her sitting on the bottom step, and a shoulder against my knee.

Over there the High Priest was again

"Man o' the O'Dorans, do you challenge?"

The drama of the ceremonial was wasted on Thomasheen James. He shouted exasperatedly.

"Dammit, you oul' puckaun! Gi'e me time! I have a coupla words to say." He threw his hands up for silence, and his high tenor carried well.

"Listen to me, all of ye! I like ye, most of ye, tough fri'ndly hounds an' able chicken-stealers. Fair an' dacent you were to me always, an' many a good day an' worse night I spent in yere company—an' will again——"

"Why not you—why not you?" a man called.

"Shut up! Ye were fri'ndly men to me, but not all of ye, for there is wan man me inimy. Don't ye know it! There he is, the skim-milk hulk o' him, Mick Andy! We tried it out wance before, an' ye needn't ax me what happened, an' him wrapped in stickin'-plaster——"

"Ax Peg Kate what happened!" roared Mick Andy. "Let me at him!"

Matt Sheridan silenced and stopped him with the back of his hand across the mouth.

"Listen to me, will ye?" Thomasheen James's voice shrilled. "See that green, white, and yalla van beyant! Half that van belongs to me an' half to Peg Kate Coffey. Ye know that. Are ye listenin'? Ye are. When Mick Andy jumps the budget this night to Peg Kate I will give him me half o' the van for a weddin' present——"

A disappointed murmur, almost a jeer, swept the and Peg Kate's shoulder twitched against my Thomasheen James struck the air with his fist and his voice was furious.

Wait, ye hounds! Listen to me last words. dy jumps the budget to-night it will be over me dead carcase. I will fight him as soon as I get me coat an' boots off."

That was not much of a "morituri te salutamus," but it sufficed. There was a sustained roar of approval as Thomasheen James came across towards me, pulling off his jacket as he came. He laid it across my arm, placed his deepsea-pilot cap on top, and looked down at me very soberly. His eyes had gone pale, but the bones of his face had set in firmer lines. He was no mean man.

"You brought me this far," he said quietly, "an' I couldn't renage you at the last." He grinned at me. "Me buryin'-ground is across in Arklow, an' you could throw me carcase in the back o' the car. I'll grow a good nettle anyway, an' you could hang me deepsea-pilot cap on it."

He took no notice of Peg Kate. As he bent over to unlace his boots I bent over with him.

"Hold him off with your left and circle left from him," I whispered. "Use your right on his wind— on his wind only, and you'll take him."

"I will," he grunted, "whin the cock lays a blue egg in a green moon."

He straightened up, kicked off his boots, and looked down at Peg Kate. Peg Kate's head was sunk forward almost to her knees, and her hands were tangled in her hair. He lightly tapped the crown of her head with one finger-tip.

"Goodbye, King o' Spain's daughter!" he said clearly, turned on his stocking heels, and made straight for his enemy across the ring. And his enemy, teeth showing, strode short quick steps to meet him. But Matt, the master of ceremonies, stepped between and propped them apart, a hand on each breast.

337

"Ye know the rules," he shouted. "A fair fight, an' let no man interfere—I 'd like to see the man that would. No kickin', no buttin', no bitin', an' time for a man to get up when he 's down, till he 's down for good an' a foot on his carcase. Are ye ready?"

"Out o' me way," roared Mick Andy.

"At it then!" cried Matt. He thrust the two away from him and walked hurriedly backwards towards the van. I stopped him from treading on Peg Kate's bare toes, and he came to my side and nudged me with an elbow.

"A nate bit o' ingineerin' betune the two of us!" he said out of the side of his mouth. "He 'll do if he outlasts Mick Andy's wind."

That was one dandy fight while it lasted. It lasted only one round, but that round lasted fifteen minutes. I expected a rough-and-tumble, savage dog-fight, but should have known better. Every tinker has to fight his way to his own level, and in that hard scramble learns the use of his hands; while Thomasheen James, dragged up among Dublin street-gamins, had acquired a good deal of the notable boxing skill of the breed. That fight was a pretty fair exhibition of old-time pugilism.

It began by the fighters making a couple of quick blows at each other and hopping away, arms sparring, to size each other up. Then Mick Andy came inching forward, his fists weaving and his head sunk into his shoulders, and Thomasheen James, head back and both hands low, circled away to the left. At once Mick Andy bored after and drove short powerful jolts alternately at head and body; and Thomasheen James propped him off with his long left and circled left from him. Three times that happened and three

338

times Thomasheen James shot that long left into Mick Andy's face. Blood began to trickle on the heavy jowl. But the young tinker would not be denied. The fourth time he bored savagely to close quarters, smashed Thomasheen James with right and left, and Thomasheen James, wilting to the punishment, thudded a hard under-hung right to the wind and got away. Mick Andy grunted, but there was blood on Thomasheen James's face now.

There was a complete contrast in styles. The younger man, short and massive, foolishly squandering his defective wind, boring in, driving short-arm jolts from all angles, made one unending savage effort to batter his foe into the ground; while the elder man, tall, rangy, in good condition, circled away behind that long, lean, tattooed, piston-like left arm, and used the right with telling effect to the wind. Once, caught between the two fires, he leaped backwards over the budget without quenching a candle, and Mick Andy, charging through the embers, took a useful swinging right under the ear. That helped.

The watching tinkers, to my surprise, made very little noise. Occasionally a woman skirled and a man silenced her with a growl.

Let it be said at once that if Mick Andy's condition had not been ruined by alcohol or if Thomasheen James's had not been toughened by a month in the harvest-fields the fight would not have lasted fifteen minutes.

Thomasheen James weathered the first five easily enough, and dealt out much more punishment than he received; he weathered the next five with difficulty and was down four times, but Mick Andy's wind was then about gone and his diaphragm almost paralysed;

and in the last five minutes Thomasheen James, groggy but still cagy, kept on evading the finishing blow, and Mick Andy kept on summoning the dregs of his energy to land it. The tinker was bleeding profusely. He knew he was in a fight all right.

In his last minute, Thomasheen James, with some wind left, tried his winning rally. He attacked and drove the young tinker right and left across the ring to where Peg Kate, watching now, was grasping and mauling my hand. There the two came to a final grapple and hung on almost helpless. I could see Thomasheen James's eyes in the flare of the van-light over the other's curled bullet head, and they were already glazed.

They hung there, heaving and panting, and then Mick Andy, with a final effort that looked feeble but must have been supreme, shoved Thomasheen James off, stepped back for distance, almost stamping on Peg Kate's feet, and set himself for the finishing blow. I saw that right-hand swing start from behind the hip.

And then it happened.

I myself, standing directly above, barely saw the flicking flash of Peg Kate's white foot. Matt Sheridan might have seen it too, but no one else could. As Mick Andy's right foot lifted with the launching blow Peg Kate's right foot flicked his bare heel sidewards, and his right foot hooked his left calf. A perfect trip. His impetus flung him forwards and downwards, and Thomasheen James's swinging right had double force. It was the most devastating blow struck in that fight. It actually threw Mick Andy back on his heels, and Thomasheen James, nothing loth, sank a left wrist-deep in a loose solar plexus. It was all over. But even as Mick Andy's knees gave, Thomasheen James, the glutton, brought a round-arm right under the left ear. The tinker fell flat on his face, rolled on his back, went over on his face again, kicked in an agony of windlessness and collapsed.

Thomasheen James looked down at him, swayed on his feet, steadied himself, and put a stockinged foot on the back of his fallen enemy. His eyes met mine, and he grinned at me weakly out of a blood-stained face.

"Just waitin' me chance," he said.

VII

The mighty yell that shattered the night proved the general popularity of Thomasheen James's victory. After that things happened quickly—and fittingly too.

A half-score of wild men—Matt Sheridan's ten—came shouting across the grass, trampling carelessly over Mick Andy's flung carcase, nearly forcing me under the body of the van, and plucked Thomasheen James and Peg Kate into the air, body and bones. They actually threw them from hand to hand as they stormed across to the budget where the candle-flames flickered to the rush. I do not know whether the two jumped over or were thrown over, but over they were. I heard Matt Sheridan's stentorian bellow: "*Ta sib posta anois*"—"now ye are bound." I saw bride and bridegroom, tossing high on supple shoulders, being galloped round and through the fires in the full circle of the clearing, the whole pack whooping about and behind them. I was there myself, leaping and whooping as madly as my neighbour.

We brought the two streaming across the open straight for the van, bundled them neck and crop inside, and banged the door. We took two minutes to cheer and laugh and pound shoulders; and then the tribes scattered off towards the fires to renew the feast. His friends had dragged Mick Andy's body into his mother's van.

I stood below and looked up at the closed door of the bridal chamber. I was sane once more, and I decided that it was time to go while the going was good. I slipped round the van and between two clumps of briars; I heard a dog growl somewhere; I heard Matt Sheridan shout my name. I kept going. Perhaps, after all, I was not quite sane or sober, for Thomasheen James's jacket and deepsea-pilot cap were still gripped tight under my arm, and I did not know.

It was a peaceful night outside the tinkers' camp: a perfect night in the mellow fall, with a full harvest moon and a delicate jewelled blue sky immensely far away behind it; and I decided that it would be pleasant to drive across the breadth of green Ireland on empty country roads. I had driven many miles in the last twenty hours, and taken, perhaps, more refreshment than was good for me, but I felt as fresh as a daisy that would be soon opening in the dew. I could make a start at any rate and see how I was going at Limerick, fifty miles away.

I went across the town square, flanked the old Episcopalian church, and clacked across the cobbles of the hotel yard at the other corner. My wife's car was the only vehicle there at that hour, and the moon was glinting cheerfully on the chromium plating. I put a foot on the running-board, and felt a wave of sentiment coming over me.

So I had cut the painter that had bound Thomasheen

James and myself, and helped to tie another painter on him! Had I tied it in a running noose round his neck, and would he strangle himself? . . . We had had some gay adventures together, and had always managed to keep our ragged flag flying. But now? . . . He would come to see me in his rounds, but he would no longer carry freedom under his hat. . . . He would have responsibilities. . . . He might even be henpecked. He would be, for Peg Kate, God bless her, was the stronger character, and, anyway, all wives henpeck all husbands when they can. . . .

"Gi'e me me deepsea-pilot cap like a good man!"

I knew that I was perfectly sober; but from whence proceeded those well-known accents? I came round slowly. Yes, that was Thomasheen James, and not his ghost, in moonlight clear as day. I could even make out the marks of battle: a fast-closing eye and a bloody graze on his cheek-bone; and his shoulders were sagging. He was in his stagged shirt-sleeves, and it was then I noticed that I had his jacket and deepsea-pilot cap under an arm.

"Yes," I said, reasoning the matter in the only way, "you would leave your wife to recover this dam' cap."

"She thrun me out."

"What? Has she donned the breeks already? Threw you out to recover her property?"

"She thrun me out for good."

"You unprincipled ruffian——"

"I didn't do nothin'. I hadn't time."

"You had better explain before I kill you finally," I said calmly, thrusting his jacket and cap into his arms.

"I tell you I didn't do not a dam' thing," he cried

343

plaintively. "The divils, an' yourself with them, pitched me into the van head-first, an' the roof o' me skull bumped a shelf, an' whin I reared up another shelf collided me timple—the bloody place is full o' shelfs—an' I done to the world as it was. I put out me two hands to steady meself an' got a hoult o' Peg Kate in the dark, an' she up an' hit me a side-winder behind the ear worse'n any Mick Andy hit me—an' didn't I pare that ladeen down to me specifications! 'Take your hands off of me,' says she. 'I'm a respect-able girl,' an' she hit me agin. An' at the same time that brute baist Paddo—she had him hid in a corner o' the van—took a fold o' me pants in his teeth. 'Call your dog off, you tinker,' says I, standing stock-still an' him mouthin' in for me ankle-bone. 'I'm no tinker,' says she. 'You're me wife anyhow,' says I. 'I'm not,' says she. 'I'm a respectable farmer's daughter from the Cork border with a business o' me own. You'll get out o' here, mister!' says she. 'Cripersalive!' says I. 'Is it for Mick Andy you're takin' me in the dark?' 'I had Paddo here for Mick Andy,' says she, 'but you'll do as well. Get out or he'll excivate you. Get out, Tommy, please! an' go back to Dublin with the boss. You'll hear from me.' Mind you, her voice was growin' sort o' soft on the verge o' tears, an', maybe, if 'twasn't for Paddo tanglin 'me feet?—Och, well! She shoved me out the back door, laivin' the fold o' me pants behind in the dog's teeth, an' I fell straight into a scarth o' briars, an'—here I am."

He started to struggle painfully into his jacket. I knew what Peg Kate had in mind, but, after all the trouble we had gone to, I still thought her conduct unreasonable or unseasonable.

"She might be kinder in the morning," I said.

"No dam' fear, the onnatural aphibian! They'll be no mornin', an' every bloody tinker in Ireland laughin' at me."

"All right! You are coming to Dublin with me."

"I am not. Haven't I done enough harm to you a'ready? I lost your sixty pounds, an' I lost me own wife. I'm done. I'm sunk. I'm rottin' on me bare feet."

I looked down at his feet. He had fought in his stocking-soles, but his feet were now bare, and one meagre leg was whitely naked to the ragged knee.

"I got a mill'on thorns in the bottom o' me socks," he explained, "so I took 'em off."

I sat down on the running-board and laughed. I was unable to stop, and I was wondering if he had enough strength left to assault me. But there was nothing in him but an indignant wail.

"That's right! That's right surely! 'Tis a great consolation to me to be able to humour you right up to the ind o' the road. Laugh away hearty, an' I will say fareyouwell for ever an' a day."

He rammed his deepsea-pilot cap firmly on his head and turned away. I had him by the shoulder before he had taken the second stride.

"Get into that car!" I shouted.

"Le' me go!"

"Get in, or you have another fight on your hands!"

"I'm in a rejooced state."

"Get in!"

I opened the door and shoved him clean across the seat head-first. I got in at his side, and we drove to Dublin.

VIII

It was again one of those brilliant brittle afternoons in mid-October, and again Thomasheen James and I were in the garden burning refuse and tidying up for the winter. I recalled the previous fall, when I had been engaged on the same task and Thomasheen James had turned up spent after his first misadventure with Peg Kate. Already I was wondering why I or my wife had not heard from her.

"Does your wife correspond with you?" I asked Thomasheen James.

"Dammit!" he exploded, impaling a cabbage leaf savagely. "Wouldn't you let me forget her?"

"She may forget you. She has nothing to remember you by now."

"What do you mane?"

"Those two five-pound notes, one of which, by the way, belongs to me——"

"Cripers!" exclaimed Thomasheen James. "Didn't I tell you? Peg Kate has them two fivers."

"What? Did I not see her——?"

"You did. But you didn't see her take them off of me agin. Yes, sir! Before she thrun me out she extracted the angvelope out o' me hip pocket. 'I'll hang on to 'em a while longer,' says she, the tinker all-out, givin' with one hand an' robbin' with th' other. Becripers! If I had a dacent shirt she'd ha' taken that as well."

"Be of a good heart," I said. "Your days of freedom are numbered."

At that proper instant a high, clear halloo rang across the lawn and over the garden hedge. Thomasheen James leaped like a shying horse and his fork fell to the ground.

"What'n hell——!"

"That's my tobacco," I said.

"Your tabaccy?" he said faintly.

"Sure. I have a standing order with a travelling shop. You know? A shop on wheels! One pound of tobacco per month. Run down to the gate and get it for me."

He stared at me open-mouthed, and every emotion known to the higher animals struggled in his face.

"You ought to be hanged long ago for conspirin'," he said.

"Hurry up!"

"Don't ax me," he besought weakly. "Me feet is stuck to the ground."

"Don't be a fool! Come along!"

I went around a corner of the hedge and across the lawn, Thomasheen James trailing slowly after. My wife was already at the gate; and Peg Kate was smiling down at her from the driving-bench of her green, white, and orange van. She had a big tin cylinder of tobacco in her hand.

Peg Kate was no longer the tinker girl. Indeed, she was not as bonny as the tinker girl, but she was bonny enough. Her dress was too neat, and most of her hair was tucked away inside a red knitted cap. Paddo, her dog, sat under the front axle and looked at us coldly.

"Ah! there's the boss himself!" cried Peg Kate, showing her teeth happily. "God spare him the health, don't he look younger every day?"

I looked at the closed half-door behind her.

"Where's my friend, Matt Sheridan?" I asked.

"Oh, the Oul' Wan! I parked him for the winter with his sister an' Mick Andy."

"That was not right of you, Peg Kate," I said reprimandingly.

"True for you," said Thomasheen James at my shoulder. "A dacent oul' puckeroo at the back of all."

"Is that the bawl of a jackass I'm hearin'?" wondered Peg Kate, ignoring Thomasheen James and reaching me down the tin canister. "There's your 'baccy, sir! 'Tis a ha'penny up in the ounce this month."

"You darn little huckster! You're learning your trade quickly. Have you met Mr O'Doran?"

She laughed, and for the first time looked directly at Thomasheen James.

"I didn't notice the tired lab'rin man before," she said. "Mr O'Doran! How are you, Mr O'Doran?"

"I'm fine, thank you, Mrs O'Doran," answered Thomasheen James, striking a spark.

Peg Kate coloured nicely in the flash of it but kept her half-mocking mood.

"Can I sell you anything, dacent man—if you have money to buy?"

"You ought to know. What have you to sell, me huckster woman?"

"Take a look!" She swung the half-door open and moved aside. "All goods open to inspection but not pawin' be dirty hands, an' if you don't find the thing you want I'll order it. Step up!"

Thomasheen James approached the iron side-step, his eyes cautiously and vindictively on Paddo under the axle.

"He won't bite you—if you know where to keep your hands," Peg Kate encouraged him. "I have your boots an' pants leg safe for you."

348

He lifted himself on the side-step and craned a long neck.

"Becripersjoe!" he exclaimed, and was awed into silence.

That travelling shop had been outfitted and stocked three months before to the orders of my wife and Peg Kate, and the two had surely played it across the board at Matt Sheridan's expense and at mine, both of us protesting futilely. To be brief, it contained everything that Thomasheen James had once enumerated, and a great deal more besides. No wonder Thomasheen James was awed into silence. But not for long. He looked up at Peg Kate in her corner of the seat.

"You' been bitin' into me resources," he said. "You never bought all them infayriour goods wi' me two fi'-pun' notes?"

"No, mister! I bought meself a weddin' present with them two. Here it is!"

A tall narrow wooden case stood by the jamb of the door. It had a hinged wooden lid, and she flicked it open. The double-barrel gun inside was never bought for a mere ten pounds; but, besides, there were a cased fishing-rod, a telescope gaff, a nefarious otter-board, a spool of plaited brass wire, a fisherman's holdall, and a canvas bag that might hold a length of net. Thomasheen James nodded his head as he considered each article, and then looked over his shoulder at me.

"'Twas hangin', I said——"

"Thim's for me rale husband when I have him," said Peg Kate. "I mane a young fella as axes me nice——"

"Don't be in any hurry, Peg Kate darling!" I cried.

"I won't then," she agreed. "Sure I'm used to waitin'."

Thomasheen James hopped off the step, backed out of reach of Paddo, and turned to me.

"You're me witness," he said. "You saw her married to me accordin' to the rules o' the time."

This had gone far enough, and he was one male appealing to another.

"I did," I said, "and the ceremony was absolutely binding."

"What do you take me for?" cried Peg Kate.

"I'll tell you that too," shouted Thomasheen James, his own man again. "A plottin', hucksterin' tinker. An' let me tell you——"

"I'll be married only the wan way," cried Peg Kate.

"Another dam' word out of you——"

My wife was dragging at my arm.

"Come on, tin-god! They will find their own way."

She went in to make tea, and I went back to my garden. I stood out of the smoke and watched the smouldering of the weeds. And I wondered if at last Thomasheen James had found anchorage. . . . At any rate, I concluded, it was the only possible anchorage. . . .

In ten or fifteen minutes I heard the clack of an axle from over the side-hedge where runs the cart-track to our two-acre paddock. The ears of the brown gelding showed over the clipped privet, and the green, white, and orange van lumbered behind. Peg Kate and Thomasheen James were on the driving-bench, and Thomasheen James held the reins. I heard Paddo barking at the horse's head.

"Hup, horse! I'll soon put life in you." Thomasheen James cast a side-glance over the hedge at me.

"Ye did me down betune the lot o' ye, but becripers! this time you'll part with that black tail-coat for good an' all."

At his second marriage Thomasheen James wore that ancient morning-coat, black, braided dress trousers, and deepsea-pilot cap.

Was it the last of his misadventures?